Open Bar

J. B. TELLER

First Edition.

Mike Tillerman, Line Editor, Content Editor.

Mary Ann Smith, Cover designer

Author's Website at JBTeller.com

ISBN- 9781735408262 Paperback

ISBN- 0781735408286 eBook

ISBN- 9781735408279-Hardback

To my loves. My family. My life.

"I don't know how much value I have in this universe...
But I do know that I made a few people happier than they
would have been without me and...
As long as I know that...
I am as rich as I ever need to be."

—Robin Williams

Open Bar

J. B. TELLER

Chapter 1

It Wasn't Perfect, Was it?

> *"The problem with the world is that everyone is a few drinks behind."*
>
> —Humphrey Bogart

My heart sinks in my chest. Was I stupid for chasing a boy to London? I put my head in my hands and cry. My heart is so broken. A deep pit forms in my body where my stomach once was —a sick feeling that I just can't shake. I throw myself back and roll in the covers. How did it go *all* wrong? *It* was perfect. *He* was perfect. *We* were perfect. I flew to London to be with him; I put my life on pause... I shudder at the thought—the stupidity of dropping everything and chasing a boy. My heart—broken. The naked pictures of me all over the tabloids. And all for what? For what? A genuine sense of dread spreads through my body, sinking and settling low in my stomach. Streams of bright sunlight creep through the curtains.

Hey, wake up. A tug at my shoulder startles me awake, "Marguerite… Marguerite. You're having a bad dream."

I bolt upright and frantically glance around. Thomas is sitting in the bed next to me, wide-eyed. "Hey, it was only a dream. You're OK. It's OK."

I rub my eyes and take in a deep breath. The dread falls away like a silk robe dropping to the ground. That's the beauty of dreams. They're only dreams. I would almost dare to say; I like nightmares better than dreams. When you wake from a nightmare, you appreciate your life so much more; the opposite of waking up from a good dream. You could be kissing Chris Evans on the beach one second, only to wake up and find out you're *alone* with nothing but your cat, or even worse, just alone.

Thomas brushes my hair behind my ear. "I won't let anything hurt you."

He was the one hurting me. I can't tell him that, though. Instead, I take a deep breath and breathe in a sigh of relief at the thought of that. "It was only a dream," I repeat as I curl into Thomas.

I've been thinking a lot lately. The thing is, London, in some ways, is not much different from San Francisco. If you Minus Marie and driving on the wrong side of the street that it. Thomas pulls the fluffy white comforter around us. I open my eyes to gaze up at the ceiling, quietly gathering all of my thoughts.

As my mind refocuses, I inhale the scent of Thomas' skin. It's a familiar smell—comfort, sexy, him—Bergamot. I shove my hand under the covers to reach for him. He is right where he is supposed to be, right next to me. I could say I'm exactly where I'm supposed to be, right next to him?

I've been in London for two entire weeks, and I still can't adjust to the fact that I'm here. In this place, with him. I reposition and cuddle back into him.

I run my fingers through his chest hair and whisper, "I don't want to, but I better get up and give my sister a quick call."

I pull myself up, letting my long hair drag across him.

Thomas reaches for me and pulls me back into him. "What do you want to do today? Do you just want to lie in this morning?"

I think about that for a second. All I want to do is stay in bed.

I cuddle back into Thomas, "I'll show you what I want to do today."

He smiles and pulls the covers over us. "I won't object."

I will never get enough of him. I fall exhausted on his chest. I could do this for the rest of my life. I swing my legs to the edge of the bed and pop up. "I'm going to shower."

"Then breakfast?" Thomas answers, grabbing his phone, shuffling through email. "Let's walk down to the coffee shop. I just have to send this email first."

I quickly shower and throw on an oversized t-shirt and leggings. A few quick strokes of mascara and some lip gloss, and I'm out the door. I grab Charlie and sit on the front stoop to daydream. I stare at my phone, contemplating calling Joan, but I shove it in my pocket instead. The morning air is crisp as I take in the sounds of the neighborhood. I let my mind wander, thinking about my family, my friends, and my life. The horrible things had to happen for me to get here. The serendipitous stuff that had to happen for me to get here. All the cogs are in the right place to get this whole thing moving. It's funny how the universe works. Sometimes things have to fall apart to fall together.

Thomas meets me at the stoop and sits down. "Enjoying the sunshine?"

I turn to him and smile. "I'm enjoying everything."

I bite my cheek in an effort not to cry. I don't know where all these emotions are coming from. Maybe I miss my family today. I don't know why. Today, I just do.

He throws an arm around me, tucking me closer to him. I lean in and kiss him on the cheek. We sit, enjoying the sun for a moment. I look at Thomas, trying to put my thoughts into words, but I can't manage it. I live for these moments that I can't put into words. My emotions are in overdrive. The nightmare has me in a state of an emotional wreck. Thomas stands and holds out his hand to pull me up. We stroll to the coffee shop two blocks over. It's quickly becoming my favorite place in the morning. The shop has a dark brown brick front with bright orange chairs and tables scattered around on the small space allotted for outdoor dining. Steele and Gage are written in script on the shop's window. Thomas strides in to order breakfast as I grab a table outside with Charlie. He has my breakfast order down; my go-to Earl Grey, dippy eggs, and soldiers. I'm feeling like a real Londoner.

Who am I kidding? I'll only be a real Londoner if:

1. I ride the tube *alone* successfully.

2. Learn to drive on the correct side of the street without dangerously forgetting and crossing into traffic.

3. Yell, "*POP OFF*" at a random person in traffic.

4. Fully understand all the slang. Boot means trunk, but it can also mean your shoe. Mate means friend, not your mating partner. Wanker does not mean wenis. Widdle Penis. Little penis with a lisp.

Thomas sits down and places my tea in front of me. "I was pondering an idea this morning."

I love how he says the word "pondering." British people make things sound so much more interesting.

He interrupts my thought. "I'd like to request your parents for a visit."

I look up, surprised, burning my tongue on my tea. "When?" the way he says, "request your parents for a visit" makes me laugh. "Are you putting in a formal request? Is there paperwork involved because if there is, I'm out."

Thomas furrows his brows, confused. "In a couple of weeks, depending on their schedule." He cautiously sips his tea, careful not to make my mistake. "I'll call them today and make all the arrangements."

My heart flutters. My two worlds are about to collide. "That would be amazing!" I exclaim.

This is precisely what I needed to hear today. I've gone long stretches without seeing my parents, but it would bring some normalcy to have them *here*. The thought of my dad sipping hot tea on the front stoop makes me laugh.

"When we get home, I'll ring your parents. Then we can go shopping. Do you want to take the tube, or would you rather take the car?" Thomas reaches over and places his hand on mine.

I blank out after the word *"home."* Does he mean *his* home, *our* home, or *just* home? It's something we haven't talked about.

Thomas grabs my knee and jiggles it. "Earth to Marguerite. Did you hear what I said?"

I shake the thought out of my head. "Oh, yes… car… hmm…."

I guess I've never thought about it. Thomas and I have been in our own little bubble for the last six weeks. I haven't even thought about how he gets around other than walking to the coffee shop. I mean, who needs to go anywhere else?

"You tell me! Which is easiest? I guess maybe the car?" I can't see myself juggling bags and riding the subway. That's what the tube is, after all. I have never ridden the bus, subway, or train. I mean, if you don't count the time, I convinced my parents to let me ride the bus to school only to fall out of it and get hurt the very first day. I've always preferred a rental car or Cooper. I think of Cooper sitting in my parent's driveway. The thought makes me feel a little sad.

Thomas grabs our plates and sits them in a tub next to the counter. He coolly salutes the barista and walks back to me, throwing his arm over my shoulder. We stroll back to his flat— home. I mentally put a pin in that thought. As we arrive back at the flat, I grab a seat on the stoop again to watch Charlie romp around in the grass of the tiny side yard for a bit. Thomas reaches down to hold my arm as he walks up the steps.

"I'm going to give your parents a ring. Then I will be ready to go shopping." Thomas' hand slides out of mine as he walks inside.

I watch Charlie sniff around in the grass. "Charlie, come on. Let's go". He looks up with a fresh mound of dirt crowning the top of his nose.

He walks in before me as I head to change into something more worthy of a shopping trip. I slowly pass Thomas, hoping to catch a snippet of his conversation with my dad.

"Hi, dad!" I yell.

Thomas turns the phone on speaker and faces it towards me. My dad's gravelly voice comes over the line. "Hi, Punky! We are coming to see you next week!"

"Sweet! I can't wait to see you guys. Love you!" I say, giving Thomas a wide grin.

I make my way to the bedroom and change into jeans, a nicer shirt, and some flats. I'm not sure what kind of shopping I'm in for today, but whatever it is, I'll be ready.

After changing, I stride out of the bedroom as Thomas finishes up his conversation. "Yes, sir. I will pick everyone up at the airport on the 24th at noon."

I glance at the date on my phone. That's only five days from now! Thomas hangs up and grabs me around my waist, spinning me in the air as my feet lift off the ground. "We have lots to do today! Your parents will be here in less than a week!"

He is more excited than I expected. It sends a warm sensation into my chest. His excitement has me bouncing on my tiptoes and smiling from ear to ear.

"OK, what do we have to do?" I grab my purse and springily walk towards the door.

"Well, we have to get a bed, for one. Sheet and a dresser." Thomas pulls out a small notepad and starts jotting down his list.

"Wouldn't it be easier if we just got them a hotel?" I assert, glancing around at the space.

"Don't be silly. We have plenty of room. This way, I can learn all about them." Thomas grabs his keys from a table by the door.

As we walk down the steps, he pushes the button on his key fob. Lights flash on a car parked across the street.

"Oh, so *that's* your car?" I add, pointing to Thomas' blue Audi R8.

"I bought it a few months back. It's sometimes faster than the tube." He smiles, opening the car door for me.

It looks like some kind of futuristic sports car. I slide in and glance in the backseat. If you want to call that a backseat, I'm not sure how people could ride back there. There are two seats but no room for people's legs. We are for sure not going to get much back there. But then again, I think we can get most things delivered. I don't see us loading a bed or a dresser, even if we had a truck.

Thomas accelerates smoothly, "Next stop—Rohde's for a bed."

I grab the seat tighter as my mind tries to wrap itself around the fact that we are driving on the wrong side of the street. Thomas pulls into a parking spot in front of a furniture showroom. It's an old stone building. Much like most shops here, the buildings are the same hundred-year-old structures. The only thing that has changed are the storefronts.

The shop looks closed as I press my face closer to the glass. Thomas knocks on the door with his knuckle. A salesman walks over and lets us in, locking the door behind us. I give him a curious look as I hold Thomas' arm tighter and reach in my pocket for my phone. I discreetly send Marie my location, but nothing else.

"Please, walk with me and tell me what kind of bed you need." The salesman ushers us to a large table in the back of the showroom.

"What kind of bed do you think your parents want? Firm or soft or something in between?" Thomas presses his hand down on the bed next to him.

"My guess would be soft." I sit on a bed, trying it out.

"Do you think we should get a double or a king?" Thomas joins me on the bed.

"Is a double the same as a queen?" I stand and try the next bed.

The salesman is following close behind us. "The double is like the *American* queen."

I laugh and muffle the joke at the tip of my tongue. "Well then, I think we only need a double."

"What do you think about this one?" Thomas bounces on the end of the bed next to me. I join him and lay back on it. "It feels like a dream."

"Is it your favorite? Like if you were picking one for yourself, would this be *the* one?" Thomas leans back, and I put my head on his arm.

"If I were picking one, I would pick this one." I casually reach over and check the price tag, 10,450 pounds! My eyes widen. "This bed is over 10,000 pounds! Why is that?"

I gaze at Thomas as he slides his hand over the top of the mattress. It sends flashbacks of every night this week.

Thomas reads my thoughts and smiles. "They are all handmade and organic. See? Feel the fabric. It's different from the beds you can buy at a mattress store. It's all hand-stitched and layered with down and organic fabrics."

I rub my forehand with my hand. "10,000 pounds for my parents to visit? A hotel would be much cheaper, and it would include a bathroom." I smile back at Thomas. "And the added benefit of more privacy."

He grabs me by the hand and spins me around. "A good bed is a must." He gestures to the salesman. "We will take one double and one Super-king in this style. Do you have any made? Would it be possible to have them delivered tomorrow?" He hands the salesman his credit card.

The salesman puffs out his chest, taking in a deep breath. "We can have it delivered and set up by noon tomorrow if that works for you."

Thomas looks at me. "We have a sofa coming in tomorrow also, so that works for us. Thank you so much for all your help."

The salesman shakes his head in acknowledgment and walks us to the door.

I scurry around the car and hop in. I can hardly hold my tongue. "A new couch, for what?"

Thomas starts the car. The engine roars to life, rumbling the seat under me. "A new couch because *we* needed one. So, where to now?" He acts like people just re-outfit an entire apartment all the time. "I want your parents to be comfortable. Now, let's get some sheets, maybe a rug, some pillows, and towels."

Thomas is weaving through traffic effortlessly. He can tell that I still haven't gotten the hang of the opposite side of the street. He reaches over and puts his hand on my knee to calm me. I nervously clamp my knees together tight.

Just the thought of a new bed, sheets, and the rumble of the engine could very well send me over the edge. "OK, where would we go for something like that?" I probe.

"I know of a shop not too far. I think we can get most of what we need there." Thomas rounds the corner and parks in front of an old brick building with a sleek modern storefront.

King and Boll Linens is printed on a metal sign swinging in the breeze. Why does every shop in London seem to have two names?

We walk up to the shop; this time, the store is open. As Thomas walks by a table of sheets, he grabs a set. "What color do you think we should go with?"

I've always been partial to white. It makes me feel like I'm at a fancy hotel. Plus, if I get something on them, I can always bleach them. That includes towels and bathroom rugs. "White, unless you object," I shout.

"Oh, they're no objections here. White it is!" Thomas looks at the tag for the size and grabs two sets. "I got them. Could you grab the towels?"

I walk over to the towel section and grab four of the whitest bath towels and two hand towels. I hold them up in the air to show Thomas. I nod towards the bath rugs and grab one.

I meet Thomas in the middle of the store. "Is this all?"

We walk towards the counter and set our things down.

Thomas pulls out his notepad and begins checking things off. "We need a comforter and a blanket. Can you think of anything else?" He makes his way back to the linens. "Pick out some new bed linens for us too. I'll grab the blanket and comforter for your parents."

My mind goes straight into the gutter, thinking of Thomas and how his hands clutch the surrounding sheets during sex. I peruse the comforters, unzipping the bags and reaching in to squeeze each one. I find one and pull it off the shelf, making a small stack on the floor next to me. I grab a fluffy blanket and a faux animal fur throw.

I'm juggling my finds to the counter when Thomas grabs the comforter from me. "I think I got everything we need. Unless you can you think of anything else?"

"Not really. What do you have in the room?" I try to think back at the only time I looked in the room.

Thomas stacks the linens on the counter. "Nothing. Just some old boxes from Uni and a rug."

I shrug my shoulders. "I think that's it, then."

"Oh, no! What about a headboard and nightstands? Oh! And a couple of lamps." Thomas scribbles in his notepad again. "Maybe a couple of fluffy robes?"

I furrow my brow and grab for Thomas' notepad. "Hold on a second. All of this sounds like a lot of stuff for a visit. Are you sure you want to buy all this stuff? You know a hotel is still an option."

"Why do you keep trying to put your parents in a hotel? Are you afraid they won't like me?" Thomas tugs his notepad back from me and slips it into his pocket.

"No, of course, they will like you! I don't want you to have to spend a lot of money when there's a perfectly good hotel close by." I bite the inside of my cheek to control the words coming out of my mouth.

"Mar, I need these things anyways. What better timing? You can help me pick things out so the flat doesn't look so masculine. Especially now that you are living here." Thomas kisses the top of my head.

I happen to think he is doing a relatively good job. His flat is lovely; it's more put together than anyone I have ever dated. It has two bedrooms, two bathrooms, and hardwood floors throughout. The kitchen is modern and primarily white. Not a single thing is out of place. He has a tiny office with floor-to-ceiling bookshelves. It's precisely how I pictured an old English library would look like. An Edison bulb hangs from an old wrought iron lamp next to a broken-in leather chair. A bed for Charlie sits on the opposite side. The office smells of leather and volatile organic compounds from the old books on the shelves. A picture of us in front of the cabin sits on his desk. The whole flat is very eclectic with layered textures, fabrics, and old books. I wonder if this is his style or something he had help with.

"OK, then… the next stop should be a furniture shop. I have a thought, though." I lean against the counter, pulling on Thomas' shirt to get his full attention. He gets the wrong idea, and a smile spreads across his face.

"What *thought* would that be?" he bends over and kisses me on the cheek.

I raise my eyebrows and bite the inside of my mouth to keep from laughing. "*Not* what you're thinking. I'll tell you in the car."

Thomas hands the saleswoman his credit card.

She looks up and beams. "I loved you in Hamlet last year."

Thomas' face softens, "Thank you. I appreciate that very much."

I still haven't figured out what to do in these situations. Do I smile? Do I hide? Do I pretend not to see her? I opt for smiling. I grab two bags and head towards the door.

Thomas is not far behind me with the rest. He clicks the button for the trunk. "So, tell me, what's *your* idea?"

"I was thinking, why don't we go to some thrift shops to find a couple of nightstands and lamps? We don't have to buy anything new. Plus, it would be fun." I duck into the car and buckle my seat belt.

Thomas smiles at me, and the corner of his eyes crinkle. "I think I know of a couple of places in Notting Hill."

I screech! "*The* Notting Hill? Richard Curtis-Hugh Grant, Notting Hill? We have to go! Absolutely! Take me there straightaway!"

I guess I have been too busy to realize that I am in the same city as my favorite romantic comedy. Not that it would have been the first thing I would have done, but it would have been darn close. We only drive a few minutes when Thomas pulls over and parks. I bound out of the car and begin speed walking up the sidewalk.

"Where are you going?" Thomas clicks the lock on the key fob.

I throw a hand in the air. "I'm going to the blue door, silly! Follow me."

"I have half a mind to tell you; you are going in the wrong direction. Here, *you* follow me." Thomas reaches around my waist, redirecting me in the opposite direction.

As we approach the blue door, it's just like I remember it in the movie. A few tourists are snapping pictures—more than I expected. I don't want to draw attention to us, so I nonchalantly walk up to the door and take a selfie.

"Here, hand me your phone." Thomas reaches out for my phone and hands it to a tourist. "Could you please take a picture of us?"

The girl on the street immediately recognizes him. I can tell by the deer in headlights look. "Yea, of course."

Thomas pulls me up the steps and holds me in his arms with a look so intense that my knees begin to buckle, and I start naming our children. No, but really… Giving in to the cheesy urge, I lean over and whisper, "I'm just a girl standing in front of a boy asking him to love her."

"I love you, Marguerite. He pulls me in and kisses me. You will never have to ask."

My cheeks flush, and my ears turn red-hot as the girl snaps a few pictures and hands the phone back to Thomas.

Thomas nods. "Thank you very much."

The girl tucks her hair behind her ear—the international flirting gesture. "You're welcome. Can you sign my map?" she pulls a map out of her purse.

Thomas signs it and hands it back to her. She rips off the corner and writes something on it, handing it back to him.

Thomas turns and intertwines his fingers in mine. He hands me the corner of the map. Her number is written on it. Who could blame her for trying? I hand it back to him, and he crumples it into a tiny ball and chunks it in a trash bin as we walk by it.

I pull up Joan and Marie's group text. I send the picture and a quick text. They know Notting Hill is my all-time favorite rom-com. Marie and I have talked about it ad nauseam. At least as far as Marie is concerned.

Just a girl standing in front of a boy asking him to love her.

"Sorry about that." Thomas looks uneasy that he might have hurt my feelings.

"No worries. I can't blame her. You're hot. It's not like you were flirting. She clearly saw that we were together." I slide my phone into my pocket, getting distracted by all the different shops. "Oh, look at *this* place!"

It's called the Last Place; it has two funky-looking white chairs in the window with British flags for seat covers. I tap on the window. "Look, I love those!"

Thomas winces, "Oh, no! We'll go inside if you promise we aren't leaving with those." He points to the two chairs I'm eyeing in the window.

I grab his hand and pull him inside. "I make no such promise."

I browse the first couple of isles, grab two interesting lamps, and carry them to the counter. I cheerfully smile at the woman behind the register. "Is this your shop?"

"It is." The woman looks up and glances at Thomas, then back at me. "Everything in the shop is refurbished or upcycled. Could I help you find anything?"

"I love this store!" I place the two lamps on the counter. "I don't think we need help finding anything. We're just going to look around."

Thomas stands behind me, casually grazing my shoulder with his hand. "We will just add what we want to the counter if that's OK?"

"Yes, here's a spot" The sales lady clears the counter to make a spot.

"Could you tell me about the two chairs in the window?" I say, pointing towards the display.

The woman's face softens. "Oh, yes, those are from an estate sale in Brighton just south of here. The man was in the Royal Army. I thought it was only fitting that I covered the chairs in the flag." She walks over and lifts one of the wooden chairs up to show the craftsmanship.

"I love that. Babe, look, they're rescue chairs!" I run my hand over the arm of the chair. "We can't leave them. They found us!" I shrug.

Thomas holds up a lamp, interrupting me. "How about this?"

I point to the chairs. "Rescue chairs…"

"Marguerite, they didn't find us. It's not like they were walking around looking for a family." He shakes his head at me.

"That's why it's even for special. How do you not see that?" I shake my head back at him.

I walk over to the counter and lift the lamps to show Thomas the ones I found.

"How about these two lamps also?" Thomas shows me the lamps he is holding in his hands.

I try not to get downright irritated that he's ignoring my comment about the two chairs in the window. Instead, I agree with the lamps. "Grab both sets. Then we can decide where they will go."

Thomas shakes his head in agreement.

The lady from the shop rolls up an end table. "This end table was a dresser at one point. It was cut in half to make two nightstands. The other is in the back. They are from the South of France. A little town called Tourrettes."

I run my hand over the wood. "It's beautiful. I love the pattern of Tigerwood. We will take both." I look to Thomas to see if he agrees.

"Don't forget the dresser; we need a dresser." Thomas whirls around and heads off to the back of the store. "Marguerite, come look with me."

I catch up to him. We walk by a row of dressers. One catches my eye. "Look, this dresser matches the nightstands." I run my hand over it. It is the same type of wood as the nightstands. "I love it! Do you like it?"

"Yes! It's perfect." Thomas gestures the saleswoman over. "We will also take this dresser. Is there anything else you want?" Thomas squeezes my hand. "Figurines, knickknacks, bobbles?"

I howl with laughter. "Knickknacks? How do you know what knickknacks are?"

"You know, I have a mother and two sisters." The corner of Thomas' mouth curls into a half-grin.

I briefly glance towards the window. Then grab a couple of pieces off the shelf. One is an English bulldog statue, and the other is a pair of oversized jacks.

Thomas grabs the bulldog from my hands. "I shall now call you M."

I cock my head to the side. "Oh, I get it! From that James Bond movie—cute."

"You know your movies." Thomas raises his eyebrows, impressed.

Thomas smiles at the saleslady and points to the window. "We'll also take both 'rescue' chairs."

A smile spreads across my face. Just when I thought he wasn't listening. "What? Are you sure? I thought you weren't interested in the rescue chairs."

"Whatever makes you happy." Thomas leans over and kisses me on top of the head.

"You make me happy." I smile at Thomas. "When could we have these delivered?" I ask, pulling out my wallet.

"We could have them delivered today or tomorrow. I would have to load the things in my lorry." The shop lady explains as she rings up our purchases.

Thomas grabs my credit card. "You aren't paying for this!" He drops my card back into the abyss of my purse.

"Tomorrow morning will be fine. Here's the address." Thomas rips out a sheet of paper from his notepad and scribbles his address on it.

I give Thomas a playful scowl and grab two of the lamps off the counter.

"You have a lovely shop. Thank you for all of your help." I casually walk towards the door while perusing the rest of the isles. Thomas catches up to me, pushing the door open before I get to it.

I place the lamps in the trunk, "Should we get all this back and start clearing out the room."

"Yes, let's do that." Thomas sits the other two lamps next to mine. He points to the trunk. "This is a boot."

I look up, puzzled. "What is?"

"This." He runs his hand over the top of the trunk.

"You mean the trunk is called a boot?" I hold my finger up to my lips.

"You got it." Thomas tucks a lock of hair behind my ear. "You'll get the hang of all this in no time."

As we drive, I study the road signs. It's the only thing that helps me not to completely freak out about being on the wrong side of the street. "Hey, what does that sign mean?" I say, pointing. "That one, right there!"

"What sign?" Thomas looks from left to right.

"The sign with the motorcycle hopping over a car circled in red." I point with my thumb backward.

"Oh! That just means no vehicles can drive there." Thomas refocuses on the road.

"OK, then! That's one thing I know now." I giggle because that isn't at all what I would have guessed. I would have assumed that Evel Knievel stunts were not allowed on that road. In my world, that's totally an option.

"Maybe you should consider getting your driver's license," Thomas utters, parking in front of the flat.

I shrug my shoulders, "Maybe."

Charlie is nearly uncontrollable as Thomas unlocks the door. "Hey, Buddy! Want to go for a walk?"

I follow, pulling the door closed behind Charlie. "Charlie, do you want to go to the park? Are you the *bestest* boy in the whole world?" I rile Charlie up by scrubbing the top of his head.

We stroll to the park, two blocks over. Thomas unsnaps Charlie's leash to let him run free in the enclosed dog park. We lean against the fence as his hand intertwines in mine. "I've been meaning to ask you something."

I swallow; what could he possibly ask?

Chapter 2

All Girls

"I shop; therefore, I am."

—HEATHER CHANDLER, HEATHERS

I CAN TELL THOMAS IS NERVOUS. He squeezes my hand a little tighter. "You've been here for two weeks, and if I don't ask you this, I'm going to hear it from my family. I would like you to meet my mom and my sisters."

I shake my head. Not in an up and down fashion, but more of just shaking. I know very little about his family. The only thing I know are the few bits and pieces from our conversations. His mom was a theater teacher, and one of his sisters is a serious photojournalist.

I straighten a little and smile. "Now, is as good of a time as any."

Thomas grabs my hand, turning me to face him. "You look nervous; you shouldn't be. They *will* love you."

"Oh." I shift a little. "I'm not nervous." At least I wasn't until you said, "Don't be nervous!" "Is tonight too early to meet them? I can have Kyle work out a reservation." Thomas checks his watch.

"Tonight would be perfect." I swallow my insecurity and think about what I'd wear. I mentally go through the things I brought in my luggage. It's still just the thrown-together things that Joan and I picked up on our adventure from California to New York a few weeks back.

"I have a couple of things I need to take care of before dinner, but I could have a car sent over for you so you can go shopping." Thomas waits for my answer.

I narrow my eyes at him. "Send a car for me? I wouldn't even know the first thing to tell the driver."

I wish Marie were here to help me explore.

Thomas sees the worry on my face. "Don't worry, I'll have Sophie, my personal shopper, go with you. She'll know all the stores to go to."

I realize my mouth is going into a tight line. I force myself to smile. "Great!"

Thomas types out a text message. His phone dings. "They will be here in ten minutes, then dinner at eight?"

I glance at my watch. The crack on my watch face has now splintered out into a hundred directions. Crap, I can't see the time. "What time is it, anyway?"

"It's just after four. You have about three and a half hours before dinner." Thomas grabs my wrist to look at my watch. "How did you break your watch?"

I run my finger over the glass face. "I cracked it in the trike accident with Joan, remember?"

Thomas pulls out his notepad from his pocket and scribbles something down.

We have rounded the block without me even noticing. As we walk up the steps to the flat, a shiny black car pulls up. A thin woman steps out of the vehicle. I eye her carefully. I've never been one to be jealous, but I've never been one to be stupid either.

Thomas hops down the steps to her and gestures back up at me. "Hi, Sophie. This is my girlfriend, Mar. You will need to take her around to all the shops."

He hands her his credit card. "Buy everything she wants."

I extend my hand. "Nice to meet you." I snatch the credit card out of Sophie's hand, giving it back to Thomas. "I don't need this. I could very well be *your* sugar mama."

"My what?" Thomas leans in and nuzzles my nose. "I don't know what that is but, I like it." He leans in closer to my ear. "I expect to be shown what a sugar mama does later."

Sophie nearly chokes. I notice she's fighting the urge to go slack-jawed.

Oblivious to her, Thomas leans over and kisses me on the mouth. He makes me feel warm and safe.

I press my forehead against his. "I'll be back in no time."

The driver opens the door for us; we hop in. I awkwardly buckle my seat belt in the deafening silence. Sophie is giving me an odd feeling, and I don't like it.

I stare at my knees until Sophie interrupts my thoughts. "So, how long have you and Tom been dating?"

I close one eye and screw up my face in thought. "About a month or so."

Sophie looks flummoxed. "You've *only* been dating a *month*, and you've moved here?"

I don't like the way she's judging me. Who does she think she is? "Well, what can I say? When you know, you know." I keep my voice even, trying to make light of her questions.

"Have you met his mother?" Her voice comes out shrill. I don't know how any of that is her business, but I answer it anyway.

"Actually, I'm meeting her tonight along with his sister's." I sit up straight, gathering my inner self. I turn to face her. "Have you met his mother?" I figure if we are asking questions here, I'll mirror hers.

Sophie's eyebrows shoot up in surprise. "Oh, plenty of times. She's a gem. We get along well and sometimes meet alone for tea."

I let that sink in. Did they meet for tea? In what capacity would they ever meet *alone* for tea? I brush it off. Maybe Thomas set her up with his mom to shop. We pull in front of a boutique shop. The driver comes around and opens the door for us. I step out and stand on the sidewalk in front of a large building. It has an elaborate wood facade with carved pillars painted black. It's precisely the chic you expect in London. I open the door and start perusing the tables stacked with every sweater imaginable. I walk around, pushing clothes back and forth on the racks in front of me.

"So, is your plan to stay in London?" Sophie asks abruptly, like we have been having a conversation this whole time. She walks up behind me, handing me an arm full of clothes.

"I'm not sure what my plan is at the moment." I hold up a thin black turtleneck. "He may just move to the U.S. with me." Although Thomas and I haven't talked about it, I add it just to get under her skin.

A saleslady walks up behind me. "Could I get a room started for you?"

I hand her the arm full of clothes. "That would be awesome. Thank you!"

"What's your name, dear?" she takes a nub of chalk out of her pocket.

"My name is Mar, but you can call me M." I giggle at the inside joke with Thomas. She writes a big letter M on a small chalkboard outside of a dressing room.

My dressing room is full, so I decide to try on what I already have. Standing in the tiny dressing room lined with mirrors, I hold up one outfit at a time. None of it is anything I would ever wear, but I am putting my trust in Sophie's professional opinion. I hold up a horrendous hot pink skirt with large pastel polka dots on it. Sophie paired it with a baby blue t-shirt. I pull them on and give myself a once over. What in the hell? I pull it off and neatly fold it on a chair.

I dig through the clothes and decide on the least offensive outfit. It's a black leather pencil skirt with a tan cashmere sweater. I look like "too hot for teacher." I reluctantly straighten it and walk out of the dressing room. "Don't you think this is a bit much for meeting his mother for the first time?"

Sophie walks around me. "No, if anything, you could go down a size." She hands me another top, in a size smaller.

I slip it on. I'm busting out of the top. I bite my lip and rub my forehead. "I'm definitely not wearing this. I look like a hooker!"

Sophie's phone rings; she holds up a finger to me. Who in the hell is she talking to? Doesn't she know I'm on a time limit here?

As Sophie walks away, a beautifully petite Asian girl with straight black hair pops up from behind a nearby rack. "Psst… Hey, come here!" She waves me over.

I walk over and fall on my knees as I round the rack. "Ouch!"

I land on a well-dressed man who is crouching on the floor. I get to my feet, readjusting my skirt that has now somehow managed to bunch up around my waist.

She whispers, "I'm Dustine. Is that your friend?" she points in Sophie's direction.

"No, no, not really." I hesitate to tell them just how I know her. "No, she's… she's *help*."

"Girl, no kind of *help* you need. I'm Alexander Chase." He twists his bleached blonde hair around his finger. "She has nothing nice to say about you."

I furrow my brow, "Why do you say that? What do you mean?"

She was on the phone when you were dressing. "She said you aren't good enough for this guy named Thomas. Apparently, they had something happen—a fling, and she thought maybe…."

They both quickly duck down, disappearing behind the rack again. Startled, I turn to see Sophie walking back my way. I walk around the rack to her, determined to sort this out. "So, Sophie… tell me, how did you meet Thomas?" I emphasize *Thomas*.

Sophie's face turns tomato red. "I met him through his agent at a party."

I'm casually moving some pieces on a rack when I spot Alexander's gold designer shoe; I tap it with my toe.

"So, have you ever had anything more than a professional relationship with him or wanted more?" I figured if she was comfortable enough to ask me personal questions, then I'm comfortable enough to ask them right back. I *am* his girlfriend, after all. I look straight at her, not blinking.

Sophie shuffles around. "Well, there was this one thing that happened." She pauses. "We had a thing right before he left for the United States."

"What thing?" I ask, stepping closer to her.

"We got a bit carried away while I was helping him pick out a suit. We had a thing, and it was mutual." Sophie arrogantly shrugs her shoulder and turns her back to me.

I fight the urge to grab her by the hair and spin her around. Dustine's hand wraps around my ankle. I glance down, and she shakes her head. Instead, I walk back into the dressing room, stunned. My mind is whirling as I tug on another outfit. I glance in the mirror as tiny tears prick my eyes. I blink them away and open the door to the dressing room.

"So, what kind of thing did you have?" I bit my cheek in an effort not to cry.

"Well… we shared a passionate kiss. Thomas kissed me. You know, it is something." Sophie's lip curls into a smile. She knows she has me frazzled.

I jerk my head back in hurt. Alexander has made his way to the far corner of the boutique. He walks this way, holding a few clothes in his arms.

Sophie's head whips around. "Excuse me!" Her eyes widen in surprise. She backs off the edge in her voice. "Alexander Chase from Alexander Designs?"

"The very one." He turns to me and gives me a wink, not offering his hand to shake Sophie's. Dustine walks up behind Alexander and leans against a table. The tension in the air is thick.

The bell to the shop dings as Thomas walks in. I feel like I am right in the middle of a tornado. Everything is spinning around me, and I'm stuck in place. I don't know whether to feel hurt, sad, or happy.

When Thomas sees my face, his smile goes into a frown. "What's wrong, Marguerite?"

I swallow the lump in my throat. "Thomas, I think we may have a misunderstanding here. I am wondering if you could clear something up for me."

Thomas' body relaxes. "Anything Love."

"Sophie seems to think that you had something together before you went to The States. The time right before you met me. I mean, if you did. That was before me, so…" I turn to examine Sophie.

She's nervously swaying and biting her fingernail. She gives me a snooty pout.

Thomas' eyes shift from mine to Sophie's.

Something happens that I haven't ever seen in Thomas. His face flashes anger. "Sophie, in hopes of honoring your dignity and your job, I agreed to ignore what happened before I left. You kissed me. I did not kiss you. I want to make that very clear. You knew that. We had a whole conversation about it. Do you want to say anything to Marguerite?"

I stare at her—waiting.

Sophie shifts back and forth on her feet. "There is nothing I want to say to Marguerite."

Anger flashes in Thomas' eyes again, but then also a hint of sadness. "Marguerite, Sophie kissed me while I was at a suit fitting. I did not return the kiss. We discussed how I didn't see her that way and how we could preserve her job and move forward. That is all."

"Thomas, why in the world would you send me somewhere with a girl that has feelings for you?" my lips tighten. Why would he keep her after that? Hell, why would he send me on a shopping excursion with her?

"I thought we had an understanding." Thomas scowls and turns to Sophie. "I thought you understood that. *You* kissed me. I let you keep your job, and now you are trying to hurt my girlfriend's feelings somehow. This is incomprehensible. You're fired! Kyle will take care of paying you."

Sophie's mouth drops open. I don't know what she thought. Did she think he was going to side with her over me and keep her job somehow?

She sputters, "I've had tea with your mother! I've been nothing but good to you."

Thomas pulls out his phone and presses a button. "Hi, mum. I have a question for you. Did you have tea with my personal shopper, Sophie?"

Well, that's one way of getting to the point. I love that about him.

His mom comes on the line in her perfect English accent. "Hi. Who—Dear?"

Thomas puts the phone on speaker and clears his voice. "My personal shopper, Sophie. Did you have tea with her at any point?"

My eyes meet Alexander's. We pause in anticipation.

"No, dear, I haven't had tea with anyone that works with you." I can almost hear the smile in her voice.

"Thanks, Mum. I'll see you tonight." Thomas slides his phone into his pocket. "Sophie, please just go."

I raise my eyebrows at her. "Shoo, then."

Dustine and Alexander step around the rack of clothes. Alexander lifts his hand, "Shoo then, you heard her."

Sophie walks out of the shop with an arrogant smirk still plastered on her face.

"I apologize. The look in Thomas' eyes makes all the anger I had building go away. I should have never kept Sophie on."

"That's OK… I know you were only trying to be nice. But if this happens again, *please* fire that person." I sigh.

Thomas hands me a tiny bag he has been holding, "I checked your location on my phone and thought this would be a nice shopping treat."

I open the bag to find a freshly baked cookie. It's one of the sweetest things anyone has ever done for me. It's just so simple, proving; women don't need fancy things; they just need something from the heart.

Dustine interrupts and extends her hand to Thomas. "I'm Dustine. This is…"

Thomas interrupts her. "Alexander Chase? I met you at Diane Ferguson's fashion party last year. You were getting an award for newcomer of the year." Thomas says, shaking his hand.

Alexander presses his other hand against his chest, over his heart. "Pleasure… how could I forget? But shoo now. I have a girl to dress."

Thomas kisses me on the top of my head. "Shooing—I love you. See you soon."

My heart melts into a hot little puddle in my chest. It feels like hot lava all the way down to the very tips of my toes.

Dustine whispers, "We are going to be new best friends, and I promise I will not try to steal your man."

Alexander looks over her shoulder, "I don't." He winks at me and spins around. "Come on, girl, we don't have time for this drama."

Chapter 3

Get Dressed

"Oh, No, My Choo!"

—Carrie Bradshaw, Sex in the City

Alexander pulls me into my dressing room. "OK…" he grabs me by my hips, then pulls off my skirt. "You have an impressive body." He twirls me around. "Yes, OK. I can work with this!" He squeezes my arm, then my waist. "Your body is fantastic!"

Even though he's looking at me from a designer's eye, I still blush. I'm rigid as he pulls a sweater over my head. Then quickly pulls it off. "That won't do."

He hands me another top. As I pull the top on, he instantaneously pulls it off. My head spins. I feel like America's Next Top Model.

"OK, put this on." He hands me a spaghetti strap silky camisole with a poncho-type shawl. I yank it on.

Dustine hands Alexander a pair of jeans. "OK, put these on too." He squats down at my feet.

"Stand up; you don't have to help me put on my jeans" I grab him by his shoulder.

The jeans seem hand-stitched. As I pull them on, I look for a tag. They look small, but they fit like a glove-all except for the length. It's too bad because I love them.

Alexander grabs me by the arm and spins me around. "Yes! These are it!" He slaps me on the ass. "See the curve of your butt; that's intentional."

"God, I hope so. Without bump, is a butt a butt otherwise?" I stare at it in the mirror. He's right; my butt looks fantastic. I pout, "I agree, but they are too long."

"That's not a problem, babe. I can fix that." He pulls a marker out of his bedazzled fanny pack that is hanging over his shoulder. He bends down and puts a tiny mark on the pants at my ankle.

I gasp. "Don't write on these until I pay for them."

Alexander laughs and blows me off. He waves his hand in the air at me. "No, babe, these are mine. I made them. Dustine grabbed them out of my bag."

Dustine opens the curtain. "Did you call me?" She hands me a metal tumbler, "Here—Drink this."

I hold it up to my nose, examining it.

My eyes widen, "Is this wine?" I think about asking her where she got the tumbler, but I don't. I take it and drink a sip instead. "Thank you."

Alexander is busy marking up the pants. Dustine hands me a pair of hoop earrings and boots. "Size eight, right?"

I stutter, "Yes, but…."

"You're running out of time. Don't yes, but' me…put them on!"

Alexander finishes marking up the jeans and pins them in place. I step out of the dressing room dressed from head to toe. I give myself a once over. So, this is what designer jeans look like. I've been buying Gap off the rack this entire time. I won't be doing that again. I run my hand over my rear in amazement.

"OK, babe, now take everything off!" Alexander practically rips the jeans back down my legs. "I'll take these and bring them by after I alter them."

My eyes widen in bashfulness. "Do you know where Thomas lives?" I question him.

"No, tell me." He uncaps his marker and begins writing on his palm. "Haverstock, gotcha."

Dustine is folding the other clothes as quickly as I can take them off. She puts them in a tiny pile on the chair in my dressing room. "Alexander, I'm going to call Genae; have her meet us at my apartment."

Alexander looks up at Dustine and shakes his head. "That's a better idea."

Did I just miss something? I quickly pay for the shawl, camisole, and earrings as Dustine stuffs her boots into my shopping bag. We step outside to the sidewalk. Alexander is practically pushing me towards the car. "Is this your car?"

The driver steps out, and I slide in. To my surprise, they both slide in next to me. Alexander looks at the driver, "10 Steele's Road, please."

I quickly type in the address and shoot it to Joan. That's strange. No reply. Not even a thought bubble.

Each house on the block looks like a mansion that was converted into individual flats.

"Come on, girl. We don't have that much time, and Genae will be here soon." Alexander stands on the sidewalk holding all the bags.

"Why are you guys doing this for me?" I hesitate to get out of the car.

Alexander grabs me by the arms and pulls me out. "We're friends. It's mate rates. Besides, it's not every day you meet the love of your life's mum."

I look to the driver. "I guess you can go for the day." He looks at me stunned but shrugs his shoulders and gets back in the car. "I could call an Uber or something when I need it." I tap the top of the vehicle and stare as he drives off.

Dustine's flat is tall and thin. We walk in on the main level, which is only comprised of an entryway and powder room. We rush up a flight of stairs to her living room. She ushers me to the couch and pours me a vodka cranberry, and sets it on the table beside me. "OK, shower, then put on my robe and come out."

Usually, I wouldn't hesitate, but I just met them. I cautiously walk to the bathroom. Dustine shuts the door behind me. I quietly turn the knob and lock it. Then begin frantically looking around for a hidden camera. I look in the cabinet, behind the robe hanging on the door and under the sink, but I find nothing. I quickly shoot Marie a text.

Met Alexander Chase of Alexander Fashion. Look him up and his best friend, Dustine. I'm at her apartment, about to take a shower. They are helping me get ready to meet Thomas' mom tonight, sending you the location.

A text bubble pops up. It's Marie.

Are you taking a shower at a rando's apartment? WTH? Try not to get murdered.

Marie's comment sets me even more on edge. I pull off my clothes and place them on the bench next to the shower. I cautiously step in. It feels bizarre to be in a stranger's shower, even if it *is* a spectacular shower. I mean, you can't get murdered in such a great shower. You can only get murdered in a dingy, rusted-out bathtub; that's the rule. As I wash my body, I increasingly become more suspicious. My imagination is getting the best of me, and I know it. My little inner voice is throwing *what-ifs* out like arrows of doubt. They could very well be filming me to make a secret porn video to sell on the dark web. Who knows, they could be watching me right now!

I begin to wash my body awkwardly in order not to look remotely sexy. I squat up and down and move my mouth erratically. I wave my arms in the air like one of those blow-up tube guys in front of car dealerships— moving erratically and getting stuck in an inappropriate position. I'm sure from the outside I look like I'm getting attacked by a bee. I pour shampoo into my hair as I continue my erratic motion. That is until I get another alarming thought. What *IF* I'm about to get murdered? I frantically try to rinse the shampoo out of my hair. Dang! Why did I put so much shampoo in my hair? Becoming more alarmed, I open my eyes despite the heavy suds running over my face, and I instantly regret it. My eyes burn fire hot.

"Crap!" I yell, bending over and cracking my head on the glass shower. I fall to my knees out of shock, more than hurt.

When I open my eyes, Dustine, Alexander, and a girl I haven't met are standing in front of the glass shower. Alexander pops open the door, "Babe, are you OK?"

I let out a blood-curdling scream. "Ah!"

I hop to my feet and fumble for something to cover myself. I reach for a floof and cover my crotch. I throw my other arm over my chest. Shock and humiliation run through me like a wave from my cheeks to my feet. How did they get in here? I know I locked the door. I run my hair under the water for a few more seconds to get the rest of the shampoo out, but my eyes are still stinging. Dustine hands me a towel as she helps me step out of the shower.

I glimpse myself in the mirror—what a pitiful sight. Water is dripping off my chin. My mascara is running down my face, my eyes are bloodshot red, and I'm surrounded by strangers. Everything feels like it is happening in slow motion. Three sets of eyes are staring at me, waiting for an explanation, but what can I say at this point? I thought I was secretly being filmed for a porno, or I thought they were murderers? I laugh. An image of that book, *How to Make Friends and Influence People,* flashes through my head.

Alexander tugs at my towel, trying to help me dry off. "We thought you hurt yourself."

I hold the towel tighter against my body. Alexander begins pressing the towel against me, trying to dry me off. You would think we've known each other forever.

"Thank you. I've got it from here." I clutch the towel tighter to myself.

The stranger looks from Alexander to Dustine and then back to me. She juts out her hand to me, "I'm Genae. I'm going to do your hair."

Genae is stunning with strawberry blond hair, a dusting of freckles across her cheeks, and hazel eyes. Her hair is flawless. It's the kind of perfect that you want a hairdresser to have. I exhale in relief. It's the same kind of relief you get when trying out a new hairstylist, and you show up just to happily realize she doesn't actually have a blue mow hawk.

Dustine hands me her robe. I wrap it around myself and drop my towel. Genae pulls me to a stool in the kitchen. She combs my hair out and examines the ends. "I'll give you a trim up, then a blowout. Is that OK?"

I raise my eyebrows, "That's more than OK. Gosh, thank you!"

The doorbell rings. Alexander skips down the flight of stairs to answer it. A slim man walks in with Alexander and puts a large black case down next to the couch, then leaves. Alexander picks it up and sets it on the kitchen table.

He opens it, and to my surprise, it's a sewing machine. "I'm going back to my roots. Back when I used to sit at my kitchen table making drag costumes in San Francisco. I can fix the length on your pants, no problem."

He takes out the pants and begins sowing the hem. I watch him make quick work of it. I glance at my watch to check the time. I'm supposed to meet Thomas' mom in an hour. Crap, I haven't even told Thomas what is happening. I shoot him a quick text.

At a friend's- Getting ready. I'll meet you there if you send me the address.
A text bubble pops up.
OK. It's called Eibbor. I'll send you the address.
I click off the phone and sit it on my lap.

"OK, you're done. Grab a look in the mirror. Then I'll do your makeup." Genae pulls the plastic cover off my shoulders.

I run to the bathroom and stop dead in my tracks in front of the mirror. She has completely transformed my hair. It's unbelievable. I shut the door and let the robe drop to the floor. I take a selfie and send it to Thomas.

A text bubble immediately pops up.

I can't wait to see more. I can't wait to hold you in my arms. It's going to take everything in me not to cancel our plans tonight and stay in bed.

I smile at the thought and slip the robe back on. Alexander, Dustine, and Genae are anxiously waiting outside the bathroom door when I walk out. Genae quickly pulls me back to the chair and applies makeup to my face.

"You don't want an overdone look. A little mascara, your brows, a little moisturizer, and lip gloss are all you need." She applies a double coat of mascara and pinches my cheek hard. "There."

"OK, OK, babe. Take this and put it on." Alexander hands me a small stack of clothes.

I only have 30 minutes to get to the restaurant. The last thing I want to do is to be late. I walk towards the bathroom and start pulling on my clothes. Alexander follows behind me and starts adjusting the fabric as I pull on and zip things. Dustine puts my earrings on, and Genae sprays my hair. I feel like I'm about to walk the runway. I strut out of the bathroom, walking to the end of the kitchen and back. I do my best runway walk. "Thanks, guys!" I say, twirling around, feeling more confident.

All the nervousness I felt is gone. All the drama from Sophie…It's funny how clothes, a little bit of makeup, and a cookie can cure anything.

"So, where are you headed?" Genae asks.

"A place called Eibbor's." I hold up the phone, showing the address Thomas sent.

"Fancy! That's a great place. I'll give you a ride. I don't mind." Dustine dangles her keys from her index finger.

"I'm just going to call a taxi, but thank you," I say, Googling local taxi companies.

Dustine waves her hand in the air, "No! I'll take you. We all will!"

I grab my bags as my newfound friends walk me out to the street where Dustine's car is parked. Funny, I didn't notice it before. It reminds me of a James Bond car from the 1960s.

Curiously I ask. "What kind of car is this?"

Dustine taps the hood. "It's a Peugeot."

I shake my head in understanding. "I like the little "*Thriller*" lion on the front. Hey, I never asked, what do you do? I know what Genae and Alexander do, but you never said."

"Oh!" Dustine lets out a small chuckle. "I'm a DJ at a nightclub."

I blow out my breath, "What? That's crazy cool!"

Dustine shrugs off my compliment but says, "That's how I met Alexander. Back when he was pouty and depressed. Isn't that right, Alexander?"

She grabs Alexander's cheek and pinches it.

"Bitch, I have never been depressed a day in my life." Alexander throws his head back and smiles at Dustine.

Dustine rolls her eyes at Alexander and shakes her head. "You should come by sometime. I work at Club Roux."

"I will!" I say, excited.

Genae and Alexander pile in the backseat, allowing me the front.

I write my number on a piece of paper. Then feel guilty that it's an international number. I write Thomas' landline number down under mine. "The top number is my cellphone. It's a California number. You can call my house phone instead."

I make a mental note to check out plans that would include international calling. Maybe I have to get a whole new plan? Or maybe it's included in my plan. I never had the need for it, so I don't know. I put a pin in that thought.

Alexander hands me his business card. "Just call *me* darling."

Dustine pulls up in front of a charming restaurant. I guess this is my stop. A valet opens my door, and I step out. Genae and Alexander hop out behind me. Alexander adjusts my shawl, and Genae fluffs my hair and gives it another spray.

I jerk my head back. "Where in the world did you get that?"

"I brought it with me." She unscrews a cap off her bracelet. "Here, drink this."

I shake my head. "Out of your bracelet?"

"Yeah, it's a flask—a Cosmo." Genae holds up her bracelet to her mouth and drinks some to show me.

She holds her wrist in front of my face again. I feel like a vampire about to drink someone's blood for survival. Reluctantly, I take a swig. "Thanks, guys. You saved me today. I'll call soon to grab lunch!" I wave and walk inside.

My eyes dart around the restaurant. I take in a deep breath to calm myself—bread—butter and the faint aroma of sweet, caramelized onions. I immediately see Thomas as he stands and walks over to me. All eyes are on us. My knees feel wobbly. I'm floating. He's the only one in the world that does that to me. Thomas grabs my hand and leans into me. His lips brush my cheek. "You—look—amazing."

I tilt my head down to hide the blush spreading across my cheeks like wildfire. We stride to a table in the corner of the restaurant. A cheerful-looking lady is sitting, flanked by two blonds. Both are tall and slim. One has uncontrollable springy hair like Thomas, and the other has a short straight bob cut to her chin. Thomas pulls out my chair. I hesitate, then sit down.

"Mum, I would like you to meet Mar. This is my mum, Catherine." I reach out my hand to shake hers. Instead, she stands; I mirror her and pull her in for a hug.

She's a doll with bright golden hair and kind blue eyes. Her cheeks are rosy, red as if she's been skiing. The two blonds stand, each giving me a polite hug, boxing me in like perfect bookends. I'm dazed as I round the table back to my seat.

I've never met a man's family. I've never wanted to, for that matter. My knees buckle as I lower down into my chair. They are only human. You are fine. My knees begin to shake under the table.

Thomas' mom looks deep into my eye, "So, Dear, how have you been getting on in London?"

I clear my throat at the whole "getting on in London" bit. I've been around Thomas long enough to pick up a few slang words. For instance, a lorry is a truck. A boot is a trunk, throwing a wobbly is throwing a fit, and pumps are gym shoes, not actually high heels. You can imagine my horror when Thomas suggested I wear my pumps for our walk to the coffee shop the other morning. I was up for trying it, even though heels aren't my thing. I bring my mind back from my British slang excursion and refocus on Thomas' mom.

"I love being here, even though I'm still getting used to people driving on the wrong side of the street." I leave out the part where Thomas and I have barely seen the light of day. "I met some new friends today; I've been shopping and out to the coffee shop down from Thomas' flat." My stomach falls to my feet—Thomas' flat—home.

One of the blondes' interrupts, "I'm Figgy. But you can call me Figs. So, tell me how you and my *ugly* brother met?"

Her short chin-length hair is cut into a blunt bob. She's wearing red lipstick and a man's white button-down dress shirt. She casually sits down, resting her foot at the edge of her chair. Her pants have a yellow and orange print on them, giving them a 1970s vibe.

Thomas reaches across the table and pushes her arm. "Stop it."

Figgy giggles, shoving a piece of bread into her mouth, ignoring him. She turns back to me and muffles, "So… do tell."

I bite my lip at the thought of Thomas singing that night. The coolness in the air and the smell of oranges on his chest.

"Well, that's a long story. My sister and I met June, June like the month while traveling. She sent us to stay at Winnie's place. We met there."

I freeze; a bolt of realization hits me. They must have seen the write-up—the pictures at the pond. TMI=TMZ. I want to plant my face into my hands, but it's too late for that. I play it off. A tiny line of sweat forms over my top lip. I blot it away with my napkin.

The other blond pipes up, "So, tell me about your road trip. What made you take a trip across the U.S.? I'm Birdie, by the way."

My eyes drift up to the spring of curls hanging over her forehead.

"That's a longer story for another time." I smile, hoping Thomas will intervene, but he doesn't.

Instead, I try to take the focus off myself.

"So, Birdie, what do you do?" I smile, hopefully looking pleasant instead of worried that I will have to go into detail about *The Wine Incident* right now.

"Oh, I'm a nature photographer for a London magazine." Birdie leans forward, resting her chin on her hand to look at me.

"So, is that why you're called Birdie?" I ask.

"No, my actual name *is* Birdie." She screws up her face. "I guess it fits, though. I've never thought of it that way. So, Mar, what do you do?"

I shift in my seat. "Oh, I own a bakery in San Francisco with my best friend, Marie."

Thomas' mom looks impressed. "Oh, do you know how to make toffee pudding? It's Tommy's favorite."

I think about that for a second. "I've learned to make a few different ones, some more on the savory side."

She looks, please. "Fine, Dear. Oh, that's fine, dear. Tommy says your parents are coming to London in a few days?"

I adjust the napkin on my lap. "Yes, I believe they are staying a week."

I look to Thomas for confirmation. He nods his head. The corner of his mouth curls into a devilish smirk. What's he smiling about. Does he know something I don't?

Thomas orders toffee pudding and tea for the table before asking, "Mar, do you mind… I am going to step outside for a second with my mum." He scoots out of his chair and wipes his mouth with his napkin.

"I don't mind at all." I smile.

Thomas kisses the top of my head, grazing his hand over my back, making my shirt slip off my shoulder, accidentally exposing my black lacy bra strap. He strides through the restaurant and out onto the street. I sit, sorting out his family dynamics in my head. Figgy is Thomas' younger sister, and Birdie is his older sister. His parents divorced when he was twelve. His dad lives just outside of London.

Figgy leans forward, interrupting my thoughts, "My brother is in love with you. You know that, right?"

I swallow. Here it is. I knew the Spanish inquisition was coming. I mentally prepared for it. "I know; I am in love with him too."

"And you're moving here?" Birdie looks me in the eye.

It sounds more like a statement than a question, but I try to answer it as truthfully as possible.

"I don't know. We haven't talked about it. I know it's something I have to figure out; we just haven't yet. I own a bakery, and my family is back in the states."

Birdie's brows furrow as she begins to fold her napkin. "Then what? How would this work? He has family here. His life is here."

My shoulders tense. I take in a deep breath to even myself. "It *will* work. We just need to figure it out." I say nervously, pulling apart the leftover bread on the table. "I'd do anything for him."

Birdie seems satisfied with my answer. She sits back in her chair and snags the last piece of bread straight out of Figgy's hand.

"How many serious relationships have you been in?" Figgy raises an eyebrow at me. I can tell she is the brass tacks of the two.

I swallow my bread with what remains in my wine glass. "Uh, none. This is the only serious relationship I've ever had. The only time I've ever been in love."

"Have you ever lived with someone?" Birdie slowly sips her wine but doesn't take her eyes off of me.

"Nope, never." I smile. "Unless you count, my best friend, Marie."

Birdie pokes out her lower lip, squints her eyes at me, and nods her head. "OK, then."

Thomas and his mother walk back to the table. She has her arm wrapped around his. They are both laughing. I love the light in his mom's eyes when she looks at him. It's a look of complete love. I catch Thomas' eye as he unbuttons his suit jacket and sits down. There's a bulge in his jacket pocket that hadn't been there before. Birdie gives Thomas a slight nod. A lesser sleuth wouldn't have noticed it, but I'm world-class with little details and body language.

Thomas reaches under the table and squeezes my knee. "Everything OK?"

I shake my head. "Your sisters had questions, but nothing I couldn't handle." I wink at him.

The server brings the toffee pudding. I've eaten enough bread to fuel two marathons, but that doesn't stop me from wanting dessert. No matter how full I am, when dessert hits the table, I can always eat more. I eye Thomas suspiciously. He is smiling, but I can tell something is different about him. Ever since he walked out to the street with his mom, he's changed. What is it? I can't put my finger on it. I know I'm not going to figure it out here; I brush my thought aside.

Thomas taps a polished spoon on his bottom lip. He smiles at me then scoops up a tiny bit of pudding. He holds it in front of my mouth. "Taste it; you won't find a better pudding in all of London."

He flies it around like a tiny airplane then feeds it to me. All the blood in my body rushes to my ears. Feeding me feels too intimate sitting here with his entire family watching my every move, *our* every move. I reach under the table and squeeze his knee to get him to understand my thoughts. Right now is when the little thought bubble from third grade would come in handy, but only if Thomas is the only one who could see it. Any other way would just be embarrassing.

I giggle, holding my napkin in front of my mouth. "I don't think I can eat anymore. The bread did me in." I say to get Thomas to stop feeling me.

The bread must have done Figgy in too. She's in a food coma and has barely made a peep since dessert.

A server walks over with his black notebook open. Thomas signs it without looking. "We'll see you next week." He says, leaning down to hug his mom.

Figgy gives him a hard squeeze. "Bye, see you next week."

She motions the server over. "Can you bring me some Primm's? I've consumed entirely too much bread."

The waiter scurries off and returns immediately with a tiny glass of Primm's. Figgy shoots it like a tequila shot. I'm not an expert in all things alcohol, but I'm pretty sure you are supposed to sip that.

I knit my eyebrows together. What's all this talk about next week? Did I forget we were doing something?

I step around Thomas and hug his mom. "It was so nice to meet you."

Catherine leans back to look at my face. "You too, Dear. I hope to see much, much more of you."

I smile, "Oh, you will. Come for dinner soon. I'll make pudding."

Thomas' mom squeezes my hand. "That will be lovely, Dear."

I watch Thomas' family leave one by one. "I think that went well, don't you?"

"My mum loved you. I think my sisters did too. My apologies for the questions; I mean, if they were too much. Figgy can be a real chav."

"No, it was no big deal. Your little sister just told me that you loved me. Well, she told me then waited for my reply." I wrap my arm around his and lean in, looking up at him.

Thomas' eyebrows shoot up. "Bloody hell! I'm sorry she put you on the spot. What did you say?"

"I said that I love you too." I stand on my tiptoes and kiss him on the cheek.

Thomas leans down and growls in my ear. "You do, do you? I am absolutely the luckiest man in the world. Let's get out of here."

I smile, "Let's…."

Chapter 4

You're Not Cooper

THE NEXT MORNING, I wake to an empty space beside me. Thomas is off to an early interview at the BBC radio station. I wash my face, pull my hair in a knot, and throw on my shoes for the walk to the coffee shop.

"Come on, Charlie!" I whistle and slap my leg. Charlie lazily drags himself out of his bed and saunters over. He's not a morning dog. He'd very happily sleep in. I clip his leash to his collar and lock the door behind me. This is the first time I've been on this walk alone. Charlie hasn't found his feet; he is clumsily stumbling around; I lift him in my arms and carry him. I walk past the spot where my life changed forever. I close my eyes and see Thomas standing there, heartbroken. I shake my head and flood my mind with the most passionate kiss I've ever had instead. A combination of all those feelings come flooding back to me—relief, love, passion, safety, and warmth.

I bend over, putting Charlie down. Taking the leap seems like a lifetime ago. I grab a seat at our usual table at the coffee shop, opting for a table outside instead of going in to order.

"Good morning," a server hands me a menu.

"Hi. Good morning!" I smile and order my usual without opening the menu. I stretch my legs out in front of me and lean back to let the sunshine warm my face. I miss Joan more than usual today. Maybe it's because I'm finally alone and I have time to think. I take my phone out of my pocket to Facetime her. It rings. Two a.m. isn't an unusual time for us. Joan is used to getting calls at this hour from me, particularly during a heated Dirty Scrabble match.

"Hi, you have reached the voicemail of Joan Becker." Joan's voicemail comes on. "Please leave a message."

She's using her maiden name again! Good for her! I fight the urge to call her back and verbally high five her over the phone. That's a big step for Joan. Instead of uncontrollably calling her until she is forced to pick up, I make a list of things I have to do before my parents arrive. Groceries will have to wait for Thomas. I still don't have a car and can't see myself riding the tube with an arm full of bags or dragging around one of those foldable carts. My phone rings, my smile goes wide. Thomas' face pops up on the screen.

"Hello!" I say as my heart jumps right out of my chest.

"Hi, sorry I had to leave you so early. I couldn't bear waking you; you looked so comfortable." I can hear the noise of the surrounding traffic. He must be in his car.

"That's OK; Charlie and I just walked down to the coffee shop. I was just contemplating figuring this whole tube thing out. How was the interview?" I absently bite a piece of toast.

"I just finished up. The interview was good; I shouldn't be too long. Speaking of the whole car thing, I do think we need to remedy that."

I gulp. Why do I need a car? We haven't exactly talked about how long I'm staying or even what I am doing here. I mean, I know what I am doing here. But really, what am I doing here? I give Charlie my last piece of bacon and sign the bill.

"Let's put a pin in that. I'm headed back to the flat now. I grab Charlie's leash and cross the street to explore the shops I haven't already. See you there."

I step onto the sidewalk a man's voice startles me. "You do realize I could give you a tickct for Jaywalking."

I jerk my head up. Thomas!

I can't keep the smile from my face. "Oh no! What can I do, officer? I can't afford a ticket on my record."

Thomas parks the car and rushes to my side. He puts his arm around me, lifting me up and pressing me into him. "I missed you all morning. Tell me, what's in the plans before your parents arrive?"

I snuggle under his shoulder. "I think we need to go to the grocery store. Even if we eat out, my dad will want a coffee way before we can get out to the coffee shop. My mom will insist on cooking. So, I have a few things on my list."

"OK, hop in. We can drop Charlie off at home." Thomas makes the quick block drive.

I unclip Charlie's collar as he scuttles through the door in front of me.

"I'll just change, then we can go." Thomas takes off his navy suit jacket and folds it over a chair as he makes his way to the bedroom.

I curl up on the bed to take an eight-minute nap. The carb crash is real. I still eat bread even though I understand that I will come crashing down like a train that has suddenly run out of track. My energy comes crashing down all around me. My body feels heavy on top of the comforter.

Thomas wraps his hand around my ankle, startling me. "Want to stay in bed? We can order what we need from the store. I mean until the deliveries start showing up. Kyle will be here soon to have it all in place."

I drag myself up. "No, it's best if I get a good look at what I'm buying." I pop up and tug in my shoes before Thomas can convince me otherwise.

As I am readjusting my messy bun, a man walks up the steps. I meet him face to face. "Hi, I'm Kyle, Tom's assistant."

"Oh, right… Hi!" He catches me off guard. I awkwardly stick out my hand to shake his. "Nice to me you."

Kyle fumbles with the fruit basket he is holding.

Thomas takes it from him. "Hi, Kyle! This is Marguerite, my girlfriend. You can call her M for short."

I furrow my brow at him. "Stop that!"

He winks at me. "Kyle, you can go in and do what you need to. All the deliveries should be here today. Sylvia is coming by to help get it all sorted. We are going to the thing I told you about earlier."

Kyle shakes his head in acknowledgment and takes the basket back from Thomas.

"What thing?" I look flummoxed.

"A 'surprise' thing… Let's take the car." He clicks the key fob and hops in.

"Listen, Marguerite. I have been pondering something for the last couple of days, and I think we should get you a car. You've been here for almost three weeks. There may be days you want to go somewhere, and I'm working. Or days you just want to go somewhere and don't want me to go."

I let that roll around in my head for a minute. "I could Uber it or whatever car service you have here."

"You could, or…." Thomas drags out his words. "We could just get you a car so you could do as you please." He reaches over and squeezes my knee.

My eyebrows furrow together. I don't want to be a jerk, but I don't want to deal with a car, mainly because I don't know what we are doing. I force a smile. I've learned this lesson already. If you don't know what to say, Mar, don't say anything.

Thomas pushes my hair behind my ear. "OK, let's put a pin in it, as you say. This makes what I have to show you very awkward, but I have a surprise for you. Kyle has been working on something for you this week. Maybe I should have run this past you before, but I didn't. I apologize in advance."

My stomach does a flip, but I keep a smile on my face. Thomas pulls around to the back of a mechanic's shop. The smell of oil and tires reminds me of my dad's service station.

"OK, close your eyes." He hops out and runs around to open my door.

Thomas covers my eyes with his hands. I apprehensively follow where he leads me—carefully putting one foot in front of the other. "OK! Open them!" He pulls his hands away.

A tiny car is parked in front of me. Surprisingly, it's smaller than Cooper. I didn't think that was possible.

"This is your car; I bought it for you this morning." Thomas waits for my reaction.

I turn and throw my arms around his neck. "I love it! It's so tiny and cute! What kind of car is it?"

"It's a 1972 Fiat 500. It's not Cooper, but I thought you might like it." A smile stretches across Thomas' face.

I walk around inspecting it. There's a tiny metal luggage rack on the back, not large enough for a piece of actual luggage. I consider what I could use it for instead. I open the door and slide into the driver's seat. The steering wheel is solid wood. I run my hands around it. The horn is a flip switch on the dash. I can't hold in my excitement.

"I love it!" I kiss Thomas on the cheek. "Oh, it comes with a picnic basket?"

Thomas opens the car door and sits in the seat next to me. "The picnic basket goes on the back, on the luggage rack. Do you *really* like it?"

I love how he didn't buy me a new sports car or try to impress me with something ridiculous. He gets me.

"Why don't you drive it home? I will have someone bring my car." Thomas nods his head at me handing me the keys. "Go ahead, start it."

Nervously, I begin counting the ways this is a bad idea. "I don't have a driver's license for one, and two, the whole driving on the opposite side of the street is still a thing for me. I mean, I can't wrap my head around it." Eagerly, I run my hands over the steering wheel again. A shiver of excitement runs up my arms. I want to drive it.

"OK, I'll drive if you keep me in check so that I don't stupidly drive on the wrong side of the road or go flying into the air off a cliff or something."

"Randomly flying off a cliff is not a thing. Is it?" Thomas apprehensively leans over and kisses me on the cheek. "I worry about you sometimes."

I reluctantly crank the engine and slowly shift into drive. "I'm sorry if I kill you today. Any last words?" I grip the steering wheel tighter; my knuckles go white.

Thomas holds his knees that are alarmingly close to his chest, "Does the seat go back?"

I look behind Thomas' seat into the backseat. "You could go back about four inches, but after that, you might as well take the front seat out and sit in the back."

Maybe that's what we end up doing if he rides with me. I make a mental note to study for the driving test. How do I take a driving test here? I wonder if I can just go to the DMV and pick up a driving manual, or maybe the DMV isn't a thing here. What is the DMV called here?

I make a right turn.

Thomas gently points. "Stay on left, darling."

I take my time and carefully pull onto the correct side of the street. The next three blocks are nerve-racking, but I think I'm getting the hang of this. I relax a little in my seat. This isn't so bad.

Thomas is smiling, enjoying the ride. "A roundabout coming up. Go slow. You got this."

I turn on my blinker. My hands begin to shake, but I'm determined to do this. I can do this. If I can drive a three-quarter-ton truck at eight,

I can drive a Fiat in London at 26. I see my opportunity; I press down on the gas, making the tiny car jerk. My mouth flattens into a straight line.

"You're doing great," Thomas says as he clutches his knees.

I pull into the roundabout integrating myself into the center circle. I make two complete rounds before I attempt to exit. I know it's all about timing, the gap, and who's turn it is. I swivel around and see my opening. I push down on the gas harder and make it out of the circle.

I nervously smile at Thomas. "That was horrible."

"But you did it." Thomas cups my knee.

I did do it; I can drive here.

Take the next left. Thomas points. I confidently take the next left and get in the right lane. Something is off; all the traffic signs are backward. Cars are parked facing the wrong way.

Thomas's phone rings. "Oh, darling, it's my agent about the movie. I've got to take this."

Before I can object, Thomas picks up the phone. "Hello."

So much for helping me drive. I hold the steering wheel steady, looking around to ensure I'm doing all the right things. A car blares its horn loudly as it passes me.

"Holy shit!" I yell. "I'm on the wrong side of the street!"

I jerk the steering wheel to the left side of the street while frantically flipping the switch for the horn. I speed up, trying to cross over to the correct side of the road. A car is coming right for us. I fight the urge to just close my eyes and pray.

"Holy shit, you cocked-up M!" Thomas grabs for the steering wheel, dropping his phone on the floorboard. He jerks the steering wheel in the opposite direction.

If it weren't for our current precarious position, I'd ask what the heck cocked-up means. I'm pretty sure it doesn't mean what I think it does. I hit a pothole. Thomas' phone goes flying through the air, then crashes down onto the floorboard between his knees. He reaches down to grab it just as I hit a bump. It flies back up as Thomas' forehead bounces off the front dash, nearly knocking him out. I over-correct, accidentally pulling too far off the side of the road. An empty car transport truck is parked on the side of the road with its ramp down. Before I know it, I've taken the ramp and sped to the top of it. I'm dangerously close to flying off the front and Boss Hogging it down fifteen feet.

Thomas shouts. "Holy fuck!" his voice goes up three octaves and down two.

I slam down on the brakes with both feet—hard—sending the car up onto its front end and the two tiny back wheels rotating high into the air. We come to a stop, crunching the front top of the hood. The motion and momentum surge us back and forth.

The car falls back down onto its tiny rubber wheels, bouncing us up and down in place.

"Made pretty good time." I smile at Thomas, quoting my favorite Christmas Vacation movie.

Thomas has both hands on the dashboard, clutching it. "Jesus Christ, M. You're going to need a lot more practice."

I open the car door and carefully step out so that I don't step off the side of the trailer.

A man is standing next to the trailer, shielding his eyes to look up at me. "Bloody hell, what'cha doing up there?"

Thomas swiftly hops out of the car. "Sorry, sir. She's just learning to drive on the opposite side of the street." Thomas winks at me. "Well, this is one to tell the family."

I laugh, putting my face in my hands, "You better not!"

"How else am I going to explain the dent on the hood?" Thomas runs his hand over the fresh crater. "I'll drive home."

I jump into the passenger seat as Thomas adjusts the driver's seat and reverses off the truck.

Despite everything, the fiat is running well without any issues other than the dent.

"So, you'll need a lot more practice." Thomas runs his warm hand over one of my knees.

I pull into the spot where Thomas usually parks and hop out to snap a picture. I text Marie and Joan.

I got a new car! Send me name ideas.

Three dots appear.

Marie- I just got the picture! So cute! Congrats! Is it a boy or a girl?

I text back quickly.

Me- It depends on what name is the cutest. But I feel like it's a boy.

Marie- hum… thinking.

Another texting bubble appears.

Marie- Tomato? Tamato? Scoot? What about Poppy or Ladybug?

Me- Keep sending me names. I'll know it when I know it.

It's seven in the morning in California. Joan should be awake by now. I wonder why she isn't texting back. Come to think of it, I haven't talked to Joan in a couple of days. That's odd for us. Even if we don't talk on the phone, we at least text.

Thomas grabs my hand as he takes wide strides to cross the street. He swings me in the air and pulls me into his arms. "Want to grab a late lunch? We could walk to Sir Richard's."

I shake my head. "Yes, I'd like that."

"Great, I'll just let Charlie out. Then we'll go." Thomas opens the door.

Charlie comes rushing out to frolic around in the grass. He looks high into a tree as though looking for something. A squirrel comes darting around the tree trunk, stopping dead in its tracks to face Charlie. Charlie begins to bark and jump up and down at the base of the tree.

"Come on, boy. Leave the squirrel alone. He hasn't done anything to you." Thomas pulls on Charlie's collar.

I have a feeling that Charlie has been watching this squirrel all day. I reach down and fluff his ears. "Has that big bad squirrel been teasing you?"

Charlie excitedly bounces on his two front paws, then roots around in the dirt with his nose. I watch Thomas throw the ball for him a few times while I try to get a hold of Joan again. I quickly send her another text.

Hey, stupid! Text me back before I have Marie drive over.

I wait for a text from Joan—still nothing. I drop my phone in my pocket, a little deflated. I pace back and forth on the sidewalk.

Thomas meets me at the gate, "What's wrong, love?"

"Oh, nothing. I just can't get a hold of Joan. I guess she's busy." I nervously reach into my pocket for my phone to make sure the ringer is on.

Thomas squats down and hugs Charlie like a child. Charlie tucks his head over Thomas' shoulder into his neck. The sight warms my heart, making me think. Does he ever want children? I never thought to ask him. I never thought to ask myself. I guess I want children. I mean, I do, right?

Thomas stands and kisses the top of my head, bringing me out of my daydream. "Let's go."

Sir Richards is only a few blocks or so from Thomas' flat. The walk is perfect. I never realized how much I like walking to places instead of driving. I think about driving the Fiat but think better of it until I get my license. As I walk arm and arm with Thomas, I don't think there's ever been a more perfect moment. My mind begins to think about *all* of our moments. The time I kicked Jeff Bowles in the balls at the pool, and he completely buckled over in perfect form. The time I successfully navigated the stairs at prom, the speech at the grand opening of Feeling Whiskey, and the night Thomas and I met. The kiss on Haverstock...

We are meeting at the entrance of Sir Richard's. "Hi, welcome to Sir Richard's. Just two?" The petite hostess leads us to a table in the back of the restaurant.

The inside of Sir Richards is made of heavy wood, red leather bench seats, and dark corners.

The hostess stops at a table in the corner, "Will this table be, OK?"

Thomas looks around, "I think we prefer the beer garden." He looks at me. "Are you OK with that?"

The hostess picks up the menus and walks us out to the beer garden.

Thomas pulls out a chair for me. "We'll take two Boddingtons."

The hostess puts a couple of menus on the table and walks off.

We sit under a large blue umbrella, hiding away from the world. I glance at the menu and quickly pick what I want. I watch as a tiny bird hops from crumb to crumb under the tables. A waiter comes by and drops off the two beers, perfectly poured. He stuffs the menus under his arm and leans against the wooden partition. "What can I get you?"

I smile, "I'll take the Cobb salad."

"I'll take the cheeseburger with everything on it." Thomas takes a sip of his beer.

I raise my finger in the air. "No onions!"

"You wouldn't kiss me with onion breath?" Thomas smiles.

"I would not kiss you with onion breath here or there; I would not kiss you on a train or a plane or a boat. I would not kiss you anywhere." I giggle.

"Oh, you think you're so clever?" Thomas tickles my sides.

"Ah! Stop!" I kick my feet in the air. I lose my balance and fall backward off the bench.

"Oh, Jesus! M, are you OK?" Thomas rushes to my side.

I just laugh. "Did I ever tell you that I'm super clumsy?"

"No, but I know now." Thomas holds his hand out to me.

The waiter grabs my other hand, looking shocked. I'm sure he is evaluating whether or not I've had too much to drink.

I smile at him and shrug my shoulders. "Clumsy…"

Satisfied, the waiter walks away without writing our order down.

Thomas leans his head on the palm of his hand. "Have you ever thought about where you would be in two years?"

I raise my eyebrows. That seems out of the blue. "No, I mean, I've done the whole how much profit I want the cupcake shop to have in two years, in five years, and ten years, but nothing beyond that."

Thomas rubs his hand over his chin. "I've been thinking a lot about it lately, and I've realized we haven't talked about our future. I'm interested in knowing what your thoughts are.

My heart gives a hard thump. I think I know where this is going, but there is *nothing* I can do about it now. It's like when you open your big mouth at Christmas dinner about something someone told you in secret, but you forgot, and everyone is waiting to hear what you have to say. You just have to say it or make up a lie so ridiculous that everyone knows you're hiding something. I sit in silence, bracing myself for Thomas' words.

"What are *your* plans for the next two years?" I pause, hoping he doesn't say something profound, and I have to sit here looking like a lump.

"If I get this part, I will do another movie which will have me traveling for work. I thought maybe you would like to come along—stay with me."

The feminist in me laces up her Army boots, throws her purse in the bushes, sets fire to the tower, and rings alarm bells off in my head. She runs over and kicks the first domino, it topples all the others down one by one. She shouts, just get up, quit my job, move to London, and bop around following a man who has a job. Well, *I* have a job too. I'm not having it! I mentally wrap a rope around her, calming her and reply. "I can't stay. I mean, if that's what you're thinking." I stop myself before I say more.

"I don't know what I was thinking. I thought you could move here, or I could move to San Francisco. I'm just trying to figure out how all this would work. I mean, I want it to work." Thomas doesn't seem at all flustered.

Why is that? I feel like I have to make all these decisions, and he isn't worried about it at all. I don't know how I expected all this to work either, but I want it to work. I meant it when I told his sister's last night.

"Maybe we can have two apartments? We can keep the flat and maybe get a new place in San Francisco; unless you want to share the apartment with Marie." I search Thomas' eyes for answers.

I think of Marie, our late-night sessions of Dirty Scrabble over a bottle of wine, our Sunday shopping at the ferry building. It makes me miss her.

"Let's table it for now. I just wanted you to be thinking about it." Thomas takes the last sip of his beer, holding my gaze. The last bits of beer foam crown the top of his lip. I've never wanted to be beer foam more in my life. The waiter passes our table as Thomas raises his hand, getting his attention. He orders himself another beer and a water for me.

"I will think about it. Maybe we can split our time. It's kind of a moving scale since your job might have you gone sometimes. Who knows, you could be filming in San Francisco." I sip my Whiskey Sour, trying to tie the cherry stem into a knot.

"Maybe if my job has me away, maybe that's the time you are back in San Francisco." Thomas sips his drink, shaking his glass to watch the cherry and orange rind collide.

I think about that. I know I have to be flexible here if I want all this to work.

I mindlessly stab at my salad, trying to make the perfect little stack on my fork. I watch as a little bird lands on the back of the chair next to me. There is a *Please Don't Feed the Birds* sign posted on the wooden fence surrounding the garden. So, I have no idea why he has decided to land here on the chair next to me. It couldn't possibly be the fact that I have crumbled up my croutons and made a tiny pile next to the chair on the ground. There is a bird congregation at my feet.

Thomas looks up at me and smiles because he has been watching me smash crouton after crouton with my fork. "You can't help yourself, can you?"

I give him a cheeky grin. "What do you mean?"

Thomas raises his eyebrows at me. "M, I've been watching you make bird crumble for the last two minutes."

"You didn't see anything." I wink at him.

Thomas settles the bill, leaving a heftier tip for the bird party. We walk arm and arm back to the flat.

I lean my head on his arm. "I know all this is new and crazy. I know we are both going to have to make sacrifices. I just want you to know; I'm *ALL* in."

"I'm in too." Thomas leans down and kisses the top of my head. "Even if it means I leave all of this and go with you. I'd follow you anywhere."

Chapter 5

In It to Win It

"You are my sun, my moon, and all of my stars."

—E.E. Cummings

I **TOSSED AND TURNED ALL NIGHT**, waking, only to stare at the ceiling. I *love* this guy. Things shouldn't be this hard. It shouldn't feel like I have to choose between my life and his. I look over at Thomas sleeping. His long eyelashes, the dusting of freckles on his chiseled cheekbones, his wild hair. It *isn't* this hard. It doesn't have to be. No one is making me choose. But, in reality, I have to. It's not like I can up and move the bakery and Marie.

I gently shake his shoulder. He sleepily opens his eyes. "Good morning, Beautiful."

I laugh, "The sun isn't up yet. I just couldn't wait to tell you. Listen, I've been thinking about this for most of the night, and I've come to a conclusion. I will move anywhere you want. I'm in."

Thomas pulls me in closer to him. "What about your family? What about your bakery—your life back in San Francisco?"

I shrug my shoulders. "I'll miss my family. I'll miss Marie and my life there. But there's only one you. Sometimes we do things for the people we love."

Thomas sighs and pulls me in closer. "Yes, sometimes we do things for the people we love…I can't believe I found you."

I whisper, "I can't believe I found you."

Thomas' chin rests on the top of my head. "Do you think anyone else in the world feels like we feel? How lucky are we?"

"We *are* the luckiest people in the *entire* world." I curl deeper into his chest. "Shall we get up and have a cup of tea?" I turn, pressing my chin on Thomas' chest to look up at him.

"Yes! I love to watch the sunrise. There is just something magical about being up before the rest of the world." Thomas slides out of bed and brushes his teeth. "I'll meet you in the kitchen. Take your time. I'll make breakfast."

I smile and roll in the covers, getting in a good stretch. He'll make breakfast? I could get used to that.

Ten minutes later, I walk into the kitchen. Thomas is standing in front of the stove, wearing only his white boxer briefs and an apron. He is staring out the window, sipping his tea and watching the sun come up. He's right; it is absolutely beautiful—he is absolutely beautiful.

I slide my arms around him. "What'cha making?"

"An omelet. Grab a seat at the counter. I'll *serve* you today." Thomas slides the omelet onto a plate and sets it in front of me.

The growl in his voice makes me want to drag him straight back to bed. I resist and happily plop myself on a stool. I stare at Thomas as he pours me a glass of cold orange juice from the fridge. Despite what he said back at the cabin, he works effortlessly in the kitchen.

"Why haven't you told me that you could cook? I thought you said you couldn't cook. Are there any other hidden talents I don't know about?" I cross my legs on the stool and smile at him.

"Stick around, my Dear. I might surprise you." He smiles, sliding onto the stool next to me. "To be honest, I can only cook a few things—eggs, Bolognese, steak, and a mighty fine grilled cheese. I'm spreading it out, though, so it can look like I can do a lot more than I can. Oh! I can make a baked potato as well."

Thomas looks so proud of himself. I hate to break it to him, but a baked potato requires zero effort.

I cut a piece of omelet with my fork and shove it in my mouth. "How is it that you are single?"

Thomas furrows his brow. "What do you mean? I'm not single."

"You know what I mean. How is it that you *were* single?" I dangle my fork in the air, then point it at him. "So?"

Thomas bends his head, blushing. "I didn't want to be with just anyone. I don't know; I was waiting for the right girl. Not just a seat filler."

"A seat filler, huh?" I smile at the way he describes things.

But now I'm also curious. Curiosity killed the cat, and I'm the cat. I haven't googled Thomas yet. I've been trying to avoid the whole thing and date him like a normal person. Marie has tried her best to fill me in. She did an extensive search on him but only got as far as to tell me he used to date an actress. I push the thought aside. His dating history could lead me down a rabbit hole I don't want to go down. If I want to know something, then I'll just ask like a normal person, right? Looking through paparazzi pictures is only going to make things worse.

As the time gets closer and closer to my parent's arrival, I begin to get nervous. Not nervous that they won't like him; just nervous in general.

Thomas pushes his plate away without taking a bite. "I know you have a list of things you want to have done today before your parents arrive tomorrow." He grabs his notebook and a pen from the counter next to him. I begin quietly humming the Blue's Clues theme song.

His lip curls into a smile. "What's that you're humming?"

"Oh, it's just a kid's show from the states. It's about a guy that writes all his ideas in his *Handy Dandy* notebook. Just like you!" I bop him on the nose with my finger.

"Oh, is that right?" He spins my stool around, so I am facing him. "Are you making fun of me, Missy?"

"Of course, I am!" I stick my tongue out at him.

He reaches over, tickling me. Tickling is like a form of torture for me. I laugh and kick at him as he drags me to the floor.

He pins me down, holding my arms above my head, trapping them and rendering them useless. "What are you going to do now? I've got you, and there's nothing you can do about it."

I smirk, "Is that right? You think you have me?"

Thomas shakes his head. "I have you alright. I'm a whole foot taller than you and at least seventy pounds heavier."

I wink at him, then reach my foot up and slap him on the side of the face with it.

"Oh! How did you get your foot up here?" Thomas grabs my foot and positions himself lower down my legs, preventing me from doing it again. But this only incites what I like to call "*Ludicrous Mode.*" It's a mode beyond all logic and reason. It's a type of panic mode I have. It was invented when Joan would hold me down and tickle my sides until it actually caused physical pain. I buck up with my hips, turning him over onto his back.

"Oh, feisty, are we? I like that." Thomas looks surprised that my hundred- and fifteen-pound body could flip him.

I have to admit, I'm a little surprised too. I reach up and bop Thomas on the nose again. "Tell me I've won, or I won't let you up."

Thomas raises one eyebrow. "You think you are holding me down?"

I shake my head, "Yep!"

Thomas reaches around my back, bracing me. He stands up as I wrap my legs around him.

"Want to take this fight into the bedroom?" Thomas slowly walks into the bedroom and lays me down on the bed.

Every part of me is screaming, "YES!"

"You know, I haven't had breakfast yet." Thomas looks up at me with a devilish look in his eyes.

"Is that right?" I smile back at him as lines of fire shoot up my legs.

He shakes his head as he slowly tugs at the belt around my robe. "That's right."

I can feel the belt slide under me as he reaches up, running his hand between my body and robe, sliding it open. I am lying on the bed, completely naked. Thomas kisses his way up on one leg, then around my belly button, then down to my pelvis. I sink heavy into the bed. My fingers wrap themselves into the cool white comforter. Goosebumps rise on my arms. My cheeks flame hot. All my energy and sensations are traveling to the middle of my body. My body convulses in tiny explosions until I throw myself back into the fluff of the pillows. I think I blacked out. When I come to, I let my mind drift before opening my eyes. I have to get into a "fight" with Thomas more often.

Thomas crawls up beside me and rests his head on my stomach. "Do we have to do errands today?"

"I wish we didn't, but we have to be adults today." I reach down and pull my fingers through his hair.

Thomas rolls over and snuggles his face into my side. "OK, if we must, then let's get cracking."

He rolls over, slapping me on the bottom before walking to the bathroom. He turns and peeks around the corner. "Come on; I've turned the water on for you."

That was better than meditation. I feel like Jell-O. I step into the shower and let the hot water run over me. I think about today, the week, the last month. I don't want this to change. I want everything to stay just the way it is. I reach up and turn the water off when I notice Thomas standing outside the shower holding a towel. He wraps it around me.

"I think we should go to the grocery store, then tidy up a bit when we get back." I pat myself dry and pull on some clothes.

"I'll meet you outside. I'm going to let Charlie out for a romp in the yard before we go." Thomas runs his hands through his hair and pulls on a pair of black jogging pants with a hole in the knee.

I grab Thomas' keys off the table as I walk out the front door. "OK, I'm ready. "I yell as I hop down the steps and stand in the yard next to Thomas.

Charlie is sniffing around, digging up clover with his nose. I call him; he looks up at me with a crown of dirt along the top of his nose. "Come on, doodle dog!"

Charlie comes running towards me with his tongue flapping out the side of his mouth. I open the front door as he runs past me obediently. If I had called Lone Lee like that, he would have taken that as an invitation to do zoomies all over the yard. I lock the door and toss the keys to Thomas.

"Do you have the list?" Thomas reaches for my door.

I hold the list up as I slide onto the seat. I watch as Thomas runs around the front of the car.

The market is only a few blocks over. I split the list in half, eager to get things done. I hand Thomas part and head off in one direction. Thomas heads off in the other. I grab a few things on my list when I come across a can with what looks like a nondescriptive blob of Spam with raisins on the label. What in the hell is this? I hold the can up and inspect it—Spotted Dick. I grimace. It's some sort of pudding. How is this even a thing? I mean, I understand the difference in slang between England and the United States but come on—Spotted Dick is taking it to the next level. How is it even sold with that kind of name? It doesn't seem appetizing. It sounds to me like some sort of penis with a venereal disease. I grab a couple of cans as pranks to send back to Marie and Joan.

As I pass an aisle, Thomas is talking to a woman at the far end. I debate whether or not to walk up to him. I casually watch from the end of the aisle, not wanting to interrupt. Who am I kidding? In any other situation, I would walk up to my boyfriend. This is no different. I turn over the Spotted Dick so that the label is facing down. There's just something obscene about it. I saunter up behind Thomas and smile, trying my best to be open and inviting. I avoid rubbing my hand on his back. A tell-tell sign of jealousy, and I've never been green in my life.

Instead, I introduce myself. "Hi, I'm Mar." I reach out my hand to shake hers.

"Hi, I'm Kelly." She shakes my hand. "I was just getting an autograph."

I smile at her. "Would you like me to take a picture of you two?"

Her eyes go wide. "Yes, that would be amazing. Would you?"

I grab her cellphone and snap a couple of pictures. "I'd love to stay and talk, but I have to get this spotted dick to the counter." Well, so much for looking cool and even. I give her her phone and start combining Thomas' cart with mine. "Stay and chat. I'll meet you when you're done."

I head to the line. Thomas is two steps behind me.

"Seems like you are getting used to me getting stopped by random people." He says as he takes over, pushing the cart.

I smile. "Oh, was she random? I wasn't completely sure when I walked up. Is there something I should say to get you out of situations like that, or do you want me to leave you to it?"

Thomas, absent, mindlessly unloads the cart onto the conveyor belt. "You don't have to be responsible for that. I can get myself out of things if I need to."

Thomas is quietly loading the groceries into the trunk of the car. I can tell he's thinking about something. "Do you ever get jealous?"

I shake my head, "No, should I? I figure I shouldn't be jealous of other women. Only a boy would make me feel the need to be jealous. A man doesn't, and you're a man. Plus, I'm a girl's girl. I don't get jealous of other girls. We all have the same problems, the same insecurities if you know what I mean. We all have to stick together."

Thomas shakes his head. "I'm your man. I've never met anyone like you, M. You could really do me in."

I wink at him, "I hope so."

We make the short drove back to the flat. I let Charlie out to romp around the yard as Thomas unloads the groceries. I watch the sun illuminate his face. The sun makes his bread stubble sparkle like golden glitter. Could this be my life? Could taking out the dog and Thomas unloading the groceries be *my* life? Is Thomas a vampire? I squint my eyes and shield them from the sun. Is this all too fast? All valid questions.

Thomas brings in the groceries and sets them on the counter. "I'll put these up."

I smile at him. "I'll go fluff the bed in their room and make sure everything is in its place to pick up my parents' tomorrow."

Thomas' phone rings as I walk into the guest bedroom; I listen. I am not as good as I pretend to be. The past few days have been a little much for me. It's not just one thing. It's a combination of everything together. Instead of fluffing the bed, I throw myself onto it, faced down. Can we just go back to the cabin and live in a bubble where real life didn't exist? I roll over and snap myself out of it. There are worse things in the world than having women stop your boyfriend while we are out shopping or him buying you a car so you can have your independence. But isn't that the opposite? Am I really independent if he bought it for me? I could have bought a car myself. I give myself a reality check and sit up.

Thomas walks in. "What are you doing, Love? Taking a brief nap?"

"No, nothing, I was just thinking. I think the last few days have been a little crazy, and it is just now hitting me. I am just trying to wrap my head around things." I smile as he sits down next to me.

"What can I do? Do you want to talk about it?" Thomas looks concerned.

I smile, but my smile turns into a tight line. "There's nothing you can do. Sophie is who she is; you are who you are, and I am who I am. That's all. I just need time to let it all soak in."

"Well, I have something that might make you feel better. My mate Ben called and invited us out for dinner and drinks. Do you want to go and maybe you can invite your new friends?" Thomas wraps his arms around me. "It'll be fun!"

I think about that for a second. I haven't called Alexander to thank him since the big mum meeting, and I have to get Dustine's boots back to her.

"Sure, I can call them." I shrug my shoulders, feeling a little deflated.

I would have jumped at the chance before. I draw in a deep, steady breath. I know I have to rally. "So, who is Ben?"

"He's one of my best mates from school." Thomas spanks me on the butt as I bounce on the bed, propping myself up.

"I'll give Alexander and Dustine a call. I look at my watch. I never remember the face is cracked until I look to check the time. I just need to stop wearing it until I can get the glass fixed. What time were you thinking?"

"Seven for dinner at the Savoy, then out for a drink or two after? Could you have your friends meet us there?" Thomas grabs my wrist to look at my watch. "That reminds me…." He stands and walks towards our bedroom. "Follow me."

Curious, I follow him. "What? What is it?"

"Close your eyes." He gently sits me on the bed as I squeeze my eyes shut.

"Hold out your hand." Thomas turns my hand palm side up. "In all the drama the other day, I forgot to give you this."

I open my eyes to see a black box in my hand. "What is it?" My mind begins to whirl.

1. Please don't let this be a wedding ring.

2. Please don't let this be the way he proposes if it is a wedding ring.

Thomas grabs it from my hand and opens it. It's a watch. He takes it out of the box and hands it to me excitedly. "Read the back!"

I turn the watch over and read the inscription. *"Love Me and the World is Mine."*

A tear pricks my eye. I lean forward, pressing my head against Thomas'. "Thank you. I needed to hear this today." I wrap the leather band around my wrist, buckling it in place.

Thomas lifts my chin with his hand. "Don't you ever forget it—It's my job never to let you."

He leans me back onto our bed and curls around me, holding me close to his chest—bergamot and freshly washed hands. "I could call this whole thing off unless you want to go. If you do, we better get moving if we are to make it on time."

I blink a few times. "What time is it?"

"It's 5:30. You haven't called your friends yet." Thomas smiles at me.

I grab my phone out of my pocket to check to see if Joan has texted—nothing. I look through my contacts for Alexander's number. I press the speaker button on the screen and listen as the phone rings.

"Hello—Alexander speaking."

I laugh. "So official. It's me, Mar."

"Shut up, Girl. What's up?" He cuts out to instruct someone in the background. "The rack on the left—the left, darling."

"Thomas and I are going out to dinner with friends tonight, and I was wondering if you, Dustine, and Genae wanted to go?" I shrug my shoulders at Thomas. "—The Savoy at seven?"

Alexander squeals on the other end of the line, "Yes, seven! I'll call Genae and Dustine. Chaio!"

The phone goes dead. "Well, I guess that's a yes!"

I open the closet to dig through my minimal supply of clothes. I need to go shopping for real this time, minus the crazy girl. I tug on the jeans Alexander gave me and freshen up my makeup.

"Kyle hired a new personal stylist. His name is Art. I had Kyle text him, and he is dropping off a few things for you in ten minutes—size six, right?" Thomas sees the confusion on my face. "I looked at the tags on some of your things in the closet."

"Oh, thanks! Kyle hired a guy?" I pull off the jeans and wrap a robe around myself.

"Well, he was the best candidate. So, yes. Kyle hired a guy." Thomas smiles at me.

I sit on the edge of the bed just as the doorbell rings. Thomas answers the door. I can hear him chatting with someone in the living room.

A tall, well-built man walks into the bedroom. "I've brought you the latest Stella McCartney and Alexander McQueen." He begins laying things out on the bed. He picks up a nude Stella McCarty seersucker dress. "This." He hands it to me. "—and this. He hands me a black trench coat wrap. "Put these on with these black Choo's."

I hold up the Jimmy Choo's. They're my size. Of course, they are. I stand in front of the mirror, feeling a little like the girl who just married the prince.

Thomas walks in and places his hand over his heart. "Wow, M! You take my breath away."

"I do!" I blush and twirl around in my dress.

"My work here is done." Art gathers up the remainder of the clothes and hangs them in the closet. "Please call me if you need me, Ms. Becker. I'll ring you next week to work out when we can meet for our shopping day."

I smile. "OK, I'll call you. Thank you so much."

Chapter 6

*I love the Night Life;
I Love to Boogie*

"People should fall in love with their eyes closed."

—Andy Warhol

JUST AS ART LEAVES, the doorbell rings. Thomas casually walks over to open the door. A man wearing a black suit and chauffeur hat is standing at the door. I wave from behind Thomas. I playfully take on an English accent. "Top O' the morning Governor."

The man's stiff face cracks into a smile. "And the rest of the day to yourself. Even though it is not morning here."

"Top O' the night to you, then." I smile.

He nods his head. "Top O' the night to you. Shall we go, Sir?" The man waves his hand in front of himself, pointing the way to the car.

Thomas shuts the door behind me as I stroll down the sidewalk to the Hackney carriage. Thomas taught me that after I called it the "nanny car" several times. It's shined to complete perfection. The tan leather seats are even shiny. I slide in; Thomas follows, sliding his hand over my knee, cupping it.

The car pulls in front of the Savoy; the sign is polished silver with green lettering. The driver comes around and opens my door. I stand on the cobblestone driveway taking in the view. The lights of downtown London are intoxicating. I feel like a moth buzzing around a light bulb. Thomas offers me his elbow as we walk into the lobby of the hotel. The floor is black and white tile and waxed to a reflective luster.

"Hey, Mate!" I turn to see a guy clap Thomas on the shoulder, pulling him in for a tight hug.

Thomas turns Ben around. "Marguerite, I would like you to meet my best mate from school, Ben!"

I offer my hand to shake his. Instead, he brings it to his lips and kisses it. "The pleasure is all mine."

Thomas shakes Ben by the shoulders. "Come on, mate, let's get some dinner."

"Well, if it isn't the Queen Bee herself. Snap! Snap! Snap!" Alexander walks up behind me, grabbing my hand to twirl me around. "This dress, Darling! I'm mad that it's not mine. Stella, that bitch. You look fabulous!"

Dustine steps around Alexander. "Move over, Queen."

She hugs me, then extends her hand out to Thomas. "I'm Dustine— nice to see you again."

Thomas shakes it. "Good to see you again as well."

The hostess guides us to a table in the back next to a large window. We are high enough up that I can see The Eye of London from here. The walls are lined in a heavy dark wood, and the tables are covered in white linen surrounded by red leather chairs. It has to be one of the most visually stunning places.

Thomas pulls out a chair for me. "My lady."

I nod and sit down. Alexander slings his bag over his shoulder and saunters in front of the table past me, and sits down. Thomas sits next to me while Dustine flanks me on the other side. Ben sits on the opposite side of Thomas, making our round table complete.

"Ben, these are my friends, Dustine and Alexander," I say, leaning back to snuggle into Thomas.

Ben nods to each, "I know Dustine. You were featured in the *London Now* magazine last month. Nice to meet you."

Alexander clears his throat, "Do me, do me, darling. Do you know me?"

Ben stands holding his tie against his chest to lean over and peck Alexander on the cheek. "Of course, you're brilliant."

Alexander presses his lips together in a straight line. "OK, you pass. You flatter me."

Alexander turns his attention to me and grabs my hand in his. He begins petting it like a cat. "Tell me everything! How was meeting the mamita the other night? Is she fantastic?"

I squeeze his hand and lean in. "She's so nice. And his sisters are great." I leave out the part about the light grilling—a sautéing, if you will?

The waiter hovers around the table, pouring water into our glasses, quiet as a church mouse.

Another waiter walks up with a white linen napkin pressed over his arm. "This is a 1966, Chateau Lafitte Rothschild. He holds a wine bottle against his arm—showing Thomas the label.

He sets it down on the table in front of Thomas.

Ben leans in, "So, Marguerite, since Thomas has practically told me everything about you, tell me something I don't know."

My eyebrows shoot up. "I don't know what you mean."

Ben scoots in closer. "I mean, tell me something I don't know, and in exchange, I'll tell you something you don't know. It's a way to get to know each other—a fun game."

Alexander begins clapping his hands and bouncing in his seat. "Oh, Fantastic!"

Thomas turns to me, "I'm sorry in advance."

"Oh, don't be. I can handle this." I furrow my brows at him. "You should be worried about your friend here."

Ben throws his head back and laughs, "I like her. But really, now stop horsing around and tell me something I don't know about yourself."

I narrow my eyes, "You don't know what you just walked into." I tap my finger on my bottom lip. "Hmm… something about myself that you don't know… Thomas' chest smells like oranges and sunshine, and it makes me weak."

Ben leans over, pressing his nose to Thomas' chest. He inhales deeply. "You're right, oranges. Who knew?"

"It's my turn, right?" I widen my smile mischievously and glance at Ben.

"Yes, it's your turn." Ben leans back, smiling at me.

"OK, tell me something about Thomas I don't know—something good." I rub my hands together in anticipation.

Ben looks at Thomas.

Thomas smiles, wringing his hands. "Oh, no, mate. I know what you're going to say."

Ben leans in and whispers, "We stole some cigarettes in boarding school, and Thomas was sick the whole night from smoking just one. The dorm master caught him, and he got into so much trouble."

"First and last time I've smoked anything." Thomas blows out his breath and laughs. He waves his hand in the air like talking about it makes him sick.

"What were we, mate, fourteen?" Ben reaches over and shoves Thomas' shoulder.

Thomas squeezes his eyes shut at the memory. "Yes, fourteen, I believe. But enough about me, Dustine, tell us something we don't know about you."

Dustine holds a finger in the air. "I moved here four years ago. Alexander convinced me."

Alexander chimes in, "I moved here five years ago from San Francisco. Dustine and I were roommates."

I'm so excited that we have something in common that I blurt out before I can stop myself. "San Francisco! I live there! I have a bakery called Feeling Whiskey!"

I have completely forgotten how much I love my life there. Thomas deflates a little. I know it, I see it, but there I can't take my excitement back now. Nor should I have to. Just because I love my life there doesn't mean I don't love him. "What neighborhood did you live in?"

"We lived off of Franklin by the Whole Foods." Alexander interrupts. "It was a dismal place, but we loved it. You know the pricing market in San Francisco, a billion dollars per square foot."

A waiter comes and sets a basket of bread down at the table. Bread is one of my all-time favorite foods, especially if it's hot. I grab a slice, pulling out the middle to nibble on it.

The waiter pours me a glass of wine and sets it back on the table. "Are you ready to order?"

I grab the menu; I haven't even looked at it. "Could you just have the chef make me something? I'm not picky. Oh, wait, not oysters, though. I can't do oysters."

Ben raises his eyebrows. "Wow, beautiful *and* low maintenance? You found yourself a unicorn, mate!"

"Isn't she perfect?" Thomas raises my hand to kiss it.

I smile, "You're not so bad yourself."

That's the understatement of the century. Thomas' hand slides over my knee and then under it. His fingers run over the soft part behind my knee.

I turn my attention to Ben, "So, do you have a girlfriend?"

Ben smirks at me, leaning back in his chair. "I don't at the moment. Why do you know someone?"

"Depends—What's your type?" I pretend to be flipping through a Rolodex and adjusting my make-believe glasses.

Dustine raises her hand, "I fancy you! I'm fun to be around."

Ben blows Dustine a kiss from across the table. "I don't have a particular type. Just someone down to earth, *fun* to be around."

I lean in, closing the gap between us. "What do you do for work?"

"What do you think I do for work?" Ben looks at me with a cheeky grin. I like this little game he thinks he's playing. I throw it back to him like a rebounded ball during Squash.

I scratch my chin. "Porn star?"

Thomas laughs, almost spitting his wine onto the table. "Bloody hell, M."

I shrug my shoulders, "It was just a guess. But was I right?" I hold my gaze on Ben. I can't let him get the better of me. I am setting the ground rules here from here and to the future of our friendship.

"You're a cheeky little minx." Thomas plants a kiss on my hand again.

Ben leans forward in his seat, "You know, Tom, if you don't wife her, I'm going to try my best to snatch her up for myself."

A mysterious grin sweeps across Thomas' face. "I'm way ahead of you, mate. Plus, she's not your flavor."

Every emotion in me thunderously crashes like a tsunami wave from my stomach to my feet and back to my stomach. I can't let on, though. I can't let on that his statement completely rocked me. Don't throw up, don't throw up. Whatever you do, Mar, don't throw up. What does he mean, he's way ahead of Ben? Is he going to ask me to marry him? I let that sink in. Could I be Mrs. Marguerite Blaine? What if he asks me to move to London forever, I mean for real? Not the 'Hey, come to London and be with me' but marry me and stay forever. Could I do that? I never thought I would be very far from my family. Maybe that was naive of me, but I never considered it. I know I said I'd do anything for him, but would I? Of course, I would. But, ugh… All the emotions are making me seasick, and it feels like everyone can tell. I have never also been in love. Who am I kidding? I've never been in love. Not like this. But if I am not willing to stay here, is it love?

I grab my wine glass and take a large gulp. I clear my throat. "Don't get ahead of yourself, boys. Nobody is going to *wife* me any time soon."

I slowly swallow down another gulp, making a joke just in case Thomas isn't kidding. Hurting him is the last thing I want to do. Especially if he thinks he might be asking me to marry him in the future. Not that I would say yes, but no use hurting someone when I could be simply making something out of nothing here.

The waiter returns, setting a couple of round plates on the table. There are seven shells on each plate. It looks like something out of our garden as a kid. I sit frozen—snails. Snails- in -butter. I can't do it. I simply can't. Another waiter is placing small glasses of white wine next to each one of us. Thomas puts a snail on his appetizer plate with silver tongs. He works at pulling it out with his tiny fork. I stare in horror. Please, the only reason these things should be here is if we are rescuing them. Make a little snail village. But I fear they are long past that unless, of course, that is little snail sunscreen instead of butter. It reminds me of when Joan and I were kids; after a hard rain, the snails would come crawling out to sun themselves on the concrete. Joan and I would spend half the day placing each one under a sturdy leaf to prevent them from cooking on the hot concrete. We called ourselves The Protector of the Snails. Texas is that way. You could fry an egg on the sidewalk on most days there. One second, it's raining, and the next, it's hot as Hades.

"What is it, Marguerite? Do you not like escargot?" Thomas puts his fork down.

I hid my eyes behind my hands. "It's not so much that I don't like it, but I'm a Protector of the Snails, you see, and I can't bring myself to eat them. But I also think they look gross floating around in the butter. The thought of their little homes boiled in a house fire; I just can't. And now here they are home and all, and it's just seems horrible. There they are just sitting there minding their own business, and then *blam*! Picked up and boiled for people to eat."

I take my napkin and wipe my mouth to hide my queasiness. I watch as Alexander doesn't give it a second thought. He takes the snail from its shell, dips it in the butter, and pops it into his mouth. I am completely fine with this. I can't change what people do, but a thought does occur to me. The more he eats, the less Thomas will eat, and let's be honest here; I don't know if I could kiss him after he ate a snail, no matter how badly I want to. And there it is, there's my limit. I didn't think I'd have a boundary with him, but it turns out I do. Onions were just a mild no; I'd rather you not, whereas snails are a hard pass. Do not pass go, do not collect 200.00 dollars. Safe word, safe word, safe word.

I cross my fingers under the table. Please let what the chef made something would actually eat. I was trying to be uncomplicated, now look where it has gotten me.

The waiter begins to bring out our entrees one by one. I watch him place a plate in front of Dustine. OK, hers looks normal. A tiny ray of hope springs up inside me. The anticipation is making me sweat. He places a plate in front of me. To my delight, it's Beef Wellington with a side of mashed potatoes and glazed carrots. Relief spreads through me as the waiter takes the escargot, replacing it with another basket of bread. A flashback of Joan eating the oysters in Louisiana pops into my mind. I laugh at the thought. It makes me miss her and feel alone even though I'm surrounded by people.

Thomas leans over. "I know you are missing Joan; I can tell. You may see her sooner than you think, but we can go if you want to."

"No, no, let's just have fun tonight. It's only because I haven't talked to her in a few days —nothing else." I say, kissing the side of Thomas' face.

"Promise to tell me if it ever is something else." Thomas raises his eyebrows at me, looking me straight in the eye.

I melt. How is he so perfect? How does he know I was missing Joan?

Alexander interrupts my thoughts, getting right to the heart of it. "So, Mar, are you going to be a Londoner, or are you headed back to San Francisco?"

I shrug my shoulders, "I guess I don't know yet. I might do a little of both."

The waiter sets the check in front of Thomas. He nonchalantly slides his credit card into the black notebook.

"Let's move this to the bar. The first round is on me!" Ben grabs his wine glass and what remains of the bottle of wine.

I grab my glass, following him, wading through the crowd with Alexander and Dustine in tow. I glance back to see Thomas signing the bill and watching me. I wink at him and do a little shimmy. He bites his bottom lip as I turn back to Ben.

When I Googled the Savoy earlier, I learned that the bar is supposedly world-famous, and I'm anxious to find out if that's true. The hostess ushers us to a booth. The walls are gold foiled with black and gold fabric booths.

I scoot in next to Ben. Alexander slides in on the other side of Ben, followed by Dustine. Thomas caps off the end of the booth next to Dustine.

"OK, let's order a round of shots." Ben holds up his hand, flagging a waiter down. "Could we please get five shots of Redbreast 21?"

I blow a kiss at Thomas from across the booth. "OK, Ben, let's get back to what you do."

"Oh, very well. I deal with money. I buy and sell businesses. I'm a businessman of sorts." Ben lifts the shot to his mouth. "Here's to Thomas. My best mate and to his girl, Mar. I love you, mate."

I smile, tapping my glass with the others. "Salut."

I shoot the whiskey, and it goes down as smooth as butter. I put the glass on the table and lean past Ben to kiss Thomas.

"Hey! Back to your corners!" Ben leans forward. "We'll have none of that."

The waiter comes by our booth, "Can I get you anything?"

"I'll have an Old Fashion," Thomas says, looking at me to order.

"I'll have an amaretto sour and another one of those shots." I nod and look over at Dustine.

She thinks for a second. "I'll just take a beer—anything German."

"I'll take a Martini—lightly shaken, Darling." Alexander smiles at the waiter as he walks off. "He's gay." Alexander watches him lean against the bar. "His ass is fabulous, isn't it?"

"How do you know he's gay?" I look at him, flummoxed.

Alexander presses his lips together in a pout. "Oh, Darling, when you know, you know."

Ben leans over to get a look at the waiter's ass. "It *is* fantastic."

Alexander looks Ben up and down. "Oh, really? You? I had no idea."

"Well, when you don't know, you don't know." Ben winks at Alexander, then takes a sip of Alexander's martini.

Alexander fans himself with his napkin. "Yummy."

Dustine raises her glass to toast. "To new friends and things we don't know cheers!"

Thomas turns his wrist over to look at his watch. "We better call it a night soon. Mar's parents are coming in tomorrow."

"Oh, Crap! Look at the time! Scoot! I've got to get to the club." Dustine rushes out of the booth. "Alexander, you'll have to get a ride from here. I stayed too long and will be late if I don't go straight from here."

We all leisurely file out one at a time. Thomas hands the waiter his credit card again.

"Oh no, mate. I've got this one." Ben flops his card onto the waiters open book. "Alexander, I'll give you a ride. My car is here."

I glance at the bill and catch the total. $1208.00! I snatch it out of the waiter's hand—six shots, a beer, and three drinks. I do the math in my head. That's, on average, $120.00 a drink! Dumbfounded, I hand the waiter the notebook back.

Ben smiles at me. "There's a reason the whiskey goes down so smooth."

"I guess so. It goes down so smooth, so you don't choke on the bill at the end." I elbow him. "Am I right? I'm right."

"Funny too! A real unicorn." Ben raises his eyebrows at Thomas.

Dustine leans in and kisses me on the cheek. "I'll call you later. I have to run. Nice to meet everyone. Thanks for dinner and the drinks." She gives us a quick wave as she heads for the door.

Thomas holds out his elbow for me. We stand out on the curb to wait for our driver.

"Want to have another drink?" Ben holds on to Alexander's arm, joining us at the curb.

"Yes, I know just the place." Alexander gleams at Ben.

Our driver pulls up. Thomas opens my door and walks around the car to get in. He taps the top of the vehicle. "Goodnight." He salutes Alexander and Ben.

Ben lifts his hand, "Night, mate."

I make myself comfortable, rolling down the window; I wave, "Toot ta Lou!"

"Motherfucker!" Alexander yells.

It was right then that I knew he and I were going to be friends for life.

I shoot him the finger, and he shoots it back. "Catch you later, Bee."

"Later, Queen." I wave as we drive off.

After brushing my teeth and washing the night off me, I crawl into bed.

Thomas turns on his side to face me, "Do you think your parents will like me?"

"Where is this coming from?" I brush his eyebrow with my thumb. "They will love you just like I love you. I mean, not exactly like I love you, but they will love you."

Thomas pulls me in to be the little spoon. Just as fast as he's asked, he has now fallen asleep. I stare at the wall trying to sort all my feelings out.

The next morning, I find Thomas sitting on the front stoop, watching Charlie run around the yard.

"I apologize. Did I wake you?"

I sit on the stoop next to him. "—a penny for your thoughts."

"I was just thinking about today and how much I love you. I don't want to ever be without you. I just want you to know that." Thomas grabs my hand, covering mine with his.

I swallow hard. Why is he telling me this? I squeeze his hand tight. "Want to go to breakfast?

"I'd love to have breakfast with you. I'd love to have breakfast with you every day for the rest of my life." Thomas pulls me to my feet and attaches the leash to Charlie.

I ponder the morning in my head as we walk a couple of blocks to our regular coffee shop. The rest of my life? The stepping outside to the street with his mother, the whole back and forth with Ben, my parents are coming. Is he about to ask me to marry him? The thought of it has me a little shell-shocked. I know I'm walking, but it feels like my feet are on autopilot. Like I'm one of those fancy show horses that walk really fast without walking anywhere at all.

Breakfast and the rest of the morning come and go in a blurry flash.

"When will the driver be here? How long does it take to get to the airport?" I look at the new watch on my wrist.

The doorbell rings. Thomas slowly glides to the door.

Chapter 7

Meet the Parents

"Come fly with me. Let's Fly, Fly Away."

—Frank Sinatra

It's George! George, the same person who picked me up from the airport when I arrived in London.

I throw myself into his arms. "What in the world? How have you been? How's your mom?" I hold him in my arms and lean back.

"Oh, mum is great. I've been well too!" George smiles at me and envelopes me in his arms for a hug. His hugs are like Christmas morning.

"Thomas, this is George! He is the very first friend I made here. Come on, Georgie, come in!" I pull him inside. "Would you like a drink?"

Thomas shakes his hand. "Hello, it's very nice to meet you. I'm Thomas."

George shakes Thomas' hand. "Nice to meet you, Sir." He looks at me. "I'm right, fine. Thank you, though."

Thomas interrupts. "Thomas. Please call me Thomas, I insist." Thomas releases George's hand.

"Very well, then. Shall we go, sir?" George hesitates. "—Thomas." He holds the door open for us.

"Why do we have a limo?" I turn to Thomas. "My parents don't need all this fancy stuff." "Dear, it's better," Thomas says. "It will be more comfortable than a town car."

I leave it at that. Besides, it's already here. The ride to the airport brings me back to the nervousness of three weeks ago. I feel very different from then. I'm nervous, but for a whole other reason. I can't believe I spent one-second debating whether or not I should get on a plane. I always thought it was crazy when people said, "I wish I met so-and-so sooner." But here I am, wishing I had met Thomas sooner. All the crazy dates I've been on have led to this; they have led to him. Thomas—with his perfect cheekbones, perfectly wild hair, his perfect eyes that look right into my soul.

I stare out the window at the passing cars, people happily on their way. Maybe going to meet loved ones, maybe to have coffee, maybe to buy groceries for their family, maybe just on their way. Their way of living their best lives. I think about my life. I think about Thomas. What am I going to do about Thomas? Could my life be here? Could I return to San Francisco and pretend that everything is normal without Thomas and our early morning walks to the coffee shop? Could I go back to a time when I didn't wake up next to Thomas? I don't think I could ever go back to a time without Thomas. It's the question that has been on my mind for the last few days. What to do now. Now that real life is setting in.

George pulls in front of the airport; Thomas and I hop out. "I'll pull around, sir. Just ring me when you are heading out."

Thomas leans down, poking his head through the open passenger window. "George, call me Thomas, please."

"I apologize. Thomas, sir." George is trying hard. I suppose he is set in his ways.

Thomas just shakes his head. "Just Thomas, not sir."

I wrap my arm around Thomas as we stand side by side in the central part of the airport.

"So, are you ready for this?" I ask.

Thomas silently answers me by kissing me on top of my head.

I throw my arms around him and hug him. "No turning back now."

As I hug Thomas, I catch a glimpse of someone who looks exactly like Joan. I jerk my head back and push Thomas aside to get a better view.

That can't be her. I call out. "Joan!" I step around Thomas. "Joan! Holy shit! Joan!"

It is her! I run to her, forgetting all about looking for mom and dad.

"What the hell are you doing here?" I grab her face and stare at her.

"You should name him Rocinante," Joan says with confidence.

I furrow my brow in confusion. "What?"

"Your car, name it Rocinante. A little past his prime but still up for the task." Joan smiles.

"Oh! Ha, yeah. That's it. That's his name! I knew I would know it when I heard it." I

Thomas walks up behind us. "Hi, Joan. How was your flight?"

"Great, grand. My flight was wonderful." She sets her carry-on down and pulls out the handle.

I turn to Thomas. "You knew? You sly fox."

"Of course, I knew." He hugs Joan tight. "This is going to be an awesome week."

Just then, I see dad walking with mom towards us. I run to them and throw my arms around them. "I'm so glad you guys made it. Come on, come meet Thomas."

Thomas walks up to dad and holds out his hand. "Hello sir, glad to meet you. How was the flight?"

"It was a long flight, but we watched a movie and tried to sleep." Dad smiles his warm crooked smile.

Mom grabs Thomas' face. "Oh, Marguerite, what a handsome boy you have found. He will make beautiful babies."

I put my hand over mom's mouth. "Slow your roll, mom. He hasn't even asked me to marry him." My heart flutters at the thought. I catch an unspoken exchange between Joan and Thomas. It's so brief that the moment I notice it is the moment I forget it.

"I'll ring George. I'll let him know that we found them." He smiles at me and tucks my hair behind my ear.

I can hear George's voice on the other end of the line. "Yes, sir. I have their luggage, and I'm waiting right in the front."

Thomas makes small talk with my dad as they walk in front of us. Mom, Joan, and I walk behind, chattering. "So, what do you guys want to see while you're here?"

Joan answers before mom has a chance. "I'd like to see everyday living stuff. The tourist stuff is great, but I would love to go to a pub."

"A pub, eh? I think we can manage that. How about you, mom?" I ask, grabbing her purse to carry.

Mom smiles. "Oh, Mija. I would love to see the Queen, the castle, and that big bridge."

"I think you mean Tower Bridge?" I shake my head in agreement with myself.

I look up ahead to Thomas and my dad. I wonder what they are talking about; whatever it is, it seems like they are getting along.

We walk out of the airport onto the sidewalk. George is standing in front of the limo, holding the door open.

He tips his hat to my mom. "Hello, ma'am."

"Marguerite, we didn't pick up our luggage." Alarm spreads across her face as she tries to get back out of the limo.

"No, mom, it's OK. George grabbed it. Don't worry." I say, trying to reassure her. I slide in next to her.

"Are you sure? How does he know which ones are ours? I'm just going to check to see if he grabs all of them." Mom scoots towards the door.

"Olivia, you know darn well you didn't pack anything so you could shop while you are here. Sit down. It will be fine." Dad says, crawling in, making himself comfortable across from us.

Thomas sits next to dad. I point my finger at him. "*This* is why you got such a big car."

There's a small cabinet back here I never noticed before. I guess I was too preoccupied with my thoughts.

I open it and laugh. "Ha! There's champagne and whiskey in here. Does anyone want something?" I hold up the bottle and show everyone.

"I'll take a glass." Joan raises a finger and points to herself.

"None for me, Mija." Mom waves her hand in front of herself.

Dad shifts in his seat. "I'll take a whiskey straight."

I pour dad some whiskey and hand it to him.

He takes this as his cue to settle in and ask questions. "Thomas, Mar was telling us that you are an actor. I have to admit; I don't know much about any of that."

I cautiously pick at the foil around the top of the champagne.

"Well, sir. I went to Cambridge. I studied acting. I did theatre for a while, but I've been very fortunate to have had some pretty significant breaks here lately."

"And all this pays you well?" Dad gets right to the point.

"Yes, sir, I'm doing well," Thomas says modestly.

I break up the rising tension. "Thomas, mom wants to visit Buckingham Palace and the Tower bridge. Joan wants to go to a pub."

Dad pipes up. "Stop trying to switch the subject. I want to see what this boy is all about." Dad laughs, stuffing an unlit cigar in his mouth. He grins that awkward, lopsided grin of his making it impossible for me to get upset. He winks at me. I just shake my head at him and mouth, "Stop it…."

While we pass the Eye of London, I point. "Look, Joan, want to try that?"

Joan lifts her glass to finish off the last bit of champagne. "Nope. I'll pass."

I laugh, "Joan, at the end of your life don't you want to say you did it all?"

"No, no, I do not." She smiles back at me.

"You're not going to fall. That's not how that works. I am sure there is maintenance on things like that." I furrow my brows at her in disbelief at how she thinks things work.

"That's the problem. You *ASS*ume they do it, and then you fall to your death." She stares out the window at the wheel, slowly turning.

George pulls in front of Thomas' flat. He opens the car door. We file out. Thomas unlocks the front door. Charlie comes barreling out like a kid on Christmas morning. He jumps straight into my dad's arms. What's with him? He's never done that before.

Thomas grabs Charlie by the collar. "I apologize, sir. I don't know what has gotten into him. I am so sorry."

Thomas looks at me, eyes wide. I can tell he is mortified.

Dad pulls out a paper towel with a piece of bacon wrapped in it.

"Dad, what in the world?" I laugh.

"Henry! Para! No necesitas eso! Mom snatches it out of his hand.

I look at Thomas, translating, "Mom just said he didn't need the bacon."

Just when I think things can't get worse, George steps past us with mom's hideous dark green and pink luggage.

I lock eyes with Joan and laugh. "I thought you made it a point to lose that."

"Are you kidding? She would have made me find it." Joan snickers.

"Thank you, George." Thomas discreetly hands George some money as he hugs him. "I hope to see you again."

"I hope the same, *Just* Thomas." He smiles.

He is being cheeky. Who knew he had it in him? I pull him in for a hug. "Please tell your mom and dad hello for me. Let's all get together for lunch sometime."

"They will be very excited, thank you." George hands me a card with his number on it. I hold it to my chest. "Until then."

George shuts the door behind him. Mom and dad stand in the living room.

Thomas grabs their luggage, ushering them into the guest bedroom. "This will be your room. If you need anything, don't hesitate to ask."

Mom runs her hand over the comforter. "This is perfect, thank you."

"Joan, you can take the room with Marguerite, and I will take the couch." He wheels her luggage into our room.

I catch dad's eye. He has made himself comfortable on the couch. Of course, he knows we sleep together, but I can tell he approves of Thomas' gesture of not sleeping together while they are visiting.

Thomas looks at his watch, "Let's kill two birds with one stone. We can have dinner at a place not too far from here if you don't mind walking to dinner."

"Oh, that's a fantastic idea." I look to mom and dad, then at Joan. "It's a pub."

"I'm in!" Joan grabs her purse and helps dad up from the couch.

It's a novelty to walk to dinner for mom and dad. I got used to it from living in San Francisco. But mom and dad live just outside city limits, so this is a rare treat. Thomas snaps a leash on Charlie's collar. We stroll out the front gate onto the sidewalk. Thomas nonchalantly slips his hand into mine. "So, tell me, Olivia, how long have you and Henry been married?"

My mom smiles, "We've been married almost 30 years."

Thomas raises his eyebrows, "That's impressive. I could only hope to have that one day." He gently squeezes my hand, and my heart beats so hard I fear it will burst right out of my chest.

As we all stand on the sidewalk in front of the flat, I point across the street. "That's my new car, Rocinante. Thomas bought it for me a couple of days ago. I'm going to get my license soon."

Dad walks across the street. "Do you have the keys, Marguerite?"

I walk over and hand him the keys out of my purse. He pops open the trunk to look at the engine. "Looks in good shape." He pulls the oil stick out and checks the oil. "Clear, good. It's a two-cylinder. Not much power but good for in town."

I smile back at him. "Isn't it perfect?"

"I didn't think you could find a smaller car than Cooper. But here it is. No driving this on the highway."

I hold two fingers up. "Scout's honor. No driving it on the highway."

Joan walks up behind me. "Scouts are boys stupid."

I stick my tongue out at her. "Loophole, stupid."

Dad shuts the trunk. "Looks like a good car. You did a good job, son." Dad claps Thomas on the shoulder.

"Son?" I look sideways at Joan.

She shrugs her shoulders. "Guess dad just adopted Thomas. We have a brother!"

"Gross—stop!" I shove her.

"Marguerite, have you been shopping yet? Could you take me shopping while we are here?" I can see mom's smile in the reflection of the storefront window she's looking into.

"Of course, I can take you shopping." I smile back at her.

"That reminds me. M, I meant to ask you this earlier. My good friend, Andrew, is having his wedding in a couple of days. I was wondering if you and your family wouldn't mind if we all went. I can't miss it."

I nod my head. "Oh, is that what your mom was talking about at dinner the other night?"

"I suppose it was. Our families are old friends, and he's a friend from university. If you decide to go, I'll have Art come by and take you, your mom, and your sister to the dress shop. I'll take your dad with me to my tailor."

"The dress shop? Is there only one?" I knit my eyebrows together.

"There is for this occasion." Thomas squeezes my hand tighter.

I raise my eyebrows. "OK, I like that. We will go if it isn't too much trouble. I mean, didn't you have to RSVP?"

"I did RSVP, but then I called around and added you and your family a few days ago when I talked to Joan about coming."

"You talked to Joan? When I couldn't get a hold of her, you had been talking to her?"

"I apologize, Joan didn't want me to tell you she was coming, and she knew if she talked to you that you would know. I promise if you had gotten too worried, I would have told her to call you. I'd rather be found out than have you worried. Tell me that you forgive me." The fold in between Thomas' eyes creases.

I reach up and rub it with my thumb. "I forgive you."

Chapter 8

Have A Look Around

"I wish I'd done everything on Earth with you."

—F. Scott Fitzgerald

THOMAS HOLDS THE DOOR FOR US as we all file in. He walks in behind us. "Reservation for Blaine."

"Right this way." The hostess ushers us to a beautifully dressed table. She walks around, setting hard-covered menus in front of each seat.

"OK, I lied." I look at Joan. "I thought we were going to Sir Richard's."

Joan looks down at her too casual shirt. Then whispers in my ear, "It's not what you wear; it's your attitude." She straights.

"Change of plans love, Kyle made this reservation for us. I thought we could take them to a pub some other time. Just not the first time I'm having dinner with your parents. I hope you understand." Thomas pulls out my chair for me.

"I do." I smile, tiptoeing to kiss him on the cheek.

I think that's the first time I have ever never shown any type of affection towards a man in front of my parents. Charlie makes himself comfortable under my feet. Dad pulls out a chair for mom. Joan is left standing next to her chair. Thomas hurriedly walks around and kisses her on the cheek as he pulls out her chair for her. Joan glances up at Thomas and beams. If she wasn't sold on him before, she is now. Dad reaches over and covers my hand with his. I can tell everyone is on edge and silently judging.

Thomas straightens his shirt and sits down next to me. "I am so glad you made it for a visit on such short notice."

Mom beams, "We wouldn't have missed it for the world."

A waiter walks over stiffly. "Can I get anyone something to drink?

Joan looks up from her menu. "I'll just take a glass of your house red."

"Sweet tea, for me." Mom smiles at the waiter.

The waiter shifts his weight from one side to the other. "Ma'am, we don't have sweet tea. I could bring you tea and some sugar."

Mom nods her head, "Yes, fine. That would be fine."

"Old Fashion for me. But only if you have a fresh orange back there. If not, then I'll just take a whiskey straight." Dad shuts his menu.

"I'll have the same." Thomas shuts his menu, mirroring my dad.

"If you are ready to order, I can take that now." The waiter looks up as another waiter walks up behind him, dropping off a plate of bread.

"I'll take the rib eye." Mom hands her menu back to the waiter.

Dad is still studying the menu. "I'll take the beef stew."

"That sounds rather delightful. I'll take the same." Thomas stacks his menu on top of mine.

"I'll just take the Cobb salad." I gather the menus and hand them to the waiter.

"What are you, a rabbit?" Joan asks me. "Get some protein."

I smile at the waiter. "OK, could you add some chicken to that, Cobb?"

"Yes, of course. And for you, ma'am?" the waiter holds his pen to his notepad, waiting for Joan.

A smile stretches across Joan's face. "I'll have the Cobb salad with chicken."

I roll my eyes at her. "What are you, a rabbit?" I slap her with my napkin. "Oh, and I'll just take a water."

The waiter shuts his notepad, tucking the menus under his arm. "Thank you. It will be out shortly."

I snatch a piece of bread from the plate. I don't know what it is about bread that I can't control myself. I spread butter on it and hand it to Thomas. He takes it, and without thinking, he grabs another and spreads butter on it, then gives it to me. Joan shoots me a confused look. I just shrug my shoulders at her. I know what she's thinking. Wouldn't it be more efficient if we just buttered our own bread?

"So, Thomas. What's in store for you now. Tell me how this being an actor thing works." Dad sips his drink.

"Well, sir. I go on auditions. If they like me and think I'm a good fit for the role. Then my agent will negotiate a contract." Thomas is making it simple.

"And you said you've been successful?" My dad doesn't take his eyes off him.

"I have sir, I've been fortunate." Thomas looks down for a second to break my dad's stare. It's not because he is intimidated. It's his way of being humble. "I've been more successful than most."

"What happens now? Marguerite is here." Dad scoots in closer to the table.

"Sir, I think that depends on what we decide. I've asked her to stay." Thomas takes a sip of his freshly made Old Fashion.

Dad grimaces. "And leave what she's built? I didn't raise my girls to depend on a man."

Thomas puts his hand to his chin. "I'm not asking her to do anything she doesn't want to do, sir. She doesn't have to depend on me. But know that taking care of her doesn't mean she depends on me."

Dad sits back, thinking. "So, are you working now?"

"I just auditioned for a movie that will be shooting in Los Angeles. I am also doing a voice-over for a cartoon. I just finished a commercial a couple of weeks ago."

I furrow my brow. "I didn't know about that. What was the commercial?"

"Oh, it was for…." Thomas blushes. "It was a tea commercial."

Joan finishes up the rest of her wine in a gulp and begins speaking in an English accent. "A spot of tea, mister. Mister, a spot of tea."

I coolly reach over and take the empty glass from her hand. It's not like Joan to get tipsy in front of mom and dad. What is wrong with her? Has something happened with Will that she isn't telling me about? I have to put a pin in it and focus on Thomas right now. I try talking to her telepathically, and she knows it. She looks down, trying to break my communication. I try harder.

Mom interrupts my telepathy to Joan. "So, tell me about your family. Your childhood."

"My mother is newly retired. She was a drama teacher. My sister, Birdie, is a nature photographer, and my other sister, Figs, is a pediatric doctor."

My eyebrows shoot up. "I don't think I knew that about Figs. I would have thought she was an art teacher."

"That's the thing about Figs. She's unassuming and has some quirks to her."

"Like what? I ask. I'm interested now."

Thomas holds up a finger. "Well, for one, she bought this old food truck and turned it into a pet circus. She rescues dogs and trains them to do tricks. On her days off, she drives it to the hospital and puts on a show for the kids."

"Really? I love that." My heart warms at the thought of her and her pet circus in front of the hospital. "I'll have to see this. I could help."

"You didn't mention your dad. Where is he?" Mom takes a sip of her tea, realizing it doesn't have sugar. She screws up her face. "Oh! Bitter!"

"My father is a scientist. He mostly does research. My mom and dad divorced when I was a teenager while I was at boarding school."

"Boarding school?" I can tell my mom has questions about that from her reaction, but she tables it.

The waiter brings out our food. He sets Thomas' hardy stew in front of him. I get a whiff of it and start to drool. Without a word, he pushes it in front of me and takes my salad. I look up and smile at him. He leans over and hands me a piece of bread, then kisses me on my forehead.

I throw my arms around him. "I love you."

It isn't necessarily that he gave me his stew. Well, it is, but it's deeper than that. He did it without a thought—completely unselfishly. I cheekily smile at him. My heart begins to flutter until it's outright booming. It's kinda like when you turn on a sprinkler, the water starts with a trickle, and by the time you know it, it's a full blow spinning cascade of aquatic chaos.

I lock eyes with my dad. I can almost see what he's thinking. Like he's played our whole life in fast-forward in his head. He dabs the corner of his eye with his napkin, tearing up, something my dad rarely does. It's not like my dad doesn't have feelings. He just doesn't cry. No one else notices dad welling up. It's our little secret. I swallow down the lump in my throat. My lip begins to quiver; I bite it hard and smile.

The waiter comes to the table. "How is everything tasting?"

"On second thought, I'll take a glass of house red," I say.

Joan puts a finger in the air. "I second that."

"Anything else?" the waiter looks around the table.

Mom shakes her head. "I don't think so; nothing for me."

Dad lifts his drink to examine it. The whiskey ball sits shiny at the bottom of his empty glass. "I might as well. I'll also take a glass of water.

Thomas wipes his mouth with his napkin, "Mr. Becker, tell me about Texas. I've always wanted to visit."

My dad smiles, "Mar told me that you wanted to be a cowboy. Like a cattle worker or a cowboy that just rides out on the land?"

Thomas' brow furrows. "Maybe a cowboy that runs cattle and that kind of stuff."

Dad leans forward. "Why haven't you done that?"

"I love acting more. Plus, I live here." Thomas tilts his head to the side. "There isn't a real opportunity here."

"You don't have to live here. You can move to the states. Leave all this behind." Dad gestures around.

"I would. I could very well move to the states. I mean, if that is what Marguerite wants." Thomas reaches over and slides his hand over my knee. "I'd go anywhere with you. If I'm asking you to move here, I could very well consider moving there."

My breath catches, and my words fail me. Would I go anywhere to be with him? What if we have children? I always thought mom, dad, and Joan would be a big part of that. All these things I never thought about. It's not like you fall in love according to someone's location. That would be being in love with the location and not the person. I think I just made my point…

If I love him, then the location shouldn't matter, and you sacrifice for the things you love. I never knew what the whole "sacrifice" thing meant until now. I grab my glass of wine and lean back in my chair, crossing my arm over my lap. Sometimes you just have to compromise. I let that twirl around in my head.

Mom interrupts. "So, Thomas, tell me about this wedding. Can I wear a fancy dress?"

"Wear as fancy of a dress as you want. Go all out. It is going to be at the Strawberry Hill House." Thomas smiles back at mom.

Mom digs for more details. "What's that? Will it be at someone's house? Like an estate?"

"Yes, an estate. It was at one point. I will be wearing a tuxedo if that helps you decide." Thomas says.

The waiter brings the already paid bill with dad's credit card and hands it to dad.

"No, sir, please. I have this." Thomas says, reaching for the check.

"Son, you are going to have to wake up pretty early to beat me at something I want to win." Dad folds the receipt and tucks it in his wallet. "—for the box." He smiles at me.

Dad has this box that he started when Joan and I were kids. It holds all kinds of keepsakes. I have never actually looked in it. I only know what he has told me he's put in it. Just recently, it has been the receipt for the tricycle Joan and I destroyed in Napa. Dad stands, pulling his pants up by the loops. Charlie lazily crawls out from under the table. I almost forgot he was there.

As we step out to the street, Thomas throws his jacket over my shoulders. Joan and mom walk beside me as Thomas and dad walk behind. I lead the way back to the flat.

"Turn up the next street. I'd like to show you something." Thomas says, gesturing with his hand.

We casually stroll up the next street. We walked this way a couple of times before to broaden my knowledge of the neighborhood. Thomas stops in front of a large gate and opens it.

I hesitantly walk in. "Why haven't you ever taken me here before?"

"I didn't have a key until now," Thomas says, walking past me with his arms behind his back. "Do you like it?"

"I love the house next door; I never knew there was a park so close." I smile up at Thomas.

Mom, Joan, and I sit on a wooden bench in the moonlight underneath a willow tree. We stare up at the large white house next door. Thomas and dad walk the perimeter of the park. They stop at the far end as I watch their body language. Thomas stands with one hand in his pocket as dad stands with his arms crossed over his chest. To anyone else, it would look like dad was closed off to the conversation, but I know dad. This is just how he stands. Joan and I crane our heads to hear. Whatever they are talking about, it is intense. The wind picks up, causing me to shiver. I shove my hands in Thomas' jacket pockets and pull it tight around me when I feel a small box. I flip it around in my hand.

My heart drops to my feet like an anvil falling from the Empire state building. I nudge Joan with my elbow and slide my hand into hers. Then I shove both our hands into the pocket of Thomas' jacket. Joan's eyebrows shoot up in surprise. She grabs my hand again and squeezes it three times. It's our way of saying I love you. Joan turns to me and takes in a deep breath. It's the kind of deep breath that follows a 1,2,3 and a jump over a cliff. Is it a ring? Am I being too assuming? Joan and I sit in silence, talking without talking—vibrating.

Mom interrupts my thoughts. "Mija, did you see that house?"

"Yes, I love it." I smile at mom, trying to focus on the here and now instead of the tiny box, I'm holding in my hand.

It's extremely hard to concentrate right now. I trace the lines of the box with my thumb. Could this be what he and dad are talking about? Is that why he invited them here? Thomas and dad start to walk back this way. Joan pulls our hands out of Thomas' jacket. We both stand up to hide our nervousness. Dad reaches out for mom and pulls her to her feet.

We carelessly walk back towards the flat. Joan and I lag behind, whispering to each other. Charlie bolts for his food bowl as Thomas opens the door. That's one thing about Charlie; he never misses the opportunity to eat.

Dad gives Thomas a big hug. "You are alright, son. You're all right, in my book."

Thomas hugs mom, tucking her tiny frame under his arm. He looks like a giant compared to mom, standing a whole foot and a couple inches taller. "Goodnight. I will see you when you wake. Please don't think you have to rush. The time change can really get the better of you."

Mom and dad walk into their room, shutting the door behind them. Thomas quickly makes his bed on the couch. He takes the jacket off my shoulders. I watch as he drapes it over the back of a chair. I was hoping he would forget about it so that I could get a chance to see what was really in the pocket. I know it isn't the right thing to do, but I hate surprises. No, that's not true. I have no patience when I know there is a surprise. Like when I was a kid, all the Christmas presents would be just sitting under the tree, taunting me. One year I snuck into the living room and opened one of my gifts. It was a baby doll that I had wanted all year. I sat on the bathroom floor playing with it before doing a terrible job of wrapping it back up.

I tiptoe to kiss Thomas. I drag out my words. "OK, I guess Joan and I are going to get some sleep. Goodnight, love."

Thomas pulls me in and buries his face in my hair. "I'll miss you."

Joan rolls her eyes, "Oh, please! Do you just want to sleep in your room Thomas? We can switch before my dad wakes up."

Thomas laughs at Joan's no-nonsense way of talking to him. "No, it's fine. I'll just sleep here and see you in the morning. It's great to see you, Joan."

Joan and I walk into the bedroom and shut the door. I grab Joan by the hand and drag her into the bathroom.

I turn on the shower to drown out our voices. "What in the world? Do you think that was an engagement ring?"

Joan pulls me to the floor. "I don't know! What else could it be?"

I look Joan in the eyes. "You were acting weird at dinner. Are you sure you don't know anything? You were acting like you knew something."

"No, the only thing I know is that he wanted to meet mom and dad. Mom called me and told me; then I got a call from Thomas the next day inviting me here. I didn't take any of your calls because I wanted to keep my coming a secret. Will was convinced you were going to fly back if I didn't answer soon." Joan grabs both of my forearms. "Do you really think?"

I run my hand through my hair. "What else could it be? I feel like I have been truly stuck on whether or not I should move here. Something was giving me that vibe. The other night he said something to his friend that struck me odd. That coupled with this….” I stop mid-sentence. My eyes go wide.

“Why don’t we sneak in and find out after he goes to sleep tonight?” Joan says, trying to calm my nerves.

“OK, deal. When Thomas falls asleep, we will crawl in and dig in his pocket.” I stand up. “I’ll shower then you unless you want to go first?”

Joan shakes her head. “No, go ahead. I’ll have to dig for my stuff out of my luggage.”

Joan and I pull on pajamas and calmly wait, listening for the flat to go still. We sit in bed holding our breath, our fingers intertwined together firmly—waiting. I become so silent that I can hear Joan breathing.

A half of an hour passes when I give Joan a thumbs up and creep to the door. Joan follows behind me, pressing herself against my back. I crack open the door and slink out. Joan squats down, and Army crawls out behind me. I slowly squat down, get on all fours, and carefully inch my way to the chair. Joan low crawls past me. My fingers are crawling over things, touching things, and feeling their way through the dark. As I catch up to Joan, I accidentally put my knee down on her hand.

Joan sucks in a breath. “Ouch!”

I squeeze my eyes tightly shut. Dang, it…

“Marguerite?” A question hangs in the darkness. “M, is that you?” Thomas calls out.

I quickly stand. “Yes! It’s me. I just missed you… and, and I came in to say goodnight again. So, goodnight!”

Joan slides the jacket off the chair. I begin to do a tiny tap dance to distract Thomas as I see Joan tuck herself into a ball and haphazardly roll back towards the bedroom.

I throw my hands in the air doing a calmer version of jazz hands… “Goodnight…” I begin to dance backward towards the bedroom as the tiny sliver of light disappears. I know Joan has made it safely back and has shut the door.

"Hey, come here." Thomas gets up from his spot on the couch and sits on the chair. "Here, lay down on the couch for a while. We can talk."

I climb under the covers and roll them around myself. Thomas reaches over his hand and holds mine. "M, could we be like this forever? Could we be this happy forever?"

"I was just thinking the same thing," I say.

The warmth and the smell of Thomas' cologne on the sheets lull me into sleepiness.

Thomas whispers, "Could I keep you forever? Could I love you forever?"

I sleepily mumble back. "I'll love you forever."

My eyelids are so heavy. The combination of warmth, Thomas' words, and the darkness takes hold of me. I fall asleep despite my unwillingness.

Chapter 9

Morning

*"If you love me for the beauty of my personality, then
I'll stay here forever."*

—Angel Taylor

THE NEXT MORNING COMES IN A BLINK. I wake to dad shaking my shoulder. Startled, I glance around. Thomas is asleep on the chair, holding my foot. Thomas' lower half and legs are stretched out on the carpet. Chairs aren't made for tall men to sleep in. Thomas wakes up and pulls himself to a sitting position. Dad is rummaging around the kitchen as Joan comes gliding out of the bedroom holding Thomas' jacket behind her.

She slyly places his jacket on the back of his chair and then hugs him from behind. "Hi, Tom. Sleep well?" She points at dad, who is now getting the coffee out of the cupboard.

I am tracking Joan with my eyes, waiting for a sign—or anything from Joan.

Joan makes eye contact with me, shrugs, and shakes her head.

Thomas stands, "I'll make coffee, sir."

I squint to see my watch. It's 5:30 in the morning.

Charlie is following dad around the kitchen in hopes of getting another piece of bacon. Thomas pours the beans in the top of the coffee maker as dad continues to rummage around in the cabinets. He pulls out a coffee mug and waits next to the coffee maker. He's like a little boy waiting for his ration of candy after supper.

Joan rounds the chair to hug me. She pulls me in for a hug and whispers, "I didn't find anything. The box was gone. It wasn't in there."

I nod my head in acknowledgment. He must have taken it out. I crack open the door to the guest bedroom. Mom is in the shower. I crawl into her empty bed and pull the covers over myself, inhaling dad's Old Spice cologne. I close my eyes and think about the day—and what it has in store for us. Mom sits on my feet.

Startled, I bolt up. "Ouch!"

"Oh, cielos! Oh, heavens! Marguerite! What are you doing in here?" Mom is standing at the foot of the bed, clutching a towel tightly around her. She pulls the comforter off me. "Go on, get out of here, and let me get dressed in peace."

It's funny how mom sounds so exhausted with me.

I slide out of bed laughing. "I love you, mom. You're so cute."

I walk back into the living room. Thomas has disappeared into the bedroom. Dad is sitting at the counter drinking his coffee. I hug him around the neck from behind. "I'm so glad you are here, dad."

Dad reaches up and holds my arms around him. "Me too, Punky. Me too."

Joan walks up behind us and wraps her arms around both of us. "What are we doing today?"

"I think we are dress shopping or sightseeing." I plop myself down next to dad and take a sip of his coffee. "Yuck! Dad! No cream?"

Dad's belly jiggles as he laughs, "That's why it's *my* coffee and not yours." He takes it from me and sits it back in front of him.

Thomas comes out of the bedroom. "The shower is free, M."

I hop off the chair and walk past Thomas. "Thanks; what are we doing today, so I know what to wear?"

"We can do whatever you want. I didn't know if you wanted to shop for a dress or if you felt like sightseeing today. Your choice."

"OK, I walk into the bathroom and turn on the shower. I Bluetooth my phone into the shower speaker and put on my favorite playlist—the Best of the '80s. Pat Benatar's *Love is a Battlefield* begins to play. I crank it up and step into the shower. Both of my worlds are here in one place. I sway to the music on autopilot. My mind drifts off in a sleepy daydream. I rinse my hair out and pour in the conditioner. I gotta rally today. I shake out my body and bring the shower head up to my mouth. *"You're begging me to go and making me stay... We are young, heartache to heartache...."* I'm holding my own little naked concert. Sometimes music is all you need to get your mind straight.

"We are strong!" I punch my arms in the air.

The steam floats around me. Foreigner comes on. It's a more mellow jam. I sway back and forth with the music. *"I wanna know what love is! I want you to show me!"*

I'm spraying water over my face and into my mouth when I catch a glimpse of Joan standing next to the glass shower door.

She startles me; I slip, hitting my butt on the soap holder—hard. I accidentally swallow a mouth full of water and choke.

She opens the glass door, "Oh, shit! Are you OK? What the hell are you doing?"

I begin to laugh. My butt hurts too bad. I turn the water off and hand her the handheld showerhead. There's only one thing you can do in this situation. Continue... *"I wanna feel what love is; I know you can show me."*

Nudity has never mattered to either Joan or me. We just don't get embarrassed with each other.

Joan joins me, *"I know you can show me. Let's talk about love."*

"The love you can feel inside," I add. I point my finger in the air and hit the high part.

Just as the song ends, Thomas slides into the bathroom. He notices that I'm still standing naked in the shower. He turns his back to me, even though he has seen me naked plenty of times. Somehow this feels, well, just wrong. Joan doesn't even flinch.

"What are you doing in here. It sounds like a bad breakup from the living room." He hands me a towel.

Joan starts to brush her hair in the mirror. "Why is Joan in here?"

I narrow my eyebrows, "Well, singing, of course."

Thomas shakes his head. "What is she doing in here while you're naked?"

I answer again with the same response. "Singing, of course."

Thomas rubs his forehead and slides out of the bathroom, confused.

Joan and I grab each other's hands and laugh.

Joan whispers, "Hey, I've looked everywhere in the bedroom. The box isn't there. Plus, I was sleeping in there. So, I don't think he could have put it in there. I think it has to be in the living room somewhere."

I pull my wet hair up in a messy bun and rub my moisturizer over my face. "Do you think it's an engagement ring? Tell me! If you knew something I don't, you'd tell me, right?"

"I don't know, Mar. If I knew, would it be better to tell you and ruin the surprise, or would it be better to keep a secret? You know, I would, of course, tell you, but I don't know anything." Joan hops up on the counter.

I think about Joan's words. She *would* tell me. Unfortunately, by the stunned expression on her face last night, I don't think she had a clue.

We aren't getting anywhere guessing; I change the subject. "So, do you know what you want to do today? Do you think we should go dress shopping or sightseeing?"

"I think mom wants to go dress shopping. Thomas was just telling her that the wedding is some kind of Lord, a family friend or something. She's beyond excited." Joan says, layering on an extra coat of mascara.

I lean against the vanity. "So, how has Will been?"

"Construction has moved up. He's been swamped, but we have been meeting to drink a glass of wine each night on the back of his truck." Joan says, turning towards me. "I filed for divorce from Frank. My lawyer reached out to his, and apparently, he had a change of heart. I haven't spoken to him, though."

"You aren't thinking of going back to him, are you?" I put my lip liner down and grab Joan by the elbow.

"Oh, hell no!" Joan jerks her head back. "I would rather lay in an ant bed with honey poured all over me."

"Good, because I was about to slap you into next week." I hold her gaze.

"That's a bit harsh, don't you think?" Joan's mouth goes into a line.

"No, Frank putting his penis in another woman is harsh." I hold my hand over my mouth, pretending to gag.

Joan claps a hand over my mouth. "Stop, you're gonna make me throw up."

I lick the inside of her palm. She jerks her hand away. "Gross!"

I laugh and whisper, "Penis."

Joan hip checks me into the sink vanity. "Come on, smalls. We can't be in here all day. Plus, when I came in here, dad was looking for something to eat, and mom was setting out food from Thomas' fridge.

"What? Oh, my God. Seriously?" I put all my supplies back in my makeup bag and shove it under the sink.

Joan and I walk out of the bedroom. I scan the room to assess the situation. Mom has Thomas and dad sitting obediently at the counter. I notice a tiny box sitting on the self in front of Thomas' BAFTA award. My eyes lock on Joan's; I look over to the shelf and back over to her. She catches on and eyeballs the shelf. She gives one slight nod, and I know she sees it.

I walk up behind Thomas and hug him around the neck. "What's going on here?"

Mom has the flour and eggs out. "What are you making?"

Mom has pinto beans boiling in a cast-iron skillet on the stovetop. "I'm making beans and tortillas."

"Will the beans be ready in time?" I walk over to stir them.

"Dejalo! Let it alone, Marguerite." Mom says, slapping at my hands.

Mom begins making little balls of dough and placing them in a bowl.

"Marguerite, I thought we should go shopping today and sightseeing tomorrow when we are completely refreshed."

Thomas raises his chin, "If you agree, then I call Art to meet you here. Maybe you should take your car, or mine if it's easier. You can practice."

"I can't take my car or yours, for that matter! I still don't have the whole driving on the other side of the street thing down. Like whom has the right of way at a four-way stop? Are there four-way stops or just roundabouts?" I absent-mindedly start to roll out tortillas. Did Thomas have a rolling pin? I hold up the rolling pin in my hand. "Mom! You brought *your* rolling pin?"

Mom's rolling pin once belonged to my grandma—the Bruja. It was one of the things mom got when my grandma passed last year.

"Si! You never know when you need it." She snatches it back from me.

I cringe. I guess if Thomas is in it for the long haul, he might as well know how crazy my family is. Not that he could get that from Joan trying to poison her ex-husband. Joan is causally standing in front of Thomas' BAFTA award.

"What's this? She picks it up.

"Oh, that's a BAFTA award for my work in Analog." Thomas walks over and stands next to Joan.

He grabs the small box off the shelf and sticks it in his pocket. I watch him closely.

Joan notices too and raises her eyebrows at me.

"Joan, come sit down." Mom sets out plates in front of each of us.

Dad is happy as a Bluebird sitting at the counter with piping hot coffee and two bean breakfast tacos.

Thomas folds his in half and takes a bite. "Oh, this is good! I've never had this before. Thank you, Mrs. Becker."

"You can call me Olivia," Mom says, proud of herself.

"OK, Olivia. Thank you." Thomas smiles at mom. His smile lights up his whole face and, in return, lights up mine.

The doorbell rings. Thomas hops up. Art, Thomas' personal stylist, walks in.

"Art, I would like you to meet Mr. Becker, M's dad. Mrs. Becker, Olivia M's mom, and Joan, M's sister. They will need dressing for Lord Andrew's wedding."

Art shakes his head in understanding. "Fabulous—I will get them measured, and all their dresses picked out today. I will make sure they have everything they need."

Mom grabs Art by the arm. "Sit, have breakfast before we go. We can't shop on an empty stomach." She sets a plate of bean tacos in front of him. "Eat—eat."

Mom never takes no for an answer. Feeding people is her way of showing people that she loves them. I can tell Art has never eaten this kind of taco before.

"Fold it, Hijo—fold it, son." Mom folds her hands together like she's about to pray. "Fold it like a book."

Art hesitantly folds the tortilla in half and takes a bite. He chews in silence. Then a smile spreads across his face. "Mrs. Becker, how in the world do you make beans taste so good? And the tortillas—soft and warm. Delicious!"

"The beans are just pinto beans with a little salt and mantequilla." Mom stops herself. "I mean butter and the tortillas just take the right amount of warm water. If I can get it, I'll use pig lard."

Dad finishes his plate and washes it in the sink.

Thomas pours dad another cup of coffee. "Mr. Becker, if it is alright with you, I'd like to spend the day with you. We can go get fitted for our tuxedos, and then I can take you to *The Speak Easy*."

"I'd like that," Dad says, sitting back down at the counter.

Joan grabs my dish as mom finishes up her food. Mom is always the last to eat, no matter how much we try to help her. Joan takes Art's dish and washes it. I hop up and put the rest of the beans in a Tupperware and scrape the skillet.

"I'm ready when you are. Now that I think about it, I will take my car. It will give me good practice."

Art widens his eyes in alarm. "Practice? You do know how to drive, right?"

"Of course! How old do you think I am? The only thing I'm still getting the hang of is driving on the opposite side of the street and some street signs."

"And driving today is something you want to try?" Art gulps his water.

"Yep!" I pull Rocinante's keys out of my purse.

Mom is just finishing up washing her plate. "I'm just going to grab my sweater."

Joan meets me at the door as Thomas walks over and kisses me on the forehead.

He hands Art a credit card. "She pays for nothing. Please make sure of that. If she pays, you are fired." He gives Art a wink. I think he's kidding, but I can't tell.

"See you in a few." I walk out to Rocinante and open the door. Art stands on the sidewalk, examining the backseat.

"What? Just get in." I lean the front seat forward for him to get in.

He gets in the back next to mom. "OK, what's the address of the dress shop?" I look in the rearview mirror at Art.

I type in the address 923 Old Church Street in Chelsea and hand Joan the phone. "OK, tell me where to turn. My car isn't equipped for Bluetooth or an aux cord yet."

Joan is scrutinizing the car's rudimentary equipment. "No kidding."

"Oh, Mija, what an economical car. When did you buy this?" Mom's five-foot body sits comfortably in the backseat.

"Thomas bought it for me a few days ago. He was worried about my independence." I smile at the dash in front of me, adjusting everything to my liking before setting off.

"What a lucky girl." I can hear the sarcasm in Art's voice, but I know he doesn't mean it rudely.

"I am lucky." I crank the engine and pull out onto the street.

Dad and Thomas are standing on the sidewalk. Joan gives dad a quick wave and an uneasy thumbs up.

I make a right turn, being very mindful of what side of the street I'm supposed to be on. My hands are clammy. I'm driving very slowly, trying to keep things straight in my head. I repeat to myself; right is wrong, left is right—Righty tighty lefty loosey. Right, isn't right? Oh, no, I'm confused. Is left, right?

"Mar, maybe you should let Art drive?" Joan looks at her watch.

Art is gripping his bag to his chest. "Absobloodylootly!"

"We're fine. Don't rush me. I'm trying to remember what side of the street I'm supposed to be on. Right is right...." I make a right turn and position Rocinante on the right side of the street. "It's like when I'm holding two drinks; mine is always in my right hand because I'm always right!" I say, giving her a smug look.

"Bloody hell! Mar, you are on the wrong side of the street!" Joan turns my head with her hand.

A car passes us, blaring its horn. I promptly jerk back to the left side of the street. "Left-is-right. Right is wrong...."

"Stop saying that. It's getting you confused." Joan checks her seat belt.

"Right is right. Left is wrong. If loving you is wrong, I don't want to be right. Right as rain!" Words are spewing uncontrollably out of my mouth. I grip the steering wheel tighter and look over my shoulder to get on the roundabout.

Art sinks in his seat. I join the roundabout without effort. "See? I'm getting the hang of this."

I lean into the steering wheel to get a better look. We have somehow positioned ourselves in the middle lane of the roundabout with no knowledge of how to get out. By the third time around, Art sits up in his seat. "Move over to the right. OK, when you get to your exit, turn on your blinker. Exit but stay on the left. I'll guide you through."

I catch a glimpse of mom in the back seat, smiling without a care in the world.

"OK, move over to the next lane. —OK, go! Move to the next lane. Go, go! Your exit is the next one; get ready. OK, exit! Stay on the left. The left!" Art is gripping the back of my seat and yelling.

I jerk Rocinante swiftly and smoothly out of the roundabout, successfully making it onto the correct side of the street. I reach up and make a checkmark in the air.

"Put your hand down, Stupid! You could have killed us back there. You don't get a point for not killing us." Joan grabs my hand and forcefully knocks it down. "OMG! I don't think you should drive, ever! Never, ever!"

"Stop it, we're fine. I have to learn somehow." I tap her hand with mine.

"I agree, but it doesn't have to be with us in the car. I'm sure there is some kind of driving school for Americans that want to drive in England."

"We didn't learn to drive going to a driving school," I smirk at Joan.

"Yeah, but we didn't have ten years of driving on the opposite side of the street ingrained in us either." Joan makes an invisible checkmark in the air.

Some of the streets here are surprisingly narrow. I think I read somewhere that the older ones were made for horse carriages, not cars. "Oh, look, mom, there's the Royal Opera House." I point out the window. I hold the steering wheel tight so as not to bump into the rickshaw sharing the very narrow road.

"Take a right." Art leans forward against my seat. "We are close."

I take a right then a left.

Art points to a parking spot. "Park here. This is the best parking you are going to get."

I pull over and hop out. The dress shop is in a tiny stone castle. Mom stands on the sidewalk and puts her purse strap over her chest.

"Right through here, ladies." Art holds the door open for us as we file in.

A well-dressed woman meets us at the door. "I'm Marissa."

Art holds out his hand to her. "I'm Art. We are here for dresses for a very important wedding."

The girl ushers us in. Rack after rack of dresses line the walls. A round green velvet sofa sits in the middle of the room. The floor is stained concrete.

"Please let me know if there is anything you need. Feel free to take anything and try it on. The dressing room is right here." She walks back to her place behind the counter.

"OK, ladies, just pore over through the dresses. Pick out a few of your favorites, and then we can go from there." Art says, grabbing a seat on the sofa.

I lay my purse down next to him and begin digging through the dresses. Mom sifts through the rack next to me.

"Olivia, don't worry about the length of the dress. We will have the dress fit for you." Art stands next to mom, pulling out each dress, giving it a once-over. "Red would be a beautiful color on you with your olive skin; if you want to be that bold."

Mom takes the dress and heads to the dressing room. Joan circles the racks.

"An emerald green would be a great color on your pale complexion." Art pulls out a dress and hands it to Joan. "And you dear could pull off almost any color. How about a maroon or a navy blue?"

He holds both up, and I grab the navy blue one and spin it around. "I'll try both."

Mom is the first to appear out of the dressing room. I quickly follow, wearing the navy blue dress. My jaw drops. I don't think I've seen my mom in anything other than something practical. "Mom, you look amazing! Wait until dad sees you in this; he might just drop dead."

Mom runs her hands down the fabric of her dress. Joan walks out and stands beside her. Art's right; the green makes her skin look flawless. I join them in the mirror book, casing mom in between us.

Art walks over with three pairs of shoes. "Here, put these heels on. I want to see the height with the dress."

I slip a gold heel onto my foot. "Don't you think this might be too fancy?"

"Oh, dear. You don't know where you are going, do you?" Art says with pity in his voice.

I turn to take in Art's expression. "Thomas said it was a family friend's wedding at an estate. A lord or something. He didn't elaborate."

"He was being modest. If you wore a ball gown, you'd fit in." Art pulls at my dress, cinching it in at the waist.

"Should we be wearing ball gowns?" I run my hand down my dress.

"Ball gowns are overrated. I think your dress is perfect. Plus, ball gowns are uncomfortable. There's just so many layers to them." He grabs Joan by the hand and twirls her around. "I don't think you have to try any more on; this dress is perfect."

Mom slips on the crystal-encrusted heels. They don't seem to be very comfortable, but they are breathtaking. Sometimes fashion is painful.

"Hang on; I'm going to send a picture to Marie." I snap a picture of us posing in the mirror. I carefully sit down on the sofa, careful not to wrinkle my dress, waiting for Marie's opinion.

Marie text back.

Oh! I like that, and I love your mom's shoes. Where are ya going?

"Apparently to a pretty fancy wedding, Thomas' friend." I type back as quickly.

Marie text back. Her message is long; I lean back to make myself more comfortable.

I meant to call you. Don't get alarmed. Mr. Horowitz went to the hospital yesterday. I have Eleanor here. I checked on him, he had a mild heart attack, but he is stable now. We are listed as his emergency contacts, as his granddaughters. I had no idea about it until the nurse asked if I was his granddaughter. I didn't skip a beat, though, and said yes. If all goes well, I can pick him up tomorrow; he'll need therapy, though. So, I'll set that up today.

I text back quickly.

Do I need to come home? I'm calling you!

I hang up and dial Marie.

The phone rings once, and Marie picks up. "Don't worry, Mar, he is fine. I would have called you if he wasn't."

I sit down and take it all in. Mr. Horowitz has been like a grandpa to me. I miss seeing his face every day on my way to run or making sure he has lunch. My heart sinks. He needed me, and I'm here. Mr. Horowitz doesn't have a family. Marie and I are all he has besides, of course, the support from mom, dad, and Joan.

I press a finger to my opposite ear and stare out the window. "OK, you tell me the moment I need to come back. I love you."

I hang up the phone with a little more heaviness in my heart. How in the world am I going to make this work? If I can't make it work, then how can I ask Thomas to come to the U.S.? It's just not fair. This isn't fair. I'm lost in a daydream when I start thinking about Taylor Swift. *'You know I love a London boy; I enjoy walking Camden....'*

I stare out the window composing myself when I notice dad and Thomas walking up the street smoking cigars. I feel like a stalker as I watch for a moment. They are laughing. Dad nudges Thomas then blows smoke into the air. They put their cigars out by a shop door and go inside.

"Is everything OK?" Mom comes up behind me, rubbing my back.

Startled, I turn quickly. "Oh, yes. Mr. Horowitz is in the hospital. He had a mild heart attack. He's OK, though."

Thank God mom didn't just see dad living his best life walking up the street smoking a cigar that he is forbidden to smoke. She would have run out in the street, fancy dress and all. I usher her away from the window and back to the mirror, just in case they walk back out.

Mom turns, showing me the back of her dress. "I think this dress is the one—and the shoes! I love them."

"Ah, do you like the dress? If the answer is yes, I'll have the designer pin it up for you." Art walks to the counter to look for the seamstress.

I catch a glimpse of a familiar face.

I squeal. "What in the world? I guess they will let anyone in here."

Alexander looks me up and down. "I guess they do."

We laugh and hug each other.

Alexander leans back to look at my face. "What are you doing, her darling?"

"I'm looking for a dress for a wedding. I love this one, though." I whirl around, shaking my rear end. "Don't I look fantastic?"

Alexander presses his lips together. "No."

Joan walks up behind me.

"Joan, Mom, this is my friend, Alexander." I grab Alexander by the arm.

Alexander takes mom's hand in his and kisses it. "Ah, un placer conocerte mama! A pleasure to meet you, mama."

"Oh, you speak Spanish?" Mom leans her head to the side.

"Of course, I do. Look at my lovely olive skin and brown eyes." Alexander holds his hands up to his expertly lined eyes. "I'm from Spain, originally. Te ves Hermosa mama. You look, beautiful mama. What's the occasion, mama?"

Mom is always happy when she has found someone to speak Spanish to. Mom grabs Alexander's arm and leans in like she's about to spill the gossip. "We are invited to a royal wedding at Strawberry Hill."

"Oh, Lord Andrew's wedding? I heard he was crunchy." Alexander scrunches up his face.

"What do you mean, crunchy?" Joan asks curiously.

"I mean, he's a real ass. I recognize him from certain circles, and he thinks he is so much better than everyone else." Alexander takes my mom by her hand and leads her to the back. "Please, pick from these dresses instead."

Art stands next to us, in awe.

"Only special people are allowed to look at these." Alexander winks at me.

He reaches in front of mom to grab three dresses off the rack. "Trust me; these are the ones."

I take one from him and hold it up. The hem is not done, and the material is hanging off it. "Alexander, the dress is ripped."

"Oh, no, love. I'm just now finishing it. I'll take your mom and sister's measurements, and I'll drop these by the day after tomorrow."

Art jerks his head back. "That's it?"

"Yep, that's it." Alexander shakes his head. "Try them on; then I'll do some measuring; they will be perfect.

I shrug my shoulders. "Ugh, I hate when people think they are better than other people. I mean, jeez, can't we all just be warmhearted and kind? I'm stealing that word, by the way." I look at Joan. "Don't be crunchy!" I laugh.

Alexander starts shifting boxes on a shelf. "What shoes do you have?" He looks down at mom's feet.

Mom sticks out her leg to show Alexander her shoe.

He inspects it. "I guess, you had no problem finding a shoe from the shelf. We hermosas mujeres españolas se juntan y pueden encontrar diamantes en un montón de mierda de caballo—We beautiful Spanish women stick together and can find diamonds in a pile of horse shit. Now, how about you, Joan?"

Joan holds out her foot showing the shoe she grabbed. Alexander looks at the dress he picked out for her and back at her shoe.

"Yes, good. How about you, queen?" He gestures for me to show him my foot.

I hold it out.

"Oh, no. Not with this dress." He turns around and pulls a box from the shelf. "Not for this princess at the ball. These are the shoes." He opens the box and holds it out to me.

The shoes are the prettiest I have ever seen. Mom's shoes are elaborate, but these are entirely over the top.

"There are precisely 126 Swarovski crystals on each shoe." Alexander holds the shoe up, spinning it around to catch the light.

I slide my foot into them. They are a bit on the not-so-flexible side, but someone wise once said that sometimes fashion is painful.

Joan squats down to look at my feet. "Do they hurt your feet?"

I saunter down the aisle and back. "They feel exactly like you think wearing 252 crystals on a shoe would feel, kinda stiff and a little heavier than the normal shoe."

I slip them off and carefully hand them back to Alexander. He returns them to the box. "I'll measure everyone and get you on your way. Go on, slip off the dresses, and put on the new ones."

We walk back to the dressing room.

"I like that boy," Mom says.

I slip off the dress and pull on the new one. The dress is maroon with crystals forming a V down and over my cleavage. A sheer piece of fabric stretches across the opening in the front. I sidestep to the sofa and throw myself onto it like a beached mermaid.

My mouth drops open as mom walks out of the dressing room. "Mom, you look amazing. Where did you get that rack?" I grab her hand and examine her dress.

Mom slaps my hand, "Para. Pórtate bien—stop it, behave yourself."

Joan nervously walks out of the dressing room; with her arms crossed over her chest.

"Put your hands down. Let me see." I tug at her arms.

"I don't think I could wear this. I mean, look at me." Joan spreads her arms out.

"Oh, darling. I'll fix that. I'll add more fabric there. Don't worry. Your girls won't be showing. How do you like it otherwise?" Alexander tugs and pulls at the top of Joan's dress. He wraps a measuring tape around her. "Yes, yes, this is going to be perfect."

"So, tell me, how did you manage an invitation to Lord Andrew's wedding?" Alexander asks, leaning in.

"Thomas said they are old family friends. He went to college with him." I shrug. "He didn't say much."

"Oh, of course. Old friends, that makes sense." Alexander laughs and stares out the window. He squints his eyes. "Isn't that Thomas?"

I crane my neck to look.

"Who is he with?" Alexander shifts from one leg to the other to get a better look.

"Oh, That's my dad." I smile.

"Oh." Alexander raises his eyebrows at me. "You're dad, huh? It looks like they are getting along well."

Thomas and dad are walking up the street looking like a couple of characters from the *Good Fellas*. Thomas is holding his chest and laughing. Dad is walking beside him with a puff of cigar smoke trailing behind him.

"What are you looking at?" Mom glides in next to me.

Her eyes widen when she sees dad walking up the street. Before I can get the first words out of my mouth, mom is rapping on the glass. "Henry Becker! Henry Becker! You put that cigar down!"

Dad doesn't notice her. He and Thomas continue to walk this way. It's almost like watching an oblivious dog walking into the house with dirty feet. He means no harm, but he gets into big trouble, nevertheless. Mom pulls up her dress so that it doesn't drag on the ground.

She flings, opens the door to the shop, and yells. "Henry Becker, you better take that cigar out of your mouth!"

Dad ducks like he has just been dive-bombed by a hawk. When he realizes it's mom, his face relaxes, and he smiles at her. All of mom's anger drains from her face. Dad crosses the street with his arms open. Thomas coolly walks next to him.

He takes mom into his arms. "Where have you been all my life?"

He holds his cigar away from her and kisses her on the nape of her neck.

"I've been right here, you old fool. Don't think that I'm just going to forget you had a cigar in your mouth. You aren't getting away that easy. Hand me the cigar." Mom holds out her hand for the cigar. Dad halfheartedly hands it to her. She snuffs it out on the sidewalk.

"Am I in trouble for letting him smoke? It wasn't apparent to me it was a rule." Thomas' eyes go wide with that puppy dog look he gives.

"Hi." I reach up and kiss him on the cheek. "You're not in trouble. They aren't your monkeys, and this isn't your circus." I smile at him.

"What if I want them to be my monkeys, and I want this to be my circus?" He knits his eyebrows together. "That was supposed to be cute. It didn't come out right. It just sounded wrong." Thomas runs his hand over his forehead.

Our metaphors went totally off track. No one is a monkey, and there is no circus.

We turn the focus back on mom.

"Henry Becker! You know you aren't supposed to smoke. If these damn cigars don't kill you, I will." She points her tiny finger in his face.

Dad smiles at mom. "You know, you are the cutest when you are mad."

That's about the worst thing you can say to a madwoman.

Dad tries to change the subject, but he just makes it worse. "We are headed to the *gentlemen's* club." Dad exaggerates the word, gentlemen.

Mom jerks her head back. "Excuse me?"

"It doesn't mean what you think." Thomas quickly interrupts. "It's more like an upscale bar—a country club of sorts. We are going to have lunch and a drink."

Dad's lack of elaboration makes mom boil.

"Go, do what you want, Henry. But you will pay the price later." Mom pretends to pout.

"You're my girl, Olivia. I'm just poking fun." Dad kisses mom on the cheek.

I love how mom still gets jealous, and dad still plays along, even though their marriage is rock solid. They still enjoy each other and haven't lost their playfulness. I can only wish to have that. Mom is all fire and spice, and dad is calm and jovial. They balance each other out.

Joan finally comes out of the bathroom. "Hi, dad! What are you doing here? Do I smell smoke?"

I squeeze Joan's arm. Don't even start."

"Well?" Joan spins. "How do you like my dress?"

Dad beams. "Your dress is beautiful, Joan."

Alexander follows us out.

"Oh, dad, this is my friend, Alexander." I step aside. "He is the one who made all the dresses."

Alexander extends his hand, and dad firmly shakes it. "Good to meet you. Nice dresses. You are talented."

Thomas nods his head. "Great to see you again, Alexander."

"And you." Alexander leans in and kisses Thomas on the cheek. "Have you heard from Ben?"

"I haven't. Have you?"

Alexander frowns. "I haven't."

Thomas frowns, "Huh, that's not like him. I'll ring him today and get the scoop."

Happy with Thomas' answer, Alexander smiles. "Thank you. So, I hear you are going to Lord Andrew's wedding."

"Yes, we are." Thomas smiles. "The dresses are fantastic. What are you doing at Madam Norva's shop?"

Alexander presses his lips together and gently puts his hand to his neck. "I bought the place from her. I needed a place to run my shop, and she was ready to pass on the torch. Her hands were just getting too bad with arthritis."

"Oh, I had no idea." Thomas begins scrolling through his phone. "I'm going to send her flowers. Back when I was first starting out, she would let me borrow suits from here for events. I'm heartbroken; I didn't know."

"You're so sweet." I kiss Thomas on the lips.

"Come, let's take these dresses off before we get them dirty. Joan, mom, and Alexander walk back up to the shop.

Thomas blushes. "OK, See you at *home*, love. Don't rush, though. I have a couple more places to take your dad; maybe we could meet for dinner?

"Yep! If you run late just call me. We will just walk up to Sir Richard's for dinner. Bye, dad." I watch Dad as he pulls a cigar out of his pocket and sticks it in his mouth without lighting it.

He turns back to the shop; he smiles at mom standing in the window, pressing her finger on the glass and pointing at him.

Alexander calls me over. "I can't let the princess go to the ball without a gown." He begins pinning up my hem. "OK, pull it off. You're ready."

Joan is next. "No pinning needed. This dress was made for you." He turns her to tug and pull at the dress. "Nope, it fits like a second skin, except for the little fabric we will add here."

Joan reaches up and pretends to write a checkmark in the air.

"You don't get a point for being an Amazon." I laugh.

"Don't I, though?" She laughs as she walks towards the dressing room.

"What are you doing tomorrow? I'll swing by and drop these off." Alexander gathers the dresses and hangs them behind the counter.

"I guess I don't know what I'm doing tomorrow. Maybe some sightseeing. Big Ben, the Tower bridge. Things like that." I hug him. "It was so good to see you."

"Do you want the shoes?" Alexander places his hands on each side of the shoebox, holding them in front of me.

"Oh, I didn't know they were for sale," I say.

"They aren't silly; I made them. But anyone asks you better tell them who I am."

"Oh, you are using me for advertisement." I laugh.

"You better believe it." He laughs. "—but, really darling. They belong with the dress. Take them." Alexander leans over and kisses me on each cheek.

"See you soon, queen. It was nice to meet you. Mama and sis." He waves. "Have fun at the wedding." Alexander opens the shop door for us and walks out to the street. "Art, come by anytime. Now that you know me. I'll help any way I can." Alexander glances around, confused. "Are you walking?"

I laugh, "No, my car is right there." I point to Rocinante.

"Oh, no, babe. Where on earth are you going to put all the things you are buying?"

"What things?" I say, confused.

"–Just in general." Alexander squints his eyes.

I shrug my shoulders. "I guess I'll take Thomas' car or just use the backseat. I mean, I'm never going to be trying to transport a dresser or anything. Maybe I'll get a tiny trailer for the back of it."

Alexander puts his hand on his collarbone. "No, don't do that."

I unlock the door; Art reluctantly gets back in the backseat with mom, and Joan hops in the front. She rolls down the window as we make a U-turn in the middle of the street.

"Toot ta Lou!" I wave at him.

"Mother!" Alexander bites his lip before getting the rest of the word out. He waves back.

"So, where do you want to go? Want to grab a pint and some fish and chips down by the river?" I ask excitedly. "Do you want to go to a van down by the river?" I laugh.

Art's eyes dart around. "What?"

"Nothing, I was making a joke. It's an old Chris Farley skit from Saturday Night live." I turn in my seat to explain it to him.

"Oh my God! Turn around!" Art grips the seat.

"OK, OK, calm yourself. I'm literally going seven miles an hour." I turn forward and point to the speedometer. "Let's go get lunch. Give me directions to a marvelous place for lunch."

"OK, take a right here—turn. Stay on the left. The left!" Art scoots to the middle of the backseat. "Take a right. OK, you can park anywhere along here. Here!"

I'm pretty sure this will be the last time Art rides with me. His nerves are shot.

The restaurant is a cute little hole in the wall on the Thames.

We grab a table as a waiter swings by to drop off some menus.

I smile, "I'll take whatever is on tap."

"Same." Joan doesn't take her eyes off her menu.

Mom smiles, "I'll take an iced tea with some sugar."

The waiter motions to Art. "And for you, sir?"

Art stares up. "I'll take a Guinness."

I raise my eyebrows. "Wow, that's a strong beer. More power to ya."

"Do you mind?" Art asks.

"No, knock yourself out." I put my menu down on the table.

Mom takes the menu from Joan and lays it on top of mine. "Let's make it easy and all order the fish and chips."

Joan leans back in her chair. "What is this river?" She points.

Chapter 10

A Proper English Lunch

"Life is uncertain. Eat dessert first."

—Ernestine Ulmer

It's the Thames; it is pronounced Tim's." Art takes a sip of his beer.

It leaves a foam mustache on his top lip.

We sit, mindlessly staring out the window, watching the ferry's go by. The water glistens like a thousand gold coins floating on the surface.

The waiter delivers the fish and chips to our table. "Fish and chips all around." He smiles.

Mom examines the crunchy crust. "Nice and crunchy." She wiggles her fork through the fish and places a piece in her mouth. "Good flavor too."

The waiter stands next to our table like he is holding his breath for mom's verdict. "How's is your lunch?"

"I'll take another beer," Joan says, sliding her empty glass back to the waiter.

"Me too." I hand my glass back, smiling. "While you are at it, bring another Guinness for my friend here." I point to Art's almost empty pint.

"Thank you, Mar." Art smiles at me then stares out the window back at the passing ferries. He swiftly turns back to me and begins to eat without looking up.

I laugh, "What's up? Why are you suddenly acting weird? Is acting weird like your thing when you drink."

Joan laughs. "Yeah, like Mar's thing is thinking she's Thor."

I blow out my breath and glance out the window. My eyes widen. Thomas and dad are slowly riding by on a polished wooden boat. The kind you'd see on Lake Como in Italy. Dad is standing next to Thomas with his chest puffed out. He has one hand on his hip and the other holding a freshly lit cigar. He is staring straight ahead, with a smug look on his face. Thomas is wearing sunglasses and holding a highball glass in the other hand. I watch in amazement. They are everywhere today.

Joan notices my wide-eyed gaze out the window. "What?" She cranes her head to see what I'm looking at. "Holy hell! Is that dad?" Mom's head snaps up. She looks out the window. "Sinvergüenza! — Scoundrel! Look at him smoking that *damn* cigar. He thinks I can't see him. Well, I see everything!"

Joan stomps her feet on the floor, laughing. She accidentally spits out a tiny bit of beer onto her bottom lip. "You don't see everything."

Mom raises her eyebrows. "Is that a bet?"

Joan looks at me sideways. She knows she just stepped in it, but instead of folding, she doubles down. "Yes, yes, that's a bet!"

"I know that you two chicas furtivas—sneaky girls rolled your father's truck out of the driveway when you were grounded. I also know you drove it out to the beach during Spring Break when you weren't supposed to." Mom looks and Joan.

Joan holds her face steady.

"—and I know Mar helped Marie sneak a boy onto the roof after dad and I went to bed. And that you illegally cut down a pole with a chainsaw." Mom holds Joan's stare.

Give up, Joan. I laugh, "She does know everything! She is, after all, the bruja's daughter."

"OK, you win this one." Joan admits defeat and takes the last sip of beer out of her glass."

Dad and Thomas' boat is just a speck now in the distance. I smile at the thought that they are getting along—not that I was worried. I just didn't know they would get along this well.

"We have the dress and shoes. Do you have anything else you want to do?" Art looks at us. "Do you want to go shopping some more, or do you have something else in mind?"

I lean on mom's shoulder. "I don't know. It doesn't look like Dad will be back any time soon. Mom, how about you? Do you want to go clothes shopping?"

"What is there to do?" Mom asks.

"There's plenty to do. What do you feel like doing? We can go from there." Art says, finishing his beer and scooting it aside.

Joan interrupts. "I'd like to try a traditional English pub."

Art looks towards mom, pausing for her suggestion. Mom shrugs her shoulders. "I want to wait for dad for sightseeing. Against my better judgment, let's do what Joan wants and go to the pub."

Art motions the waiter over and signs the bill. "I know the perfect place. It's called Coach and Horses. It's a piano bar at night and one of the oldest pubs in London."

"I have an idea." I look at Joan. "Do you have a marker in your purse?"

Joan looks puzzled. "No, but I can ask the waiter for one."

I shake my head.

Joan raises her hand to get the waiter's attention. "Do you happen to have a marker we could borrow?"

"I don't, but I'll go to the back to get one." The waiter turns on his heels.

He quickly returns and hands Joan the marker.

Joan hands it to me. I spread out a thick napkin and write. "Coach and Horses, NOW! Tell Dustine."

We stand to leave. I tuck a few pounds under my plate.

"Oh, no, girl, you can't drive. You've had too much to drink." Mom grabs me by the arm.

"OK, you're right. We will just call a cab." I smile at mom.

"Nonsense, I'll drive. I haven't been drinking." Mom reaches into my purse and takes the keys.

Joan shakes her head, looking worried. "Mom, have you ever driven in a place like England where they drive on the opposite side of the street?"

"Basta—stop it. It can't be that hard. Your sister did it." She walks out to the street with us following behind her.

My mouth drops. "Oh, burn!"

Joan and I sit in the backseat. It feels like we are kids again, being driven around by the adults.

I clap mom on the shoulder. "I trust you. I need you to drive by the dress shop before we head to the pub."

Mom cranks the engine and turns on her blinker. She pulls onto the road with ease. Art directs her back to the dress shop.

"Pull in front and honk," I say, siding forward in my seat.

Mom pulls in front of the shop and flips the switch to honk. Rocinante's horn sounds like a barking seal. I hold my napkin against mom's driver's side window.

"Honk again." I urge mom.

Mom honks the horn again as Alexander walks out of the shop and reads my sign. Mom pops Rocinante in gear, making the tiny car jump. Mom swiftly speeds off. Seconds later, I get a text.

"You want me and Dustine to meet you at Coach and Horses…Now?"

I quickly text back. *"Indeed."* I smile at my phone like he can see me.

"Take the next left. Then a right on the next street." Art points, sounding a lot calmer than he did when I was driving.

Mom lifts her chin and watches the traffic as she hums along.

"Take a right here!" Art frantically points, sending mom's anxiety straight through the roof. "Right! We are going to miss it!"

Mom uncontrollably jerks the steering wheel. Two of Rocinante's wheels lift off the ground, tipping him sideways. It feels like we are in one of those old black and white slapstick comedies. I look out the window. Rocinante's two small rubber wheels are rotating in the air. Joan and I throw our weight to the side that's in the air, leveling him out. Rocinante's two wheels hit the ground, bouncing. Mom is now on the wrong side of the street.

"Left! Get on the left!" Art yells.

Mom jerks the car and turns back to the left, almost making a complete circle.

"No, I meant turn right but stay on the left!" Art is so hysterical now that he is completely yelling out random directions.

Mom doesn't skip a beat. She returns to the same street and stays on the left.

"I was going to the left side of the street. Did you think I suddenly forgot? I'm not the one that has been drinking." Mom furrows her brows at Art. "You sit there and be quiet. You are not good under pressure. Joan, you tell me how to get to Coach and Horses."

Joan pulls out her phone and types the name into Google Maps.

"I see that you have officially made it to the twentieth century." I laugh and poke her in the ribs.

"Only because I don't have a real map." Joan sticks her tongue out at me.

"Google Maps is a real map, *and* it's probably more up to date than your stone tablet." I pinch her cheek.

Mom glances at Joan in the rearview mirror. "Where am I going, Joan? Stop arguing with your sister and give me directions!"

Joan immediately becomes defensive. "She was arguing with me first! She says, looking back down at her phone. "Mom, you missed the turn. Take the next left."

Mom swivels in the seat to see if anyone is coming.

"Mom here. Jeez! It's right there! The street is right there!" Joan yells.

Mom unintentionally jumps the curb. Hopping the curb in such a small car feels like we are physically skidding on our butts instead of having a leather seat under us. Our front fender hits the curb making its wheels creak. A loud metallic scratching sound makes me cringe. I turn just in time to see one of my hub caps rolling down the street in the opposite direction.

"Mom, take the next left. The building is brown and white—park anywhere." Joan exits out of her Google maps and throws her phone in her purse.

Mom pulls up, parallel parking right in front of the building.

As she reverses, I look back to guide her. "Mom, I don't think there is enough room. You'll never get into that spot unless someone physically picks up this car and places it there."

"Nonsense." Mom reverses into the space with ease.

I hop out to get a look at her parking job. She hasn't left any room between the car in front of her or the car behind her. I walk around Rocinante. She has literally left two inches at both ends.

"How in the world are you getting out of this spot?" I ask, looking at the wheel with the missing hubcap and the large crater in the hood from my earlier fiasco.

"The same way I got in, with finesse." Mom smiles.

I have a flashback of parking Cooper next to my apartment steps. Dad was right; just because it fits doesn't mean that you should park there. The Coach and Horses is a brown and white building with high-top tables lining the front sidewalk. The building looks like it is straight out of Mary Poppins. If Dick Van Dyke slides off the roof covered in soot, I wouldn't at all be surprised. A horn blares behind us. I turn to see Alexander stepping out of a blue F-type Jag three cars back.

"You bitch! You interrupted my whole day; thank you." Alexander kisses me on each cheek.

I hold my hand on my chest. "Me? Did I mess up your day? You're the one that decided to come!"

Alexander grabs me by the arm, wrapping his around mine. "Come on!"

"Is Dustine coming?" I lean into Alexander's shoulder.

"She will be around in a bit. She was just getting up." Alexander pushes the door open.

The hostess greets us and seats us at a large table next to a piano.

Joan runs her finger across the keys. "Is someone playing today?"

The hostess shakes her head. "Yes, we have a singalong at night."

Joan raises her eyebrows at me. I know exactly what she's thinking. Never will we miss an opportunity to sing karaoke.

"Do you sing Alexander?" Joan asks.

"Do I sing?" He laughs. "Do I sing? Does a drag queen know how to wing her eyeliner?"

"I'll take that as a yes." Joan laughs.

A waitress rushes up. "What can I get you? We have Guinness on tap, of course, Speckled Hen, and a few beers from the Camden Town Brewery."

"I'll have any light beer from Camden Brewery." I smile.

"Same." Joan smiles.

"I'll have a tea." Mom smiles, looking at the advertisement in the plastic holder on the table.

"Come on, mom, have something." Mom wrinkles her brows. "OK, I'll have an Amaretto Sour with a cherry; make that two cherries."

"Beer, Guinness. Please. Thank you." Art folds his menu. "We've eaten, but perhaps we'll order something a little later."

Dustine walks through the door. I immediately spot her and stand. "Hey, sorry if we woke you." I look at my watch. "It's passed one."

Dustine hugs me. "I know, it's OK. It was a long night."

Dustine, I would like you to meet my mother, Olivia, and my sister, Joan. This is Art; he is Thomas' friend."

I'm still grappling with the whole personal shopper thing. It makes me uncomfortable. Art stands and shakes Dustine's hand, introducing himself. "I am Thomas' personal shopper."

Joan nods her head. "Nice to meet you, Dustine."

Dustine grabs a seat next to Joan. "I'll take a whiskey—straight."

Alexander blows out his breath vibrating his lips. Then winks at Dustine. "Are you going straight for the hard stuff?"

Dustine shrugs, "Guess so."

The place is crowded. The noise of people talking, drinking, and laughing travels around the room, creating an electric atmosphere of a variety of people. People are having business meetings, tourists, regulars, and your run-of-the-mill diehards at the bar. The wooden floor is worn and dips in the middle from people walking the same path throughout the restaurant. The tile under the piano seat is worn so thin that the concrete is showing. I read the back of the menu. Coach and Horses is the oldest pub in Mayfield. Beer coasters are cover the top of the bar top. Tufted leather seats line the walls.

We are two beers in when Alexander reaches over and starts tapping a piano key. First, he taps softly, but then he progressively taps harder when we don't pay attention. He continues until everyone in the room is dead silent and looking at him. He slides onto the piano bench and begins playing the intro to *I Will Survive*. Eighty percent of the world would know this song anywhere. If you've ever gotten drunk with your girlfriends after a bad breakup, you'll recognize it. It has a very distinctive intro.

Alexander plays the piano effortlessly. He throws his head to the side and sings. *"At first, I was afraid; I was petrified...."*

I stand and sidestep my way around the table to the piano, dancing and snapping my fingers the whole way.

Joan follows me; she sits on the bench next to Alexander. *"It took all the strength I had not to fall apart...."*

Mom makes eye contact with me. She throws her head back and chugs the last bit of her drink. She dances her way over.

When she gets to the piano, she waves Art over. "Come on, tonto—silly." We are playing a sort of karaoke Red Rover game.

Art stands in front of his seat, hesitant. Mom joins Alexander, singing loudly in Spanish. Joan and I flank her, moving in unison. "Sobrevivire! —survive!"

Mom is living out her fantasy of being a diva in the 1970s. I have to admit. I didn't know mom had it in her. I've never seen this side of her. It's like her dancing and singing has somehow made Joan stronger. Joan sings every single word with clarity and passion, exhausting all her emotions. Alexander doesn't skip a bit and goes straight into his next song.

He swivels his legs around to face the restaurant, then stands to walk around. *I hate the world today. Yesterday I cried. Must have been a relief to see a softer side.* He goes from person to person, singing. Putting on a show comes naturally to him.

We join him—singing each part that feels fitting to each of us.

I yell, "I'm a bitch."

Joan follows, *"I'm a lover. I'm a child."*

After the second chorus, mom gets the hang of it and shouts, "I'm a mother," at her part.

The crowd is really getting into it. I watch as the hostess strategically ping pongs her way over to the piano. I have a feeling she's about to shut this whole thing down. I lock eyes with her and shake my head, pleading with her. She shrugs her shoulders in agreement and walks off.

I take over as I sit on the piano seat and hammer out the beginning of *Total Eclipse of the Heart by Bonnie Tyler.* "Turn around…"

My squad joins me back at the piano. I sing the main part as the crowd sings the course.

"I really need you tonight." I'm enthusiastically acting it out. *"Nothing I can say total eclipse of the heart.*

Although Art is dancing with us, I have yet to hear him sing. I glance at him and smile, encouraging him to join.

He sheepishly looks down. So, I nudge him with my shoulder.

He bites his lip. *"Turn around bright eyes."* Art's voice cracks as he hits the high note. *"Turn around bright eyes, turn around."*

My mouth goes into a wide grin; I begin to clap and throw my arm around Art's shoulders. "See, it wasn't that bad. We are all here just to have fun."

We must have set off a chain of events because a tall, burly man joins us. I scoot over to share the bench with him.

"Hi, I'm Steve." He shakes my hand.

I smile. "Hi Steven, I'm Mar."

I look up to notice Dustine walking out of the restaurant. She didn't even say goodbye. I stand to watch her leave. To my surprise, she quickly returns with two small amps, a mic, and an electric guitar. She plugs the amps and guitar in next to the piano and hands Steve the microphone.

"What are we playing?" She lifts one foot onto the amp in front of her, resting the guitar on her knee.

"Purple Rain," Steven yells into the mic in Dustine's direction.

Dustine's fingers slide over the strings. The crowd erupts in excitement. Steve sings. *"I never meant to cause you any sorrow."*

It sends goosebumps up my arm.

I always forget how much I love this song until I hear it. His voice is rich and raspy with a lot of texture to it; it's surprising coming from him. I had a friend in high school who loved Prince. I thought she was crazy until she made me listen to 1999 and followed it up with Little Red Corvette. I was smitten.

We stand in awe of Steve. Alexander grabs two butter knives from our table and begins taping out the drumming parts on the table next to Dustine. I imagine rain falling from the ceiling and purple lights illuminating the makeshift stage.

As Steve's second song comes to an end. The crowd begins to quiet down. Joan, mom, and I slump down in our seats, laughing.

Alexander grabs a chair and sits in front of us. "Are you guys always this fun?"

I smirk, "We are always up for *some* fun. How about you? Where did you get those singing chops?"

Alexander's hand rests over my hand on the table. "I used to do drag on Haight Street in San Francisco."

"Shut up! You did not! Prove it!" Joan laughs.

"I sure did. Watch this." Alexander walks back towards the piano. Exaggerating his walk —it's more calculated; it's more of a saunter. As he strides past Dustine, his well-manicured nails glide over the table as he casually grabs the microphone and turns it on.

He unbuttons the top three buttons of his shirt and lifts it to his mouth. *"There were nights when the wind was so cold."*

He runs his perfectly groomed hands through his dark silky hair.

I slowly stand and lean against my seat. Alexander sounds precisely like Celine Dion. If I close my eyes, I wouldn't be able to tell the difference. I can feel the wave of confusion from the lunch crowd as one by one turns in their seats to face Alexander.

He transitions into the next song. *"Every night in my dreams, I see you, I feel you."*

I look around at the people sitting at their tables. Each one of them are completely slack-jawed. Alexander must know how good he is. I think about joining him, but instead, I stand completely frozen. Why he isn't a singer is beyond; besides the fact that he is a fabulous designer. It's just not fair sometimes how much talent one person can have.

After Alexander finishes the song, I hear, "Another please, you lovely creature."

Alexander looks up, takes in a deep breath, and looks around at the crowd, absorbing all the energy from the room. He closes his eyes, overacting the longing. *"The whispers in the morning."*

He must know every Celine Dion song in existence. Mom rests her chin on her hand, enjoying the show Alexander is putting on.

Dustine puts her guitar down and scoots onto the bench alongside Art. She smiles as she sways against him. As Alexander finishes his song, the crowd roars in applause.

Alexander stands up from the piano seat, bending his head down; he puts his hand over his heart. "Thank you."

He saunters back to our booth.

Dustine raises her hands up to Alexander, grabbing him by the hand. "Sit down, you attention whore."

Alexander shoves Dustine's shoulder and sits down.

Joan wraps her arm around mine and leans her head down on my shoulder. "I miss you. I miss this kind of stuff with you. Would it be selfish of me to ask you to come home? Don't listen to me; I'm drunk."

My heart sinks in my chest. I miss her too. Why can't I have all of this back in San Francisco?

The waiter walks up laughing. She nods to a man standing at the bar. "Your tab is on Lawrence, the man at the bar."

An older man with grey hair gives a modest wave and disappears through the doors to the kitchen.

"He's notoriously shy. He wanted me to tell you that you were wonderful." She looks at Alexander. "Do I know you from somewhere?"

Before Alexander can introduce himself, I chime in. "He's only Chase Alexander—the best fashion designer London has ever seen."

I may have gone overboard here, but I did just have about four beers in the span of three hours.

Alexander blushes and tilts his head down, acting coy. "Thank you very much."

Art checks his watch. "I have an appointment. Shall we go?"

I begin gathering my purse.

Mom stands up. "Well, well, well, I guess I'm driving since I'm the only one completely sober."

She walks out to the sidewalk. We follow her in a straight line like ducklings following their mother.

Alexander kisses me on the cheek. "See you soon. I had a fun time."

"Me too," I say.

"It was so nice to meet everyone," Mom says, giving hugs out like she's giving out candy. "Get in the car, Chicas traviesas—mischievous girls."

Joan and I hop in the back. Art jumps in the front next to mom. I guess he likes to see death coming.

"OK, give me the directions back to the house." Mom cranks the engine and carefully pulls onto the street. Never once mentioning that, she almost tipped the car over.

Joan reaches for my hand and holds it. Surprisingly, we make it back to the flat without a single incident. I guess mom learned her lesson when she tipped Rocinante on two wheels.

Chapter 11

Two Fools, Does That Include Me?

"Completely and perfectly incandescently happy."

—JANE AUSTEN

MOM PARKS IN FRONT OF THE FLAT facing the wrong way. I don't bother telling her because, to be honest, I just want to get out of the car safely. We made it here without incident; I don't want to tempt fate.

Art steps out of Rocinante, he holds the seat for Joan. "It was so nice meeting you. I had a fun time today. So much fun that it didn't feel like work."

"Thank you so much for your help." I extend my hand to shake his.

Joan grabs our shoes and bags from the truck. She gives Art a wave and meets me on the sidewalk. I can see Charlie through the glass in the door as I unlock it. He runs to the yard to relieve himself. Poor guy, who knows how long he has been holding it.

Mom passes me and heads to the bedroom. "I'm going to lay down for a few minutes."

Joan sets the bags on the coffee table, then joins me on the stoop to watch Charlie. "How are you feeling about all of this?"

I shrug my shoulders. "I don't know. I mean, I love Thomas. But I miss you guys. I miss Marie. I know I can hop a plane and come and see everyone, but it feels different—harder. I had a really hard time the other day wrapping my head around people being around, taking pictures, or having to be in the spotlight. I don't know if I'm explaining it right. It's just a lot to think about, you know? First world problems."

Joan wraps her arm over my shoulders. "It is, sis. Just do one thing at a time. Speaking of one thing at a time. You don't think he's about to ask you to marry him, do you? I mean, what was that box?"

I think back to the small box in his pocket; it was on the shelf, then it wasn't. I inhale and straighten my spine to calm myself.

"I don't think he is thinking about marrying me. I mean, at least not right now." I let that roll around in my head. "Maybe it was just a gift, and I'm letting my overthinking get away from me."

I think back to the night I met his family. Why did he and his mother go out to the street? Why did his sister give him a nod at dinner? Everything inside me feels like it's buzzing—vibrating. I put my head in my hands. What if he *does* ask me to marry him, then what?

Joan must be thinking the same thing because the following words out of her mouth are, "What are you going to say if he asks you to marry him?"

Before I can answer, a shiny black car pulls up next to Rocinante. I look up to see a driver opening the back door.

Dad steps out with an unlit cigar hanging out of his mouth. "Hi, girls!"

I look around dad, waiting for Thomas. Thomas crawls out of the backseat on his hands and knees. He stands and clutches the side of the car to steady himself.

Dad smiles, "The boy can't keep up."

I jump to my feet and rush to Thomas. "Oh, my God! What in the world? Are you OK? How much did you drink? Are you sick?"

Dad claps Thomas on the back. "He's not sick—he's just drunk. He'll be fine. A little sleep, and he will be right as rain."

Joan claps her hands over her mouth, waiting for my reaction.

I look at dad with a stern look. "Dad, what happened? Why?"

"Hey, it's not my fault the boy tried to keep up with me." Dad puts his arm around Thomas' waist and helps him into the flat.

Dad helps Thomas to the couch and sits him down.

I examine the espresso maker for the button to turn it on. The Delonghi machine quietly comes to life. I select a double shot, and the coffee begins to grind. I lock it into place and turn the knob for espresso. Amber liquid begins slowly pouring out of the two-sided spout. The color is beautiful and oddly satisfying to watch. I don't particularly like espresso, but I love the smell of it. After the liquid stops dripping, I pour a bit of steamed milk into it to make a Cortado. A Cortado is a 1:1 ratio of espresso and steamed milk. I learned that from the barista at our local coffee shop. It was a lot easier than I thought.

I take the tiny glass of dark liquid over to Thomas, who is now completely laid out on the couch. He has one foot over the back of the sofa and one on the floor. "Hey." I shake him. "Here, drink this. It will help."

Dad carefully watches me from the other side of the sofa. I squat down in front of Thomas as he sits up, taking the glass from me. "I will *never* drink with your father again."

What he says reminds me of that Toby Keith Song, *I'll Never Smoke Weed with Willy Again,* and it makes me laugh. Joan must be thinking the same thing because she starts humming the song, which only makes me laugh harder.

I smirk, "I should have told you my dad is a joker." I turn and look at dad. "You did this on purpose! You hardly ever drink more than a drink or two. You're being a rascal, *and* you know it."

Dad smiles at me and winks. "I needed to see if he could roll with the punches."

I press my lips together, giving him another stern look. "Dad…"

Mom comes out of the bedroom. "What did he do now?"

She rounds the couch without taking her eyes off dad.

"He drank all day, leaving Thomas no other choice other than to be polite and try to keep up," I say, pointing at dad.

"Henry Becker! Stop being so Travieso—naughty." She smirks at dad.

By the look on her face, I have a feeling she doesn't mean what she said at all. I sit on the couch next to Thomas. He leans his head on my shoulder as I rub it. Charlie jumps on his lap and curls in.

"Ah, my head is throbbing. No, Charlie, I can't right now." Thomas runs his fingers through his hair, pulling it tight.

"Why don't you take a shower and lay down. Drink your Cortado and go shower." I pat Thomas on the back as he gets up to shower.

I watch Thomas disappear into the bedroom and close the door.

Dad is sitting in the recliner like Marlon Brando from the Godfather. As soon as the door to the bedroom shuts, dad turns to me. "I like him. He is in love with you. He's a smart young man."

I jerk my head back at dad's bluntness. "How do you know that?"

Dad leans in closer to me. "He told me so today. He asked me for your hand in marriage."

Bile rises in my throat. I swallow it down hard. My voice comes out like a teenage boy going through puberty. "Today? He asked you today?"

Mom and Joan lean in closer.

Mom's mouth drops open. "And?"

"And I gave him my permission." Dad smiles at mom. "He's a good man. I put him through some hoops today."

"Henry! I don't know how I feel about it. But I will refer to your judgment. I love how he asked you. It's very gentlemanly of him." Mom nods her head like she's made up her mind and agrees with dad.

Joan leans back on the couch. "I knew it. I guess we know what that box was."

Dad nods his head. "I saw the ring."

"You saw the ring?" My mouth goes tight as my eyebrows go up. This is real. He has a ring.

Dad smiles, "Yes, I saw the ring today when he asked me. It's a lovely family heirloom —his great grandmother's."

I think about June, June like the month. "Is it from his grandmother June?"

"No, he told me her name was Rose. His mother's grandma." Dad says. "It's a beautiful vintage piece. He took it to the jeweler and had a two-carat center stone put in it and a hidden sapphire on the inside of the ring for loyalty."

I raise my eyebrows. "Two carats…wow!" I stretch my hand out in front of me to look at my ring finger. "I'll be right back; I'm going to go check on him. Then maybe we can go to dinner?"

I walk into the bedroom, and Thomas is sleeping on the bed, curled up in his bathrobe.

I shake his shoulder and whisper. "Hey, we thought we would get freshened up and walk to dinner."

Thomas groans. "Oh God, M. I'm so out of sorts right now."

"You sleep, and we will go for a walk around and a bite to eat." I rub his back.

"I feel so bad that you have to go without me." Thomas pushes his face into the pillow. "I'll rally."

"No, don't rally. It will be good to go out and do some catching up with my parents." I kiss him on the forehead and pull the covers over him.

I walk back into the living room. Mom and dad are on the couch as Joan is snooping around Thomas' flat. I whisper. "Why are you snooping? And don't say you aren't. I know you better than that."

Joan gives me a coy smile. "You don't know what you don't know. Besides, I'm looking for anything suspicious." She walks around pretending to hold a magnifying glass to different parts of the bookshelf.

"Stop that stupid, and let's get out of here." I grab my purse off the table by the door. "Let's go for a walk then a late dinner?"

Mom helps dad off the couch and follows behind as I lock the door.

"Let's take the long way." I lead the way a block in the opposite direction. There is a cute little shop I want to stop at."

"What kind of shop is it?" Joan asks.

"It's a paper shop. You know the kind that sells stationery and pens and stuff." I say, smiling.

"Figures. Are you looking for something or just going for more pens?" Joan frowns at me.

"I'm just browsing. And if a pen speaks to me, then I will have no choice other than to rehome it. It would be horrible to leave it there." I shrug my shoulder.

"That's just your way of saying we are going to buy pens," Joan says flatly.

"OK, yep! I'm going to buy more pens." I grin at her.

The stationary shop is a bright little shop with a yellow door. Rows and rows of hot pink, gold, and aqua stationery line the walls. This shop has every color pen, marker, or pencil imaginable.

A girl wearing a pink gingham dress walks up to us, holding a wicker basket. "Would you like a basket?"

"No, thank you." Joan points at me and takes the basket from the girl. "She can only have what she can carry. She's a hoarder."

Embarrassed, I slug Joan on the shoulder. "I am not a hoarder."

I grab a set of new gel calligraphy pens, a box of rainbow Sharpies, and a stationary set with pink clouds on the envelopes. I make a makeshift basket by holding the bottom of my shirt and piling my found treasures in it.

Joan sees me and shakes her head.

I laugh, "Where there's a will, there's a way."

I browse through the last few aisles, then take my stash to the counter. The lady at the counter rings me up and thankfully gives me a bag. The sun is going down, making the sky glow violet over the shops and rows of flats. Have you ever had a moment in your life where it just felt perfect? One moment, where everything just fit and felt right? This is it. I'm having one right here on the street, surrounded by my family. Should we hand to dinner, or do you see anything you want to look at?

Joan looks at her watch. We better go, right, dad?

Dad clears his throat. "Yes, yes, right."

We pass the flat again. Some of the lights are on inside, including the front porch. I could have sworn I turned everything off; that's odd.

"Can we go past that garden we visited last night? I want to see it while it's still light out. "Joan says. "Was it this way?" She points and begins walking.

"I guess we are going this way." I follow. "It's next to my favorite house in London. It's a win-win. Let's go!"

Chapter 12

The Great Gatsby

*"He looked at her the way all women want to be looked
at by a man."*

—F. Scott Fitzgerald

WE PASS THE ENORMOUS IRON gates of the secret garden that Thomas
bought us to last night. I point up at the house. "That's my favorite house
in all of London."

We walk towards the driveway. The driveway has square pavers with
perfectly cut grass in between each. A lady is standing on the front steps
locking the door. I notice she is holding a for sale sign under one of her
arms. I didn't know this place was for sale. My heart sinks. Not that I
wanted to buy or could buy it. All the little imaginary stories about who
lived here go up in a puff of smoke and glitter.

I make a pouting face to Joan. "Oh, no… it's being sold. I felt better
when it wasn't for sale…."

"Excuse me," Joan yells to the woman standing at the door. "Is this
place for sale?"

The woman turns to look at Joan. "It was."

I never noticed a for-sale sign in front of it.

"I know this is a long shot, but do you think we could maybe walk through it? We won't get the chance to do it again since it's sold." Joan pleads with the realtor and extends her hand. "I'm Joan, and this is my family. Mar, Henry, and Olivia."

We all give a synchronized happy wave.

"I guess it couldn't hurt. I'm called Stephanie." She turns, unlocking the door for us and letting us in.

As we walk into the foyer, the floors are polished white marble. A bit fancier than I would have liked, but the house calls for it. There's a grand mahogany staircase leading upstairs. I stand, looking up the open foyer to the second floor in awe. A massive crystal and gold chandler hangs from a heavy chain down the two stories: illuminating and making a beautiful shadow pattern on the walls. On the ornate table sits under it.

Mom is doing her own tour. "Oh my! Henry, come and look at the kitchen!" Mom pulls dad into the kitchen.

Curious, Joan and I follow. The kitchen hasn't been updated in years, but I love that. It's timeless. The oven is the most beautiful dark blue with gold accents. It has so many doors on it that I'm not sure what they are all used for.

I point at it. "Mom, what are all the doors for?"

Mom walks over. "Oh, Mija—girl. Those compartments are for storage, keeping things warm, and baking."

I open one of the oven doors. Inside, one of the doors has a recipe timing guide painted on it. "Jelly rolls are set at 176° for 10 minutes. Have you ever seen anything so adorable?" I motion Joan over. "See, it's your kind of oven. The recipe temperature guide is chiseled right here on its door."

Despite herself, Joan throws her head back and laughs. "Funny."

The kitchen floor is black and white checker marble. I run my hand over the white countertops. The cabinets are white with glass inserts in them. Three wrought iron lights hang over the kitchen island. I lean over, pressing my face to the cool countertop.

"Gosh, I really love this place," I say into the air, to no one in particular. Joan is opening all the cabinets one by one until she reaches a door.

She opens it and sticks her head in it to peer around. "What is this?"

Dad walks over and looks. "Oh, it's a dumbwaiter."

My head pops up, and I smirk. Never being one to miss an opportunity to aggravate Joan, I say, "Oh, that's definitely for you."

Joan hops in and pulls her knees to her chest. I walk over and push the button.

The dumbwaiter slowly lifts Joan up into the shaft. "Hey, find me! I don't know where this is going! Mar! Mar!"

I can hear the slight alarm in Joan's voice.

I shout, "Marco!" as I run up the giant staircase.

I faintly hear Joan yell, "Polo!"

I open a door and stick my head in, "Marco!"

"Polo," I hear Joan in the distance.

I shut the door and run to the next. "Marco!"

Joan is stepping out of the dumbwaiter.

"I found you!" I smile, looking around the room.

The wallpaper is baby pink with flecks of gold weaved into it. The window is encased in an intricate wood design with a large bench seat for reading. Next to the window is a double door leading out onto the balcony. The lock is jammed. I press my face up against the glass, trying to see the view. Is this house attached to the garden we were in last night? Is it their yard? The yard is pitch black. I can see what looks like a shadow.

"Hey, Joan. Come look. Does it look like someone is walking in the garden?

Joan presses her face to the glass and squints. "No, stupid. You always think things are haunted. Come on. Let's go check out the bathroom."

Joan grabs my hand and pulls me towards the bathroom. The bathroom is enormous. I imagine Betty Davis in a satin bathroom powdering her chest. The most beautiful wooden tub sits in the corner. It has four huge gold lion's feet on the bottom of it. I put my foot next to one. It's bigger than my whole foot.

"Do you think they cast these out of a real lion's foot?" I squat down to examine it closer. The tile on the floor are hundreds of white octagons. I open the glass door to the shower and peek inside. Oversized shower spouts face in all directions. That must feel like a tsunami. I'm not sure I would like that, but at least I'd be clean.

Joan leans in behind me. "Wow! Think about all the sexy time you can have in here!"

"Yeah, I could power wash my legs and never have to shave again." I turn the water on to check the pressure. "Woah, see?"

As we walk back into the bedroom, Stephanie is standing next to the window staring blankly out of it. "This is such a lovely place."

"How many bedrooms does it have?" Mom asks, joining us from the hall.

"It has five bedrooms, four full baths, and a powder room. The garden below is also included with the house. The base-level has a pool and a sauna. There is a two-car garage with two extra parking spots. The house is four stories if you count the pool level. Stephanie is reading a list from her paper.

I knit my eyebrows together. "Didn't we come in on the base level?"

"No, we came in on the second level. The base-level opens onto the garden." Stephanie smiles at me, hugging her paperwork to her chest.

"You mean there's a pool inside the house?" I squeal.

I wonder how I missed the doors when we were in the garden last night. It makes sense. It was dark. Plus, other things were occupying my mind, like the tiny box in Thomas' pocket.

"Let's walk down to the pool level." I grab mom by the hand as we begin to descend the staircase.

"Here, let me show you something. I think it's one of the coolest features of the house." Stephanie walks over to what looks like a small coat closet and opens the door. We stand curiously behind her. It's an elevator!

She laughs, thrown off guard by my excitement. "Yes, it's a two-person elevator. The couple that lived here before had it put in because the wife had arthritis."

"Where does it open up to on the fourth floor?" I ask.

"It opens up into a library. The door is hidden, so you wouldn't immediately know it's a door." Stephanie says, looking down at her watch to check the time.

Enthusiastically, Joan and I immediately jump in. "Stay here, mom. We will be right back; then you can take it down to the pool."

The brass door slides open. Joan and I step out into a very ornate library. The door shuts behind us as we spin around, taking it all in. Heavy built-in mahogany bookshelves line the walls. The floor has a very intricately designed tile pattern. The walls are covered in green velvet wallpaper, the kind that has a raised pattern you can feel with your hands. I run my hand up and down it, feeling the fuzz. I wonder what the people did that lived here before. I imagine the grand dinner parties in the dining room or the international business meetings held in this office. The house is straight out of the Great Gatsby. I walk around the bookshelves pushing and pulling each book, hoping to trigger a secret door.

"You are looking for a secret door, aren't you?" Joan narrows her eyes at me.

Just as she says it, I hear a click. The bookshelf springs open. My mouth drops open.

"See?" I pull the bookcase door open wider and peer in. I bust out laughing, "Oh, my Gosh! It's a bathroom!"

"Shut up! Move, let me see." Joan pushes me aside. "Huh, who would have thought?

—Top secret bathroom meetings."

"It's a bathroom panic room. When the shit hits the fan, don't skip a beat, just run to the *Bathroom Panic Room*!" I giggle.

I shut the door concealing its secret behind the bookcase. Joan and I ride the elevator back down to the third floor. Dad has finally caught up with mom and is standing at the elevator entrance as Joan, and I step out. "Switch, we'll meet you down on the pool level."

As soon as the door shuts, Joan and I race down the stairs to see if we can beat the elevator. It's an old childhood game that we'd use to play.

We beat mom and dad down and stand in front of the elevator doors feeling proud of ourselves.

Dad puts his arm against the door to keep the door from shutting on mom. Mom steps out and smiles. "Wow, this is a beautiful place. I'm impressed."

Stephanie catches up to us, huffing. She pushes a button on the wall. Two massive glass doors begin to slide open.

I run to them, then turn back to Stephanie. "Are these the doors to the garden?

She nods. "Yes."

I clap my hands and turn around to see Thomas down on one knee.

Chapter 13

A Rose Garden

"Never let the fear of striking out keep you from playing the game."

—Babe Ruth

The garden is filled with baby pink roses as far as the eye can see. A thousand little twinkling lights are wrapped around the trees. Strings of star-shaped lights dangle from the willow tree in the middle of the garden; strangely enough, an old boombox from the '80s is wired to a branch. What's an old boombox doing in a tree? Marie hops over a bush and presses the button. *Can't Take My Eyes Off of You* begins softly playing in the background. I'm impressed. How in the world did he find a Frank Valli cassette tape? I guess Amazon does really sell everything these days.

Standing in shock, I look around at all the faces. Marie! Marie is here! —and Will is here! Mom, dad, and Joan are standing arm and arm. Catherine, Birdie, and Figs are beaming at me. I run to Thomas. My body feels like it's floating up through the Milky Way. I feel like I'm an astronaut—like Neil Armstrong bouncing one foot down at a time on the moon without gravity. Until my feet touch the ground hard right in front of Thomas like the gravity switch was just turned back on.

I grab him by the shoulders, balancing myself. "What is going on?" I point at him. "You weren't drunk at all!"

I look wide-eyed at Joan. If she and mom knew what was happening, why didn't they have me change before dinner? Now, I'm going to look like a slob in all my engagement photos —forever!

Thomas looks deep into my eyes. He's balancing on one knee, wearing a very well-tailored blue tuxedo, and his hair is perfectly combed. Thomas carefully squats down on one knee. Even on one knee, we are almost at eye level. My toes go completely numb. I swallow hard as my knees wobble. His hands begin to shake as he holds out a tiny box—the same box from the bookshelf. "Marguerite, I know we have only known each other for a few weeks. But in that time, I've fallen madly, profoundly in love with you, and I don't want to spend another minute not having you as my fiancée. I have asked your father for your hand, now I'm asking you. Will you do me the biggest honor in the world and marry me?"

He opens the tiny wooden box and holds it firmly in his hand. It's an art deco ring with a two-carat diamond in the middle. It's the most beautiful ring I have ever seen. I can feel everyone's eyes on me, holding their breath—waiting. I look up to see my mom wiping tears from her cheeks. Then I look back at Thomas and smile. Everything is in slow motion. A ball of warm happiness starts from my toes and travels up into my chest. I feel like I'm about to faint with love drunkenness. With all my force, I throw my arms around Thomas just as my knees buckle. He loses his balance and falls backward.

Thomas crashes down hard backward.

I land on him. "Yes! Yes! A thousand times yes!" I kiss him hard.

He gets to his feet and pulls me up to stand. He places his hands on my hips and presses his forehead against mine. "Only us, only right now—Mrs. Blaine."

I shake my head. "Only us, only right now—Mr. Blaine."

A flash goes off. We turn to see a man peaking over the fence, holding a camera.

"Tom! Tom, do you have a statement? Can I get a picture of the ring?" He snaps a few more pictures before we fully comprehend what is happening.

I watch as Thomas fumbles with his words. "You can't be here. This is a private occasion —private property!"

"I'm on public property." He sneers and snaps a few more pictures.

My blood begins to boil. How can he be allowed to do this? One of my top pet peeves is people getting away with things that they shouldn't. I turn to look at Joan. Speechless, I don't know what to do.

Joan nods at me. I know that look. It's about to go down, and I might get engaged and unengaged all in one night.

I hear a gasp from Thomas' mom as Joan catapults herself up onto the wall. Joan makes it to the top of the wall in one springy leap. She snatches the guy by his shoulders. "You aren't ruining my *little* sister's night." She begins to shake him—hard.

My mouth drops open. "Get him, Joan."

Mom takes off one of her shoes and throws it at him, hitting him right on the top of the head. "Sal de aquí que nosey hombre—Get out of here you nosey man!" She takes off her other shoe and lifts it high in the air.

Thomas' eyes grow wide. I feel like my family is a bunch of circus performers, and he is just finding out. I can only imagine what he is thinking right now. Maybe he didn't realize how crazy my family is. Maybe he is reconsidering. Maybe he's impressed? I glance over to see Figgy, Thomas' younger sister, laughing.

I watch as dad unlatches the gate and disappears behind the garden wall.

"Hey! Hey!" I hear the man yell from the wall. "You can't do that!"

Joan still has a tight hold of the man's shoulders.

"Joan, let him go!" Dad yells from the other side of the wall.

We all run to the open gate just in time to see dad yank the man down by both of his legs. The man falls about three feet to the ground, ripping the knee of his pants.

Dad holds out his hand. "Erase the photos in front of me or give me your camera!"

"You can't take my camera! I'll ring the police!" the photographer backs away from dad.

Dad reaches in his pocket and shoves three one-hundred-dollar bills into the front of the man's shirt pocket.

He then yanks the camera from the man's hands. "You really ought to be more polite. This is a private moment, and you are ruining it. Now, get out of here!"

Dad kicks at the man's butt. As the man scurries off, I notice a four-inch burn hole on the back of his trousers.

I cover my mouth to muffle my laugh. "Did you light his pants on fire?"

"No, no, I would never do that. I simply made it a little uncomfortable for him to stay." Dad smiles his crooked smile at me.

We file back into the backyard. Catherine is now standing next to mom, laughing and cleaning mom's shoe off. She hands mom her shoe. Mom slips it back onto her foot. Relief rushes over me. Maybe they don't think we are crazy after all. Maybe all this will be OK.

I run to Marie. "I can't believe you are here! I have so much to show you!" I throw my head back in excitement. "I have so much to tell you!"

Marie grabs my hand. "Let me see the ring!" She squeals." Oh my gosh, Mar! What the hell?

"I know, right?" I hold out my hand. It's the first time I've really gotten a good look at it. I wish I had gotten a manicure. My scraggly nails aren't worthy of such a beautiful ring. I'm going to have to have my nails done for the rest of my life!

Joan rushes to my side with her hand cupping her elbow. "Show me the goods!"

I hold out my hand to her. "It was his grandmother's." I clasp my hand over the ring and press it to my chest. "I love that."

"Why are you holding your elbow? Let me see." I pull Joan's hand away from her elbow. "How is it that you always seem to hurt yourself? I laugh.

"It seems to me you are the common denominator here; I'm just saying." Joan takes a napkin and wraps it around her elbow.

Thomas walks over to me, guiding his mother towards me.

She looks up at me, her cheeks flush. "I hope that you love the ring just as much as my mother did." She grabs both of my hands, cupping them in hers. "Welcome to the family, Dear."

Dad is surveying the wall like an attack dog when a distinguished older man wearing a kilt walk through the gate.

Thomas' mom raises her hand, "Fin! Fin over here."

Thomas turns, and his eyebrows shoot up in shock. "Father, I didn't know if you were going to make it."

"Right might chap, I wouldn't have missed it for the world." He claps Thomas on the shoulder.

"Marguerite, I would like you to meet my father, Fin." Thomas gestures to his father.

I extend my hand. "Very nice to meet you, Sir."

He raises my hand to his lips. "Pleasure is *all* mine." Jeez, so this is where Thomas gets it.

Dad looks Fin up and down. Not many kilts in Texas. If there is one thing my dad isn't is judgmental. Dad has always been very open-minded and eager to learn new things. Dad grips Fin's hand with a firm handshake. "Good to meet you. I'm Henry, Mar's dad, and this is my wife, Olivia."

Mom holds out her thin petite hand to shake Fin's. "It's nice to meet you, Fin."

"I'm Joan, Mar's sister." Joan shakes Fin's hand briefly. "This is my boyfriend, Will."

Will shakes his head. "Good to meet you, sir."

"Will! Look at you, taking time off from work." I give him a tight hug.

"I brought you something." Will reaches into his pocket and pulls out a small Tupperware box.

I smile widely. "Don't tell me this is what I think it is. I take it from him and open it.

I unwrap the tiny loaf. The smell hits my nose. It's a yeasty, buttery, warm smell. A scent that makes you feel warm and cozy inside—bread—my all-time favorite. I pop a piece in my mouth. It doesn't disappoint.

"Thank you, Will. It was the perfect gift." I fold the tiny loaf back in its wrapper.

"No problem, I made it yesterday. So, congratulations!"

A loud metallic high-pitched screech rings out. I cover my ears. Thomas softly speaks into the microphone. "It took some doing to get everyone in the right place at the right time. I would like to thank everyone for coming tonight—for making time in their busy schedule to join us. For hopping a plane and flying across the pond at a moment's notice. For driving across town, for setting up, for all the work behind the scenes."

Thomas looks around at all the smiling faces beaming up at him. He is taking it all in.

"I would like to take this time to say one more thing." He gestures me up to him and shoves one hand in his pocket.

If he has another ring in there, I think I'll pass out.

Thomas smiles at me, noticing my confusion. "I have one more gift for you." Close your eyes. Don't worry, it's good."

Just before I close my eyes, I give Marie that *If stuff goes down, I'm going to need you to go psycho* look. I shake off the nervousness and close my eyes.

Thomas wraps his arms around me, hugging me. "OK, I want you to open your hand."

I hold my hand out and open it. Thomas swirls his finger around on my palm, tracing a line up and down each finger. Then he presses something metal and cold into my palm. I close my hand around it. What is this? It feels like a key.

Chapter 14

The Great Gatsby

"What the my heck?"

—ROBBIE EKLUND

MY WHOLE BODY FEELS LIKE JELL-O. I feel like I'm going to turn into a blob of putty on the grass. A house? A whole house? Of course, a whole house. Is half a house a thing?

"Welcome home, love. I closed on the house today after bringing your dad by for a second opinion. I knew that it was your favorite. I confirmed it when I brought you into the garden last night."

Confused, I point at the house. "This house? Why?"

"What do you mean why? It's an engagement gift." Thomas reaches out for both of my hands.

I begin to shake involuntarily. "The ring is an engagement gift. Dinner is an engagement gift; hell, at the very tippity top, a car would be an engagement gift. Not a house."

"It is an engagement gift if I want it to be. Just answer one question. Now forget about if we are going to live in London or San Francisco.

Forget about jobs, family, or anything else. Answer this one question. Do you love the house?" Thomas squeezes my hands.

"I absolutely love it. It's amazing! Thank you." I put the key in my pocket. I feel like I should make some sort of announcement but, what? I grab the microphone. "Hi, everyone. As you can imagine, all this is a shock to me. So, I apologize. I'm just a little shell-shocked. Thank you for coming; it means the world to me that everyone could be here for this."

Marie hands me a glass of wine. I hold it in the air. "Thank you. Salut!" I swallow the wine in one large gulp.

Thomas raises his glass and smiles at dad. Dad gives him a wink. "They're not making more land."

I hand the microphone back to Thomas and step down onto the grass. I don't know whether to freak out, cry or do both. I don't know what to say.

I shove my hand into my pocket and squeeze the key tight in my hand. "This house is mine—mine? Here in London?"

Jeez, that was a stupid question. Although, that's a thought. Wouldn't it be cool to be able to teleport?

Thomas wraps his arms around me from behind. "Everything OK?"

I wave my hand around in a circle. "This house? This whole house is mine?" I step back and take it all in. It is beautiful. "I'm sorry." I cover my mouth with my hand. "Wow! I'm just in shock right now. Thank you!" How do you accept a major gift like this? I throw my arms up around Thomas' neck. "You sure know how to surprise me! I love the whole thing. The engagement, the surprise, the house. I love you."

Marie is passing out plastic champagne glasses, and Joan follows her, filling each one up, one by one.

Dad picks up the microphone and raises his glass high into the air. "To my youngest daughter and Thomas. May you always be this happy. May the days not pass too fast. May you always see the sunshine even on the gloomiest of days. May you always be as happy as your mother and I have been."

Dad takes a swig of his champagne and wipes a tear from his eye.

Fin walks up calmly, scooping the champagne glass out of my dad's hand.

He begins reciting an old Irish prayer. *"May the road rise to meet you, may the wind be always at your back, may the sunshine warm your face, and the rain fall soft upon your fields."*

I reach up and kiss dad on the cheek. "You are such a rascal—you *and* mom. You knew about it this whole day and didn't tell me. You told me the small part to distract me from the big part. I see how you are."

Figgy, Birdie, and Marie are sitting off to the side, laughing. Will and Joan walk around the yard. Will is examining the blue hydrangea bushes.

I walk up, curious. "What? Is something wrong with them?"

"No, nothing is wrong with them. They are very healthy. As a matter of fact, if you want them bluer, all you have to do is plant some pennies in the ground next to them. The cooper will make their color better." Will says, rubbing one of their leaves between his fingers.

"Huh, well, you learn something every day." I eye mom as she walks over.

"I'm going to take some of these cuttings home with me." Mom walks along the fence, checking out all the plants.

I laugh, "Take what you want." I know she will anyway. She does what she wants, especially when it comes to plants. One time we visited a botanical garden without our knowledge; mom was taking cactus cuttings. It was only until Joan borrowed a pen that we found out. Mom had put several cuttings in her purse. Joan's hands were covered in cactus thorns, and we had to throw away mom's purse. There just wasn't any way back from that.

Thomas walks up behind me, putting his arms around my waist. "Shall we all go and have *that* bite to eat you were talking about earlier?"

I knit my brows together. "You are such *the* actor."

Thomas smirks. "What do you mean?"

I pinch his cheek. "I'm going to be watching you from now on. I was so worried about you. But that's it! Now that I know that your abilities spill over into real life, I'll never believe you again. Never!"

"Awe, M! Don't be sour at me! It was for a good cause." He grabs my hand and holds up the ring. "I'd say the tiny lie was worth it."

Normally I would say something snarky here, but falling in love has knocked it completely out of me. I'm all butterflies and rainbows. I shake my head at the thought and bat my eyelashes at Thomas—good grief.

Chapter 15

Papa Paparazzi

"Chase you down until you love me."

—Lady Gaga

Thomas raises his glass and taps the ring box on it. "I would like to thank everyone again for coming, but now we should move this party to dinner. It's been a very long day for everyone, and I'm sure we could all use something to eat."

As Thomas opens the garden gate, flashes go off like a strobe light at a disco. I grab Thomas' arm and raise my hand to my face to shield my eyes. I'm disorientated and dizzy. Someone grabs me by the arm and pulls me through the sea of photographers. They push me into a small black bus—followed by dad, mom, and Joan.

"What in the world is going on out there?" Marie pushes past me, plopping herself down on a seat.

"I guess the other guy had friends." I shrug my shoulders.

Will joins Joan. "Are you OK? That's crazy! I've never seen anything like it."

"Yeah, there's a lot of people out there." Joan sits on her knees, staring out the window.

Birdie and Figs make it on the bus and grab a seat.

Figs presses her face closer to the window. "It's been getting more and more like that these days. I guess it's the price you pay?"

I rub the back of my neck, "I guess."

Fin and Catherine step onto the bus. They sit down and fold themselves in neat little proper packages at the front of the bus. I search around for Thomas. He hasn't made it on. I walk back down the aisle towards the doors. Kyle, Thomas' assistant, is standing inside of the doors. He must have been the one to pull me in.

"You don't want to go out there." He presses himself against the door. "Thomas will be here shortly. Don't go, Mar."

"The hell I don't—move, please." I place my hand on Kyle's shoulder. "Please." Usually, this wouldn't bother me, but I have lost my patience. It is my special night, after all.

The bus doors fold open; I step out and stand next to Thomas.

He raises his hand. "I assure you, if you give me a second, I will answer your questions."

A hush goes over the photographers.

He wraps an arm around me. "I asked this lovely lady, Marguerite Becker, tonight to marry me. I am very fortunate that she said yes."

Thomas gestures to me. I hold up my hand to show the ring. Flashes start to go off.

"There is nothing more to report other than it has been a very long day, and we are headed to dinner. Thank you and goodnight." Thomas lifts his hand in the air and waves. He puts his other hand on my back and guides me back towards the doors of the bus.

The doors open. I step on the first step then turn around to kiss Thomas. I place both hands on his face and pull him towards me. I kiss him worthy of this night. I don't care who is watching—the crowd of paparazzi cheer. The flashes blind me. I can't see a thing.

I wave, smiling into the brightness. "Goodnight!"

We slump in the first empty row and giggle.

"Can you believe we are engaged?" I snuggle into Thomas' shoulder. "I'm going to be your wife. Marguerite Blaine. I like the sound of that."

The bus driver pulls away from the curb as we stand to face our family. I must admit that this is a little overwhelming to me. It isn't like we got engaged, and our family all met us at Maggiano's to celebrate. Getting engaged like this is a whole other level. Kyle begins handing out drinks like he's a flight attendant.

As he finishes, Will stands. "To Mar and Thomas!"

I catch the tears in dad's eyes, and I hold his stare, then smile. I nod my head and pat my chest with my hand.

"We are taking the bus to the Venti de Caste for dinner, and then it will drop you at your desired locations." Thomas smiles. "I hope everyone is hungry."

I notice that four or five photographers have jumped in their cars and are now following us. Is this how it's going to be—forever? Will we never have another private moment? Will, there be pictures of me with made up headlines like *Thomas Blaine's Wife is Sick*, when it's only that I'm not wearing makeup, and this is how I normally look. I mean, who gets all dressed up to go to the grocery store? I swear, the paparazzi didn't seem like this last week. We walked to the coffee shop without a photographer in sight. I really started to believe the whole thing about it being normal here.

The bus driver pulls to the back of the building.

I look up at Thomas, confused. "What are we doing back here? Are we going through the kitchen or something?"

I guess with the good comes the bad. Being famous isn't all it's cracked up to be. Thomas notices my confusion. "What is it, M? Do you want to go somewhere else?"

I shake my head, "No, no, this is good. I was just thinking how funny it is that we are going through the back door through the ally, that's all."

"It's to hide us from the paparazzi," Thomas says, trying to help me understand.

I shake my head. "No, absolutely not. I'm not hiding. Let's go through the front. Let them see us. We can't let this change us. Let them get as many pictures as they want. If we start running now, we will never stop. Plus, if anyone can get our picture, then they won't be worth as much, and people will lose interest in us."

I might be naïve in my thinking, but I refuse to let the spotlight change us; change me!

Bruce Springsteen's Born to Run pops into my head.

"Drive around the front, chap," Thomas asks the bus driver. "Looks like we will be going through the front doors." Thomas looks at me. "I like the way you think."

The bus pulls up to the front of the restaurant. We pile out and towards the building.

I wave my hand around. "See? It's not that hard. Eventually, they will have to go away, or we will have to get better at ignoring them, right?"

Thomas winces, "I would normally agree with you, but my publicist says that it could get a lot worse, especially if the new movie is as big of a deal as he thinks. And on top of that, our engagement will be a big deal because I have been single for so long. They thought I had a secret love life. Even my male friends were asked if they were my partners. I am just warning you. When I was just a stage actor, it wasn't like this—and even now, it isn't as bad as it could be."

Dad is walking behind us. He is posing—doing his Arnold Schwarzenegger poses and showing his muscles. He is batting his eyelashes and waving. He pretends to lift his make-believe skirt and twirl around, for heaven's sake.

"Dad, what the heck?" I spread my hands out, asking.

What in the world has gotten into him? Mom is dancing the Merengue next to him. Well, that's one thing; they'll never be accused of being boring. Joan and Will follow mom in a makeshift conga line, pulling everyone else in behind them. Marie brings up the caboose by waving to the paparazzi like she's royalty. We all make it into the lobby as the hostess shuts the doors behind us.

A man in a dark suit rushes over. "Mr. Blaine! I thought you were coming in through the back. My apologies for the miscommunication and lack of planning on our part in the front."

He guides us to a sizable private table.

The table is in a recess, almost in its own tiny room. Two heavy emerald, green drapes hang on either side of the wall. Scones symmetrically line the walls. They pull shut to form a barrier between the table and the rest of the restaurant. Several bottles of champagne sit in various spots on the table. Thomas pulls out a chair for me to sit down.

Marie grabs the seat next to me and wraps her arms around me, giving me a sideways hug. "I'm so happy for you, Mar. He is such a nice guy."

"He is, isn't he? He gets me, you know?" I bump her with my shoulder.

The man in the dark suit returns, pulling the heavy curtains closed. "Glenn, your waiter will be right in. I am Grant Kent; it would be my pleasure to get you anything in the meantime."

Thomas grabs my hand and runs his thumb over my ring finger. "Pretty."

I'm actually doing this. I have a giant rock on my hand—from a guy I'm completely bonkers for. I smile at him and feel the light and love beam out of my eyes. Finding Thomas makes Fart Fandango Chris, the squirrel guy, and all the other lousy dates worth it.

Thomas leans over and whispers in my ear. "I'm crazy about you, M. I really am."

My stomach flip-flops back and forth in my body. I feel the blood rush from all parts of my body and up to my cheeks.

I snuggle into the bend of his neck. "I'm crazy about you."

The waiter splits the curtains and walks in. "My name is Glenn. I will be your waiter for the night. The chef has prepared a special meal for you—that will be out shortly. In the meantime, can I get drinks other than champagne while you wait?"

He starts with Catherine and mom, then goes around the table clockwise. He is not writing one thing down. How in the world is he going to remember all this? He nods his head and disappears behind the curtains again. The heavy curtains drown out any noise coming from the central part of the restaurant.

I stand, "I'd like to introduce everyone again. This is Olivia and Henry, my mom and dad. My sister Joan and her boyfriend Will. And last but not least, my best friend, Marie Danielle."

Thomas stands next to me, "Everyone, this is my father, Fin, he's a research scientist. My mother Catherine, she's in theater. My sister, Birdie she's a nature photographer, and my other sister Figgy is a pediatric doctor."

Well, heck, I didn't know we were giving out people's resumes. Is that a thing here? I begin pointing around the table. "Marie and I own a bakery in San Francisco. Joan is an artist and owns a gallery in California. Will owns a restaurant also in California. My mom is a stay-at-home mom without anyone to stay home for. She is now retired since Joan and I are gone. My dad is also retired but owns a hundred or so gas stations in Texas."

I smile and sit down. That whole introduction was weird. We make small talk, and it looks like everyone is enjoying themselves. Could this be this good? Something must be wrong here. I feel doubt creep in. This is too perfect to be authentic. I let the thought roll around in my head. It rolls there just long enough to catch Joan's attention. She knows my face all too well. She raises her eyebrows at me. She's asking me a question. I can tell. I imagine one of her eyebrows going into a question mark. That's how well I know her face, and I guess she knows mine.

Four waiters usher in plate after plate. Pristine white plates are placed on the table in front of us. Slices of prime rib and scoops of mashed potatoes accompany the asparagus. My mouth begins to water. I study

Will as he is dissecting the dinner with his eyes —judging it. I smirk at his judginess. I know that's not a word, but it should be. It's like the word ginormous or ignoramus. Those weren't words until people used them so much that they became words. Will notices me staring at him. I give him a wide grin and shake my finger back and forth at him.

After the staff sets down the last plate, mom reaches over and grabs dad's hand. Dad grabs Joan's, and it continues, making it around the table until it gets to Thomas. He gently smiles at me and takes my hand, then his mother's finishing off our prayer circle.

Mom bows her head, "Come Lord Jesus be our guest and let this food by thee be blessed —amen."

Slicing through the prime rib is like slicing through butter. I make a little prime rib and mash potato stack on my fork. Figs is watching me; I lift my fork in the air waving it at her. I then put it in my mouth and smile. She makes a little stack too. She puts it in her mouth and shakes her head, agreeing with me that this is definitely the way to eat prime rib. We have our own little back and forth as I study each person at the table—their manners, their faces, how they love each other. Dad is happy. I can tell by the wrinkles on the corners of his eyes. Mom is reserved but happy. Joan is in love with Will. Will is completely smitten. Marie is content to be spending time with me. She's proud. All is right with the world at this moment. Thomas is doing that upside-down thing with his fork. I laugh at the memory of trying it myself.

As dinner begins to wind down, I fold my napkin and place it on the table. Thomas runs his hand over my knee before pulling my seat out. Glenn returns and ties the curtains back into place as we file back out of the restaurant into the lobby.

Fin looks at his watch. "I better get going. I have an early day tomorrow. I have a car coming. It was so good to meet you, Mar." He kisses my hand again. He shakes my dad's hand and kisses mom's cheek. When he gets to Catherine, he pulls her in tight. "You looked beautiful tonight, Cat." He hugs Birdie and Figgy. "Bye girls, see you soon. A shiny black car pulls up, and Fin hops in. He gives us a wave as his car disappears.

"Will and I are going to walk around the city for a while. I'll see you in the morning—for breakfast?" Joan says, turning back towards Will.

"That's my cue also. I don't even know what day it is. I'm headed back to the hotel." Marie gives me a tight hug. "See you in the morning."

"Wait, are you walking?" I ask.

Marie looks at Joan. "Is it OK if we walk past the hotel while you guys are out?"

Joan nods her head. "Sure, we will make sure Marie gets back to the hotel; it isn't far."

"Yeah, OK. We will meet in the morning for breakfast and some sightseeing?" I smile.

We board the bus and wave to Will, Joan, and Marie standing on the sidewalk. This just feels weird. I should be exploring the city with Joan. Maybe that's their way of saying they are going back to the hotel for alone time. In any case, I feel horrible. We ride in silence all the way back to our new house to drop people back at their cars.

Birdie, Figs, and Catherine hop out. "We'll see you at the wedding."

Thomas and I wave, then slump back down in our seats. Getting engaged really takes it out of you emotionally. The bus rolls to a stop in front of the townhouse. Today has been one of the longest days I have ever had. That includes the time I stayed up all night cramming for my Anthropology final. The long day pulls everyone's shoulders down, rounding them as we shuffle to the front door. When Thomas opens the door, Charlie bounds out of the house to the yard. I sit on the stoop to watch him.

Thomas sits down beside me, throwing his arm around my shoulder. "What's wrong, M? You haven't been yourself all night."

I pull my knees up to my chest. I cross my arms around them and rest my cheek on them. "I'm not sure. I mean, I'm happy but… this should be the best night of my life. And right now, something is eating at me, and I can't put my finger on it."

"Do you *not* want to get married?" Thomas pulls back to get a better look at me. "I mean, did I put you on the spot? Did you feel pressured to say yes? That's not at all what I was trying to do."

I shake my head. "No, no, I didn't feel pressured. I think seeing my parents and having my family here just made me realize how much I miss them." I stare down at the giant ring on my hand.

Thomas pulls me into him. "You don't have to choose, M. I guess buying the house was the wrong thing to do. I think to you it said. 'Our home is here. And I'm sorry that that scared you. I was just trying to buy you something you loved. With all that being said, I do want you to know what you're getting yourself into. I may have to travel a lot. It all depends on my job. Life will be different. Things will be different." Thomas looks up at me with that puppy dog look on his face.

I press my face into my knees and take a deep breath. Why can't we live in that little bubble we were in back at the cabin? Because that's not real life, that's why. I turn to face Thomas. "Let's just put a pin in it for now. I'm too tired to think about it."

Charlie pushes his head into my hand. "Oh, Charlie, come on, you doodle dog."

I stand, still tucked under Thomas' arm, and walk back into the flat. I hesitate as I turn and stand in front of Thomas' bedroom door—our bedroom door. I wish we could cuddle tonight. It feels like I just rejected him, and now I'm leaving again. Is this considered being a runaway bride? Am I considered a runaway bride? I feel like I'm standing on the side of the train tracks, waiting for a train to come by. I reach up, grab the handle, and get pulled into this new life 100 miles an hour.

Thomas kisses my forehead. "Parting is such sweet sorrow."

I look up at him. He holds my gaze, then presses his lips against mine—kissing me deeply. He's the runaway train. He's who I grabbed; he is pulling me into my new life 100 miles an hour. Thomas slides his hand around the back of my neck and pulls me in closer. I wrap my arms around his waist and down to his butt—what a fabulous ass. Everything inside me wants him. All of him. But there is something morally wrong with having sex in the very next room to my parents.

I pull back, "We can't do this."

Thomas shakes his head. "You're right."

He grabs me by the hand and pulls me towards the front door. I quietly slip on my running shoes, flatting the backs down with my heels. Thomas snatches his keys off the table and locks the door behind us.

I giggle. "Where are we going?" I say as I jog next to him.

He turns and kisses me. "You'll see."

I smile. "I know where we are going—our house."

Thomas pulls me into a dark shop doorway and presses me against the door. He pleads with his eyes and cups one of my breasts. His mouth is hot on mine.

"Come on, M." He pulls me by my hand.

We make it up the walkway and to the front steps. Thomas unlocks the door and pulls me in.

Chapter 16

The Christening

"We all have a purpose, and mine is to love this life with you."

—Dirty Heads

THOMAS PUSHES ME DOWN onto the wooden stairs. He pulls my panties down, crumpling them in his hand and tossing them onto the floor. He kisses my inner knee as he works his way up my inner thigh. He flattens his tongue against me. I feel every taste bud and bump. It is a fabulous mixture of wet, rough, and smooth, all at the same time. My body involuntarily throws itself upward and back down hard. I feel like melting straight into the wood, like hot wax filling in every crack and pore in the wood.

I intertwine my fingers in his hair. His crazy, fantastic hair. His wild, mind of its own, hair.

"Slow down—wait," I whisper.

"Wait, for what?" Thomas leans back down and continues.

He slides his arms under my legs, lifting them higher into the air. He places each hand on the step next to my face. I stare at the veins traveling up his forearms. Every movement of his tongue edges me closer to the edge. Kind of like the water at the beach touching the shore and retreating. Until all at once, a huge wave crashes over you, knocking you down, and you lose all sense of where you are—like that.

Thomas is my ocean. His blue-green eyes are my favorite color. The color I use to color my sky, the one that I can never get enough of. He pulls me to my feet. My knees are wobbling as Thomas scoops me up and carries me to the kitchen. I lean into his chest—bergamot. I jerk as he lays me on the cold marble countertop. I reach down and unbuckle his belt and unsnap the button on his pants.

He kicks them off his feet and crawls on top of the counter, hovering over me. The look in his eyes is intense, deep, and devouring. Yes, the marble is cold and hard, but at this point, I'm willing to take one for the team, even though this feels like a mortuary slab. Thomas spreads my legs with his. It's happening! This is happening. Sound the alarm! Our new kitchen island—christened. A smirk teases the corner of Thomas' mouth.

"What? What is it?" I ask.

He smiles. "This was hotter in my head." He presses his forehead against mine.

We both laugh at the situation.

"I was just thinking the same thing," I say as I sit up.

Thomas carefully edges himself off the hard marble. "Let's go find some carpet."

I tiptoe naked behind Thomas as he walks upstairs. We go from room to room. Why is there no carpet in this house?

Thomas turns around and kisses me. "M, I can't wait any longer."

He lifts me off my feet and presses me against the wall, pinning me there. His warm body rubs against me. Every curve, every line, every bulging lean muscle is too much for me to handle. My toes curl tight as my body quakes against his. Thomas is close behind me. His trembling body holds me in place against the wall. Sweat drips down my stomach. I'm not sure if it's his or mine or where I begin, and he ends. I could get used to this.

Out of breath, Thomas whispers in my ear. "First thing we buy for this house are rugs." He laughs, pressing his face against the side of mine.

Thomas lowers me to my feet. "I guess we christened the bedroom."

"And the stairs." I laugh.

"And the kitchen." Thomas smiles. "We should get back, though, and try to get some sleep before sightseeing tomorrow."

I look down at my watch. "It *is* tomorrow." I hop down the stairs and retrieve the bottom half of my clothes. "Can we just look around before we go? I mean, now that I know this is our place?"

"Of course! I'll tell you a little of the history of the place. It belonged to a couple named Charles and Judy, who were married for 63 years. They bought it in 1966 from a couple who built it in 1917. Charles and Judy didn't have children, so the place quietly came up for sale last week."

I run my hand over the banister. "I feel a good vibe here. It feels welcoming. I can almost see the guest, the dinner parties, and all the good times that were had here."

Thomas walks over to the large stone mantle in the living room. "I was told that the stone around the fireplace was brought here from Spain."

I walk over and place my hands on the stone. On the opposite side of the living room are heavy white floor-to-ceiling bookshelves. I love this house. A massive crystal chandelier hangs in the foyer over the marble floor. It has a very Great Gatsby vibe.

Thomas slides his arms around my waist. "Do you love it, sweetheart?"

I smile, "I adore this place."

"Well, good because it's all yours. If you get sick of me, I can live in the flat. Like Woody Allen and his wife." Thomas gives me a cheeky smile.

Smirking, I knock him on the shoulder. "If I get tired of you, you won't be moving to the flat; I'll just kill you off."

"I don't like the sound of that. How about you don't get tired of me, and I won't move to the flat like Woody Allen?" Thomas locks the door behind us.

The night air is cooler now; I tuck myself under Thomas's arm as we stroll back towards the flat. A flash goes off. I turn in the direction it is coming from. A man is crouching down in the bushes.

I walk over. "Hey—you there. Come out. What are you doing? Why are you hiding in the bushes?"

A sheepish bald man steps out of the bushes.

"Why are you hiding there?" I ask, furrowing my brow.

"I'm with the H and H Press. Your engagement is big news." He puts his camera up to his eye and snaps a picture.

I shake my head. "Yeah, I get that. But why must you hide in the bushes? Why not just ask us for a picture?"

He looks confused, waiting for the catch. "Could I get a picture, please?"

"See, that wasn't so hard." I reach out my hand to shake his. "I'm Marguerite. But you can call me Mar. What's your name?"

The man reluctantly holds out his hand to shake mine. "I'm called Oliver."

Oliver nervously looks around.

"Alright, Oliver. What is it that you want to know?" Thomas follows my lead.

"When is the wedding? How long have you been dating? Mar, what do you do? Will you live in London?" Oliver spits out questions like an auctioneer spitting out prices.

I think to myself, great questions. I wish I had all the answers myself.

I start, "Well, we've been dating a short time now. I own a bakery in San Francisco, but I think we will live here. And being just engaged today, we haven't set a date."

The man is holding out a recorder in front of my face. "Where are you from? Are you pregnant? Why the rush to marry?"

I think to myself, are we rushing? Am I ready for the forever and ever? Hell, yes, I am. I bring my attention back to the man standing in front of me. "Wait a second now. Don't be rude. First, no, I'm not pregnant. And two, I'm from Texas, so you better mind your manners."

"Right on. I apologize." Oliver looks at his feet, embarrassed.

"OK, if you have what you need. Then grab a picture, and we'll call it a night." I say, smiling at him. "But next time, just ask. You get more bees with honey than you do with salt. You'd be surprised what people will do if you are just a decent human being. Stop hiding in the bushes, for heaven's sake. If I were alone, I would have tased you."

Oliver laughs, "You'd tase me?"

"Indeed, I would have. That or I would have hit you with the closes thing I could find." I laugh, looking him straight in the eyes.

"Alright then." Oliver extends his hand to me.

I reach out and shake it again like we are making a deal.

"I like you, Mar. I like you very much. My apologies for my behavior." He smiles at me.

"Apology accepted." I smile back at him. "No more hiding in the bushes."

Thomas smiles and puts an arm around me.

Oliver snaps a couple of pictures. "Thank you so much, Mar and Tom. I appreciate the time you took to stop and do this for me."

"You're welcome." I wave at Oliver over Thomas' shoulder as we walk back to the flat.

As we round the corner to the flat, dad is sitting on the front stoop with Charlie.

"Dad! What are you doing out here?" I ask, sitting next to him.

"I just came out to get a little fresh air, and I wondered where you two wandered off too." Dad smiles up at me.

"You mean you came out to smoke and didn't want mom to know?" I lean back to look at him and hold out my hand.

He lays an unlit cigar in my hand. "I wasn't smoking it. I just hold it in my mouth."

I squint my eyes at him. "OK, well… I'm watching you." I stand and kiss the top of his head. "Goodnight, dad."

Thomas points to his face. "Right here. Kiss me right here."

I lean over and kiss his cheek. "Goodnight."

He squeezes my hands. "Goodnight, my love—until tomorrow. Even though it is already tomorrow."

Thomas sits next to dad, holding Charlie in his lap. I look out from the living room window. Gosh, to be a fly on the wall with ears right now. I watch as Thomas throws his head back, laughing. He hammers dad on the shoulder. My dad shakes his head up and down. What in the world could they be talking about? Could this be real? Could life be this perfect? I feel like, at some point, the other shoe is going to drop. Maybe I'm thinking about it so much that I'm trying to destroy it from the inside out? I bite my lip. I have to stop this nonsense and just go to sleep.

I turn the shower on and stand in front of the mirror, examining myself. Do I look any different now than I did before Thomas asked me to marry him? I hold my hand up and finally get a good look at the engagement ring. There really couldn't be a more perfect ring. I slip it off my finger and twirl it around, looking at all the details. There's an engraving on the inside along with a single sapphire—*1921 with all my love*. It is followed by *2021*. Thomas must have had the new date engraved in it. His great grandma wore this on her finger. I think about who she was. Who was her husband? Where they lived, what historical events they lived through… I sit it down on the shelf and step into the shower. The water runs over me, washing away all the lingering thoughts from the day. I wrap a towel around myself and get in bed without putting on my pajamas. This has been the longest day of my life.

Chapter 17

Are You a Prince?

"Out of all the places in the world, you are my favorite."

—JB Teller

Morning comes with a knock at my door. Thomas pokes his head in. "Good morning, love. Your parents are already up."

I lift my wrist to face—seven a.m. "Ugh…" I let out my breath.

"She's making something called Migas." He gives me a wide smile.

I laugh at the way he pronounces Migas. "OK, I'm up."

I brush my teeth and throw on a pair of shorts and a t-shirt.

Mom is cutting up corn tortillas and frying them in a pan as I grab a seat next to dad. Dad is holding up a cup of black coffee.

I peer into his cup. "I see you haven't wrapped your head around having hot tea instead."

"No, and I don't think I ever will." Dad takes a swallow of his coffee. "It's like drinking dirty water."

My eyebrows shoot up. "Dad!"

Dad shakes his head and shrugs his shoulders. "What? The boy didn't invent it."

Thomas shrugs his shoulders, agreeing. "I didn't."

I narrow my eyes. "Still."

Mom cracks the eggs into the skillet effortlessly. "Everybody is on their way here."

Thomas pulls out his notebook. "Perfect, I have the most impeccable day planned for us. First, we will tour Big Ben; then we will tour Buckingham palace and the gardens. Then to end the night, we will do the Eye of London."

The doorbell rings. Thomas smiles, standing to answer it. Marie, Joan, Will, and Kyle are standing on the front steps with about seven photographers standing behind them on the sidewalk snapping pictures. Joan rushes past Thomas, followed by Will. Marie is waving as Kyle pushes her in.

"They have been snapping our pictures since we rounded the corner from the hotel. I didn't know what to do other than just keep walking." Joan throws herself down on the couch.

Kyle shuts the door behind him and presses his back against it. "Awe, mate. It's a madhouse out there. I got a call from Adaline this morning. She said that your prescreening of your movie dropped last night."

He flops down a magazine and a couple of newspapers on the coffee table.

The picture we posed for late last night is on the cover of one of the papers. I glance at it. I pick it up and show it to mom and dad.

"This puts a tiny little rinky-dink in our plans today. I'm going to call Adeline." Thomas steps into the bedroom.

I chuckle, "Do you mean a tiny little wrinkle dinkle in the plan?"

Thomas pulls a face and snorts. "Wrinkle dinkle, what is that? I've never heard that before."

Joan walks over and begins to sing. *"Skinamirinky dinky dink, Skinamirinky dinky do."*

I join her. *"I love you…I love you in the morning and in the afternoon. I love you in the evening and underneath the moon."*

Marie puts her arm around Joan. *"Skinamirinky dinky dink. Skinamirinky dinky do."* We begin swaying like we are in an Irish bar regaling Irish folk songs.

Mom walks over, holding the spatula in her hand. "Oh, Mar, you look beautiful in that picture. When was that? Was it last night? It looks like what you were wearing last night."

I nod my head. "Yes, Thomas and I walked over to the new house to look around. Then we talked on the porch with dad."

Mom's eyebrows knit together, forming two lines in between them. "Henry, why were you outside?"

"Charlie had to go to the bathroom. I took him out." Dad looks at me, and I laugh because I know the truth.

And just like that, this is how a white lie turns into a not-so-white lie. But what was I supposed to say? Thomas and I couldn't keep our hands off each other, and dad was pseudo smoking on the front steps? There are just some things you don't say.

Mom gestures everyone over. She lines out Migas on plates like when we were kids. Kyle looks confused.

"Kyle, it's good. I promise. Just eat it." I say, amused. "If I can try beans on toast. You can try tortillas and eggs."

Will happily takes a plate and leans against the wall.

"Hi, mama." Marie hugs mom as she swipes a plate off the counter.

Thomas comes out of the bedroom. "A tiny change of plans. We are still going to do all the sightseeing stuff. But we will have company and a different car. No worries. I have it figured out."

I hand Thomas the stack of papers. "Looks like we made the news."

Beaming, he flips through the paper to the article about us.

"You made quite the impression on Oliver." He folds the magazine to the article and hands it back to me.

I skim the article. "Oliver said I was charming and kind. That's awfully nice of him to say."

Mom comes over and takes it out of my hand. She begins scanning the article. "He said *Thomas* is the lucky one." Mom smirks. "This man knows what he is talking about. Marguerite, you are a treasure."

Thomas slides his arm around my waist, pulling me to him. "You have that right. I should ever be so lucky." He looks at his watch. The car will be here in about an hour."

What kind of car can carry eight people? Maybe England has a clown car we can all fit in. I stand next to the sink taking people's plates and raising them off before shoving them into the dishwasher.

"OK, I'm going to get ready." I look at Thomas for advice. "What do you think I should wear?"

"Wear something smart." He says.

I think he forgets that I'm still learning British talk. I throw my hands in the air. "What do you mean, smart? Like, does my outfit need to know quantum physics?

"No, you cheeky minx. I mean, wear something comfortable but nice." Thomas tries explaining it when Kyle jumps in.

"It just means wear something you could meet the queen in but not uncomfortable where you are a wreck the rest of the day," Kyle says.

I jerk my head back, "Are we meeting *the* queen today?"

"No, but we are going to Buckingham Palace. Dress for that." Thomas runs a hand through his hair.

I poke him on his side. "I'm only joking. I'm not a complete idiot."

I walk towards the bedroom. Joan and Marie follow. Marie tries bouncing on the bed but sinks instead.

She lays back. "What kind of bed is this? It is divine." She runs her hands over the sheets. "Don't mind me. I'll just be right here."

Joan starts sectioning off my hair. "So, show me the ring."

I grab the ring off the shelf and hand it to Joan.

"For heaven's sakes, Mar. What are you going to do, flag down planes with this?" Joan holds it up to the light. She hands it back to me. I casually slip it back onto my finger.

Joan blow dries my hair as I rub moisturizer all over my face. I eye Marie curled up on the bed.

I nudge Joan. "Did Marie not sleep last night?"

"How would I know? The time difference is probably throwing her off." Joan runs a round brush through my hair.

"I'm not sleeping. I'm just resting my eyes." Marie turns on her side and sits up. "Where are your clothes? I'll help you pick something out."

I gesture to the closet. "In the closet, but I'm not sure I have something *smart*…all my clothes are dumb."

Marie pulls out a pair of white chinos and a blue button-up. "How about this?"

I shake my head. "I guess it is as good as any."

Marie flops herself back down onto the bed. She rolls around in the top comforter. "It smells like oranges." She presses her face into the pillow and inhales deeply. "Let me know when you are ready. I'll just be here."

I pull them on and walk out to the living room to wait for everyone else. Thomas points to our bedroom, asking if he could go in. I shrug my shoulders and nod my hand. Thomas opens the door. Marie is sprawled out on the bed. I crane my head past Joan, who is brushing her hair in the mirror. I watch him as he grabs a few things from the closet and heads to the bathroom. Marie makes no effort to move. I lean my head back on the couch as mom walks out of the guest room. You've got to be kidding me.

"Mom!" I stand up, pointing at my outfit. "What the heck?"

Thomas casually walks out of the bedroom. "No, No, No! You too?"

We are all wearing some variation of the same outfit. Thomas is wearing light tan chinos and a dark blue long sleeve shirt rolled up to his elbows.

Dad walks out of the room, wearing the male version of mom's outfit.

"Come on, guys! Dad and I are changing? We don't want to look basic, and frankly, all of us dressed the same makes us look, well…like we are all at an insurance convention." I rub my forehead. "I'm changing."

I grab the first thing in the closet—a white t-shirt dress and my cognac flats. If dad comes out wearing anything remotely like this, I'm calling it a day. I walk back into the living room. Thomas' brows shoot up. There's absolutely no hiding his approval. I blush.

Kyle looks at his phone. "The driver is here."

The doorbell rings. Dad, who is now standing by the door, answers it. Two men, wearing all black, walk in. They both have small black earpieces hanging out of their ears like secret service.

Thomas extends his hand. "I'm Tom."

One man pulls his sunglasses down. "I'm called Robert. This here is Stu. We are your security."

Robert is wearing a black suit jacket that reminds me of Chris Farley's *Saturday Night Live* skit, *Fat Man in a Little Coat*. Robert is nowhere near being fat. He has muscles on muscles. Stu is a medium-built man with bouncy red hair. He is wearing the same attire as Robert, but his fits more appropriately.

"Good to meet you." Thomas grabs my hand. "This is Mar, my fiancée. Olivia, Henry—her parents. Joan—her sister. Will—my friend and Marie—her best friend. Oh, and my assistance Kyle." I feel like he is going from most important to least important. Like if the shit hits the fan, here's the list.

"Right, then. Shall we go?" Robert holds the door as we file out to a bus— a black party bus. The windows are blacked out with heavy-duty tint. Well, I guess there is no other way to get this many people around. I mentally take a headcount—eleven people, including the driver. It's an entire baseball team. Photographers are lined up at the gate, snapping pictures. Stu is blocking them with his back when I look up to see a familiar face. It's Oliver! Oliver is standing on the other side of the bus door, making a little walkway for us to get straight on the bus.

I make eye contact with him. He bows his head at me. "Mar."

I beam at him. "Oliver! It's nice to see you again." I touch his arm as I walk by.

"Same Mar, could I take your picture?" he adjusts his camera.

"Absolutely." I pull Thomas to my side to face Oliver. "See? Honey gets more flies, now, doesn't it?"

Oliver looks down. "It indeed does."

I stop to chat. "I loved the write-up and pictures. It was very nice of you."

Oliver looks up at me, smiling. "It was very easy to write kind things about someone so kind."

Kyle pushes me from behind, guiding me onto the bus. I don't let on, but I'm incredibly taken aback by it. I smile and wave to the onlookers.

As I take my seat, I look Kyle straight in the eye. "Don't ever push me. I'm not and never will be cattle. I know you mean well, but please just don't push me. I'll stop and talk to whom I please."

Thomas' lips go into a line. "I never have to worry about you, M. I never have to worry if you will get swallowed up in all this."

I pretend to slug him on the chin. "You got that right, *mate*."

He rolls his eyes at me. Then turns his attention to Kyle, giving him a stern look. "Don't touch her. She does what she wants and only what she wants."

A ripple of excitement rolls up my spine. No, not excitement, that's not it. Lust? Longing? I can't put my finger on it. Caveman appeal? Whatever it is, I like this side of Thomas. I catch my dad's look of approval. Stu and Robert are the last to step onto the bus. The folding doors shut behind them. Robert sits next to us as Stu sits across. The seam of Robert's suit jacket is about to rip up the middle of his back. I force myself not to stare, waiting for the inevitable. It's like that game you played at the arcade as a kid, where the little metal hand would scoot coins to the edge, but none of them would ever fall. So, they are left tittering there instead.

I look at Marie, who widens her eyes at me. I shake my head in an effort not to laugh. Like the image would just fall out of my ear. She knows what I'm thinking because it's exactly what she's thinking. She looks at Joan. Joan immediately looks down and bites her lip without even a hint of looking my way.

We ride past Regent's Park. I stare out the window at all the things that are different and all the things that are the same as my little spot in San Francisco. I like the way people talk and all the miniature cars. Why doesn't the U.S. have an assortment of tiny cars? I mean tiny. We sure could use them in some of the cities. Parking would be more accessible. That's one of the reasons I love Cooper so much. The U.S. has the Smart car, but again it's an import. I guess there is more of a need for tiny vehicles in Europe. The roads are smaller in some places here. People walk a lot here too. Unless the distance is longer, then they take the underground. I'll have to figure the underground out soon. But one thing at a time.

As we get closer to Buckingham Palace, I feel like this is the London I know. Only because of all the generic pictures I've seen, or all the romantic movies Marie and I have watched. There's always a boy who pretends not to be a prince but ends up being a prince. You know the drill. He then falls for the girl, who is a peasant. Then they live happily ever after. Yada-yada.

We park and walk through a building with three massive arches. I glance around. No paparazzi, which I must admit is a relief. Stu and Robert flank our sides.

"Henry, did you see this? This is Princess Diana's memorial walk." Mom makes the sign of the cross. "Bless her. She was such a sweet soul."

The sidewalk is lined with long white spears with a gold cross at the top. We reach the gate and peer in from behind the massive black fence surrounding it. Will and Joan lead. We follow them inside. The colossal golden staircase I have ever seen is the main attraction. The steps are covered in red carpet. I head up one side as Thomas heads up the other.

We meet at the top and look down at Joan. She digs out her phone and snaps a picture of us. Then we trade-off. She and Will do the same. Mom and dad follow, then Marie. Marie is the lone single person here, but that doesn't bother her.

"Come on, Stu and Robert. Come take a picture with me." Stu and Robert bookcase Marie in between them.

"Alright then, Let's not be a couple of boring chaps." Stu nods his chin at Robert as he grabs Marie under her arms while Robert grabs her legs.

They lift her up Cleopatra style as Joan snaps another picture. That's more like it. What is life if you can't have a little fun once in a while?

We continue to the estate rooms as Thomas tells us what little history he knows about each room. I have to admit; I do love a man that knows things. Not a man that thinks he knows *it all* but a man that knows things. He knows where he's going, knows what he wants, and knows how to get it—that kind of man.

We walk out into the expansive lawn behind the palace. It stretches as far as the eye can see. The grass is striped dark and light green. I often wondered how people get their lawns to do that. The gravel path crunches under our feet as we walk along it. A short, pudgy man walking towards us makes eye contact with Thomas. A wide smile spreads across his face. He begins running towards us. I don't know whether to shove Stu at him or stand completely still. I chose the latter. His face is red and round.

"You wanker! You didn't tell me you'd be here today. Did you call Andrew?" the man shakes Thomas by the shoulders.

Something in Thomas' wide eyes throws me off. "Gregory, this is Mar and her family."

Thomas is stretching his words.

"I'll ring Andrew. I'm sure he is still here." Gregory runs his thumb over his phone and puts it up to his ear.

Thomas grabs Gregory by the hand. "Nah, mate. Don't call Andrew."

Gregory holds his phone in the air. "Too late, mate. Ello! Andrew? You won't believe the wanker I found creeping around your family yard. Come out; we are by the pond."

I listen to Gregory's one-sided conversation. "Right then. We'll come back up."

I shoot a confused look up at Thomas. He shakes his head. Don't freak out. I can explain. I know I didn't explain it well. This isn't his family's yard. That's just something Gregory likes to kid about, especially if we are at a pub."

"OK, explain quickly," I say as we begin walking back up to the palace. "Is your friend not a Lord? Is he a *prince* or something? Are you? Have you been hiding the fact that you are a prince?" I joke.

I have to admit, when Thomas told us his friend was a Lord, I didn't really know what it meant.

Thomas throws his hands in the air. "No, no, nothing like that. Well, kind of like that but not really. He *is* a Lord. His father is a lord. It's hard to explain. But no, he's not a prince. This is not his place, nor is he related to the Queen. And it's not like we are going to walk up here, and the Queen is going to pop out for a spot of tea. I'm not sure what he is doing here. His family are old family friends. We became close at Eton College as kids."

I swivel around to face Joan. I mouth, "What the hell?"

Mom pinches me on my side. I straighten, then wink at her.

As we walk back into the palace, a trim-looking man walks towards us. He's dressed in khakis and a white polo shirt. I don't know what I was expecting. I've never met a Lord before. A brief flash of Jesus pops into my head, I laugh. That's not right. Thor, the God of Thunder, pops in my head, then Jesus again wearing gladiator sandals.

"Halò!" His hello sounds like William Wallace in Braveheart.

I whisper out of the side of my mouth towards Joan and Marie. "Freeeddooomm!"

Joan slyly kicks the back of my heel. She straightens and smiles.

"Andrew, I would like you to meet my fiancé Marguerite and her family. Henry, Olivia, Joan, Marie, and Will."

"Bloody hell, mate, she's a stunner." He slugs Thomas on the arm.

"She is, isn't she? Where's Patrice?" Thomas smiles, taking my hand.

"Oh, you know, somewhere off fretting over the flowers or the food…." Andrew examines me. "What are you doing today, dashing around with the family in tow?"

"Well, we got the dresses and tuxes for the wedding. Thank God Mar knew the designer at the dress shop. So, we were able to get something perfect." Thomas says, smiling.

Andrew looks at me with something in his eye. Is it curiosity? Surprise? Confusion? In fact. Whatever it is, it gives me an uneasy feeling, and I don't like it.

"Today is just a day of sightseeing. We are pretending to be tourists." Thomas exclaims happily.

Marie pipes up. "We *are tourists*."

"You *are* coming to my stag party tonight, aren't you? It's the last night. Patrice and I just got back from our Stag and Hen week. Come out with us. Mar and the girls can meet up with Patrice and her friends."

That's the last thing I want to do. I don't want to spend the night hanging out with girls I don't know, but I'll play nice. It won't be that back; at least Joan and Marie are here.

"Come on, mate. It will be total rubbish if you aren't there." Andrew's voice whines.

"OK, OK. I'll go." Thomas looks at me. "If it is OK with you, darling."

I am not going to say no here. I smile, "Yes, of course! Go have fun."

I can't expect him to spend all his time with me, but still, I feel a little gutted. Especially since my family is in town.

"You are *whipped,* my friend—*Whipped!* When did you start asking for permission?" Andrew blows out his breath.

"Oh, come on, mate. Don't be a wanker. It's the polite thing to do. I care about Mar's feelings." Thomas slugs Andrew on the arm hard enough to let him know he is joking but not joking. Thomas caps it off by giving Andrew a stern look.

My dad steps closer to Andrew. Oh, gosh! Please don't let this be a fight. I could see it now. Dad, on the lawn of Buckingham Palace, wrestling around. I rest my hand on dad's shoulder. Thomas seems to notice.

Mom notices and distracts dad. "Look, Henry! Did you see this history on Big Ben?" She nudges him with the pamphlet she is holding.

Reluctantly dad turns to look at the booklet. The whole vibration is much higher now. There's an overall uneasiness.

"OK, mate. I'll see you after dinner tonight. But only if you promise not to be a wanker. If you are going to indeed be a wanker; you can be a wanker without me." Thomas holds Andrew's gaze.

Andrew's face brightens. "I apologize, mate. I've overstepped. I was only kidding." He turns his attention to us. "It was a pleasure to meet everyone. I'm so glad you will make it to the wedding."

Andrew walks off with his arm draped over Gregory. I blow out my breath. That could have been bad. We all need to loosen up. Andrew leaves a pit in my stomach. Alexander was right, this guy is an ass, and there's something about that guy that I don't like. I look at Joan and roll my eyes.

Thomas turns to look at me. "I apologize for Andrew's behavior. He's an ass. Shall we move along?"

We visit Big Ben, the London Eye, and the Tower of London. It goes by in an exhausting haze.

The bus driver drops us back at the flat. I walk in, dragging with the rest of the gang right behind me.

"You know we are going to have to rally," I say.

Marie throws herself down on the couch and takes off her shoes, rubbing her feet. "I don't think I'm going to get these puppies in heels or anything cute tonight."

Like the Grinch's heart, Marie's feet grew ten sizes today.

Mom and dad quietly walk into the bedroom and shut the door. That's their cue that they are wiped and are going to bed. I don't plan on seeing them for the rest of the night.

"I'm going to walk back to the hotel to shower and get ready." Will kisses Joan. "I'll see you later tonight.

Joan kisses Will and slumps down next to Marie.

"Thomas, is a *hen* party like a bachelorette party?" I stare up at him as I lean against Marie.

"It's more of a weeklong thing where the women go on holiday. It isn't as wild as the American one-night bachelorette party. It's more of a spa week, like a week at the shore, something of that nature."

I scowl at the "*American one-night bachelorette party*" like Americans are so uncivilized. I try to hold my tongue, but I find it almost impossible when I think someone is saying something I disagree with. "Do you think Americans are uncivilized or something?" Well, so much for trying.

The tension in the air vibrates. Nobody got over the whole Andrew comment. It wasn't like we spent any more time thinking about it. It's just something that rubbed everyone wrong. And we all quietly swept it under the rug for the sake of not starting a fight on the Queen's lawn.

Thomas looks me right in the eye. "M, no, not at all. That's not what I was saying at all. I was just trying to explain it."

"OK, then, what is tonight about if they already spent the week being civilized somewhere?" I raise my eyebrows at Thomas, looking smug.

Are we having our first fight? Maybe it isn't a fight. It just feels like one. It feels like all the emotions from the last week are boiling to the top. Like macaroni cooking on the stove, it's about to boil over, but can you reach it in time to remove it from the heat before boiling over and causing a huge mess?

"Tonight is just the roundup, the ending of the Hen party, the catchall," Thomas says, pulling out this phone. "You are to meet in the Luggage Room. Kyle has made the arrangements. The car will be around in an hour."

I throw up my hand and point a Thomas. "Absolutely not. I'm driving. You didn't even ask me if I cared to be chauffeured around tonight."

Thomas jerks his head back in surprise. "M, don't. I was just trying to be nice. After the other day, I just wasn't sure. I didn't want you to have to drive, especially if you are drinking tonight. Besides, you don't have a bloody driver's license."

I can feel the blood crawling up my neck to my ears. "Then why did you get me a *bloody* car then? Cart before the horse, huh? AND you didn't have a problem suggesting it earlier!" I throw my arms out in anger.

Oh, crap. Stop Marguerite. Stop while you're ahead. You are being hurtful, and for what? You are picking a fight, and you know it. I imagine a tiny guy in a fire truck circling me, dowsing me with water, but I'm like a train going off the rails. I can't stop. I feel like I'm suffocating, and the walls are getting closer and closer to me. Everything is bubbling to the top. I force it back down and just standstill in the middle of the living room with everyone's eyes on me.

Why do I always lash out when I feel out of control? Maybe there are too many changes at once? I couldn't expect it to be all roses and sunshine all the time. But I didn't expect to lash out over a comment from a guy that doesn't even matter. And a comment that under any other circumstance would have just rolled off my back. There is something deeper here, but I decide to put a pin in it. At this point, my *"put a pin in it"* board is looking more like the great black hole that I'll never go back and revisit.

Chapter 18

Independence Day

"Life itself is a privilege, but to live life to the fullest -well, that is a choice."

—ANDY ANDREWS

I WRAP MY ARMS AROUND THOMAS. "I'm sorry. I'm feeling overwhelmed; there is no excuse; I'm sorry."

Thomas rests his forehead against mine. "It's OK. You're OK." He pulls me tighter into his chest. If it weren't for family standing around, I would stay here. "It's only us, only now. All this is happening fast for me too. There are lots of changes, but they are good changes. But I can see how it is getting overwhelming. You have moved all the way across the pond. I haven't moved anywhere. Everything is OK; you're OK."

All the stress and high vibrations roll off my shoulders. "OK, we will get dressed, but we are taking a taxi that I arranged. I don't need a driver. Just grant me that." I kiss Thomas on the mouth to let him know that all is good between us.

Joan and Mar walk into the bedroom as I follow.

I slap my hand on my forehead. "Dang, dang, dang! You guys don't have clothes here."

I think about telling Thomas but, I can't need him for clothes when I don't want him to get me a driver, and I practically burned the house down out there.

I point my finger in the air. "I know who to call."

I push a couple of buttons, the phone rings. Alexander's voice comes on the line. "Bitch, where have you been? You got engaged! Dustine and I were just talking about you, and then we saw the news. What's the word, Chiquitita?"

"Well, we are invited to the last day of hen's week for Lord Andrew's bride, and I just realized I don't have anything to wear since it is last minute. Do you think you could help?" I ask, pleading. "I swear one of these days; I'm going to pay you back for everything you've done for me."

"Oh, bitch, please! Did you get invited to Patrice's bachelorette party? I'll help! You've got to look amazing. Where are you? What do you need?" I can hear the excitement in Alexander's voice.

"I'm at the flat. How about you come with us?" It should be a good time. As you know, my sister is here, and my best friend flew in for the engagement. So, I'll need something for the three of us to wear. If you join us, I promise we will have a great time. Call Dustine, ask if she wants to come."

"What are the sizes?" I hear Alexander flipping through racks of clothing.

"You know mine and Joan. Marie is a size eight to ten if that helps."

I hear Alexander writing it down. "Where is the party?"

"A place called the Luggage Room. Do you know it?" I look at Joan for confirmation.

"I know it, and I know exactly what to bring. I'll meet you in twenty. I'll call Dustine, but I think she works tonight." Alexander hangs up the phone before I can say bye.

I hang up, feeling proud of myself. I'm in London, and I am getting things done. I know people here. I don't have to depend on Thomas to figure everything out for me. I have never been that kind of girl. I like to do things my way.

The doorbell rings. I poke my head out of the bedroom. Thomas looks confused as he walks over to answer it.

"Hey, handsome." Alexander kisses Thomas on the cheek. "Congrats on your engagement."

"Hey, no small talk. Get in here." I wave at Thomas. "Mind your business." I wink.

Alexander walks in carrying an arm full of clothes. "Here witch I bought you some clothes."

Marie stands. "I'm Marie. I'm Mar's best friend."

Alexander looks Marie up and down. "Yass—yaasss. *You* will do." He begins pulling things out of bags and holding them up to Marie.

Marie screws up her face. "I'll do? What do you mean I'll do? Shouldn't that be the other way around?"

"Oh, no, dear. I got it right. The clothes wear you. You don't wear the clothes."

Alexander lays out an outfit. "This one is it. Put this on."

"Oh, are you sure? I'm not sure this will look good on me." Marie holds it up and spins it around on the satin hanger it rests on."

Alexander hands Joan an outfit. She takes it without hesitation.

I smile at Marie. "Trust me. His clothes fit like a glove."

Marie shrugs her shoulders and heads to the bathroom with Joan. I strip off my clothes and put on the outfit Alexander hands to me. I pull on a pair of black pants that feel like butter. I can't wrap my head around what kind of fabric this is.

"I know these aren't just cotton. What kind of fabric are these?"

"It's a blend of cotton, spandex, and silk," Alexander says, running his hand down my leg over the fabric.

I pull on the lopsided sweater over my satin bodysuit and adjust it to bear my shoulder. Alexander squats down beside me, handing me a pair of stilettos. I hold them up to look at them. They're black with pencil-thin heels.

"Louboutin?" I slip them on and begin to sing. "*These expensive, these is red bottoms These is bloody shoes.*"

Alexander gets to his feet next to me and starts snapping his fingers. "*Hit the store; I can get 'em bot— I don't wanna choose.*" Alexander twirls me around, "Yes, girl. Now spin me!"

I twirl Alexander under my arm. "What are you wearing?"

Alexander unzips a garment bag. He pulls out a black tailored jacket and a pair of high-waisted wide-leg black satin pants. He strips down to his very small colorful briefs and glides on his pants and jacket without putting a shirt on underneath.

Alexander has this sexiness about him. He's mysterious and overconfident, which gives him an allure that makes him feel unattainable. His body is slender, beautiful, and completely hairless. A thin gold chain loops around his neck and hangs to his naval. I look up to see Joan walking out of the bathroom. She's wearing a royal blue vintage-looking micro dress with a puffed sleeve. I must admit, it isn't something I would have ever picked out for her, but I guess that's why I'm not a fashion designer. She looks fantastic. Which only means I must bring her back down from space.

"You look like a giraffe," I say deadpan, giving her a wink.

"Shut up; I *do not*. You look like a troll— all 5'3" of you." She laughs as she hits me on the side of the head with a pillow.

"Stop, you're gonna mess up my troll hair!" I lift my hand to straighten it.

Marie steps out of the bathroom. She's wearing a light pink baby doll dress with fishnet stocking and black Louboutin's. "Oh, no, this is not happening! I can't wear this! You can almost see my butt!"

The bottom of Marie's butt cheeks are very visible.

"Almost isn't, actually. Plus, you look hot. You *need* to wear this. It says you're single and ready to mingle." I say, eyeing her.

Marie pulls at the dress. "I'm not sure this outfit says *mingle*. It mostly says hooker for hire —a lady of the night. And why do you get to wear pants, and Joan and I are wearing half dresses?"

Alexander walks up and pulls a string at the back of the dress. It releases the fabric. The dress falls to just above Marie's knee. "Silly girl, you did not untie the dress. You were wearing it like a belt." He turns Marie around and adjusts her outfit. "There, now that's right. Go look."

All three of us stand in front of Alexander for inspection. He walks around us like he is inspecting a new car. "Perfect. Absolutely perfect. Yes, go."

I quiet rapping sounds at the bedroom door. "M, is everyone dressed? Can I come in?"

Thomas cracks open the door, gliding in. God, he looks fantastic in a suit.

Alexander walks around Thomas expecting his suit. "It isn't mine, but damn, you are looking fine in that suit."

Thomas blushes at the way Alexander is looking at him. "If you stare any longer, love, I'm going to charge you."

Alexander laughs, tucking one arm under the other and resting his hand on his collarbone. "Something, I'd gladly pay."

Thomas smiles and runs his hand over Alexander's cheek. "Cheeky fellow." Thomas then turns his focus on me. "I'm taking off. I wish you wouldn't drive, but obviously, do what you want." He kisses me on the forehead.

"Oh, she's not driving. Especially if it's that little car parked out front. We simply will not fit." Alexander points in the general direction of the front drive. "That little car is a death trap."

"Good, that makes me feel better. I'm glad you won't have to worry about driving or parking tonight." Thomas straightens his shirt. "See you tonight. I don't know when I'll be back but call if you need me. I'm picking up Will, then headed out."

I watch him as he slips back out of the room. I think to myself, that's mine —he's all mine.

Alexander turns back towards me. "Tisk, tisk, let's get back to the task at hand. Grab your bags, ladies. We'll take my car."

I lock the door behind us. As we walk out to the street, Alexander pushes his key fob. A beep and flashing lights come from a shiny black Jag parked in front of my Fiat. Joan and Marie slide into the backseat.

Alexander checks himself in the mirror. "Dustine and Genae are meeting us at the Luggage Room. We will show these *snoots* how to party.

We pull up in front of a modest large black door. Alexander hands his keys to a man standing discreetly next to it. I sure hope that was the valet. I don't see a valet stand. I shift my eye to question Joan. I know she's thinking the same thing. Just as I shift back to look at the valet. Another man, dressed the same, runs up and pushes the wall next to the first man. A secret panel opens, displaying a row of keys. Ah, I get it. That's clever. We step into the bar. The walls are cream-colored fabric with nailhead tacks arranged to make symmetrical large rectangles around the room. The stairs are white marble with large black veins running through them. Small groupings of dark leather couches are scattered about. I scan the room. In the rush and excitement of the day, I completely forgot that I have no idea what this girl looks like. I look for a large group of girls — nothing. Oh my gosh, how did I forget this?

I turn and look at Marie and Alexander. "You're gonna laugh, but I have no idea what this girl looks like." I throw my hands in the air.

Joan pulls me by the arm. "Let's Google it. We can figure this out. What was the guy's name?"

"Andrew, I think. Hers was…" I think for a second. "Patricia? No, it wasn't that. When I was a kid, a friend's mom had the same name. I picture her in my mind with her bright red lipstick, her well-put-together outfit —her accent. And it hits me like a ton of bricks. "Patrice! Google that!"

I try to wait patiently, but Joan is taking entirely too long. I snatch the phone out of her hand. My thumbs have never moved so fast. A list of websites pops up. I click on one, and a picture loads. It's scary but, Google does really know everything. I show the screen to everyone. We scan the room —nothing. As we make it to the back of the bar, we spot a few women huddled together in the most proper seated posture I have ever seen, ridged and ridiculous. This ought to be fun.

I walk up, smiling. "Patrice?"

A thin blonde looks up from her table. "Yes?"

I stick out my hand to shake hers. "I'm Mar. This is my sister, Joan, my best friend Marie, and my dear friend Alexander. I'm Thomas' fiancé. Thomas Blaine."

The awkward pause makes me uncomfortable. I begin to do what I do when I am uncomfortable. I fill the silence with talking.

"Scooch on over." I sit down next to Patrice and bump her with my butt. "Scooch, scooch."

Joan, Alexander, and Marie file into the booth next to me.

Patrice sheepishly smiles at us. "These are my friends, Kitty, Laura, Julie, and Krystal."

Patrice is wearing a baby pink cardigan over a white dress. Her friends are wearing variations of basically the same outfit.

"So, what's the plan for tonight?" I ask with a devilish look in my eye.

Patrice looks around at her friends. "*This* is the plan."

"Just sitting here, sipping a perfectly crafted cocktail —on your last night of singlehood?" I shake my head. "This can't be."

I look at Joan to telepathically tell her that we must do something about this. She gets what I am sending her because she gives me a sharp nod.

Alexander notices Joan and I nodding back and forth to each other.

I whisper in Alexander's ear. "We are thinking of turning this into a real bachelorette party. You think you can swing that?"

"Honey, *swinging* is my middle name." He winks at me, putting his phone to his ear and excusing himself from the table.

I fill the silence. "So, Patrice, what do you do?"

"I, well —I…" she furrows her brows. "I do a lot of charity work."

"That's noble. What kind of charity?" I smile politely. This is about as fun as standing in line at the Apple store waiting to be seen.

Alexander interrupts me. "OK, bitches it's on!"

My smile goes into a wide grin. "Patrice, can we kidnap you and your friends for a bit?"

"Kidnap?" Patrice's face goes into alarm mode.

"Stop that! We aren't going to kidnap you for real. Is that even a worry here? Do you think I'm some sort of kidnapper where Liam Neeson will have to show up to find you?" I narrow my eyes at her.

Alexander looks at his phone. "It should be any minute now. I'll leave my car here."

We shuffle to get out of the booth. "Come on! We are taking you out of here. We are breaking you out of this craziness to go have some real fun."

I place my hand in Patrice's and pull her towards the door. Just as we reach the sidewalk, a black Mercedes van pulls up.

I look at Alexander, perplexed. "Is this us?"

He throws his hands in the air. "What? It's what I could do at such short notice."

A man hops out of the driver's seat and opens the back doors to the van. Even for me, this is stretching it. The van doesn't have seats. It is completely empty except for the lines of racks hanging above. It looks like a giant mobile closet or a subway car.

"Well, get in!" Alexander holds out his hand for each of us to step up.

I hop in first to show that I'm on board with this whole idea—Marie follows. Joan ushers each one of the girls up before she jumps in herself. Alexander pulls the door closed, shutting us in. The driver starts the engine. We tightly hold onto the metal poles above our heads like we are riding the subway.

I tap Patrice on the arm. "Are you doing, OK?"

She smiles wide at me. "This is the most fun I've had in a long time! I don't even care where we are going!"

I grimace, "If getting in the back of a van is the most fun you've had in a long time, then we have to change that."

"We are going to the Roux; Dustine is DJing tonight. I called Genae; she'll meet us." Alexander casually holds onto the bar above him.

"I've always wanted to go to Roux. I've never been." Patrice giggles and nudges one of her friends.

Alexander nips Patrice on the nose, "You're in for a treat then."

Chapter 19

Get in the Van

"Why do they call it rush hour when nothing moves?"

—Robin Williams

As the van pulls up to the front of the club, the driver swings open the doors like he is letting barn animals out to the pasture. Flashes of light surround us. At least fifty photographers are standing on the cobbled street. I feel like I'm in some kind of art exhibit in a Lady Gaga stunt.

Alexander turns and whispers, "Follow my lead. Do what I do."

Alexander holds up his arm to showcase each one of us like we are in a pop-up fashion show. We hop out one by one like we are exiting a plane over a drop zone. As Patrice jumps out of the van, an audible gasp comes from the crowd, and the cameras shift. Alexander holds Patrice's hand in his and twirls her under his arm. Marie throws her hand in the air and waves. A couple of doormen block the crowd and accompany us inside. The club is exactly what you expect, hot, loud, and fantastic.

The manager meets us at the door. "I'm called Reese. Dustine told me you would be arriving."

Alexander kisses Reese on the cheek. "Thank you for being so accommodating so quickly."

Reese bows his head, "My pleasure."

We grab a table by the dance floor. I catch Dustine's eye from her perch in the DJ booth. She's wearing a bobbed black wig tied up into two pigtails with heavily lined eyeliner. It must be her DJ persona. I throw up my arm and wave.

A cocktail waitress walks up, carrying an ice bucket under her arm and a bottle of champagne with glasses in between her fingers. "I'm Mod; I will be running your bottle service."

She sets the champagne down. Dustine yells into the microphone then begins to scratch out and digitize a mix between Rain Radio and Calvin Harris. It always baffles me how great DJs mix music to create a whole new song. It's so loud in here that my eyeballs are vibrating.

Mod screams over the noise. "I'll be back!"

I shake my head to the music. "Let's dance!"

I grab Joan by the hand. She reaches behind her and grabs Marie's. Marie holds Patrice's —like the *Barrel of Monkeys* game we played as kids. We shuffle towards the dance floor in a line. Joan's dancing has always had a touch of Elaine from Seinfeld. But she's happy, and that's all that matters. We circle around her, dancing. That's the thing; you don't have to be the prettiest, the best or the best dancer, or the most educated. People are attracted to people who are happy and fun —they're magnetic! Patrice is stiff. I grab her by the hands and sway them back and forth until she starts to loosen up and copy me.

"You got it!" I yell.

I let go of Patrice's hands. Krystal, Julie, Kitty, and Laura slowly move in and dance beside her. Joan, Marie, and I start a conga line around them. I know it doesn't go with the music, but it's fun. That's all that matters.

The waitress returns to our table, carrying a large tray of shots. We start the conga line back to the table, absorbing Patrice and her friends into the line with us.

I grab my shot and raise it into the air. "To Patrice and Andrew."

Patrice shoots her shot and motions the cocktail waitress over. "Could we have a couple of bottles of Domaine Leroy Richebourg 1949?"

The waitress screws up her face. "We don't have that here."

Joan butts in. "Could we have eight amaretto sours?"

"You aren't at The Savoy, honey." Alexander pats Patrice on the arm.

I don't think she has ever been told no. It's interesting to see. No worries though, we'll knock that pretentiousness and properness right out of her. The drinks arrive. Patrice lifts her glass to eye level. "There's a cherry in it! Cherries are my favorite!"

Dustine walks up to the table. She smiles. "Hi, I'm Dustine. How's the chicken party going?"

Krystal's smile goes into a line. "It's called a *hen* party."

Dustine nods at Krystal. "That's what I said. So, where are you headed after here?"

I look at Alexander. Then back at Joan. I throw my hands in the air. "Karaoke? What about the place we did karaoke the other day? Coach and Horses, right?"

Genae walks up behind Dustine. "Hey! Finally! I finally caught up with you guys!"

Genae scoots in closer. "I'm Genae. Nice to meet everyone!"

Alexander kisses her. "I'm glad you stopped messing around and made it."

"You know me, never late." She says sarcastically.

I make all the introductions as Alexander calls for the van.

Marie hops up. "Come on, ladies. Chug your drinks. Let's get this party on the road."

Everyone lifts their drinks and chugs them, leaving their ice at the bottom of their glasses. We stack a few pounds under a glass as we make a beeline towards the front door.

I hug Dustine, "I'll see you soon?"

"Oh, no! I'm coming with you guys. The shift just changed." Dustine wraps her arm around my, locking our elbows.

As we step outside, camera flashes begin to go off again. It's a surreal moment. Joan, Marie, and I begin to practice our Charlie's Angels poses for the crowd. My phone rings. I dig in my purse and pull it out. It's Thomas.

I grab my spot in our makeshift subway van as I put the phone up to my ear. "Hi! Hello?"

The phone sounds dead. I check it to see if I accidentally hung up. Thomas' face is still on the screen, and the timer is going, but I don't hear anything.

I put it back up to my ear. "Hello! Thomas. Hello?"

"Hello, love!" Thomas finally says on the other end of the line.

"Are you calling your *girlfriend*? Hang up! Unbelievable!" I hear another male voice along with Thomas', then a bunch of rustling. Silence. Crackling. Sound.

"Give me my phone back, mate." I can hear Thomas say in the background. Then nothing —the phone is dead silent. Not a dial tone, not a ding, not a sound.

I drop my phone back into my purse.

"Who was that?" Joan nudges me.

"It was Thomas, but I think something happened to his phone," I say, a little confused.

Ding —Joan digs her phone out of her purse. "It's Will."

Thomas' asshole friend threw his phone in the river. My phone is dying. Why can't I be in bed with you staring at the skyline?

"What did he say?" I look over to glance at Joan's phone.

"Apparently, Andrew threw Thomas' phone in the river. Will's phone is dying, and it's only the beginning of the night, and Will, who gets along with everyone, is already regretting going.

"He threw Thomas' phone in the river? What an ass!" I furrow my brow. "Well, I'm not going to let that ass ruin our night. He can try to ruin Patrice's life. That would be her choice, but he isn't ruining ours."

Patrice is a few feet away from us; I glance over at her, feeling a little sorry for her. I often wonder how women end up with assholes.

Alexander's assistant zips through traffic as we hold on for dear life in the back. Marie is pulling herself up into a ball, not letting her feet touch the ground. She throws one leg over the rail. She's hanging on like a sloth dangling from a tree. I laugh because I know she's feeling the shot and drink back at Roux.

We make the short ride to Coach and Horses and file out of the back of the van like a bunch of paratroopers jumping out of a plane. No photographers. We made it here before anyone else could follow us. It's crowded tonight. We shove our way through the crowd and wedge ourselves into a booth.

A familiar man walks over to our table. "I am Lawrence. I remember you from the other day." He reaches out to shake my hand. "Are you here to put on another performance?"

"Maybe." I smile. "This is my sister Joan, my best friend Marie, Genae, and Chase Alexander." I point to each person as I make their introductions.

Lawrence stops in his tracks as though he's seen a ghost. "Patrice Ashley Byron —pleasure."

Patrice holds out her hand to him to shake his. He instead grabs it and kisses the top of it.

I smile and continue without skipping a beat. "This is my friends Patrice, Krystal, Laura, Kitty, and Julie."

"The pleasure is all mine." He puts his hand over his chest. "Enjoy yourselves tonight. Please let me know if there is anything you need. I'll be right over there at the bar." Lawrence points at the bar behind him.

The bar is crowded. The sea of people are laughing, drinking, and cheering on the piano player. We go virtually unnoticed—something both Patrice and I like. Although she gets way more attention than I do, but still. It's a nice change. A cocktail waitress bumps her way to our table with a round of drinks. Drinks we didn't order.

Alexander halfway stands up, tapping his ring on his glass. "I'd like to propose a toast." He nods his head towards me. "To Mar, my amazing new friend."

I smile, holding my glass in the air. "To new friends, to old friends, and Patrice's wedding!"

I'm not for sure, but I see something quickly flash across Patrice's face before it disappears, and she smiles, holding up her glass.

The crowd backs to our table, forming a makeshift barrier between us and the bar.

"So, let's play a game. Here, hand me that saltshaker." Alexander holds out his hand. "I'm going to ask a question then spin this, whoever it lands on answers the question then asks one, and so on. What's said at this table stays at this table. Capeesh?" Alexander spins the shaker. It lands on Joan. He lifts his brows. "OK, Joan, during your childhood, when did you know you hated Mar?"

My mouth drops open, turning my grimace into a laugh. "Oh, I know! It was that one time I mixed M&M's and Skittles together and gave them to her.

Joan laughs, "No, it was the time she was running around kicking boys in the nuts." Her mouth goes into a wide smile. "No! I take it back. It was the time she snapped my bra in front of Chris Powell, a guy I liked."

I shrug my shoulders and puff out my bottom lip. "All character building. You're welcome."

Joan spins the shaker. It lands on Dustine. "OK, Dustine." Joan stops and thinks for a second. "What was your worst date?"

"Oh, that's easy. "Back in the states. A guy that wouldn't stop talking about himself. Then asked me to pay for dinner. Not only mine but his too." Dustine shakes her head.

I joke. "Hey, I think I know that guy."

Dustine shakes her head at me and points. "Small dating pool in San Francisco." The shaker lands on Patrice. Dustine slaps her hands together. "Have you ever done it in Buckingham Palace?"

Patrice glances around to see if anyone is listening. "We *have* never done it in the palace." She emphasis the word, *have* and winks at Dustine. "That's my answer."

I hold out the shaker like a microphone. "Is that your final answer?"

"Final answer." She takes the shaker and spins it. It lands on Alexander. OK, kiss the next person that makes eye contact with you. Guy or girl doesn't matter."

"What? When did this turn into truth or dare?" Alexander smirks. "Fine, I'll do it." He climbs on the booth, getting on his knees to look above the crowd. He scans the room and locks eyes with someone.

"Skootch bitch. Do you want me to do this or not?" One by one, we file out of the booth.

Alexander stands and adjusts his blazer. He never drops his gaze. We make a path for him through the crowd. In true Alexander fashion, he glides through, dramatically. He's locked eyes with a short strawberry blond man with a boyish face. We stand in behind him, waiting for his next move. He puts a hand on each side of the man's face and kisses him. Patrice goes slacked-jawed. I almost wet myself from laughter. Alexander turns on his heels and walks back to our table. We follow him, closing the opening in the crowd.

"I can't believe you did that!" I sink into the booth. "It's like that time in Grease where Michelle Pfeiffer kisses the new guy."

My obsession with music deeply extends into musicals, especially Grease.

I glance back at the man. He's standing in the middle of the bar, dumbfounded, and trying to decide if it's a good idea to come over here. Alexander sits up straighter—peacocking. Oh brother. Alexander picks up the shaker again; he deviously looks around and spins it. It lands on Marie.

Marie scoots over, bumping Genae. "It didn't land on me; it landed on Krystal!"

I eye her like a disappointed mother. "It landed on you, and you know it did. "OK. But I'm going to need a drink because I know where this game is going." Marie lifts her hand into the air and waves the waitress over. "Ten tequila shots. Por Favor."

I frantically wave my hand in the air. "No, no tequila for me. I'll do a schnapps of any sort. Apple or peach…." OK, nine shots of tequila and one shot of something fruity." Marie rolls her eyes at me.

Alexander giggles and pats Marie on the hand. OK, stop stalling. I dare you to request and sing Midnight Train to Georgia."

Marie throws her shot down her throat and slams the tiny glass on the table. "Done. Let's do this."

That's one thing about Marie; she doesn't get embarrassed.

Marie squeezes her way to the piano player. She sits at the edge of the bench and whispers in his ear. She smiles, waving Joan and me over. Someone hands her a mic. If I remember correctly, Marie can't sing. Well, she can sing but not in tune. Joan and I make our way to the piano as Marie pulls herself on top of it to lay across it like a lounge singer.

She raises the mic to her lips. "LA proved too much for the man…."

Joan and I dance in sync next to the piano, adding the backup vocals. "Leaving…going back to find."

"Going back to find." I strain to look over Joan's shoulder, peaking over to add my own chorus in a higher chord to her backup vocals.

One by one, the crowd turns to watch us. Marie is now lying flat with her back pressed against the top of the piano. She crosses her legs at the knees. She switches each leg, holding one straight in the air at a time. As the song comes to an end, I wave the rest of our crew up. Alexander is the first to shove his way to the piano to grab the mic from Marie. He whispers something to the pianist, then puts a finger in the air and twirls it around. He looks down at the floor, holding the mic close to his chest as the piano player starts pounding on the piano.

His head flips up on cue. *"Tonight, for the first time…for the first time in history, it's going to start raining, men!"*

We start jumping up and down around the piano, hyping up the crowd. Alexander is whipping his head back and forth to the beat.

Patrice and her crew dance their way to Alexander and begin singing. "And for the first time, I'm going to get soaking wet!"

"Is that Patrice Ashley Byron?" I hear someone ask before snapping a picture.

Patrice and I make eye contact. She shrugs her shoulders at me. "You can't hide all the time. Nor do you want to."

She continues to dance without a care in the world. I love that about her; maybe she's not at all what I thought. We make our way back to our booth after the song ends. Another round gets sent to our table as we sit down.

Simultaneously we hold the shots in the air. "Friends! Friends forever!"

Someone in the distance snaps another few pictures. Instead of getting annoyed, we embrace it. Every time we see a flash, we change poses. If you can't beat them, join them. It's not like we are trying to hide. OK, who's next?" Krystal asks, looking around at everyone.

"Mine!" Marie narrows her eyes at everyone, not to miss her opportunity; she quickly spins the shaker.

It lands on Joan, and she nearly jumps out of her seat.

Joan points her finger at Marie. "You better watch yourself. "OK. Shhh!" Marie puts her finger to her lips. "It won't be bad; I won't make you kiss anyone or anything. I dare you to buy the whole bar shots."

Joan pulls out her wallet, opens it then shuts it.

"Do it, you cow. We know you can afford it." Marie slugs Joan on the arm.

Joan stands up in her seat and cups her hands around her mouth. "Hi everyone! Hello!"

People start turning around.

"Hello! Hi." Joan waves her hands in the air. "Hi, I'm Joan, and the next round of tequila is on me!"

Everyone starts clapping. One man turns to Joan. "Right on, mate!"

Joan holds her card out for the waitress. "I guess the next round is on me."

The waitress happily takes the card and begins bringing trays of tequila shots to each table. We are the last table she serves, handing the bill and card back to Joan.

I glance over at the bill. £1947.07! I'm glad I'm not her. Joan adds the tip and hands it back to the waitress.

"You just spend $3000.00; you know that, right?" I swallow hard. "That's crazy."

"It's not every day my little sister gets engaged; you know?" Joan leans over, wedging herself against me.

I shrug my shoulders. "Just so you know, when you get engaged, we are going on a vacation. I will not be throwing $3,000.00 down for tequila shots." I watch her closely when I say engaged for any flicker of anything, but nothing. If she's thought about it, she isn't showing it.

Wait, come to think about out, I just might throw $3,000.00 down on tequila shots. It's not every day that my sister gets married either. What comes around goes around, I say. Funny thing about how you treat people. Most people will say karma is a bitch, but I think karma is only a bitch *if* you are. I mean, isn't that the whole thing about karma? If you aren't an ass, then karma isn't a bitch. The same thing works on people. If you are nice to people, then people are nice to you. Unless you are an ass, then refer back to why karma is a bitch. I should get a shirt made: *Karma Isn't a Bitch, You Are.*

Joan knocks back her shot and sets her glass down on the table. "OK, I've got one. Mar, I'd like you to get up and lead the Cotton Eye Joe. Most people won't know it, so you'll have to teach it."

"No way! What the hell?" I smile, sipping my schnapps.

"What the hell, what? Get up and figure it out." Joan shoos me with her hand. "Go on! You can do it!"

I sheepishly walk up to Lawrence at the bar. "Hi. First, I know this is going to sound weird, but could I possibly lead a dance? I mean, would you mind if I teach the crowd how to dance to a certain song? We are playing a game, and I was dared to teach the crowd how to do a certain country dance. Is there a speaker or something I can hook my phone to?"

Lawrence's face lights up. "Of course, dear. Follow me." I shoot Joan a dirty look.

Lawrence takes me to a small closet. He pulls out an amp and hands it to me while he continues digging in the closet. He pulls out a mic stand and a mic. What in the world does he exactly think I'm about to do? He shuts the closet door and takes the amp from me.

"Follow me. I'll get you set up." Lawrence leads me to a plug in the wall. He plugs in the amp and microphone. I set up the mic stand as he places the mic in it.

"There you go, dear. Do what you want." Lawrence returns to his spot at the bar to watch.

I tap the top of the mic to check if it is working. A loud, high-pitched sound reverberates out of it. The people in front of the amp press their hands over their ears. I guess that's one way to get people's attention.

I lift my hand in the air. "Hi, I'm Mar, and I'd like to teach you a little dance from Texas we call the *Cotton Eye Joe*. It's the most country song you'll ever hear." I reach down and plug my phone into the amp. I fiddle with the music app looking for the song. "OK, get in a line. Like a pinwheel." I move people into place. "It's just something you have to watch and then pick up. Here I'll show you."

People start to form a pinwheel shape on the dance floor. I motion for Marie and Joan to help me show everyone how the dance is done. They walk over, each putting an arm over my shoulders. I motion to Lawrence to push play on my phone. We go through the kicking and back and forth in a circle until most of the crowd has it down. The song progressively gets faster. Dustine, Genae, and Alexander join, pulling along Krystal, Kitty, Laura, and Julie with them.

Dustine grabs the microphone from the stand and starts yelling out random things pretending to be an auctioneer. "A little faster now! Do I hear a pound, a pound! Do I hear two pounds?"

Patrice joins our line, in between Joan and me. We laugh, trying to keep up as the music begins to speed up. If you don't laugh dancing the *Cotton Eye Joe*, then you have issues. It is impossible to dance it without smiling from ear to ear.

She blurts, "How do you ever keep up?"

Joan smiles, kicking her leg high into the air. "You just try your best. If you can't keep up, just start running. Plus, trying to keep up makes it so funny."

Patrice puts more weight on Joan and me as we lift her off her feet and swing her along with us. This makes us laugh even more. The song ends with us out of breath and dizzy —dizzy from the excitement, the drinks, and the spinning.

Patrice grabs Dustine by the forearm. You have to promise to come and DJ at my wedding and play this song!"

"At—your—wedding? Are you sure about that?" Dustine is hesitant. "OK…"

It's the kind of "OK" that people say to crazy people, or drunk people, or people that need to hear a little white lie.

We all slump back into the booth in hysterics, huffing. Joan drums her knees, jazzed. "So, now what?"

I smirk. "Well, I believe it is my turn to spin the shaker."

I spin it, and it lands on Laura. Laura is a petite little thing with vibrant red hair. When the shaker lands on her, she throws both of her hands in front of her chest like she's trying to push someone off her. "Oh, no! No, thank you!"

"Nope, you are playing. You never said you weren't, so you are." I shake my head at her. "It doesn't work like that." I reach up and scratch my chin like in thinking, just to make her nervous. I turn to her. "What should I ask? Men, crime, sex…I settle. Have you ever ridden a bull?"

I'm just joking with her, but her eyes go wide. "Uh, not ever!"

I laugh, "Me either. I was just checking. That's not your real question or dare." I tap my finger on my chin. "No, I'm going to dare you to do something. Let me think."

Her anxiety is visible. I watch as she scoots down in her seat. "OK, I got one. Everyone is going to write a song down. You'll pick one at random. Then you will have to stand on the booth seat and sing it. At least the words you know."

Laura fans her hands in front of her. "No, nope, I can't do that."

She wraps her arms around Patrice's and hides her face in Patrice's neck.

"Here, this will help. I hand her a shot. Just Schnapp's this time. I don't care who you are; more than three tequila shots in a short amount of time will take you down. I dig in my bag to pull out my mini yellow legal pad.

I rip off a piece and scribble down a song. I wad it up and pass the pen and paper around the table. I throw my wadded-up piece of paper in the empty peanut bowl. Everyone randomly tosses their paper in the bowl, one by one.

I swirl the papers around and hand them to Laura. "OK, pick."

Laura closes her eyes and picks one. She slowly opens it up and reads the name out loud. "Driver's License -Olivia Rodrigo. I'm not sure I remember the words."

I quickly open my music app and type in the song. Laura puts her face in her hands as we start to chant. "Laura-LaURA- LAURA!" until she finally gets to her feet.

She steadies herself on the booth cushion. She holds my phone, knees trembling. "Hi, my name is Laura."

No one turns to look at her.

Patrice nudges her. "I don't think they can hear you."

Laura sheepishly looks down at her feet and draws in a deep breath. "Hi! My name is Laura! I'm going to sing a song. It's called Driver's License."

She stares down at the phone as it begins to play. One by one, people start to turn around. The piano payer begins to join in. Laura isn't on key, but that's the fun of it. With every note, she begins opening up, and it makes me smile. She's still visibly nervous. Her body begins to sway a little under her uneasiness. I stand up next to her, wrapping my hand in hers and joining in.

I take the attention off Laura and onto myself. I screech out piercingly and off-key. "I guess you didn't mean what you wrote in that song about me!"

Joan busts out laughing.

"What am I if not fun?" I smile at her like I did when we were kids—overexaggerated and ridiculous.

Laura begins to smile from ear to ear, relaxing. She giggles and grabs my arm to steady herself. I nod for her to finish it off with dramatics. She looks straight into the crowd. *"Cuz' you said forever now I drive alone past your street."*

We all clap enthusiastically for Laura. "See? You were great, *and* better yet, you didn't die!"

A look of pride spreads across Laura's face.

Laura sits back down in the booth. "Why do you make people do things they don't want to?"

I screw up my face at her. Well, that went south quick. "Didn't you have fun?" I ask.

"Well, yes." She looks at me, confused.

I don't think Laura knows how to feel.

I give her a big hug. "If you had fun, then that's all that matters. You wouldn't have done it otherwise, right?"

She timidly shakes her head. "Well, no. I guess not."

"See, and you had fun! Just take that. It's just a game. Just for fun." I shake her, loosening up her stiffness.

She smiles. "I'm just not used to being the center of attention."

I knock her on the shoulder. "Well. You gotta change that."

Joan shoots out of the booth and makes her way to the bar. She leans in next to Lawrence and is having some sort of exchange with the bartender.

I amble up beside her. "What'cha doing over here all by your lonesome?"

"I think we need to cool it on the shots. I'm explaining to Raul here how to make a Lava Flow." Joan leans over the bar, showing him how to pour the right amount of strawberry daiquiri on the bottom.

I point two fingers at her, forming a small pistol. "Gotcha! Good call."

Joan and the waitress make it back to our table, carrying a colorful tray of tropical drinks. They are a bit out of place here. The first time I had a Lava Flow was at Margaritaville in Hawaii. Joan and I ordered steak and drank Lava Flows while we listened to a local band. We ended up walking back to our hotel using the beach instead of the sidewalk. It was magic. Lava Flows are my happy place.

Chapter 20

Onward and Upward

"We are all broken, that's how the light gets in."

—Ernest Hemingway

"Hey, hand me the menu. We better start eating something." The waitress looks confused. "Sorry, love. The only thing I can offer you is peanuts and maybe some mints. The kitchen is closed."

Patrice, now three sheets to the wind, tries standing up. "Onward and upward!" she stands with one foot on a chair next to us like she's a sea captain with a telescope looking out to sea.

"OK, OK… one more song for the road while we finish our drinks." I hold up my drink to toast. "Salut friends!"

I plug in my phone to the app again and join everyone gathered around the piano. The crowd instinctively makes space for us. I look at Joan, "Bye, Bye, Bye?"

"I want to see you out that door…." Joan nods her head. "Is that the one?"

"Yep, that's it. OK, guys. We are doing that old NSYNC song, *Bye, Bye, Bye*.

Krystal claps her hands. "Oh, I know this one!"

Joan, Marie, and I line up, holding our arms out to the sides, like scarecrows hanging in a cornfield. Before the music starts, I start to giggle. I bump Marie with my butt. "Do you remember the dance?"

She rolls her eyes at me, "Of course I do. Do you?"

I smile, "Of course. Are you ready? Go hard or go home."

Marie goes limp and hangs her head. It's taking everything in me not to lose it.

I whisper to Joan. "Ready?"

Joan knows this dance. She learned it when she was in the pep squad. Marie and I learned it waiting for Joan to give us a ride home. A happy product of not officially having my driver's license.

Joan lets her head go limp. I take in a deep breath. *We* are doing this! The marionette music starts.

Marie pops her head upright on cue. *"Hey, hey! Bye Bye…"*

To my surprise, Patrice's group knows it too. I guess I don't know what I thought. NSYNC was a big deal back in the day. We sync our dancing.

A few people behind us join in. *"Now it's time to leave and fake it alone."*

I added the change to the lyric after Joan's first lackluster sexual experience in college. Even now, it makes me laugh. Fortunately, Joan can laugh about it now too. I wonder what ever happened to that guy. Somewhere getting sexual advice, I hope. Alexander leads the way to the door. I unhook my phone from the amp, and I follow.

Just as I reach the door, I throw up an arm and sing. *"Bye, bye, bye."*

Chapter 21

Marco, Polo!

"My heart beats as much as I can breathe."

—Marco Polo

THE VAN IS WAITING FOR US as we exit the bar. We all hop in, grabbing a spot to hang onto.

"Headed to Polo on Bishopsgate," Alexander tells his assistant. His long black satin pants flow in the breeze as he joins us in the back of the van.

Polo is a 24-hour eatery that serves alcohol 24 hours a day. It has a long tufted burgundy bench that runs the length of the front dining area. A giant stuffed brown bear hangs from the wall to greet you. White subway tiles cover the seats, and old bricks cover the walls. I have never seen subway tiles arranged like that to make a bench. It's clever. I read the sign at the door. It was established in 1959. Wow! This place has been open for 60 years! I love when a business has a history.

I grab a stack of menus, following Genae and the group to the back. Genae looks over her shoulder. "Let's sit back here. There's plenty of space."

We cramp into three tables. I glance at the menu. "Hey, look! They have a burger challenge?"

"What's that about? Joan asks, looking over the menu.

"You have to eat five burgers in fifteen minutes." I open my mouth and point down my throat, making a gagging gesture. If I ate more than one burger, I'd feel miserable, not to mention five!

Marie slams her menu shut; her eyes are starting to glaze over with drunkenness. "I'm having the Traditional English breakfast."

I flip through the menu to the traditional English breakfast. "Marie, I don't think you want that; it looks pretty heavy."

Marie nods her head once, hard. No use arguing with her at this point. With her level of drunkenness, it would be fruitless for me to argue with her. It's like trying to get a seven-year into the shower; they need to shower but can't rationalize why they do.

The waitress glides up with a tray of water. "Have you had enough time to look over the menu? Do you have any questions?"

I lift my hand in the air, raising my finger. "I have a question. How many people do this hamburger challenge weekly?"

Joan knocks me with her elbow. "Just order something and stop asking questions."

"I'll just have the pancakes." I smile and hand the menu back.

"Could I get anyone anything to drink, other than water?" the waitress pulls out her notepad.

"Hot chocolate for me." I smile and look at Joan.

"Same." Joan slides her menu over.

"I'll have a hot toddy *and* the traditional English breakfast," Marie says, making her menu do the wave on the bar.

For some reason, I can't stomach the thought of beans right now. Maybe it's all the booze in my system. Maybe it's because toast with beans doesn't sound good. But Marie's order almost sends me over the edge.

Genae and Patrice are huddled together in a booth. Krystal is sitting on the long bench propped against the wall with Kitty, Julie, and Lauren stacked up, leaning one by one against each other.

The waitress finishes taking everyone's order and walks off. Patrice looks up, slurring her speech to no one in particular. "Do you think I'm doing the wrong thing? Do you think Andrew is an asshole?"

I look around to see if anyone is going to answer her. I think a second. Do I answer her or pretend that I didn't hear her? She sits up straighter, looking around this time. Alexander shrugs his shoulders at me. Joan lifts a finger to her mouth and shakes her head. Usually, I wouldn't have a problem telling someone that I think their boyfriend is an ass. But right now, I have the power to potentially ruin things. I don't want to do that, especially since I don't know Andrew all that well.

I tiptoe around it. "I think Andrew is different, and if you love him, that's all that matters. You are the only one sleeping next to him at night."

Patrice sheepishly looks down.

I put my hand under her chin. "Don't look down now. Now is the time. Either you know, or you don't. Do you love him?"

"I love him." She nods her head.

"Well, then there isn't anything else." I hear the words coming out of my mouth, but they sound like someone else's. Like someone else is talking straight to me. Love is all that matters. Everything else is not important.

The waitress returns with our drinks. I grab my drink and start sipping to prevent myself from giving any potentially ill-advised advice.

Lauren raises her hand, calling the waitress over. "Could we get a round of kamikazes over here?"

I hold my hand up to my mouth, trying not to vomit. "Please none for me. I'm at my limit."

"Plus, the three drinks I had tonight are all I want. It was more than enough." Joan holds her hand up, waving. "Skip me."

Marie begins dancing in her seat. "Yes! Bring me another! Let's dance, guys."

She stands up, grabbing my hand. "Come on MARshmellow. Come on and dance."

I don't know if Maire really wants to dance or if she's just doing it to get me out of a sticky situation. But I love her for it. She's probably had too much to drink. She rarely calls me MARshmellow. It's a nickname we came up with in elementary school. We didn't have nicknames and wanted to seem cool, so we came up with our own. Mine was MARshmellow, and hers was Peppermint Patty. Marie pulls me to my feet.

"Let's dance like we used to. Come on MARSHMELLOW!" Marie shuffles the songs on her playlist then picks one.

California Gurls begins to play. Marie grabs my hands and starts jumping around. She's contagious. We start acting out the song like we did when we were teenagers dancing in my bedroom, with Marie dreaming of living in California.

I hold out my hand for Joan. "Come on, Joan. You know you want to."

We dance on our makeshift dancefloor. Sweat, laughter, and emotions abound.

"My feet hurt!" Marie kicks off her shoes.

"Ugh! Don't do that!" I try handing Marie back her shoes. "You don't know what's on this floor!"

Marie slurs her words. "It's fine. I'm fine."

The waitress begins delivering our plates and Kamikazes. Thank God.

I motion to Marie. "Hey, Marie, your food is here."

Marie dances and twirls her way back to her seat. Getting food into Marie is a good thing at this point. As Marie's plate arrives, the sweet smell of beans floats through the air, hitting my nose. For whatever reason, the sight and smell of beans right now is too much for me. It's like the PTSD you get when you smell the alcohol that left you dying in a field when your parents had no idea where you were or that you were up to no good. That. I grab my plate and switch seats with Joan. Joan smiles and sits down. She immediately throws a hand over her mouth.

"I can't! Nope!" She stands up and runs around, looking for the bathroom.

"There, over there!" Genae points.

I follow close behind her, opening the bathroom door before she can. Joan just makes it to the toilet before she throws up what little she has in her stomach.

"Oh, jeez, Joan, Are you ok?" She's the only person in the world that could throw up in front of me and not have me blowing chunks myself.

"Oh, God, Mar." Joan lowers herself down in front of the toilet.

I pull Joan's hair around my hand, holding it firmly.

"I hate throwing up." Joan moans. "I feel so sick. I didn't even drink that much."

I raise my eyebrows. "I mean, beans and toast are not everyone's favorite."

Joan's whole body tenses as she leans over the toilet again. "Don't, don't say beans."

The back of Joan's neck begins to feel clammy. I begin waving my hand over it.

Alexander walks in. "Oh, Lawrd. Honey, you are being a shitty drunk right now." He grabs a paper towel and soaks it in the sink. "Here."

I take it and place it on the back of Joan's neck.

"She didn't drink that much." I think she may have eaten something bad earlier, or she just doesn't like the smell of the beans." I clamp a hand over my mouth, realizing I said the forbidden word —beans. Beans, the thing that shall not be named or spoken of.

"Ok, I'm done. I think. It was just like a wave of nausea. But it's gone now." Joan slowly stands up.

I hand her the wet paper towel so that she could clean herself up. She walks over to the sink and splashes water on her face. She presses her hand over her stomach. "I'm sorry. That was weird."

"Yeah, it's not like your pregnant or something." It feels surreal as the words come out of my mouth. I jerk my head hard in her direction; it feels like heaven and earth just shifted, and someone is playing with the gravity switch. "You're not pregnant, right?"

"Don't be stupid. I have an IUD. I can't be pregnant." I can see the wheels turning in Joan's head. She's counting. I know it.

"You're counting, aren't you?" I hold her by the shoulders. All the buzzing from the drinks completely drains out of me.

Alexander steps in closer. "When was your last cycle? Your last red beast?"

Joan ignores the fact that it isn't any of Alexander's business. She begins to count out loud.

"I was having my period when you were in the hospital. I remember that I was hormonal. That's why I thought I was maybe making up stuff in my head when I thought Frank was cheating. I thought I was being menstrual." Joan holds up her hand. "It's been nine-ish weeks." She says slowly. Thinking about each word, making sure she's correct. "Holy shit!! It's been nine weeks! I've been so busy with the divorce I haven't even thought about my period!"

I lean against the sink. "OK, let's not jump to conclusions. You've stressed out. Periods do weird things when you are under stress."

"We'll just stop by The Convenience store, no biggie," Alexander says with a wave.

No biggie? Joan could be pregnant, and I'm a world away. That's a very big deal! He has no idea.

I grab Joan by the hands. "OK, Let's go, Joan. We shouldn't worry about it until we know. And even then, we shouldn't worry about it."

Joan's whole demeanor changes. She's walking slower, more deliberate. "I was drinking tonight!"

"Let's not even cross that bridge. I bet a ton of women have had plenty to drink before they knew they were pregnant. Come on, don't melt down on me now. You don't even know if you are." As I get back to the table, I tap Marie on the shoulder. "Hey, we have to go."

Marie stands up mid bite. Despite her buzz, she knows in the tone of my voice that it's a no-questions-asked situation.

Patrice hands the waitress her credit card. One by one, the girls pluck themselves out of their seats and head back out to the van. As soon as the van doors shut, I start rallying people.

"OK, people, we are all women here. We've all been in the situation or have known someone in this situation. Joan has missed her period, and we need to get a test. Everyone circles around me like we are about to deploy on a secret mission out of the back of our minivan paratrooper style.

Alexander opens the door to the van and steps in. "OK, we are headed to The Convenient store. Get into your places. Places everybody, places."

We all line up, holding onto the racks above us.

"I'll jump out and get the pregnancy test. You meet me in the bathroom." I nod my chin in the air at her, waiting for her to agree.

"Let me do it! I never get to do stuff like this." Patrice chimes in.

I make a mental note; we need to get Patrice out more.

"OK, you get the test and meet us in the bathroom." I point to Patrice.

The van comes to a stop. Alexander opens the door and peeks out. "OK, no paps. We're clear."

Joan and I make a beeline to the restroom. While Patrice casually walks into the store.

Joan and I hunker down in the accessible stall and wait. The seconds feel like hours.

"What's taking her so long?" the anxiety in Joan's voice has me pacing and circling in the tiny stall.

"I don't know, but I'll go check. I'll be back." I squeeze Joan's hand.

I open the bathroom door. I glance around and see Patrice standing in line to pay. Three men with cameras begin snapping pictures. I speed walk over to Patrice as she throws her hand with the test in the air, shielding her eyes from the flashes.

I leap over to Patrice and grab it. "Nothing to see here. It's mine. Go!"

Well, that was as believable as Santa Claus is to a seventeen-year-old. I pay and shove the test into my bag.

I drag Patrice towards the bathroom as the paparazzi follow us. I close the door tight behind us. To my surprise, everyone from the van is now quietly standing in the bathroom.

"Hey," I whisper. Hey, Joan."

Alexander presses his body against the bathroom door as I step into the bathroom stall.

Joan sits on the toilet. She takes a long and very deliberate deep breath. "What if I'm pregnant, Mar? I can't do this alone."

I grab both of her hands tight. "You aren't alone. You have Will. You have mom and dad, and you have *me*. You'll always have me."

I unwrap the test and hand it to her. I squat down against the wall as Joan uses it.

"How long do we have to wait?" Joan asks, standing up and holding the stick securely in her hand.

I read the back of the box. "It says two minutes. Two lines means you're pregnant. One line means you're not, and three lines means you're having a zebra."

I yell out, "Someone start a two-minute timer."

Joan blows out her breath and laughs. "You're so stupid."

I shrug my shoulders. "There's nothing you can do about it." I pull her in for a hug. "Joan, if you're pregnant, I'll be there. It's not like you're a kid anymore."

Someone's phone goes off. "OK, it's been two minutes."

I pull Joan back to look her in the eyes. "Do you want me to look, or do you want to?"

"You look." She nudges me.

She squeezes her eyes shut and hands me the stick. "There will never be another time will I ever be comfortable holding something you peed on. I'm just saying."

Joan bumps me. I hold the stick up to look at it. Two very pink lines...

Chapter 22

Two Pink Lines

"People who say they sleep like a baby usually don't have one."

—Leo J. Burke

My legs go wobbly. "Joan- YOU-ARE-PREGNANT!" I sound like Maury Povich. Will YOU-ARE-THE-FATHER! Or even better…Luke, I-am-your-father…I can't control myself.

Joan reaches up and holds my hand. I turn the test over to show her.

"I'm pregnant! Oh my God!" she wraps her arms around me, squeezing me tighter.

"You're pregnant!" I yell; I pull her up and down in my arms, forcing her to jump with me. "I'm going to be an aunt! Is this a good thing? Are you excited?"

Joan doesn't say a word. She just shakes her head up and down, then yells. "I'm gonna be a mom!"

My smile is a permanent toothy grin across my face. "You're gonna be a mom!"

I open the bathroom stall. Everyone floods in and surrounds Joan, hugging her.

"Now what? Are you going to tell Will? Of course, you are going to tell Will." I beam at Joan. I look at her in a different light. I can't explain it, but she looks different. She's glowing; maybe that's just a figment of my imagination. "Are you ready for this?"

"I'm ready." She looks around. "Please, don't say anything. I want to tell Will."

I point my finger around the circle in silent warning. Each person raises their hands, agreeing to be silent. I feel like screaming from the rooftops, but I know this is Joan's to tell.

As we open the door to the bathroom, a sea of flashes illuminates the already very bright fluorescent lights of the convenient store. Alexander tucks Patrice under his arm as we dash the van.

"Marguerite, are you pregnant with Thomas Blaine's baby? Does he know? Is Lady Patrice pregnant? What's the story?" a cameraman shouts.

I look up, alarmed. Crap, he thinks I'm pregnant! How did all of this become so complicated? I wave my hand in the air. "No comment."

The last light from the flashes creeps through as Alexander shuts the van doors. We scream. The sound in the van goes into a flutter of chatter and happiness as it pulls away. I catch Joan's eye and smile at her.

My heart feels as big as it's ever been as I reach out for Joan's, squeezing it three times and shaking my head. "I'm so happy."

Joan smiles. "Me too! Now I have to figure out a good way to tell Will."

"Do you think he will be happy or freaked out?" I wait for Joan's answer, quietly judging Will even though he isn't even here or doesn't know anything about the test. After Frank, he will always be under my very watchful eye. It doesn't mean I don't like him.

"I think he will be thrilled. We've talked about how he wants a big family. It's something he missed as a kid, especially after losing his parents." Joan's face relaxes.

I laugh, "I guess there's gonna be a shotgun wedding! I've always wanted to go to a shotgun wedding."

"No, I don't want to get married. Will and I have talked about it; he knows. I don't want to do the next thing or what everyone thinks I should do. I want to do what I want to do. I'm not living for anyone else but myself. Well, myself and this nugget." Joan points to her stomach.

"No shotgun wedding then. Just you and the baby. You're a strong independent woman." I say, swinging my fist in front of myself and holding my arm flexed like Rosie the Riveter.

We drop Patrice and her friends back at the Luggage Room.

"See you, darling," Alexander says as Patrice's friends get out of the van.

Patrice hands Dustine her number. "Please say you will come and do that dance and a few fun songs. You know, change it up a little."

Dustine smiles and nods her head. "It would be my pleasure."

We step out of the van. And form a circle like we are huddling up for the big play.

"Friends forever. Strong women." We chant, bouncing up and down. "Strong women do what they please. *We* do what we please."

We break and aggressively, high-fiving each other.

"See ya!"

Alexander gives his assistant my address. We hop back into the back of the van. The night, the booze, and the enormity of the news leave us deflated.

As we pull up to the front of the flat, I hold out my hand to help Joan out of the van. I can tell I'm going to be that kind of aunt. I kiss Alexander on the cheek. "Thanks for everything tonight. I'll call you."

Marie blows Alexander air kisses.

We quietly unlock the door and sneak into the bedroom. Mom and dad must be fast asleep. I throw myself on the bed.

"Someone shower, then I'll go." I'm trying to buy enough time to take a short nap.

Marie sits on the end of the bed then slides down onto the floor. She leans over and lays flat on her back. "I don't feel good. I'll go after MARshmellow."

I hang my foot off the bed, resting it on Marie's knee.

Joan walks into the bathroom and turns on the shower. "I'll go."

I close my eyes and doze off.

"Hey, stupid, I'm done. It's your turn." Joan pulls on the clothes she had on earlier.

She left the water running so that I could just jump in—a big no-no for my water-saving mom. I get in and sit on the floor of the shower. I haphazardly put shampoo in my hair; I'm so tired I scrub my face clean with Thomas' bar soap. I rinse my hair out and wrap it in a towel. I'll brush it out tomorrow.

Joan has set out my pajamas. I tuck them under my arm as I squat down to Marie. "Your turn."

Marie turns over on all fours and crawls into the bathroom.

"You OK? Here let me help you." I step over Marie and pull her dress over her head. Get in."

Marie crawls over the tub into the shower and sits under the showerhead. I scrub her hair then condition it. "You had a good time tonight." I make small talk with Marie. She isn't talking back, but I know she's listening. "You should have stopped at the bar." I laugh.

Marie nods her head.

"And those beans…ugh…." I wring Marie's hair out and reach for a towel.

Marie begins to gag.

"Oh, man, don't do it!" I hold an arm over my mouth, counting my breaths, focusing on the sound of my breathing instead of Marie's gagging.

Marie bends forward and throws up on the floor of the shower. It was all she wrote. I lean over and involuntarily start to forcefully gag. I squat down and put my head over the toilet and barf.

"What the hell is going on in here?" Joan opens the bathroom door wide.

Without another word, Joan bents over the sink, emptying out the remains of her stomach. It's like a bad chain link reaction that no one can stop.

Joan begins to run the water in the sink, washing her bile down. She reaches over and turns the shower back on Marie. "The sink is clean. Wash your face." She taps me on the shoulder.

I stand, trying to compose myself. I gag a couple of more times before I get myself clean.

"Here, help me with Marie," Joan says.

We lift Marie as I put Thomas' robe around her.

"Here." I hand Marie the mouthwash. "Here, swig this."

Joan and I sit on the couch in silence. We are talking, not talking.

Marie comes in and sits next to me. "I feel so much better after I threw up. I think I had food poisoning."

I roll my eyes at her. "More like alcohol poisoning."

Joan won't even look at us. None of us can chance it.

We doze off hard before Marie's snoring wakes me.

I tap Joan. "What time is it?"

"I don't know; check your watch." Joan scoots up on the couch. In her sleep, she has slid down.

Chapter 23

The Thames

I CHECK THE TIME ON MY WATCH and stare out the window. It's just past 3 a.m. when I see a black town car pull up in front of the flat. Thomas steps out of the car, pauses then turns back to the car. He leans his arm on top of the roof of it. I press my face closer to the glass. An arm reaches out of the car and pushes Thomas. Thomas stumbles backward, then readjusting his stance.

"Come on, Mate. Don't do this." Thomas crosses his arms and steps back further as Andrew steps out of the car.

I whisper to Joan and Marie. "Get over here quick —hurry come here!"

They hop off the couch and open the curtain to look out.

"I think Andrew is drunk." I reach down and crack open the window so I can hear.

"All night, you have been going on and on about that American girl." Andrew slurs his words. "And now she's pregnant! Tell. Me, that's why you're marrying her! You don't know her!"

"Hey, hey. Stop!" Will puts a flat hand against Andrew's chest.

"What? Mar isn't pregnant! Mate, don't test me. You very well know her name, and she's my fiancé, not just some random girl I am hooking up with." Thomas puts his hand on Andrew's shoulders.

"She is pregnant. The paparazzi got pictures of her tonight holding a pregnancy test. You don't know her as well as you think you do!" Andrew stumbles towards Thomas.

I can't tell if Thomas is holding Andrew up or pushing him back as a woman steps out of the car. I can't believe my eyes. I blink a few times, trying to clear my vision. I open the curtain wider. Could it be? I angrily press my mouth into a tight line. What the hell? It's Sophie! What's she doing with them? I thought this was a boy's night. I fight the urge to kick the door open John Wayne style and start Kung Fu Fighting.

"You know, Mate, you've become a royal wanker since you started dating that girl." Andrew pushes his finger into Thomas' chest.

Thomas furrows his brow. "Me? I've become *the* wanker? This isn't Uni. You aren't going to just get away with things. At some point, people aren't going to care who you are. We can't be together all the time. I have a job, a fiancée, a life. I am super confused why you are so mad right now. What's going on here?"

Andrew shoves Thomas, tipping him off balance. Thomas falls backward and lands on the sidewalk, ripping his pants. To my surprise, he bounces back up like his butt is made of rubber.

"No, no. Stop!" Will's voice elevates.

Before I know it, Thomas' right fist connects with Andrew's right eye. Andrew staggers backward. He then reaches up and clocks Thomas upwards under his chin. Bone on bone solid contact. I cringe. Thomas' chin begins to dribble blood down his neck. Andrew's eye is swelling shut. Thomas grabs Andrew by the shoulders and forcefully pushes him back. Will runs his hands through his hair. Stopping them at this point is futile. The damage is done.

Will seizes Andrew hard by the arms and swings him towards the car. Sophie walks towards Andrew and guides him back to the car.

He spins around her and stands right in front of Thomas again. "Bloody hell! You serious *wanker*, you've given me a black eye on my wedding week." Andrew reaches up and feels his eye socket with the tips of his fingers.

"Move back, Mate. I don't want to give you a matching one on the other side. You've had too much to drink, and you're sauced." Thomas bends to look Andrew in the eyes, making sure he understands the severity of the situation.

Will grabs Andrew's shirt, shoving him. "Go home. This isn't good for anyone."

In an effort to get away from the situation, Thomas turns towards the flat. Joan, Marie, and I duck down, quickly, Army crawling into the bedroom. I hear the mechanism in the front door click. We are holding our breath when Thomas walks into the bedroom. The blood on his chin is splintering into a dark red line. Marie and Joan shuffle past Thomas into the living room.

Thomas wraps his arms around my waist. "M, are you pregnant?"

Thomas' arms radiate warmth, love, safety. "M, if you are, then that's wonderful! That's wonderful news!"

I put my hands on his arm, then pull them away to look at him. "No, I'm not pregnant. It isn't my secret to tell. You have to trust me on this one."

"OK. I trust you. If you can't tell me then, I'll wait." Thomas sits on the bed.

I meet Thomas' eyes. "I saw everything. I was watching." I walk to the bathroom to grab a warm wet washcloth to clean his chin. "What in the world? First, why was Sophie there? Second, good for you for punching Andrew; he deserved it."

Thomas raises his hands in defense. "Before you get crossed, let me explain." He falls back into the bed. "Ah, M. It was horrible. Andrew was acting crazy. He threw my phone in the Thames, then Will's phone died, and some hookers showed up. I don't know if they were part of the party or if they just thought it was easy money because we were having a Rooster party. Then somehow Sophie showed up while I was trying to figure out how I was going to reach you, get home or do anything without my phone." Thomas begins to talk faster, pulling at the front of his hair. Something he does when he is frustrated. "Andrew insisted Sophie ride with us. I didn't have a choice. He was being completely disrespectful, so I socked him in the eye. Will tried to get him to calm down by holding him back; then, I punched him in the eye. We'll be good, though; guys are like that. It just takes a good sock in the eye sometimes to set a friend straight."

I sit on the bed next to him. "I saw all that. Is he really a friend if you have to hit him to set him straight?" I fiddle with the comforter underneath him. "He doesn't like me much."

"The thing about Andrew is that he is used to getting his way. He doesn't like to be second to anyone. Which is strange because he's Gregory's best friend." Thomas sits up in bed. The cut on his chin is turning purple.

"Was Gregory there tonight?" I tighten my grip around the washcloth I'm holding in my hand. "I just don't understand how you ended up stuck in a car with Sophie, especially with all the drama she caused."

"I'm not sure how or why she was even with us. I think she was trying to be with Andrew." Thomas leans into me, wrapping his arms around me. "I'm just glad to be home."

"OK, I can't say I understand all of this, but I trust you. We had a great night. We rode in the back of Alexander's van. It didn't have seats. We had to hang on like we were riding the subway. We sang karaoke." I giggle at the memory.

Thomas shoots upright, rubbing his eyes. "That's right; I was trying to call you! The paparazzi were posting pictures in real-time. My agent alerted me. That was until Andrew threw my phone into the river! I saw you guys hopping into a black van. I swear you are going to be the death of me." Thomas grits his teeth together, accentuating the muscles in his jaw. "He very rightly deserved that sock on the cheek."

I smile at the way Thomas talks. I put a soft finger on his bottom lip. "He very rightly did, did he?"

He laughs. "I want to stay here and just snuggle, but it isn't proper. Plus, Joan, Marie, and Will can't share a couch."

"I think they are taking a cab back to the hotel." I slide my hand down his arm as he stands.

"Even so. It's bad enough that I've been fighting. I don't want to disrespect your parents even more." Thomas kisses me on the forehead. "Until tomorrow."

I smirk at Thomas. "I know something that will make you feel better."

"M, we can't. Your parents are in the next room." Thomas gestures towards the door.

"Flip off the light. We can be very quiet." I begin unsnapping his pants and slowly pulling them down. I put my finger up to my lips. "Ssshhh… just be quiet."

My mouth is an inch away from his. I can feel his hot breath blowing against my lips. I graze my lips over his. "Lean back."

My teeth skim his neck, he shivers. "You are driving me crazy."

I push him down on the bed and slowly straddle him. Thomas takes in a deep breath; his eyes roll backward.

A smile stretches across my face. "Am I?" I giggle.

Thomas grabs my hips and rocks them back and forth in place. "M, you are an insatiable little minx."

Sweat begins to crawl down my stomach. "I know."

My toes curls as Thomas pulls me to him hard. A low growl comes from his throat as I collapse onto his chest. Thomas crumples into me. We lay silent for a long minute.

Thomas scoots to the end of the bed.

"Stay..." I reach for his thigh as he quietly slips out of bed.

"You know I want to, but I don't want to be even more disrespectful," Thomas says, pulling on his pajamas and slipping out of the room.

Just as Thomas slips out of our bedroom, my phone dings. It's Joan.

Black nanny car. RGE 1226, male, mid-forties —Charles. We took a cab back to the hotel. We'll see you for breakfast. Don't be too hard on him. He looked rough.

I quickly text back.

All is good. Andrew is an ass. See you in the morning. Text me when you get there. Are you going to tell him?

Joan texted back.

Yes, I just want it to be kind of special. I don't know. Let's talk tomorrow.

I text back.

Copy that Mama Bear...

I drop the phone at my side and roll myself in the comforter. Now what? Do we still go to the wedding? Is it something we can miss, especially if Thomas is in it? I'd never ask him to miss a wedding because his friend got drunk and said some not-so-nice things.

I reach over and turn off the lamp. Lying still, I restlessly stare up at the ceiling. My mind can't shut off. I begin listing every aphorism type phrase I can think of, trying to console myself. You never live in a bubble. No one does. Some things aren't like you expect. You take the good with the bad. Eat to live; don't live to eat. A barking dog never bites. God, I can't control myself. My brain is on autopilot. East or west, home is the best. That one hits me hard. Just go to sleep, Mar. You are overthinking, and this isn't helping. You're making it worse.

The alarm on my phone startles me awake. I'm tightly wrapped like a burrito. I wiggle to get my hand free to grab it. I try to focus on the time. It's seven a.m. UGH…God, why did I set my alarm for seven a.m.? Riddle me that Universe. Why must I push my limits? I roll my head back into the pillow and wrap it around my face. I stomp the bed. Fine, I'll get up, but I won't like it. I drag myself to the bathroom. I glance in the mirror. My mascara is smudged all under my eyes. I look like The Grumpy cat from a few years ago. How in the world was Thomas even attracted to that? That's next level. We are still on the don't come into the bathroom; I don't poop level.

I turn on the shower and step in. Popping open the shampoo, I pour some in my hair, twirl it around and stand frozen in blankness under the running water. The kind of blankness that when you come back, you have no idea where you've been or how long you have been there. And you've gotten absolutely nothing accomplished. The shampoo has been completely rinsed out of my hair. I reapply, this time being more deliberate. Coffee will do me good; four hours of sleep is not enough. I'm *an eight hours a night* kind of girl.

As I step out of the shower, the smell of dad's coffee has crept its way into the bathroom. Funny how you don't notice any smells before you get into the shower, but you can smell everything when you step out. I don't know why that happens. Is it because I showered, that it cleared my nose, and now I can smell, or is it that I'm just not awake enough to notice anything? Universal questions, whatever the answer is, I won't solve it now. My mouth starts to salivate when I get a whiff of the freshly made tortillas. I throw on a t-shirt dress and walk out into the living room.

Joan, Marie, Will, and my parents are all gathered around in the kitchen. Thomas is still knocked out on the couch. I grab his ankle as I walk by and shake it. I swear that man could sleep through anything.

Mom kisses me on the cheek as I steal a tortilla from the stack and roll it into a tight spiral. I take a bite of it. It's like taking that first sip of coffee for coffee lovers. It hits your soul and sucks you back in time to sitting around my grandma's table patiently waiting for the plate of refried beans and fresh tortillas. Thomas sits up from the couch. His chin has a dark line on it with a deep purple bruise.

Mom rounds the kitchen counter and heads straight for Thomas. She sits on the couch next to him. His hair is standing straight up.

I walk by and tap it. "Floof."

Thomas reaches up and tries to flatten it down. It isn't working; in fact, it's just making it worse.

"What happened, Mojito?" mom soothingly touches his chin. "Did you get into a fight?"

I can tell that Thomas is hesitant to tell mom, but he does. "I did get into a rumpus of sorts last night with Andrew. He was a bit out of sorts in his thinking, so I had to set him straight, that's all."

Dad stands up and leans against the couch, holding his cup of coffee. "What was the fight about?"

Thomas waves his hand in the air to lessen the enormity of it. "He kept calling Mar *that American girl,*" and I wasn't having it. He was drunk and out of line."

Dad calculatingly sips his coffee, holding eye contact with Thomas. "Alright then. It was warranted. And he is good now?"

"Yes, sir. He will not be disrespectful to Mar again." Thomas reaches up for my hand. "I promise I will never let anyone harm or disrespect her. You have my word."

Dad nods his head. "Good, son. Good."

Chapter 24

The Bruja Always Knows

"Keep the flowers; buy me tacos."

—ANONYMOUS

BREAKING THE TENSION, Joan interrupts. "Oh, I forgot, I brought you something." Joan lifts the bag from the ground next to her feet. "Here."

I take it from her and reach inside. I immediately get a lump in my throat, and I bite my lip to keep from crying, but tears spill over my bottom lashes before I can stop them. "You got me a Dirty Scrabble board? Thank You! It's only the best gift ever!"

Joan takes it from me. "Here, you can keep it on your coffee table. Just like you and Marie do." Joan begins setting it up. "I just bought one also. We can Facetime our Dirty Scrabble games."

My bottom lip pokes out. "Guys…"

Marie stands and wraps her arms around me. She imitates Humphrey Bogart. "We'll always have Dirty Scrabble."

I laugh, "You mean, Will always have Paris?"

Marie shakes her head, "That too!"

Joan digs around, looking for just the right Scrabble pieces. She pulls out the tiles one by one and carefully places a word. D*I*C*K*L*I*C*I*O*U*S

Thomas' eyes widen.

Mom laughs. "Cabra tonta —you silly goat!"

Dad just shakes his head. He walks back into the kitchen and begins digging through the cupboards. That's the thing with dad, he means no harm, but if you give him permission, he will make himself completely at home.

I skip over. "Hey, what are you looking for, pops?"

"The coffee, we ran out." Dad continues to open one cupboard after the other.

Thomas pops up from the couch. "Here, Sir. I have another bag right here." He reaches in the cupboard above dad's head. "I'll make you some." Thomas begins pouring beans into the hopper. "Who wants another cup?"

"Me." Will raises his hand.

"—guess I'll take another." Joan holds up her empty cup.

I glance at Joan. I am sending telepathic hesitations about caffeine to her. She turns, ignoring my attempt at communication.

"How about you, Mum? Do you fancy a cup of coffee?" Thomas sweetly asks.

Mom waves her hands in front of her. "No, no. I've never had coffee. I don't think I'll like it."

Joan's head shoots up. "Mom, you've had coffee! I know for a fact you have. Mar and I went to Starbucks and asked if you wanted some; you said no but then took Mar's when we got back."

"No, I don't remember that. I haven't coffee because I know I don't like it." Mom says.

Joan rolls her eyes.

"Oh, young lady, you'll have to try it. If I make you a cup, will you try it?" Thomas bats his eyelashes at mom. "For me?"

"Oh, fine. I'll try it." Mom blows out her breath like she's exhausted with the whole conversation.

Thomas happily pushes the button on the coffee maker. He pours mom the first cup. "OK, do you want anything in it? Like milk, cream, or sugar? Or milk, cream, and sugar?"

"No! Nonsense. I'll take it like that." Mom holds out her hand for the cup.

We all stare in anticipation. Black coffee for a first-time coffee drinker is not a good idea. Hell, black coffee for anybody is a horrible idea. Unless, of course, you're John Wayne or lack tastebuds. Either way, mom is neither. It's almost like when you're in college, and everyone convinces you that beer is the thing. That it's something amazing and that it tastes so good. Then you taste it, and beer is *not* the thing. It's gross matter of fact. And you can't see how anyone could choose this as an option. It's only until much later that you like it. And even then, I'm not quite sure how it happens, but it does. Maybe your tastebuds change; maybe you try it so many times that you eventually like it.

Mom cautiously lifts the cup to her mouth and takes a sip. "You son of a bitch! This is poison! You poisoned me! What are you trying to do, kill me?"

I laugh at her involuntary cursing. It's like burning your hand on the tortilla skillet. You spit out a line of every curse word you know, including all of the Spanish curse words you know for added flavor.

Thomas looks at me, shocked. "It's only coffee! I promise. It's only coffee!"

"Don't worry. It's only Joan that poisons people. Eh, am I right, Joan?" I wink at Joan. "You should have had it with cream and sugar, mom. It's too strong, black —crazy woman."

"No, never again. I don't know how anyone can drink this." She hands the cup back to Thomas. "Thank you, but no."

Thomas pours the coffee out into the sink and rinses out the cup.

Will smiles, relieved it wasn't him that gave mom her first cup of coffee. "So, what's on the agenda today?"

Thomas looks at his watch. "Well, we can go for breakfast, then we will have to start getting ready for the wedding after that. I have a team coming to help."

Will has been a fly on the wall this whole trip. I guess because the entire purpose of this trip was for my parents to meet Thomas. He is completely flying under the radar. He's like the dress fluffer at the Oscars. You know they are there, but they work unnoticed.

"How about this —how about I make breakfast, and we just hang out for a bit before we have to get ready. I don't know what that entails, but I can imagine quite a bit since your friend is who he is." Will says, waiting for Thomas' answer.

"He is, but it isn't anything like a royal wedding you've seen on television. It's more relaxed, a lot less formal. It's not televised or anything like that." Thomas leans on the back of the couch with his arms over his chest.

Will begins looking through the fridge, surveying the produce. The fridge is completely full since we knew mom and dad were coming. I feel confident that he will find what he needs.

He begins pulling out the cardboard container that stores the eggs. "Do you have a sieve?"

Thomas looks puzzled.

Will makes a circular motion with his hands. "It's like a strainer or a flour sifter."

Thomas holds up his silver spaghetti strainer. "Will this do?"

"It will have to." Will takes it from Thomas and sets it on the counter.

Will begins chopping and dicing vegetables with ease. I watch in a wondered trance. If I tried dicing things like that, I'd chop my fingers off. Thomas makes a motion that he is headed to the bathroom to brush his teeth. I give him a slight nod.

Joan hops up. "Is there something I can help with?"

Will hands Joan the butter. "You can chip this."

Joan takes the butter and begins slicing off pieces. I can tell she's feeling nauseous.

"Hey, I love slicing butter. Let me do it." I guess I've been weird for so long; no one flinches at my odd request.

Joan hands me the knife and whispers. "Thank you."

Will cracks all the eggs and strains them through the sieve into a bowl. He throws the chopped vegetables into a pan to sauté them. After cooking a bit, he gently tosses in the eggs and sliced butter. He expertly flips the eggs in half, making a large omelet.

Joan starts running the bread through the toaster. She starts taking small bites out of the first slice. She and Will work like a very well-oiled machine. Will cuts the omelet into seven pieces. He artfully places them on a plate. He then takes the toast and slices it, stacking it into a toast tower. Don't get me wrong, how well you make a dish is a lot of it, but the presentation makes all the difference.

Will pulls out a stool for Joan. He scoots her in and casually stands behind her. Mom is circling Joan. Then she points right at her. Crap, she knows.

She speaks in Spanish so that we are the only ones that understand. "Estas embarazada chica! —You're pregnant, girl!

Joan looks at mom; then mom looks at me. I look down to avoid her eye contact.

Thomas walks out of the bedroom and puts a hand to his chest. "Ah, mate, that smells divine."

Thank God for Thomas. He obliviously walked in and interrupted our invisible conversation.

Will waves Thomas off. "It was easy."

Thomas grabs his plate and leans against the counter.

I spoon eggs into my mouth and begin tapping my spoon on my plate —thinking. "So, we can take our time eating. Did everyone bring what they need, or does anyone need to run back to the hotel?"

Marie looks up from her cross-legged position at the counter. "I brought everything I could think of. I hope my outfit is ok." She points to the giant suitcase by the door.

Joan screws up her face. "I think I have it all. Everything except the dress."

Will points to the hanging bag next to Marie's luggage. "I have everything."

I finish my plate and begin taking dishes to the sink. I rinse as Joan stacks them strategically in the dishwasher. You could cut the tension with a knife, or maybe I'm the only one that feels that way.

"I feel so full." Marie waddles to the couch to sit next to Thomas. She falls asleep.

I guess last night took it out of her—a flashback of her throwing up in the bathroom flashes in my head. I squeeze my eyes tight to block out the image. Thomas leans his head back, resting it on the back of the couch. He folds his hands in his lap and gently falls asleep next to Marie.

I dry my hands on a kitchen towel. Mom and dad exit the living room and head back to their room without saying a word. Will sits down on a chair in the living room and curls in. Going out the night before a big event should be outlawed. We are all wiped and too proud to say it. I nod to Joan; she follows me to the bedroom.

I crawl in bed and lay flat on my face. Joan joins me, forcing me to be the little spoon.

I whisper. "That was freaking close. What the hell? How in the heck did mom figure that out?"

Joan laughs, "She's related to Grandma witch; what did you expect?"

"Have you figured out how you are going to tell Will?" I turn to face Joan.

"I figure I'll just carry around the stick, and when I feel the time is right, I'll tell him." Joan closes her eyes.

"Gross, but I guess that's as good of a plan as any." I close my eyes and doze off with her.

Chapter 25

Royal Mess

"Don't stop me now, cuz I'm having a good time."

—Queen

Thomas shakes me awake. "Love, wake up. Alexander is here with the dresses. And the rest of the team is in the living room."

I sit up groggily. "Oh, man. How long did we sleep?"

Thomas looks at his watch. "At least a couple of hours."

Joan turns over and sits up. She has a crusty circle next to the corner of her mouth. Ugh, she must have been just as tired as I was, and she's pregnant. I can't even imagine.

Without opening her eyes, she murmurs. "Do we need to get up now?" She sounds like she did when we were young, and she wanted to sleep in.

I pinch her. "Yes, we need to get up."

Alexander walks into the bedroom and slaps Joan on the butt. "Get up! Princesses can't be late to the ball."

"Ugh…princesses need their beauty sleep." Joan pushes her face into the pillow.

I laugh. "No amount of sleep is going to make you Sleeping Beauty. Get up, cow."

Joan lifts her leg and kicks me. I laugh and slap her foot away.

I walk into the living room. It has turned into a pre-Oscar makeup, design, and wardrobe backstage event.

Mom is sitting at the counter getting her nails done while another person is setting her hair.

A manicurist is trying her best to snip dad's nails and run a file over them. He is narrowing his eyes at her while snatching his hand back. I give her an *I'm sorry* look as she makes eye contact with me. I look at dad, giving him a deadpan look, then I frown. He shrugs his shoulders, reluctantly giving his hand back to her.

Marie is still sitting on the couch, absorbing it all. "Get up, sweetheart." Alexander hands Marie a couple of dresses. "Try these on."

"But I brought a dress." Marie holds the dresses looking confused.

Alexander waves his hand in the air. "Oh, aren't you cute? Yes, but it isn't one of mine. In which case, it isn't good enough."

Marie's eyebrows shoot up. "How do you even know my size?"

Alexander looks at Marie like she's just grown a second head. "Oh, dear. You can't be in this business if you can't sight measure. You're an eight. Your shoe is and eight also. Now go."

Marie walks towards the bathroom, holding the dresses off the ground.

"Come out after you get the first one on," Alexander yells after her.

A lady comes around the coffee table and grabs me by the hand. "Ok, I'm your stylist for today. Let me see your nails." She looks at my fingernails. "No, Marco, you'll have to come and do a nude nail on her."

A small man holding a black case sits down in front of me. He begins working on my nails. Someone else shoves a barstool under me.

Marie comes out of the bedroom. She twirls around, letting the dress fan out in all directions.

"Ok, go back in and put the other one on." Alexander shoos her back into the room.

Marco is sitting on a box, working on my fingernails, when another similar man joins him to look at my feet. My head begins to swirl. I feel like I can't catch my breath. I try to calm myself and take in a deep breath. I can't. I'm trying hard not to panic. I try again. I can't. I stand up in alarm.

Thomas runs over. "M, what's wrong?"

"I can't catch my breath." I can hear the panic in my own voice as I push out the words.

I try to rationalize with myself. I can talk, so I am breathing. Calm down, Mar. You *are* ok. Why is it so loud in here? Why am I so hot?

"Hey, hey, hey! M look at me. Just calm down. Follow me. Breath in with me. Ready?" Thomas begins slowly breathing in until his lungs are completely full. I do the same.

"Ok, we are going to do it again. Ready?" He holds my hands, taking in a slow, measured breath. One, two, three, four—

I smile, and a small tear pricks my eye. "I'm ok." I lean my forehead on his chest.

He raises his hands, lifting my head to his. He presses his forehead to mine. He puts a hand on each side of our eyes, blocking everyone else out. "It's only us, only right now."

I swallow hard and nod my head. "Only us, only now."

My mom catches my eye. A look of concern is etched on her face. Did I just have some sort of panic attack? A hush goes over the living room.

I lift my hand. "I'm ok. I think I may have gotten overwhelmed and a little too hot." I smile nervously, thinking of the real fear I had from not being able to breathe. I've never had that before. I continue to take slow, methodical breaths without calling any more attention to myself.

Joan presses her hand in mine and squeezes it three times. It sends a warm feeling that whirls around my chest. Some people talk about finding your soulmate in life. Joan is mine. Your soulmate doesn't have to be your lover or partner. Your soulmate is just your person. Your ride or die. The person who will help bury a body, no questions asked. I give Joan a small smile and get back to prep.

"I'm Maria." She begins pulling at my hair as she brushes it. "I'm going to do an updo."

I feel pulled into all different directions. I gently close my eyes and think about the first time I saw Thomas standing over me in the pasture. The grass mark on my head and the tiny goat chewing my pants. Him singing at the piano. Life seemed so much simpler back then before we added our real lives into the mix, before we had to make sacrifices to be together—before friends and compromises. Before getting on a plane and flying halfway across the world. I stare at the wall, daydreaming. It's been a lot to take in—the paparazzi, the new house, the car, the new life —here. Maria is putting the last pin in my hair before spraying it.

She swivels me around to face another woman who is standing by a rolling case. "I'm Kelly. I'm doing your makeup."

I look wide-eyed at Joan. Mom instilled in us at an early age to never use someone else's makeup that we'd somehow end up with pink eye or something.

"Oh, no. No, thank you. I can do my makeup." I say.

Kelly scrunches up her face. "No, no, this is a different kind of makeup. It's made for the cameras. The lights. It's so you won't look washed out."

She sees my hesitation. "Everything is clean. You aren't sharing dirty brushes with anyone. I clean all my stuff in between clients."

I shake my head. I better not look crazy. "I'll let you do this, but just don't make me look like a clown or a hooker or a clown hooker."

I'm serious, and she knows it.

"Ok, gotcha. Don't make you look like a clown, hooker, or clown hooker." She laughs.

I catch Thomas staring at me from the other side of the room. I can't tell if he is staring because he thinks I'm the most beautiful girl in the world or the craziest. I'm going with the most beautiful girl in the world, based on his previous conversations and actions.

I give him a little wave and a hardy wink. I pull a silly face. He shakes his head and goofily smiles back at me.

Marie comes out of the bedroom wearing her second dress.

"Oh, Darling. That's the one. Pull it off and come get your hair done." Alexander gestures Marie back into the room.

I'm sitting in a robe on the couch as Marie takes my spot on the stool. Marcos begins looking at her cuticles. These are good. One by one, as people are done, they find various seats on the couch to wait.

"Come get your dress on." Alexander gestures me to the bedroom. I slip it on as Alexander straightens it. "You look absolutely perfect, Mar," Alexander says as he steps back to give me a once over.

Thomas walks over and slides my engagement ring on my freshly manicured hand. "You don't want to forget this, darling."

I smile. "Never."

Joan and Marie sit rigidly on the couch in their new dresses. Dad is walking around, bending up and down at the waist.

"We have two cars coming. Your mom and dad will ride with us. Joan, Will, and Marie will ride in the other car." Thomas says, looking out the window. "They're here. Shall we?"

I gather my gown and slowly shimmy to the door.

"Oh, no darling —here." Alexander slips a gold bracelet onto my wrist and then clips a tiny ring to it sewn into the bottom of the dress.

Huh, that's clever.

"This holds up your dress without you having to hold it. It's super handy when you are dancing." He does the same to Joan and Mom.

"Thank you." I kiss him on the cheek.

"Don't forget to tell them who you are wearing if they ask." Alexander makes kissy noises all around my face, careful not to touch my makeup.

Chapter 26

Royal Wedding

"When I saw you, I fell in love, and you smiled because you knew."

—William Shakespeare

I NERVOUSLY PRESS MY KNEES TOGETHER as we ride in the stop-and-go traffic. We ride through Notting Hill and travel along the Thames River. The neighborhoods are crammed full of row houses with thick moss-lined roofs. Homes with rock fences are dotted along the drive. It is speckled with homes with rock fences. We follow the line of cars to a red brick fence. There's a pea gravel driveway leading up to the castle. It is buried under a heavy royal blue carpet. Would this be considered a castle? It's bright white with gothic-style windows. If you ask me, I would have said that there was no way there was a castle here. Whatever it is, it's strangely beautiful.

Thomas slides out of the car and holds out his hand for me. I slide out, looking up at the expanse of the building. Flashes go off from the paparazzi outside the gate. I wave, Oliver, catches my eye. I look directly at him and smile. I focus on him and breathe in slowly. Mom and dad step out behind us. We pose together for a picture.

Thomas guides me out of the way as Joan's car pulls up with Will and Marie. Marie and Joan step out of the car, almost sparkling. Look at us. Who would have thought three months ago that we would all be standing in these dresses attending a wedding in London? I guess this is what happens when you say yes, a little more, and no a little less. As we walk in, I try to absorb everything. The walls are bright red. The ceiling is white with a very ornate gold lace design on it. It looks like a very fancy wedding cake with golden royal piping.

"I hate to do this to you, love, but I have to go. We have pictures to take and a few other duties. You have assigned seating. I'll meet you after the ceremony." Thomas kisses me on the cheek as not to mess up my lipstick.

I shake my head. "Yeah, no problem. Go. We will just have a look around, then make it to our seats." I smile to reassure Thomas that everything is just fine.

Marie walks up and interlaces her arm in mine, mainly to help hold herself up. "These shoes suck."

"I don't think it's the shoes. I think it's because we aren't used to wearing anything other than running shoes." I giggle.

"What are we talking about here?" Will walks up behind us, wedging himself between us.

"Oh, nothing, we were just talking about how no woman in their right mind should wear heels. What's the purpose? I'm Goggling that later. Who invented high-heeled shoes anyways? I bet it was a man. I mean, what was the thought process there? Was it? How can we make women taller? Or hey, why don't we put tiny little stilts on women's shoes. Let's see how that goes. Not like we don't already have enough crap to juggle. Marie's feet hurt already. And I'm about to cry because I've lost all feeling in my right pinky toe." I put all my weight on my left foot. "Why couldn't I be taller, so heels weren't an option for me?"

Will puts an arm around my waist and lifts me slightly off the ground. Not enough to tell that my feet aren't touching the ground but enough to relieve the pressure. He's an angel. "OK, wiggle your toes to get the blood back down to that little toe."

"That's better, thank you," I say.

"Want to find our seats? —get off our feet for a bit?" Joan says.

"Yep, great idea. I would hate to have to creep in during the ceremony." I follow the crowd.

We are ushered into a long hall. Wooden chairs line the walls on each side of a makeshift aisle, four deep on each side. Joan, Will, Marie, and I sit in the row behind mom and dad. I slip the shoes off my feet just enough to relieve the pressure off my toes.

I watch as Thomas, and the rest of the men shuffle around, getting into position. The trumpets startle me as I'm lost in thought, wiggling my toes, and reciting This Little Piggy Went to Market. As a kid, I never thought about the song too much. I always assumed the first little pig went shopping, but what if it wasn't like that at all? What if he went to market? Like the market to be bought and sent to the butcher and then eaten? I almost kick my loose shoes into the air. I stand, my foot searching for the right fit in my shoe. The sound of the crowd turning to look at the bride sounds like soldiers turning in formation. A smile stretches across my face. I muffle a giggle as I think about last night. Patrice makes eye contact with me as she glides by with her father holding her arm. I wink at her. She smiles and gives me a wink back.

I don't know the protocol here. I stand until everyone else gives me the signal by sitting down first.

I sit back down and whisper to Joan. "So pretty."

Joan nods her head.

I get lost in a daydream as the priest, some random person, and the vows dissipate into a low buzzing in my ear. How many people are going to talk at this wedding? It seems like each person has a ten-minute dissertation on love, life, and weddings. I wiggle in my seat to bring the blood back to my butt. Thomas is staring at me. I see everything in his gaze. Our life, the coffee dates, our children, the rocking chairs we sit in as we grow old. A peace comes over me. I will never begin to know how this happened. How he found me. How we found each other. How we fell in love so fast. My eyes meet his. I know one thing, I love him. He smiles because he knows it. The clapping pulls me out of my daydream as Joan tugs on my arm to stand. Birdie, Figs, and Catherine is sitting on the opposite side of the aisle from us. I smile in acknowledgment. Patrice and Andrew walk out into the long hall, arm, and arm. I turn as I follow them with my eyes.

"You know, you shouldn't show up here looking more beautiful than the bride. Looking as good as you do should be a crime." Thomas growls low in my ear.

My cheeks immediately flush. How did he get over here so quickly?

I gesture to myself. "You know, I can't turn this off."

He smiles. "You are hilarious. I don't think I'll ever get enough of you."

"Well, I would hope not since you put a ring on it." I hold my ring finger in the air.

"Let's go to lunch. We must walk to the other side of the building. They have lunch then the reception." Thomas guides me down the aisle as we nonchalantly follow the crowd.

I squeeze his arm tighter. The thought of us walking down the aisle hits me like a ton of bricks. I feel a little woozy. I need to hit the open bar. All the same, players are here—mom, dad, Joan, Marie, and Will. I look up at Thomas. He notices my nervousness. He cups his hand over my hand that is gripping his and squeezes it three times. It's the same thing Joan does to say I love you. I love that he does it too.

The most enormous wedding cake I have ever seen is sitting on an ornate wooden table at the entrance. It must be at least ten feet tall if you count the table. The frosting is off-white buttercream. I can tell by looking at it. It's one thing I picked up from Marie. Each tier has white royal icing piped onto it to look like lace. That's a ton of work. Marie makes wedding cakes all the time, and it is so nerve-racking, especially knowing that you are responsible for something so important. Now that I think about it, I'll ask Marie to make my cake. Not that anybody else is an option. A bolt of excitement goes through me. I get to pick out a wedding cake. I'm getting married! Joan is pregnant, and I'm getting married.

The dining hall looks much like the wedding hall but three times as large. The walls are lined with red paint capped off with the same white and gold ceiling. The only difference is instead of chairs lining the hall, there are tables covered in white tablecloths, crystal, gold silverware, and heavy china. In the middle of each table sits a large vase with every white flower imaginable. We stroll around looking at the place cards to find our table. After finding it, we sit down. Waiters are delivering plates to tables. Their movements are straight out of Swan Lake. If they didn't have plates in their hands, it would seem like they were putting on some sort of dinner ballet.

A waiter sits a white appetizer plate in front of me. There is a tiny salmon square in the middle of it with a round crab cake on the side. I look around the table at all the different silverware. Big forks, little forks, big spoons, little spoons…. Suddenly, I feel a little out of place. I swear I knew what each fork was before I sat down. It's not like I'm a cavewoman. I try to look around the large vase in the middle of the table at Joan. I can't see her, so I try to send her a message telepathically. She must have gotten it because she holds a fork awkwardly out to the side of the vase so I can see it. I nod my head, even though she can't see me. I look back at mom. She has been talking to me this whole time. I had no idea. I try to play it off.

I throw my head back and laugh. "That is so funny!"

"Marguerite, what is so funny about your dog dying as a kid?" mom scowls at me.

My eyes widen, and I swallow. "Oh my gosh, mom. I wasn't even listening. I'm so sorry. I was trying to figure out what fork to use and when."

"Ridícula —ridiculous." Mom picks up a fork and shoves it into my hand.

"Why the heck are you talking about my dead dog anyways? Jeez, have you hit that age where you think you have to give the death report?" I squint my eyes at her. "You're ridícula."

Mom waves her hand at me dismissively.

I shove the last piece of salmon in my mouth as the waiter whirls around, replacing my plate with dinner.

I eat half of my steak and pass the other half to my dad, who gladly takes it. On each plate, there is a perfectly cooked filet mignon, three asparagus stalks, and a fancy white potato patty with some sort of crest pressed on the top of it. Crest pressed on it or not; potatoes are my love language. Dad scoots his potato onto my plate with his butter knife. Steak is his love language.

"I'm doing your wedding cake. I'm not even asking." Marie says as a waiter places a piece of cake in front of her.

Huh, I guess they have a whole different cake in the back that they serve us, peasants. Their wedding cake can't be fake, can it? I sniffed the frosting. Don't tell me they just frosted a bunch of plastic tiers for show.

I give Marie a wide smile. "Absolutely! You are for sure making my wedding cake. I wouldn't have it any other way."

I sink my fork into my piece of cake and sniff it. "Is that lemon?"

Marie lifts hers to her nose. "Hum, lemon, and something else. I can't put my finger on it. Orange maybe." She places the piece in her mouth, holding it there. "I'm going to reverse engineer this. I got it! Its elderflower. It's the same stuff you make good lemonade out of! If used the wrong way, it's somewhat toxic. Do you think Patrice is trying to kill Andrew?"

I smile, "I would!"

Joan laughs, "You get that from me."

I laugh before I can stop myself.

"How is it that you can talk about killing someone, and I fall more in love with you every second?" Thomas kisses me on the cheek.

I smile, "Cuz you know I'm kidding."

"Or is she? Maybe the murder gene runs in the family?" Marie drags out her words. "Maybe you're a closet serial killer, like Dexter?"

I roll my eyes. Marie's fascination with serial killers has been at an all-time high since moving to San Francisco. She watched a documentary on The Golden State Killer and the Zodiac Killer, and now she's in deep. She even falls asleep to CSI. It all started when we were in college. Joan, Marie, and I would huddle on the couch watching forensic files and try to break the case before the show would. Knowing very well that the show only tells you what they want you to know until the very end.

"Maybe *I* am." Thomas' face goes into a sinister smirk like the clown from It.

How can he be so sexy one second and scary as hell looking the next? I point at him with my fork. "Don't ever do that again."

Two men roll the massive cake to the corner of the hall as a crew of well dress people pull open makeshift walls. The walls fold back to expose a large dance floor.

"Hello, can everyone hear me?" a man in a black tuxedo taps the top of his microphone. "I would like to introduce Lord Andrew and Lady Patrice. Patrice and Andrew clasp their hands together and walk to the middle of the dance floor. The first notes of the song plays.

It's Harry Connick Jr.; It *Had to Be You*. He must not be that bad if he likes Harry. Who am I kidding? He is *that* bad. I just feel sorry for Patrice, who must deal with him for the rest of her life. Maybe I'm being too judgmental, maybe he's a nice guy, and the stress of the wedding got to him. I shake my head. No, I'm no longer making excuses for people that are just assholes.

"Are you ready to dance the night away?" Thomas twirls me in place.

I wiggle my toes and rally. "Absolutely!"

Thomas pulls me up to my feet and walks me to the dance floor. Joan and Will join us.

Thomas glides on his feet effortlessly. "Is there *anything* you can't do?"

"I can't take my eyes off of you; that's one thing I can't do." Thomas' stare bores into me, making me blush.

Thomas twirls me around.

"You know that Marie is going to make our wedding cake?" I lean closer into his chest.

"You can buy a cake at the market for all I care as long as you are meeting me at the end of that aisle." Thomas presses his lips to the top of my head.

"Gosh, mom and Marie will never let that happen. So that you know." I smile at him.

"Oh, I know." Thomas smiles back at me. "But so that you know, I'm up for running away to Rome and getting married."

"I'll keep that in mind if I turn into some sort of bridezilla. You could yeet me out of here and whisk me away to Rome." I giggle.

"OK, yeeting it is if you turn into Godzilla." He smiles as he pulls me against him. "Can you believe we are getting married? That just three short months ago we hardly knew each other?"

"I can't believe how fast any of this has happened. But I'm glad it did." I lead Thomas off the dance floor to rest my feet.

Joan and Marie must have the same idea because they follow me. I slip my shoes off under the table then take a large gulp of wine. I need something to kill the pain.

Birdie and Figs make it over to our table.

"Hi. I love your dress. Who made it?" Figs ask.

I grin. "I'm glad you asked. Chase Alexander of Alexander Fashions."

"It's beautiful." Birdie adds.

Catherine walks over. Thomas grabs an empty seat and adds it to our table. "Here, mom, have a seat."

She leans over and starts a conversation with mom. I scan the room, looking at all the beautiful dresses, when I notice a familiar face.

Dustine is here? I wave and mouth, "Yay! You're here!"

She smiles back at me as she pulls the curtain back and wheels out a large DJ setup. I perk up. Is this about to go down? When I hear the first few notes of the next song.

I immediately jump out of my seat. "Come on!" I run to the dance floor, minus my shoes and pulling Joan and Marie behind me.

Thomas meets me on the dance floor, handing me his socks. "Here. You never know what's on this floor."

I laugh, "Thanks."

Patrice, Krystal, and a couple of girls from the other night run towards us.

Patrice is excited. "Can you believe we are about to do this? I practiced!"

I'm not sure what we are about to do, but if the Cotton Eye Joe is involved, then it's bound to be a good time.

Patrice grabs my arm. "OK, OK, get in line. Let's do this!"

We lock arms as I slowly remind them of the steps. "OK, remember, it's going to get faster. Ready?"

We laugh, dancing faster now. We clutch onto each other as the sheer speed tugs at us.

Thomas joins me, grabbing onto my waist. "You surprise me every day."

He throws his arm over me and studies my feet to pick up the steps. Will wedges himself in between Joan and Marie. Mom and dad form a line in front of us with a couple. They pulled to the dance floor with them. I watch as Andrew hesitantly shuffles over to Patrice.

He laughs, "What is this, Patrice?"

It's the first time I've seen joy on his face. It must suck to go around being such a jerk. I can feel the whole vibe in the hall change. The string quartet is sitting in awe as they wait.

I reach up and waggle Andrew's cheek. "See, you aren't so bad when you aren't being a total wanker."

I can't believe I said that. Well, it's already out there. He can use it to hate me even more. Or he could use it for an actual reason to hate me now. There's nothing like insulting someone at their own wedding to put you on the *hate* list. Dustine blends Cotton Eye Joe seamlessly with The Chicken Dance. It takes natural talent to do that. I tuck my hands under my armpits and poke around like a chicken. Marie is next to me, pretending to play the accordion. Out of all the people dancing, dad is having the most fun.

What was once a formal, follow the rules wedding is turning into an absolute hoe down. I let the world whirl around me as I take a mental note of everyone around me. Will and Joan are having the time of their lives. Will is beaming, his love for Joan almost visible, tangible. I'm not talking about the love or happiness you can see on his face. I mean something you can walk up to and almost physically touch.

Dustine slows the music down to a couple's song. I'm so thankful as I hobble off to my seat with Joan and Marie following. I wiggle my toes under the table. I try to slip my shoes back on, but my feet have swollen up a tad. I am never wearing heels again —never. OK, I lie. I will wear heels again. Just not right now. I will not wear heels for ten minutes.

"What's wrong? Is it you're feet?" Joan says, leaning over to grab my hand. "Mine are killing me too." She reaches down and rubs her feet.

I glance at her feet. Her ankles are nonexistent. "What happened, Joan? You have cankles."

"Here. Put your feet on my lap under the table. I'll rub them." Will slaps his knee.

"So, what happens later? There isn't some other ceremony or anything, right?" I ask, settling, turning my feet sideways, reliving the throbbing.

"No, just more dancing and then fireworks." Thomas smiles at me. "As soon as it gets dark enough, there will be a firework display when the couple leaves, then more dancing until the guest start to leave. Once the guest begin to leave, things will start to shut down."

Waiters float around like ghosts filling up champagne glasses. The string quartet begins to play again.

"Would you like to dance?" Thomas holds out his hand to me.

I smile, taking it.

Thomas pulls me in close. "So, Ms. Becker, are you ready to be Mrs. Marguerite Blaine?"

I think about that for a second. In grade school, I remember writing my name over and over in as many styles as possible, changing pens and colors. When other little girls wrote their names with their crush's last names, I always just wrote my name. I never had a last name to include.

"Earth to M. Hello?" Thomas pulls me back from his chest. "Are you OK?"

I shake my head. "Oh my gosh! Yes, I was just thinking about when I was in elementary school. I didn't have anyone's last name to add to mine."

He presses his face to my ear. "Well, you do now. Mrs. Marguerite Blaine."

An imaginary skywriter flies through my mind spelling out my name in puffy contrails.

Thomas lifts me off my feet ever so slightly. I force myself not to think about what this looks like because I can tell you it feels like I'm a ragdoll being carried around by a huge person. I catch Dustine's eye. She smiles at me and waves as the string quartet's song ends. She seamlessly takes over. How does she do that? One, she must have something worked out with the quartet, and two, she's just that good. No one else in the world could pull this off.

John Legend's song, *All of Me,* begins to play. Thomas hugs me around the waist and lifts me completely off my feet. Not an inch off the ground like before, but completely off the ground. He sways to the music with me helpless in his arms.

"You know we look crazy right now." Beyonce's *Crazy in Love* begins playing in my head, and I fight the urge to act out the dance moves hanging a foot off the ground. Although that would look pretty funny.

Thomas presses his mouth against my ear. "All of me loves all of you...."

The same warm feeling spreads through my body and down to my toes, giving my toes the much-needed blood. Over Thomas' shoulder, I see the first fireworks through the window. "Hey, the fireworks are starting."

Thomas puts me back down on my feet. "Let's go see."

I slip on my shoes without taking Thomas' socks off. "We are going out to watch the fireworks. Where's Joan?" I ask mom.

Mom lifts her hand from the serious conversation with Catherine. "Oh, she and Will went outside a while ago."

Thomas and I find a spot on the grass. I kick off my shoes again like I'm allergic to them. I sit in between Thomas' legs. He wraps them around me, making me a makeshift chair. The hill is very steep; Thomas locks his legs around me, securing me in place. I get comfortable and lean back against him, watching as one spectacular firework after the other lights up the night sky. I watch Joan and Will cross the grass hill in front of us. Will sits down in the grass and pulls Joan down next to him. Thomas' warm arms wrap around me, and all is right in the world. I look up to see Marie walking our way.

"Will I spoil the romantic mood if I sit with you?" Marie smiles as she slides down next to us, not waiting for our answer.

We stare in silence at the gold, red and blue fire lighting up the sky making Joan and Will a black silhouette in front of us.

Marie squeezes my elbow and whispers. "What is that?"

I squint my eyes. "What?"

"That! Is he proposing?" she points, craning her neck to see.

"I don't know." I squint my eyes. "Let me try to get a better look."

Chapter 27

Humpty Dumpty Had a Great Fall

"When I fall in love, it will be forever."

—Jane Austen

I GET ON MY FEET and crouch down to get a better look. I can't see very well. I try to get a closer look. I get to my feet without standing and peddle my way over, inching closer. I look like one of those dancers that look like they're floating, but all they are really doing is making very fast and small movements with their feet. I transition to my knees as my feet begin to cramp. Dang feet! I pull the layers of tule and fabric up to expose my knees to the grass. I sashay over, sliding over the damp grass.

Will holds out what looks like a ring. He glides it on her finger. I move a tiny bit closer. Joan pulls out the pregnancy stick out of her pocket and hands it to Will. I make bigger strides on my knees when I accidentally put one of my knees down on a tiny, jagged rock, making me jerk in pain. It's just enough to tilt me off balance, sending me tangled in the layers of my dress and hurling down the hill. I land with a hard thud against Joan and Will's backs.

"Hiya." I sit up, pulling grass blades out of my knees and straightening my hair.

"Hiya, whatever! Mar, what the hell happened?" Joan turns to look at me.

"What the hell happened is right!" I distinctly look at her ring finger. "You tell me!"

Joan holds up her hand. "This? It's not what you think."

Will raises his hand behind Joan like he's a schoolboy asking a question.

I point. "Yes, you—you in the back. What?"

"I want to know what to expect here. Is it going to be you barreling in every time your sister has something happen?" Will asks.

"Yep! That's what you can expect. It's kinda the deal. You get her; you get me. Not in a sister's wife sort of way but in an 'I'm all up in your business sort of way.' Are you OK with that?" I lean towards him, narrowing my eyes.

"Yep, I'm OK with that." I was just checking. The pregnancy test is still in his hand.

"Then what is it?" I have no choice other than to double down here.

I wasn't planning on crashing her engagement or ruining her special moment, but that rock and my knee had other plans.

Joan holds out her hand to me. "It's a promise ring."

"Like in high school?" I screw up my face.

"More like, I'm not ready to get married, so this is a promise. More like for when I am ready." Joan twirls the ring on her finger.

I grab Joan's hand. "A sapphire?"

"Yes, a sapphire for loyalty." Will smiles.

He really knows how to hit home. A sapphire for loyalty is just what I expected from him. I have to get out of here before I make it worse. "OK, then goodbye!"

I don't address the pregnancy test or even let on that I see it or that I know anything about it.

I stand, shift my dress back into place, and walk back to Thomas and Marie.

"He gave her a promise ring with a sapphire, not a diamond—a sapphire. It's for loyalty, and I love that." I plop myself down next to Marie. "And she gave him the test. I screwed that one up." I look at Thomas. "Oh, by the way, Joan is pregnant. It's a zebra."

Thomas nods in understanding. "I see why you couldn't tell me."

I change the subject to get my mind off completely ruining Joan's moment.

"So, what's next? Maybe you'll meet someone too?" I shove Marie with my shoulder.

"Tallyho! I found you!" A man holding two wine glasses sits down next to Marie.

I raise my eyebrows. Tallyho? Who says that?

He hands a glass to Marie. "I'm called Scott—pleasure."

Thomas nods his head. "Pleasure."

I awkwardly stare at Marie, willing her to say something, say anything. She's about to hook up with a leprechaun.

"Mar, this is Scott; I met him inside. He is a London boy like Thomas." Marie bats her eyes at him.

"Oh, right then." Thomas is doing the nice guy thing he does, but I know he is vetting him. "Whereabouts do you live."

"Right, mate. I live in Camden. I'm in finance. I work in The Gherkin downtown." Scott reassures Thomas. "I know Andrew from Uni. I briefly played on the rugby team before I got my teeth rattled if you know what I mean?"

"Right, are you Jerry's friend?" Thomas is double downing him. "He played on the rugby team too."

Scott's face goes into a wide grin. "Yes, Jerry, Andrew, and Hugh."

Thomas shakes his head. "I played rugby the following year. It must have been after you left the team. Funny how our paths didn't cross."

"No, right. I met you once at the pub we used to go to called Hide Nor Hair." Scott tries to get Thomas to remember.

Thomas is satisfied with that answer. "Right, I apologize, mate. I didn't recognize you. This is my fiancée M, and of course, you met her best friend, Marie."

What if Marie falls in love with Scott? What if Marie ends up moving to London? I know I'm getting ahead of myself, but what am I if not hopeful? What if she falls in love with Scott and he moves back to the states? Marie has the bakery. Hell, I have a bakery. This is hard. Joan is pregnant; I promised I'd be there. What do people do when they fall in love with someone that doesn't live in the states? I guess that's the epic battle; where do we end up living? Who could stand to lose everything to build a life somewhere new? I look up at Thomas, studying his face. Would I regret this? In ten years, would I regret moving? If I make him come to the states, would he regret it? Could I live here and not see Joan or the baby regularly?

A loud bang interrupts my thoughts. It must be the grand finale. I watch as Andrew and Patrice drive off—Patrice hanging halfway out the window blowing kisses.

I make it to my feet. Thomas tucks me under his arm as we walk back to the castle. "I wonder where mom and dad wandered off to. I haven't seen them since dinner."

Joan and Will walk next to us.

"Have you seen mom?" Joan asks.

I shake my head. "No, I was just saying that."

"Well, we have some exciting news to tell them; they have to be around here somewhere." Joan says, searching the crowd."

I point. "There they are."

Dad is sitting on the grass with mom in his lap. He has a cigar hanging out of the corner of his mouth, laughing. I smile; I could only hope to be that happy. We all could only hope to be that happy.

I tap dad on the shoulder as we pass by. "We'll meet you inside. Joan has something to tell us all."

"So, now what?" I push against Thomas.

"So, I'll have the car take Joan, Will, and Marie back to their hotel. We'll take the other. We will meet in the morning for breakfast." Thomas looks for everyone's approval.

"I'll catch a ride with Scott." I'll see everyone in the morning.

I have to admit; I don't like that idea.

"Send me the dets and the location. You know the drill." I scowl at Marie.

"I know, I know. Don't worry." Marie tightens her lips, scowling back at me. "I'm a big girl."

I roll my eyes at her. I know she's right.

Mom and dad walk up behind us. "What are we talking about."

I shake my head and laugh, "Oh, nothing."

I wave my arms, showcasing Joan like Vanna White showcases a letter. "Joan has something to tell us."

"Mom, Dad, I'm pregnant!" she nervously says.

"And she's having a zebra." I'm trying to break up the tension.

Dad swoops in and hugs Joan. "That is the best news. Isn't that right, Olivia?"

Dad turns to mom. "I already know. I told her this morning. Congratulations, Mija."

Dad claps Will's hand in his. "Congratulations."

Mom notices the ring on Joan's hand. "Did you get engaged?"

Joan looks down at her ring and spins it on her finger. "No, this is a promise ring when I am ready to get married again."

"Everything is wonderful." Mom leans into dad. "This has been a perfect trip, Henry."

We walk out to the gravel drive to wait for our car.

I hug Joan. "See ya. Congratulations, sister, I'm sorry I almost ruined you telling Will."

"You didn't almost ruin it; it's going to be a hilarious story to tell later." Joan releases me.

Will holds out his arms. "Do I get a hug?"

I hug him. "If I must." I wink.

I watch Marie as she gets into a Porsche in front of us. My phone dings almost immediately.

Black Porsche Taycan, Scott, inviting you to track my location.

I throw my hand up and wave. Marie rolls down her window and gives me a thumbs up.

"No, No! Where is Marie going?" Mom fumbles in her bag, pulling out a receipt and a putt-putt golf pencil.

I grab her hands. "Mom, what are you doing?"

"I'm writing down everything I know while it is fresh in my mind." Mom is straining to look around me.

My mouth drops open. "That's where we get it from! You are why Joan and I are so neurotic!"

I look at Joan and point at mom. "See? She's the reason!"

"Mom, we have been doing this for years. We always send each other the details of where we are and who we are with, along with the location tracker. Don't worry. But it's good to know where we got it from, and that crazy runs in our family." Joan throws an arm around mom's waist, nestling her chin on mom's shoulder.

"It's not crazy; it's responsible…Chicas cabeza dura—hardheaded girls." She tucks the receipt back into her handbag.

"Why do you have a putt-putt pencil in your handbag anyways? But, besides that, the real question is, why you thought it was necessary to transfer it from your purse to the tiny handbag you brought to a royal wedding." I smile. "I don't care what you say; that's a little crazy. I hold up my fingers, indicating she's a little crazy. "You're this much crazy."

She grabs my hand. "If I am crazy, you girls made me that way."

Our driver opens the car door. I wave at Joan and Will. "See ya!"

Joan nods at me. "In the morning!"

Chapter 28

Mr. Perfect

*"One is loved because one is loved. No reason is
needed for loving."*

—Paulo Coelho

I GROGGILY KISS MOM and dad goodnight as I hobble towards the bedroom. "See you in the morning. But not too early. We'll go for breakfast."

I drop the shoes from hell in at the bedroom door.

Thomas follows me. "Why don't you jump in the shower, and I'll rub your feet when you get out?"

I close my eyes. "How are you so perfect all the time?"

Thomas screws up his face. "You think I'm perfect? Ah, M, I'm not perfect."

"Well, you're perfect for me." I tippy-toe up and kiss him on the neck.

Thomas nods his head. "If two people fit, then they are perfect for each other. Obviously, I'm far from perfect to the outside world, but I am perfect for you. And that's all that matters. And that's all I need."

I kiss him on the cheek. "That's all *I* need."

He presses his head against mine. "Go take a shower. I'll be here when you get back."

I turn and shut the bathroom door behind me. When is the shoe going to fall? It can't be this good. And it for sure can't be this good all the time. I don't know what turned me so cynical, but here I am waiting for the shoe to drop. I unzip my dress and wiggle it down to the floor. I hang it on the velvet hanger it came on. I brush my teeth in a haze of thoughts and emotions. Am I the dumbest girl in the world for not wanting to stay here?

I jerk my head back. That's the first time I realized that. That's the first time I've fully let that come to the surface. I don't want to stay. The house, the engagement, the man, everything's so perfect, but there is something else. There's that pesky little thing called location. And I thought I was fine with it, but obviously, it's like bad seafood; it comes bubbling up to the surface. Plus, now Joan needs me. I run the water to get it hot.

I mindlessly step into the shower. I pour shampoo on my hand and scrub the layered-on makeup off my face. My makeup remover is next to the sink, and I'm too lazy to hop out and grab it.

I hear the door creak open. Goosebumps cover my body. I'm almost too afraid to call out. I frantically rub the soap out of my eyes. My irrational fear of being murdered in the shower is in overdrive.

I jerk the curtain open just to see Thomas standing in front of the sink flossing his teeth. "Hello, love. I need to get ready for bed."

Relief washes through me. I rest my head on my arm and watch the soap bubbles float over my toes.

I scream from the top of my lungs. "Spider!" I jump straight into the air, hitting my arm on the shower door as I try grabbing for it. My feet hit the bottom of the soapy tub. The shampoo and soap make both of my feet slip out from under me. I come crashing down hard and hit the back of my head on the edge of the tub.

"Oh, Jesus M! Crap, your bleeding! Hold still." Thomas drops to his knees to cup my head.

I blink my eyes; everything is blurry. I reach back to touch my head. I feel something wet and sticky.

"What happened? Thomas grabs a towel and presses it to the back of my head. "I'm adding pressure. Sit up slowly."

"Oh God, where did the spider go? I begin kicking my legs.

"The spider? It probably ran off." Thomas stands up and looks around the bathtub. He begins to laugh. "Oh no, M…." He picks up something from the drain. "It's your false eyelashes. You must have forgotten to take them off before washing your face."

I want to laugh, but all I feel like doing is crying. Thomas takes the towel off the back of my head to survey the damage. "M. I'm sorry to say, but I think you are going to need a couple of stitches."

I start to cry.

"Oh, no, M don't cry. It's all under your hair. No one will ever see it." Thomas says, placing his hand back on my head.

"That's not why I'm crying," I say in-between sobs.

Confused, Thomas asks, "Then what's wrong?"

"I'm terrified of needles…like I would rather get into a fistfight than have someone poke me with a needle. I've been so scared ever since I was a kid. One time when my mom took me for the flu shot, I bolted through the side door and out into the field. The doctor had to run me down, which made it worse. He gave me the shot right there in the field.

Thomas kisses me on the forehead. "It doesn't mean you don't need it. Come on. Can you try to stand?"

"I think so." I laugh at the sight of my wet eyelash laying limp on the toilet lid.

"Here, hold the towel to your head. I'll go get you some clothes." Thomas ushers me into the bedroom and sits me down on the bed. "Here, lift your feet."

He loops my feet through my panties then follows them up with a pair of his joggers.

He wraps a bra over my chest and snaps it in the back. "Here, you can wear one of my button-ups, so we don't have to go over your head."

I stagger to my feet as Thomas leads me to the front door.

"I'm just going to knock on your parent's door just to let them know." Thomas walks over to the door and gently knocks on it. "Mr. Becker. I'm driving Marguerite to the ER. She slipped in the shower and needs a couple of stitches."

Dad gets out of bed and comes into the living room. "Punky, do you want me to come with you."

"I shake my head. "No, dad, I don't know how long this is gonna take. Just go back to sleep; we'll be back."

Thomas walks me down the cement sidewalk to the car. "OK, M, get in." he holds the door open and shuts it behind me.

Thomas' calm is all gone as he shifts through the few blocks to the ER. He speeds through red lights without even a pause.

I clutch at the door handle. "Hey, you know if you kill me on the way to the hospital, I'm coming back as a ghost to haunt you."

"I'm not going to kill you, M. But there is a time to be calm, and there's a time to drive fast. This is a time to drive fast." He says without taking his eyes off the road.

"It's not like I'm bleeding to death!" I press the towel harder to my head.

The Audi's tires screech to a halt in front of the emergency room doors. Thomas helps me out of the car and ushers me to a seat.

"Hello, my fiancée has fallen in the shower and has a pretty good bash on the back of her head." Thomas starts to pull cards and his ID out of his wallet. "She isn't from here. Whatever you need, just put it on this card."

The shock is wearing off, and the pain is starting to kick in. I take the towel off my head to readjust the pressure. My hands run over something I hadn't noticed before. It feels like a piece of plastic. I gently touch it, exploring the edges.

"Oh no! no! no! M. Don't touch that," Thomas says as he rushes over to help fold the towel back, putting it back in place.

"What is in my hair?" I try to reach back to touch it again.

"Nope, don't." Thomas grabs for my hand.

"What is it?" my voice goes up an octave.

"Well…it's…it's your razor head that was on the edge of the tub. I took the handle off when you didn't notice." Thomas grabs both of my hands in his, trying to calm me.

"A razor?" I begin to feel nauseous. "Ugh…I don't feel so great." I hold my chest. "I think I'm going to barf."

"Hey, hey, hey. You're OK. It's OK." Thomas squeezes my hands.

My eyes begin to flicker. Then blackness.

The next thing I know, Thomas is running his thumb over my hand. "You're all done, love. They removed the blade and stitched you up. It came out easily. We can go now."

I press my forehead against Thomas and cringe at the thought of the blade. The next time I have to deal with a needle, I'm just going to pass out and skip it all. That's the way to do it. Joan is going to have a field day with all of this.

Thomas wraps his arm around me as I slide to my feet. "OK, let's go home."

Home—my home—his home—our home? "Maybe we can catch a few hours of sleep before breakfast," I say.

Thomas looks at his watch. "You aren't expected to do anything, M. Why don't you rest today? It's already 5:45 a.m."

"It's doesn't hurt anymore." I reach back and touch my head. The stitches feel like tiny spider legs, which makes me feel queasy all over again. I smile.

Thomas winces. "Only because they numbed the whole area before stitching you up."

I jerk my head back. "They stuck needles in my head to numb it just to stick needles in my head to stitch it? That totally makes sense."

Thomas kisses my hand. "It's all over now. Let's get you home and into bed."

Mom and dad are sitting on the front stoop with Charlie when we pull up.

"What happened, clumsy?" mom asks.

I shrug my shoulders and shake my head. "Don't ask; I'm just stupid. My eyelash fell off, and I thought it was a spider. I freaked out and hit my head." I bow my head down to show where they put the stitches. "I got six stitches right here. My razor was stuck in my head."

"Marguerite, how is that even possible? Is there a mat in the bottom of the tub? I'll go to the store tomorrow and buy one."

I sit down on the step next to mom.

"Better yet, I'll rip the whole thing out." Thomas sits down next to dad, circling his knees with his arms.

I laugh. "That's ridiculous."

We stare in silence at the sun slowly creeping over the roofs, shooting rays of sunshine between the townhouses. Charlie wedges himself between us.

I take a deep breath in. "I'm going to take a nap for the next couple of hours; then, we can go for something to eat."

"I'm going to clean the bathroom and nap too." Thomas stands.

"I cleaned it already." Mom waves her hand dismissively. "Nothing a little bleach and vinegar can't fix."

Thomas helps me up from the stoop. "Let's get you some sleep."

He says it like we could go buy it somewhere. At least my head doesn't hurt. Thomas pulls the covers down as I crawl into bed and press my face into the pillows.

He makes circles on my back with his hand. "Can I get you anything?"

I reach up and pull him down next to me. "Just lay down here so I can sleep."

Joan busts through the bedroom, howling! "You got stitches, stupid? Normally, I'd make up a lie to make this a good story but falling in the tub because of your eyelashes is funny enough. Sit up, let me see."

I sit up and lean my head towards her.

"Ah! That's a pretty good gash. How many stitches?" Joan touches my arm.

I look at Thomas. "Ten, I think." He says.

"Did they check you for brain damage while they were at it?" Joan hammers me on the knee.

"Yes, as far as they could tell, I didn't get a concussion. But I did pass out when Thomas told me my razor was stuck in my head." I laugh at the memory of my lash on the toilet lid.

"Oh my God! Yuck! Don't tell me anything else. I'm glad you are OK."

Marie comes bouncing in. "Hiya!"

I'd ask her what she's so happy about, but for some reason, I feel like this isn't the appropriate time for that. She gives me a look; I look at Joan, and Joan looks back at Marie. Like a visual ring around the Rosie. I giggle and roll my eyes.

"What's on the agenda today. Do you feel up to anything, or do we just want to go for breakfast and hang out?" Joan asks.

"I'm up for anything today. How about breakfast, then a walk around Regent's Park? Then later we can go to Big Ben and whatever else anyone wants to see." I say, making a tentative plan.

"We have to sign a couple of things. So, we will have to swing by the new townhouse after breakfast." Thomas muffles from the bathroom where he is brushing his teeth. "We'll walk."

I slide out of bed and walk to the living room.

"I heard you hit your head. Are you OK?" Will hugs me.

"Yes, the worst thing is the thought of the stitches," I say, sitting at the kitchen counter. "I think the plan is to go to breakfast, stop at the townhouse, then sightsee. If that works for everybody."

Mom carries her walking shoes to the couch and starts lacing them up.

"OK, I'm ready if everyone is ready." Thomas snaps on Charlie's leash. "How about Georgie's for breakfast?"

I nod. "Yes, Georgie's sounds great."

I wash my face and change. "I'm ready."

As we make it to the sidewalk, I turn my attention to Marie. "So, what happened last night? Tell me everything."

Chapter 29

Tourist Trap

"No artist tolerates reality."

—NIETZSCHE

JOAN LETS THE LATCH LOCK on the gate behind her. I wave her over. "Marie was just about to spill the beans. Spill it, sister!"

"He showed me around. Then asked if I wanted a coffee. We walked to a local coffee shop and had coffee, then we spent all night walking around and talking. He was the perfect gentleman. He eventually drove me back to the hotel. He kissed me and that was it. Then we said, goodnight." Marie smiles.

"Ooh, la la!" I straighten as I see mom slowing to wait for us.

We are passing the townhouse when mom asks. "Mar, what are you going to do with a house this big?"

"Well, the very first thing I'm going to do is buy one of those robes from the 1960s with the feather boa attached and answer the door. It will be hot pink. I'll even wear matching high heels with it." I laugh, giving her a cheeky grin.

"Nina tonta—silly girl." She shakes her head. "Thomas needs you."

I sped up to catch up with Thomas.

"M, let's sign these papers since we are already here. Do you mind?" Thomas asks, gesturing towards the towering townhouse. "Do you have the keys?"

I dig in my purse for Rocinante's keyring. "Here."

Thomas takes the keys, unlocking the door. Papers are spread out on the entry table. Thomas begins systematically going through each piece with dad right by his side.

"All done?" I glance over his shoulder.

Thomas scatters the papers out. "Yes, but you need to sign some of these. It's the inspection and some other things."

I look at dad for reassurance.

"I've read through them, Punky. They look all good to me." Dad gives me his famous crooked smile. It's a reassuring smile and exactly what I needed.

I breathe a nervous breath out. "Buy land they aren't making anymore, or something like that, right, dad?"

Dad winks at me. "Something like that."

I think about my name. Marguerite Becker…soon to be Marguerite Blaine… Marguerite Becker-Blaine. This is my life. Joan poisoning me was just the beginning of this fairytale that I kinda just fell into. Maybe if Joan hadn't poisoned me, I would have never found Thomas. Do you believe that? Or do you believe if you are meant to be, you will find each other no matter what?

If Frank was a stand-up guy, we might not be here right now. In a weird way, I have Frank to thank. And by thanking Frank, I mean I'll give him a pass on not getting kicked in the nuts again. If Frank hadn't done what he did, there would be no Will. So, I guess it's true what people say; everything *does* happen for a reason. I guess I did find out if Thomas was a reason, season, or a lifetime. Frank was a reason. Joan learned. Will is turning from a season turned into a lifetime. And Thomas is definitely a lifetime.

It's funny how something so wrong can make something else into something so right. Even if you can't see it at the time. I heard something a while back. It didn't mean anything to me at the time, but now I know it as truth. It goes something like this—it's worth growing old for. Thomas is worth growing old for. I feel this to my core.

I reach down and sign the places Thomas points to. "M, if you want to read through all this, we have time. I don't want to rush you."

I wave him off. "Dad read it. I'm good with that."

I stack all the papers together into a neat pile, handing them back to him.

We make quick work of breakfast and head back to the flat.

"How are we getting around today? Another party bus?" I ask, plopping myself down on the couch.

"No, we have an SUV coming. It will seat all of us, plus the driver doubles as security. I have it covered."

Everyone is lounging in various places in the living room when the doorbell rings. An average-looking man is standing at the door.

Thomas extends his hand. "Phil?"

The man smiles. "Yes, I'm Phil. I hear we all want to see the sights today."

Mom jumps up from the couch and grabs her purse. She spreads out the pamphlets in her hand like she's playing a hand of Poker. "I want to see Big Ben, and I want to drive over Tower Bridge."

"I want to eat at a traditional English pub." Joan chimes in. "I'm still starving."

I swear, ever since Joan found out she was pregnant, she has all of a sudden been starving. I don't know if that's psychosomatic or if she really is starving. Even though we just ate, Will unwraps a breakfast bar that he gets from his pocket and hands it to her.

"What else do you have in there?" I smile, pretending to peer into his jacket pocket.

"I have a small orange juice and some crackers." Will pulls out the contents of his coat.

"Good man." I hand him a chocolate bar. "For Joan, just in case."

I call out to dad. "Dad, is there anything you want to do?"

Dad thinks about that for a second. "I would like to make a phone call in one of those red phone booths."

Thomas shakes his head. "I think we could handle all that."

Of all the things he could do in London, he wants to make a phone call.

"Marie, is there anything you might want to do?" Thomas asks.

"I mean maybe, if we have time, I'd love to do the Eye of London. But make that the last thing."

"OK. The Tower Bridge, lunch at a pub, the clock, a phone call, and the Eye of London. Do I have everything?" Thomas jots it down on his handy dandy notebook. "The first stop is Big Ben; then we can have lunch, do the Ferris wheel, and head over Tower Bridge. If we see a phone booth, we can stop to make a call."

Thomas stands by the door, holding it open.

I grab my purse and follow mom and dad out to the SUV. Mom gets in the front seat. Out of all the people in this vehicle, mom is the one most interested in seeing the sights.

Chapter 30

The Night Begins to Shine

"When I look at you, I see the story in your eyes."

—B.E.R.

WE PASS BY WESTMINSTER ABBY before Phil pulls into a parking lot. We jumble out of the SUV and walk towards Big Ben's clock tower.

Mom pulls out her tourist map; it only shows the five or six things of interest down here. It's cute that she thinks she's leading us. Thomas and I are right behind her and dad. Thomas gently directs her by pointing out things that she might be interested in, so she goes the way he needs her.

"Look, Mrs. Becker, that purse is beautiful." Thomas points at a window display.

Mom walks over and stares at it in the window. "Oh, it's a nice one."

Thomas knows that dad is a big WWII buff. He points the way to a Churchill Statue. Dad walks up to it and poses by it, letting his round belly poke out as he stuffs a cigar in his mouth.

Mom glares at him. "Henry Becker, you old goat."

"Mr. Becker, did you know Churchill took his granddaughter on most of his vacations later in his life?"

Dad smiles at Thomas for his attempt at Churchill trivia. "I did know that, and her name is Celia. Did you know he was very fond of his parakeet Toby?"

Thomas shakes his head at dad. "Impressive."

As Thomas closes the app on his phone, I glance at it. He's reading Churchill trivia. I love him even more.

Joan and Will have stopped and walked into a shop.

Marie casually follows them in. they are looking at baby clothes.

I walk in and pick up a small pink onesie with tiny roses on the collar. "Isn't this adorable?"

"Not more adorable than this." Will holds up a tiny blue onesie with a dog on it."

I walk to the counter with my it. Like buying, this will decide the sex of the baby. I hand it to Joan. "It's a girl."

Mom walks in and presses her hand over Joan's stomach. "No, you're wrong. It's a boy."

"Mom, how do you even know that? I'm not even showing yet." Joan laughs nervously.

"Oh, Mijita, I know." Mom starts looking at baby clothes. "My mama used to help deliver babies."

"Of course, she did." She hands the bag back to me.

I head to the counter and exchange it for the blue onesie with the dog. I hand it to Will, "I guess you're having a boy."

He takes it from me, smiling.

We walk another block before we see the top of Big Ben. It's under construction. We walk around the outside and read the plaques instead. I snap a picture of mom and dad standing in front of it. I make a mental note to add a funny title to the picture in my photo album.

After exhausting the construction zone, we see the top of the Eye of London.

"Marie, there's the Ferris wheel. Let's go!"

Marie's face brightens into a smile. "You sure?"

"Yes, I'm sure!" I start walking in that direction.

Will walks up to the ticket counter. "Seven, please. Seven and a half if you count this nugget." He rubs Joan's flat belly.

Will is over the moon, and I can already tell that he's going to be *that* kind of dad. The kind that tells dad jokes and is ridiculously oversharing dad stories. I am extremely happy for Joan. I wonder if being pregnant will cure Joan of heights.

"They are sold out until seven o'clock tonight. I got the tickets. Should we go to the next stop?" Will puts the tickets in his wallet.

"Let's head to Tower Bridge then have lunch," Thomas says as we all begin walking back the way we came.

"Dad, look!" I point. "There's a phone booth.

Dad slaps his hands together. "What time is it in Texas?"

I mentally do the math. "It's noon here, so it should be six a.m. there. Who are you calling?"

Dad holds his index finger in the air. "I'm going to call Tex. See how he's doing."

I don't even know if he can make a call from here or if there's even a phone in the phone booth. Are phone booths even a thing now that everyone has a cellphone nowadays? We crowd around the phone booth as dad steps in. Huh? Who knew? There is an actual phone in here.

Dad picks up the receiver and looks at Thomas.

"Dial 100, you'll get an operator," Thomas says.

Dad taps in the number. "Could you please connect me to 361-643-2981 for a collect call?"

Dad holds the phone up; it's ringing.

"Hello?" I can hear Tex on the other end of the line.

"Hey! It's me! I'm calling you from one of those red phone booths in London! How ya doing, old pal?" Dad is always happy to talk to Tex.

We listen to dad's one-sided conversation. "Marguerite got engaged! Yes! I'll tell her. And Joan is pregnant. Yes, Will. They are happy. OK, I'll talk to you soon, everything good there? Bye."

Dad hangs up the phone, smiling his crooked grin. "Tex says hello and that he is happy for you girls."

Thomas gets stopped by a couple of women holding a map of London. We awkwardly stand a few feet away from him as he signs autographs. As we stand there, more and more people begin to notice. This is the part that always gets me. Do I stand here? Do I go there? I opt for standing with my family, waiting.

Thomas turns to look at me. He holds his hand out for me and motions me over. I gingerly walk over and stand by him. He puts an arm around me as he takes out a black sharpie from his jacket. His handy dandy notebook falls to the ground. I pick it up and laugh. While he's signing autographs and taking pictures, I flip through his notebook to the beginning and read.

Meet a girl tonight. She's hilarious and fantastic.

My stomach falls to my feet. Should I be reading this? But it's like a car accident. I can't look away. So, I continue.

She's the one, I know it. I'm going to marry that girl. She had a grass stain on her forehead. She's beautiful, but it's like she doesn't know it. Her heart is the biggest I've ever seen.

I flip the page.

Missing Mar today.

My heart sinks. I hate this. He sees me flipping through his notebook and smiles at me. My heart melts right there on the spot. Just when I thought I couldn't love him more, I do. Phil whispers in Thomas' ear and pulls him away from the forming crowd.

Thomas raises his hand in the air, waving. "Nice to see everyone."

Thomas tucks me into his arm and begins to walk off.

I give Joan a look. "Form a tight group. Let's get back to the car."

People are snapping selfies as we walk back to the SUV. Thomas is being very polite. I guess no one gets a class in acting polite and preserving your privacy. Or is that even possible?

As we make it back to the SUV, Phil clicks the lock. Mom hurries into the front seat. Will guides Joan into the backseat, making sure she is safe. Marie joins them in the backseat as Thomas, dad, and I take the middle seat. We laugh in relief as Phil puts it in gear and drives off.

"Well, what's the next stop?" Mom asks, sweeping the whole famous thing under the rug.

Curiously I ask, "Mom, what do you think about all the people trying to stop Thomas and take pictures?"

Mom waves her hand, "Oh, Mijita. It's his job. You just got to learn to cope with it."

I'm surprised by her answer. It beats the answer she used to give us as kids. If anything hurt, say our arm or something, she would say cut it off. I guess she's getting nicer in her old age. Her logic as a kid was brutal and terrifying. But it taught Joan and me not to complain. In her own way, she was telling us it could be worse.

"Take a right here, mate," Thomas tells Phil. "Then a right. Park in that parking lot right there."

Phil pulls into a small parking lot. We jump out as he pays the parking attendant.

"OK, Joan, this is an authentic English pub. I hope you like it." Thomas holds the door open.

Thomas points at the sign. "The Red Rabbit. Winston Churchill used to drink here."

That has my dad's attention. The pub is dark and has an underline age to it. It's old, I can tell. I look around while we wait for someone to seat us. The bar is wood and very ornate. There's a sign next to the bar.

"Hey, on this very sight, used to be a medieval tavern. Charles Dickens used to drink here. He knew the owner. That's cool." I say.

We grab two tables and drag them together. Will grabs a stack of menus and passes them around. Dad is standing reading a plaque under a picture of Churchill.

The waitress comes bouncing up with a tray of water. "I'm Veronica. The special today is the pie sampler. I'll let you look at the menu. Can I get you anything else to drink?"

Mom starts, "I'll take a sweet tea."

"We only have regular tea, but I can bring you sugar." She says as she writes it down.

"I'll do just a water," I say. "And she will just have a water also," I say, pointing at Joan.

Joan gives me a dirty look.

"Stop it; you aren't a camel. You have to drink water, especially now that you are pregnant." I say, narrowing my eyes at her.

She nods her head, agreeing with me.

"I'll have whatever local beer you have on tap," Will says, then immediately looks at Joan. "I mean, unless you want me to go on the wagon with you for support."

"No, it's fine." Joan kisses Will on the cheek for his consideration.

Thomas piggybacks onto Will's order. "I'll do the same."

As the waitress's eye meets Thomas. I can tell she recognizes him, but she keeps it professional. I appreciate that. I watch her as she types in our drink order at the kiosk, then whispers something to the man behind the bar. He turns and looks over at us. I pretend I don't notice; I drink my water instead.

Veronica comes back carrying two beers. She sets them on the table. "Have you had a chance to look at the menu? I'll start with you." She presses her pen to her notepad and looks at mom.

She takes our order. We make small talk as we wait.

Will is rubbing Joan's shoulders. He says something that I have been dreading all day. "We leave tomorrow at one p.m. We can take a taxi there."

I know he doesn't mean to hurt my feelings, but this conversation is killing me.

"No, we will want to go and see everyone off. We'll get a car." Thomas says, pulling me in a little closer.

I feel sad, and I know he can tell. He's trying to comfort me by rubbing my knee. I can feel the stinging in my eyes. I blink the tear away that I know is coming. I won't be there for Joan's first baby appointment. I don't even know if she wants me to go. That's probably stepping on Will's toes, but I still feel bad just thinking about missing it.

Veronica carries a large tray of food over her shoulder, saving me from myself. I swallow the lump in my throat. Joan and dad ordered Sheppard's pie. Mom, of course, ordered the special. Thomas and I copied mom by ordering the pie sampler and a salad to split. Will ordered the fish and chips and a flight of beers.

Thomas takes a beer from Wil's wooden tray. He hands one to dad and takes another for himself. He raises the glass in the air. "I have a toast. Congratulations to Will and Joan." He lifts his drink higher, clinking it to dad and Will's glasses before drinking it.

Joan smiles then starts making quick work of her meal.

"I guess you're having a linebacker. Am I right, Joan?" I raise my eyebrows up and down at her.

"Stupid," Joan whispers under her breath.

"Stupider…" I knock her on her knee.

Joan finishes her plate before anyone else. She folds her napkin and sets it on the side of her bowl. She leans back in her seat, resting her back.

Dad raises his hand to get the waitress's attention. "We'll take the check when you get a chance."

"It's already been paid for, sir. I'm sorry." She hands Thomas the receipt to sign.

Thomas smirks, "You'll have to be faster if you want to do something I want to do."

Dad looks shocked. "You son of a gun!" He points his finger at Thomas. "You're learning."

Thomas shrugs his shoulders. "I guess I am."

"Oh! Scoot! Scoot!" Joan hops up from the table, glancing around frantically. She runs out the door with Will close behind her.

Marie dumps the contents of her shopping bag onto the table and throws it to me. I run behind Will. Joan is dry heaving on the sidewalk by the door.

I hand her the shopping bag. "Here, Joan." I rub her back. "Just do what you have to."

A couple passes us, giving us a dirty look.

I shake my head. "The food is awful."

Mom meets us outside. She presses her wet napkin on the back of Joan's neck. "You'll be alright, Mijita."

Joan stands, taking the napkin from mom. "I didn't throw up. Thank God. I just feel like I am."

Joan takes it a little slower as we head to the car.

Phil is waiting for us in the front seat. Noticing Joan's slower walk, he hops out and opens the door for her.

"Where to now? Shall we head to Tower Bridge, or do we need to go back?" Phil asks, looking at Joan in the rearview mirror.

"No, no, let's go. I'll be ok." Joan leans her head onto Will's shoulder.

Mom bundles up her jacket as we begin the walk across the long bridge, getting to the first tower. The tour guide ushers us in. We watch a brief show and head up the stairs to the walkway.

"My gosh, you would have thought you could have made it further away from the door. You should have seen those people's faces." I laugh and throw an arm around Joan. "It was hilarious."

"You blamed it on the food." Will chuckles.

I shrug my shoulders. "What can I say? I revert to sarcasm when I don't know what to say."

I notice the walkway before Joan does. Its floor-to-ceiling glass and metal girders. I don't know what I was thinking. Well, I guess I thought it was just a walkway like the one on the Golden Gate Bridge. The floor is glass also. You can look straight down the 137 feet down to the Thames River below. As we step on the walkway, I try to distract Joan from the floor. She is already terrified of heights. I spin around and begin singing an old Annie song. I throw my arms out to the side, "Let's go to the movies, let's go to the show…." I tap dance my way to her and back out onto the bridge. She follows me, dancing along. We get about 20 feet onto the catwalk before Joan notices that the floor is glass.

She swiftly gets to her knees and begins to crawl backward. "Oh my God! Oh my God! Will, Will!" She reaches her hand out.

Will squats down beside her. "Joan, you are OK. Do you want me to carry you?"

No! Nope! No! Get me off of here!" Joan begins frantically crawling with her eyes closed.

She turns herself around and begins crawling further onto the skyway. I watch in awe as the situation gets worse. It's kind of amusing, I laugh.

Mom pinches me on the arm. "Don't laugh at your sister."

"Joan, Joan. Stop, you're going the wrong way." Will gently puts his hand on her shoulder.

She screams, scaring everybody else on the bridge. A baby starts crying in the distance.

"Joan, I'm going to pick you up. Keep your eyes closed. I'll give you a piggyback ride the rest of the way." Will puts his hand in hers and begins pulling her to her feet.

"OK, Scoot over. Do you feel me? Hop on my back." Will steadies himself.

Joan squeezes her eyes shut tight and hops on his back.

"See? Your OK." Will wraps his arms around Joan's legs.

We all begin walking across the bridge again. Thomas is pointing out points of interest to us. Joan's head is lying flat on Will's back.

We make it to the second tower, and I just can't help myself. "Why are these stairs made of glass and not the other ones?"

Joan clutches Will tighter.

"I'm just kidding! Jeez! Are you going to continue to be a baby and have your boyfriend carry you down all these steps?"

Joan cautiously opens her eyes, one at a time. "Oh, I'm OK."

She slowly slides off Will's back until she touches her feet to the ground.

I draw out my words. "So, how are we getting back? I take it we aren't walking back across?"

Joan's legs wobble underneath her. I got my answer.

"We can take a double-decker back over. Maybe see some things along the way." Thomas answers.

Joan nods, agreeing. Will holds Joan's hand tightly in his as we go down the stairs. Will get Joan a set on the first level of the double-decker as the rest of us head to the top.

Mom snaps pictures as the tour guide points out different places before we cross back over the bridge, this time not with Joan on Will's back.

The sun is going down as we make it back to the Eye of London. Mom and dad are splitting a newspaper funnel full of fries. Dad is dipping them in tater sauce.

We walk around Jubilee Park, eating ice cream and reminiscing about the trip. I stare up at the illuminated pink Ferris wheel. It looks like a giant wedding ring. I glance down at my finger, then hold it up and snap a picture with the Eye of London in the background. What a crazy week. Everything has changed.

Chapter 31

The Decision

"You'll be mine, and I'll be yours. All I know since yesterday, everything has changed."

—Taylor Swift

I sink into the couch. Mom kisses me on top of the head; I wince. I forgot about my stitches until now.

"Go to bed. I don't even see how you're awake now. Dad and I will see you in the morning." Mom drags her hand over my shoulder.

"Night, Punky, get some rest." Dad squeezes my hand.

"Goodnight, guys." I wave and walk towards my bedroom and slump down on the bed.

Thomas walks out of the bathroom with his toothbrush in his mouth. "You must be exhausted."

I begin to cry.

"Oh, no, M! Are you sad your parents are leaving?" Thomas sits beside me, concerned.

I put my face in my hands. "Yes, but no. I'm just drained. I get over emotional when I haven't had enough sleep."

"Is that really all it is?" Thomas rubs my back with his toothbrush hanging out of his mouth.

"Yes, that's all it is." I know what I'm saying, but my face isn't matching the tears spilling down my cheeks.

"Well, get some sleep. We'll have a good breakfast before everyone leaves tomorrow. We'll have time to spend with them." I stand in front of the bathroom mirror on autopilot. I squeeze a blob of toothpaste on the end of my toothbrush and turn it on.

"You know, we don't have to stay here," Thomas says, rinsing his mouth out.

I stop brushing my teeth to look at him. "We don't? I came here to be with you; we're engaged. I made a choice."

"Yeah, but that was before Joan was pregnant. I can tell you want to go back. You don't have to sacrifice that for me. I told you that." Thomas pulls me into his arms.

I begin to sob uncontrollably. "You'd do that for me?"

"I'd do anything for you." Thomas says.

"What about the townhouse? Charlie? All your stuff here?" I ask. "You have so much here—so many loose ends. We still have all of the clothes from Alexander. I didn't get to say goodbye."

"M, calm down. Kyle can get all the clothes back to Alexander. Your friends here are only a phone call away. We'll take Charlie with us." Thomas tucks my hair behind my ear.

I sit on the bed, silent…thinking.

"We'll worry about everything else later," Thomas says, pulling down the covers for me. "What do you say, M?"

"I say, I don't deserve you." I kiss him as I slide under the sheets. "What about your family?"

"What about them? I can hop a plane, you know? This isn't the Stone Age. We'll split time between here and the states. So?" Thomas waits for my answer.

I inhale a deep breath. And shake my head hard up and down. "Yes! Yes, yes, yes!" I pull him to me and squeeze him tight. "I can't wait to tell everyone!"

"I'm glad you're happy. That's all I want you to be." Thomas slides out of my grip. "I better get to the couch before I fall asleep here.

"Stay, who cares? Stay with me tonight." Thomas crawls back in bed and wraps his arms around me, making me the little spoon.

I drift off to sleep.

The next morning, I wake to Charlie sleeping at the foot of the bed and Thomas nowhere to be found. I quietly tiptoe out to the living room. Thomas is spread out on the couch with one leg hanging off. I'm so excited I'm bursting at the seams.

Dad comes sluggishly walking out of the guest bedroom, rubbing his eyes.

"Dad," I whisper. "Guess what?"

"What?" he pours the coffee beans in the hopper. "What is it, Punky? Is everything OK?"

"Yes, yes, everything is OK!" I can't contain my excitement; I screech. "We are coming back to the states with everyone today!"

Mom comes swiftly, stumbling out of the bedroom, "Did I hear you correctly? Are you and Thomas coming back to the states with us today?"

Thomas sits up on the couch. His floof is in full effect, springing in all directions. He gives me a wide grin. "Are you packed?"

I bound over and throw myself on his lap. "Not yet, but I will be! Oh, we have to get tickets!"

"No, don't worry. I had Kyle get us tickets last night. And Alexander is dropping by this morning after breakfast." Thomas bounces me on his knees then stands up.

I dance my way into the kitchen. "Don't tell Joan. Let me do it!"

I throw my things back in my suitcase and hide it in the closet. I'm in the shower when everyone arrives for breakfast. I hear them in the living room; I quickly rinse my hair and throw on my clothes.

"Hey!" I walk over to Joan with my arms open wide. "Guess what?"

"What, stupid?" she sits down on the couch and looks up at me.

"Well…Thomas and I are coming back to the states with you guys today!" I jump up and down.

"For how long?" Joan jumps to her feet to hug me.

I shrug my shoulders. "For as long as we want."

"Shut the front door!" Marie joins our crazy circle jumping.

"OK! Let's eat and get this show on the road!" Will holds up a bag of pastries.

After breakfast, Thomas goes into the bedroom to pack. The doorbell rings. I pop up to answer it. Alexander is standing in the doorway. Before I can say anything, he squawks. "Bitch, you're leaving me?" he fake kisses me on each cheek. "I'm only kidding."

I step aside as he walks in.

I hand him the dresses. "Thank you so much, Alexander. You have been a great friend."

Alexander jerks his head back. "You act like this is forever. Stop that. Dustine and I will come and see you. Maybe we will even bring Patrice." He shoves my shoulder.

I open the door for him. "I'll see you soon. Pride?"

"Yes, I'll come for Pride. Mark it down." Alexander says, walking out the door.

"See you at Pride!" I yell after him before I shut the door.

Thomas comes out of the bedroom rolling his luggage.

"Are we going to see your mom or sisters before we go?" I ask.

Thomas shakes his head. "No, mom and Birdie are out of town, and Figs is at work. They'll come to see us in a couple of weeks. I talked to my mom last night after you went to bed."

So, that's where he ran off too; I should have known he wouldn't disrespect dad. I nip him on the chin. "I should have known."

Thomas smiles, "You were so excited; I needed to call Kyle and make sure things were arranged."

The doorbell rings. Thomas opens it.

"Speaking of the devil." Kyle is standing at the door.

"Come in, come in," I shout behind Thomas.

Kyle is holding a folder that he lays out on the counter. "OK, your tickets and Charlie's vet pass are in here." He hands Thomas his passport. "Here's your passport; that should be it."

Thomas claps Kyle on the shoulder. "I'll call you. I'll need you to have the fridge cleaned out and put our cars in storage." Thomas hands Kyle our extra set of keys.

Kyle shakes his head. "OK, see you." He waves as he leaves.

Thomas turns to us, clapping his hands together. "OK, the car is coming around shortly. Are we all ready?"

Will begins lining up all our luggage at the door.

Mom gives the bedroom a once-over. "I got everything."

The doorbell rings as Will rolls the last luggage in place. He opens it.

George is standing in the doorway, holding his hat in his hand.

"Good morning, Marguerite!" he smiles. "It's good to see you again."

"George! You're driving us to the airport?" I question.

"It would seem so." George's thick accent is something I love about him. "Can I take your luggage to the car?"

Everyone loads in the SUV George is driving. Thomas has Charlie in his travel kennel. I turn and lock the door behind us.

I buckle my seatbelt and end this trip the same way I began it, in George's car. I give the flat one last look as we head to the airport—only this time *with* Thomas.

"A bend in the road is not the end of the road unless you fail to make the turn."

—Helen Keller

To my loves. Rob, for being my inspiration, my partner in crime, for our love story, and for being my safe place to land. Robbie, for being my hero, my best friend, for being the person I try to be better for.
I stand in awe of you. You are a Rockstar.
For Joann, my ride or die.

Note to my readers,

First, hi! I hope you enjoyed my book. I had a heck of a great time writing it. Thank you as always for all the love and support. If you enjoyed my book, please consider posting a review. Since I am an Indie author, reviews help me out tremendously. Through my writing journey, I have made some great new friends. It has been an absolute dream to share my stories with such a fantastic group of people.

From the bottom of my heart, thank you.

As always, you can reach me on my social media or just by a simple email. I love getting feedback or a note.

 jbrteller@gmail.com

 www.jbteller.com

 Instagram @jbrteller

 Twitter @JBTeller1

 Or on Facebook @JB Teller

9 781735 408262